The Posilecheata
A Day Trip to Posillipo

Pompeo Sarnelli

The Posilecheata
A Day Trip to Posillipo

Translation and Introduction by Hermann W. Haller

Agincourt Press
New York, 2025

Opuntia is an imprint of Agincourt Press
Luigi Ballerini and Gianluca Rizzo, Editors
Agincourt Press is a non-profit organization chaired by Berardo Paradiso

ISBN: 978-1-946328-66-3

AGINCOURT PRESS
P.O. Box 1039
Cooper Station
New York, NY 10003
www.agincourtbooks.com

Table of Contents

Frontispiece of Pompeo Sarnelli's first edition of *POSILECHEATA de Masillo Reppone de Gnanopoli,* printed in Naples in 1684. (Biblioteca Nazionale Centrale, Firenze)

Introduction

Hermann W. Haller

Within the great Neapolitan literary production in dialect, with poets and play-wrights of the sixteenth and seventeenth centuries such as Giovan Battista Del Tufo, Giulio Cesare Cortese, Felippo Sgruttendio De Scafato, Giambattista Basile, Andrea Perrucci, Nicola Stigliola, the *Posilecheata* is a small jewel with an optimistic vision of humanity created by the young polygraph Pompeo Sarnelli, alias Masillo Reppone de Gnanopoli. Together with Basile's masterpiece, which was its source of inspiration, it stands out as one of the very few narrative prose texts in Italy's literary dialect canon.[i] The five fairy tales exude the author's imagination and fantasy, passion for the Neapolitan language and culture, erudite knowledge of history and art, and daily exposure to all facets of humanity. They were published in 1684 during what has been called the Golden Age of Naples in the sixteenth and seventeenth centuries, when the capital of the Kingdom governed by Spanish viceroys underwent a demographic explosion, becoming one of the largest cities of early Modern Europe.[ii]

The *Posilecheata* is playfully framed as a feast among friends in Posillipo on the Gulf of Naples, on a day that ends with festivities at sea celebrating the viceroy. The book opens with a preface in which Sarnelli defends his work and the written use of the Neapolitan language, which he considers superior to the sophisticated codified Tuscan and superior to Northern dialects. Following Baroque hyperbolic precepts the *cornice* introduces a Lucullan banquet prepared for Masillo by his friend Pietruccio but enjoyed mostly by an un-invited guest, Rabelaisian Doctor Marchionno, whose gargantuan appetite is accompanied by a symposium of comments, proverbs, and puns. The reader and listener is overwhelmed by the host's generous accommodation; by the doctor's forwardness, wit, and intelligence; and by the richly diverse Neapolitan gastronomic terminology. The magically transformative potentials of erudite discourse grounded in history, art and anthropology stands in contrast to the *vajassa* Cianna's and her four daughters' popular songs and narratives at the end of the feast.

The *Posilecheata*'s five literary fairytales share a moral and didactic purpose with opening and closing proverbs and statements in support of justice and empathy for the weak and marginalized.[iii] They focus on the magic of transformation and a happy resolution and defeat of trickeries. Unlike the dominant male protagonists of the cornice, the *Posilecheata*'s tales celebrate women protagonists who face adversity, such as goodhearted Pacecca, the wife and victim of the cook Cocchiarone (Cunto I); royal Pomponiella, who is cursed at birth by a fairy to turn into a serpent on her wedding night but is saved thanks to a loyal servant (Cunto II); Ciccia, who is married to a king but betrayed by a spiteful stepmother (Cunto III); Cecca, who is tricked by her brother Mineco's wife yet finds wealth and happiness (Cunto IV); and Nunziella, whose generosity to beggars is rewarded by the fairies (Cunto V). The stories' female villains such as Pascadozzia, the king's stepmother (Cunto III); Belluccia, the wife of Cecca's brother (Cunto IV); or Rosecachiuove, an impersonation of stinginess (Cunto V), are in the end all defeated through fairies' interventions or thanks to saviors. All stories share transformative events due to magic spells: Pacecca becomes a Queen who brings a murdered prince back to life; Pomponiella turns into a serpent on her wedding night; Jannuzzo becomes a statue but is revived by a speaking bird; Nunziella is abused by her stingy mother yet rewarded for her empathy for the poor. Perhaps indirectly, the *Posilecheata* reflects symbolically the hierarchical structure and social tensions of mid-seventeenth century Neapolitan society made up of privileged aristocrats, business people, clergy, and a large working class population drawn to the capital from Southern regions in hope of better lives.

Born on January 16, 1649 in the Apulian town of Polignano, Luca Vito Pompeo Sarnelli grew up with his brother and two sisters in a middle-class family, encouraged to pursue ecclesiastic and military training by his father Francesco, a soldier in the army of the Kingdom of Naples. At age fourteen the young Pompeo moved to Naples to study theology, law, and science. He was ordained as a priest in 1672 and became a Neapolitan citizen a few years later. While preparing his ecclesiastic and legal career in a post-Tridentine environment, Sarnelli began to work as an assistant and consultant of Antonio Bulifon, an anti-conformist French entrepreneur who arrived in 1670, opening a bookstore at San Biagio that would become a successful publishing house and important meeting place for writers and intellectuals through the end of the century.[iv] During these years, Sarnelli began to pursue his philological, linguistic, historical, and literary ambitions as a polygraph. Among his early publications are *Il filo d'Arianna*, an erudite interpretation of an ancient headstone in the church of San Domenico Maggiore; an edition of Giambattista Basile's Neapolitan masterpiece, *Lo cunto de li cunti*; a successful Latin school grammar; and translations from French of *Gli avvenimenti di Fortunato e de' suoi figli* and, from Latin, of Giovanni Della Porta's *Chirofisonomia*. In the early 1680s he composed in Latin *Bestiarum Schola,* a collection of short Aesopian fables with moralizing religious and political illustrations and, in Neapolitan, *Posilecheata,* the fairy tales that would ensure his lasting fame. In 1679 Sarnelli was appointed as assistant to the Dominican Cardinal Vincenzo Maria Orsini,[v] whom he followed to Manfredonia, Cesena, and Benevento through 1692, the year he became bishop of Bisceglie, a diocese he governed through the end of his life in 1724.

During the years that followed his 1681 *Lauree* in Church Law and Theology, Sarnelli's publications turned increasingly ecclesiastic and erudite. They include church chronicles, hagiographical texts, and didactic manuals for priests. However, even while writing an enormous number of ecclesiastic texts, his early literary calling continued to resurface sporadically.

Although no detailed biographical account is known beyond the record of his printed work and parts of a diary edited and translated by Angelo Custodero,[vi] Naples—as the capital and cultural epicenter of the Kingdom—was the locus of what could be considered the three most consequential encounters in Sarnelli's life. They comprise the linguistic and literary discovery of Giambattista Basile and his Baroque masterpiece written in Neapolitan; his assignments with Antonio Bulifon, who engaged Sarnelli as a consultant and editor; and his appointment by Cardinal Francesco Maria Orsini, which led to a church career. Naples is also the city where Sarnelli, the native of Puglia, developed his polyglossia by studying and practicing Latin and Greek, Italian and Neapolitan, French, and likely Spanish.

Sarnelli the linguist, philologist, translator and editor

While studying and working as an assistant at Bulifon's bookstore, Sarnelli pursued his philological and linguistic interests as the author of a Latin school grammar, as translator and editor of *Degli avvenimenti di Fortunato e de' suoi figli* (1676) and of Della Porta's *Chirofisonomia*, included in the scientific treatise, *Della Magia naturale* (1677). By this time, he had grown fond of Neapolitan dialect literature. The painstaking revision and "correjeture" carried out for the 1674 edition of Basile's *Cunto de li cunti* with its new title, *Il Pentamerone*, vividly illustrates his expert knowledge of spoken and written Neapolitan and his familiarity with Neapolitan literary dialects. In the five-page foreword, *A li vertoluse lejeture Napolitane*,[vii] signed with the pseudonym Masillo Reppone—but accompanied by a sonnet whose initial letters yield the real name of Pompeo Sarnelli—he draws up his personal linguistic history. As a foreigner who fell in love with Neapolitan, preferring it to Latin, Sarnelli claims the need for correcting a corrupted earlier edition of Basile's *Cunto*, reminding the reader of the discrepancy between spoken and written Neapolitan, a language lacking dictionaries—unlike Tuscan, Latin, and Greek. A sample comparison of passages from the *Introduttione* and *Lo cunto dell'huerco* of Basile's posthumous 1637 edition with Sarnelli's *Pentamerone* shows predominantly orthographic changes (*Eracleto* > *Aracreto, malenconia* > *malanconia, adanza* > *addanza, mastro Grillo* > *masto Grillo, etate* > *aietate, miezo a le gamme* > *'nmiezo a le gamme, succiesso* > *socciesso*), and a slightly revised punctuation. Some corrections such as betacism (*viento* > *biento, votato* > *botato, vino* > *bino*) or assimilation (*quindece* > *quinnece*) seem to suggest an effort to make Basile's text more Neapolitan. While the detailed corrections tend to be minor, except for occasional lexical substitutions (*scorzeta* > *scorza, na more* > *na noce, ceste* > *vesiche*),[viii] they show Sarnelli as an ambitious linguist who promised, in the *Introduttione* to the *Posilecheata*, to offer "ciento regole d'Artocrafia ... e frase de lo parlare Napolitano..., coi millanta belle asseruattiune" [one hundred orthographic rules... and phrases of spoken Neapolitan ..., with one thousand beautiful observations], something he never accomplished.

Sarnelli was clearly aware of Italy's geolinguistic stratification and astounding variety of regional languages, and of the sixteenth-century debates on the *questione della lingua*. In his prefatory letter to the readers of the *Posilecheata* he mentions the *Vocabolario della Crusca* published in 1612, while offering a strong defense of Neapolitan by stating boldly that "Vale cchiù na parola napoletana chiantuta che tutte li vocabole de la Crusca" [A robust Neapolitan word is worth more than all the words of the Crusca],[ix] before disparaging Tuscan, the foundation of the Italian standard language: "E po' co sta lengua toscana avite frusciato lo tafanàrio a miezo munno" [With this Tuscan language you screwed up half the world]. To advocate the superiority

Frontispiece of Pompeo Sarnelli's edition of Giambattista Basile's *Pentamerone* or *Cunto de li cunte* [nuovamente restampato, e co tutte le zeremonie corrietto] printed by Bulifon in 1674. (Biblioteca Nazionale Centrale, Firenze).

of Neapolitan over other regional languages, he tells the humorous story of a compatriot who was derided for his speech on a visit to Lombardy. To defend himself, the Neapolitan asks the Lombard to translate three Neapolitan words into his language—*io, casa, capo*—and to repeat them quickly as *mi, ca, cò* with a scatological outcome, stating parahypotaxically that "Lengua che no' la 'ntienne e tu la caca" [you shit a language that you don't understand]. The Neapolitan visitor then cherishes his own robust speech by deriding Lombard apocope (*pa* for *pane*).[x]

Sarnelli's appreciation of the expressive potential of the Neapolitan language is seen, for example, in the more than one hundred curses hurled in equal proportions at a beggar and at courtiers (Cunto 5, *Head and Tail*). Of all these, many are found in Basile's *Cunto*. For more than twenty curses, Emanuele Rocco's *Vocabolario del dialetto napolitano* (1882-1891)[xi] includes citations from both Basile and Sarnelli (*guaguina, perogliosa, affocapeccerille, scanfarda, mantrune, pappalasagne, mmoccame chisso*), while eighteen curses have quotes only for Sarnelli, among them *ciernepédeta, spetalera, sorchiamucco, scianchella, zantragliosa, cacciannante, sautam'adduosso, zengrille, sbrammaglia, babane, caca-zeremonie*. The young priest Sarnelli clearly did not shy away from celebrating the rich Neapolitan curse words found in Basile's *Cunto* and *Lettere*,[xii] as well as in everyday spoken language.

Sarnelli's advocacy of the Neapolitan language is enhanced by a strong defense of dialect literature, a relatively youthful production opting deliberately for a cultivated dialect in lieu of the dominant literary Tuscan that had been codified in the sixteenth and early seventeenth centuries.[xiii] Sarnelli challenges critics who associate the use of regional languages exclusively with comedies by calling the prejudice an *asinata*. With his *Posilecheata* he follows in Basile's footsteps by choosing a dialect for prose, by that time a literary genre privileging Tuscan exclusively. By using Neapolitan, he challenges the dominant literary practice with a bold subversive choice that will have only very few followers across the canon.

The Polygraph at Work: Masillo Reppone vs. Pompeo Sarnelli

Throughout his numerous publications, Sarnelli tried to carefully separate his more experimental literary works from his erudite writings by signing them with pseudonyms in the form of anagrams. Among these, Masillo Reppone da Gnanopoli is the preferred signature for *Posilecheata, Degli avvenimenti di Fortunato e de' suoi figli,* and the edition of Basile's *Pentamerone.* Esopo Primnellio is used for *Bestiarum Schola*; Epompo Narselli for his multilingual play, *Il vero Tesoro*; and Salomone Lipper for the *Diario napoletano.* These pseudonyms were likely used to conceal the origins of the more secular works by a young author who had been ordained a priest in 1672. The pseudonyms also allow a tentative grouping of his literary works, or what Reppone has a friend define as "cunte dell'uorco" in his Preface, "ogre tales," as opposed to erudite works, "tant'opere grave de considerazione" addressed to a different kind of readers.

Among the works signed by Masillo Reppone, *Degli avvenimenti di Fortunato e de' suoi figli* (1676) is more than a translation from French, as the text is rearranged into two books, each with thirty chapters presenting, respectively, the stories of Fortunato and his son Andolosia, with creative additions of Reppone's own narratives and inventions.

Bestiarum schola (1680), a comical-serious Latin composition with 110 educational *Lezioni* about human behavior through analogies with the world of animals, illustrates the variety of genres chosen by the young Masillo, his linguistic versatility, and what Antonio Iurilli called an "insatiable voracity for books,"[xiv] an unbridled passion for knowledge to be disseminated in print, not without some indiscriminate use of sources. Inspired by Aesop's fables, the somewhat pessimistic animal metaphors are reflections that combine religious moralism with Baroque bizarreness. As a "schola," their didactic purpose is to revert the moral decline of society observed by the young priest. With their playful style, the short fables signed by Aesopo Primnellio e' Mnianopoli are defined as "false narratives of things that are similar to the truth,"[xv] aimed at simultaneously instructing and entertaining. The thematic exchanges between two animals consist of a "lesson" for humans: they recommend home schooling (Eagle and Owl, ii); avoiding prejudice (Two Hens visiting in China, xxxiii); foreign travel (Swan and Sparrow, xl); abstaining from excessive drinking (Owl and Bat, xlvi). They promote the need for patience and assiduity (Ant and Cicada, liii) and the futility of social pride, as all humans face the same destinies (Lion and Dog, lxxiv). As precursors of the great European tradition of fables the short texts could be memorized easily, thus serving also as an aid to the study of Latin.[xvi] A charming yet sarcastic exchange between father *Orso* and son *Orsetto*—likely an imaginary dialogue between Reppone and his mentor Orsini—concludes *Bestiarum Schola* with 48 questions and common-sense answers about friendship, marriage, food and banquets, wealth, aging, and social class. With his *Bestiarum Schola*, Reppone offered universal thoughts on human behavior, as well as veiled political reflections on the Spanish government of his time, influenced perhaps by Carlo Celano, the Neapolitan lawyer and writer who was suspected of supporting the 1647 Masaniello insurrection against Spanish rule and the aristocratic class.

Baroque bizarreness and religious moralism are found also in the light comedy in verse in three acts, *Il vero Tesoro de' Santi Corpi de' Gloriosi Martiri Mauro Vescovo Pantaleone, e Sergio Cavalieri Romani*, published in Naples in 1709 with both Sarnelli's real name and the rather transparent anagram Epompo Narselli. The humorous plurilingual play about the relics of the patron saints of Bisceglie found in the Middle Ages combines history and legend. The story, which was previously printed in *L'Arca del Testamento in Biseglia* (1694), is aimed at promoting faith among the town's citizens through entertainment. In the multilingual play, the Italian-speaking hermits deride wealth, while the Neapolitan-speaking Cienzo praises poverty and modesty and the patron saints of Bisceglie. The play celebrates the Italian cities and their people: Naples is gentle, Rome saintly, Venice wealthy, Milan big, Florence beautiful, Bologna fat, Ravenna ancient, Padua learned, Ferrara civil, Genoa conceited, and Lucca industrious. It also features a catalogue of national idiosyncrasies: Italians are considered judicious, the Spanish ingenious, the French correct, Germans sincere, the Polish friendly hosts, the Flemish industrious, the Greeks eloquent, the Africans astute, and the English are praised for loving their people. At war, Italians are considered resourceful, the Spanish diligent, the French courageous, and the Germans tidy and obedient.

Periegetic and historical works

Sarnelli's profound interest in the city and cultural treasures of Naples and its surrounding areas is demonstrated by two guides for foreign visitors, both published with Antonio Bulifon in 1685, one year after the *Posilecheata*. The pocket-size guides are based on a rich tradition of periegetic works describing the city and its history, such as those authored by Cesare D'Engenio Caracciolo, Carlo De Lellis, and Giuseppe Mormile.[xvii] The guides also draw from Giovanni Antonio Summonte's *Historia della Città e Regno di Napoli* (1601), reprinted by Bulifon in 1675. As the subtitles of Sarnelli's *Guide de' forestieri*

Map of the city of Naples designed by Johannes Federicus Pesche. Second edition of *Guida de' forestieri curiosi di vedere ed intendere le cose più notabili della real città di Napoli* (1688). Eds. Federica de Rosa, Alessandro Rullo and Simona Starita (https://www.memofonte.it/ricerche/napoli/#pompeo-sarnelli)

indicate they are based on the "lettura dei buoni autori"—that is to say, Sarnelli's mining previous works and selecting "cose notabili". The numerous illustrations by Bulifon made the guidebooks useful to the educated tourist, prompting frequent reprints and revised editions through the end of the eighteenth century. The guides remind us of the attraction Naples and its surrounding areas exerted on international visitors in early Modern Europe. They also represent important sources for reconstructing the architectural and social history of the city.

The *Guida de' forestieri* of Naples opens with a preface by Bulifon crediting Sarnelli and listing his works.[xviii] The *Guida* is divided into three parts. Part One discusses the city's ancient and modern history; its contemporary structure and government; its seven *borghi*; and attractive palaces, fountains and gardens. Part Two reviews a selection of more than 150 churches and religious institutions listed in an index at the end of the book, thus emphasizing post-Tridentine "sacred Naples." Part Three describes Posillipo, Mergellina,

Chiaja, the Sebeto river, and Mount Vesuvius and its numerous eruptions. A catalogue of important libraries brings to mind the city's vibrant intellectual life. General notes are added on the seven provinces of the Kingdom of Naples, its 144 towns and 148 rivers, twelve lakes, seven harbors and seven islands, and its numerous titled aristocrats. Barely three years later, a second, slightly revised edition of the Neapolitan *Guida* was printed with a detailed map of the city and new illustrations.

Sarnelli's *Guida* was very successful, due to its manageable format and innovative maps and illustrations.[xix] It reflects the importance of Naples, which became an obligatory stop of the Grand Tour in the eighteenth century.

For an extended visit to the surrounding areas, Sarnelli and Bulifon published a second guide in the same year titled *Guida de' forestieri curiosi di vedere e considerare le cose notabili di Pozzoli, Baja, Miseno, Cuma ed altri luoghi circonvicini*, based in part on Ferrante Loffredo's short guide, *L'Antichità di Pozzolo et luoghi convicini*, edited by Sarnelli ten years earlier. These nearby towns of the volcanic Phlegrean Fields attracted visitors for their thermal baths and respective health benefits, as well as for their archeological sites. Following a dedication to Diego Ibagnes Della Madriz, Bishop of Pozzuoli, and a Preface to the Readers by Bulifon, the short guide of twenty-three chapters and some one hundred pages describes the towns' notable villas, temples, lakes, caves, and surrounding mountains. The guide follows a route from Pozzuoli to Agnano, the *Solfatara* volcano known for its sulfurous vapors, Averno, Baja, Miseno and Cuma, towns that in antiquity were popular with Greeks and Romans. Chapter 4 on Pozzuoli recounts its history from the Romans to the Germanic invaders and chronicles the area's repeated earthquakes. To broaden this *Guida*'s interest for a diverse group of tourists, Sarnelli adds information on the volcanic eruptions and on the various thermal baths' healing potentials for diseases affecting the heart, lungs, internal organs, eyes, and ears. An Italian-French edition with Bulifon's translation printed in 1697 is indicative of the guide's broad interest at a time when French had become the language of international relations and diplomacy, a role similar to today's English as a global lingua franca. Several revised editions were printed through the late eighteenth century.[xx] The two guides were without a doubt one of Bulifon's and Sarnelli's most lucrative publications for a very large audience.[xxi] Unsurprisingly, some of the guides' contents crisscross parts of Sarnelli's oeuvre.

Ecclesiastic writings

With his appointment as the assistant of the Dominican cardinal Orsini, and particularly after the mid-1680s, Sarnelli's writings turned increasingly ecclesiastic. During his church career in Cesena and Benevento and as bishop of Bisceglie, he authored more than ten religious works with hundreds of pages devoid of a critical or polemical perspective, grounded in the Catholic Church's conservative official doctrine.[xxii] Signed with Sarnelli's real name the works share a similar structure. A dedication, preface to the readers, and chapter index are followed by the main body of text and an analytical subject and name index at the end. The books are written in a Standard Italian language "senza pompa di frase, senza affettazione di parole" [without pompous and pretentious language], inviting a conciliatory dialogue in order to avoid the attention of Spanish inquisitors. Sarnelli displays his erudition by including frequent citations in Latin without an Italian translation referring to Greek, Roman, and medieval sources. The following is a list of Sarnelli's ecclesiastic writings in chronological order of their publication:

1678	*Dello specchio del clero secolare*
1680	*Cronologia de' vescovi et arcivescovi sipontini*
1686	*Antica Basilicografia*
1686-1716	*Lettere ecclesiastiche* (ten volumes)
1688	*Il clero secolare nel suo splendore o vero della vita comune chericale*
	Memorie dell'Insigne Collegio di S. Spirito di Benevento
1691	*Memorie cronologiche dei vescovi ed arcivescovi di Benevento*
1694	*L'Arca del Testamento in Biseglia*
1705	*Lezioni scritturali alla mente, ed al cuore*
1708	*Filalete Dialogo delle cose spirituali, ed invisibili*
1723	*Lume a' Principianti nello studio delle Materie ecclesiastiche, e scritturali*

Several texts, such as *Il clero secolare nel suo splendore,* offer guidance on how to lead a good Christian life, while most are directed at the clergy with a didactic intent. Many repeat topics discussed in previous texts. They concern music played in church, priests' appropriate haircuts and clothes, flagellation as punishment, baptism, chastity and fornication, modesty of speech, and how the clergy should deal with relatives.

Each of the ten volumes of *Lettere ecclesiastiche* consists of some forty to fifty letters between five and seven pages long. They answer a question raised by real or fictitious individuals. Volume One includes the above-mentioned topics and, in addition, potentially delicate issues such as mental oration and Sarnelli's cautious sympathy for quietism, next to more mundane themes—for example, how to decorate the church during holidays. In the moralistic letters of Volume Two Sarnelli addresses drinking and eating habits of priests, card games, and a description of the 1688 earthquake in Benevento, which is described in great detail in *Memorie dell'Insigne Collegio di S. Spirito di Benevento*. Later volumes highlight brotherly love among bishops, Christian modesty in speaking and writing, and the rejection of curses.

Unlike the chronicles and lists of church leaders and feudal lords (*Cronologia de' vescovi et arcivescovi sipontini*; *Memorie cronologiche dei vescovi ed arcivescovi di Benevento*), the short manuals printed in *Il clero secolare nel suo splendore o vero della vita comune chericale* and *Memorie dell'Insigne Collegio di S. Spirito di Benevento* are concise treatises on the rules of clerical life, including chastity, avoidance of lying and lust, obedience, and respect for hierarchy. In particular, the *Memorie* of the Collegio of Benevento illustrate Sarnelli's taste for lively chronicles and news coverage, as they describe the Benevento earthquake of 1688 when close to 1,400 people died and both Sarnelli and Orsini were injured and buried under the rubble.[xxiii] The destructive power of the event is perceived as God's punishment for past sins. Sarnelli's account of the ensuing flood caused by the Sebeto river ("pianse il fiume Sabato, veduto uscir, come per gran dolore, dal suo letto") [the Sebeto river wept as if in great pain when leaving its bed] shows his love for Baroque metaphors and style, while chronicling Benevento's history from the fourth through the seventeenth century documents Sarnelli's interest in history.

Among Sarnelli's didactic texts is an elegant pocket-size edition of 525 pages titled *Filalete Dialogo delle cose spirituali, ed invisibili* (1708), a dialogue with Filalete (a pseudonym derived from an ancient Greek name meaning 'lover of truth') on the world's creation, original sin, superstition, hope, devils, Divine Providence, silent prayer, and the ears as a conduit of virtues to the soul. Throughout his church career Sarnelli's writings reflect an educational mission, as the forty *quesiti* of *Lume a' Principianti nello studio delle Materie Ecclesiastiche, e scritturali* document, a volume directed at future generations of priests. In most of these works, Sarnelli adopts an Italian language that is close to the spoken register, a style defined as "piano, familiare, come se parlassi dimesticamente con coloro a' quali hò scritto" (in a plain, simple and familiar style, as if speaking commonly and in a friendly manner with those for whom I wrote).[xxiv] As his occasional correspondence with the Florentine librarian, book collector, and cultural organizer Antonio Magliabechi seems to suggest,[xxv] Sarnelli was eager to receive recognition and support for his books from learned circles.

Positioned somewhat between Sarnelli's popular Guides to Naples and his ecclesiastic writings, *Antica Basilicografia* (1686) is an erudite work in fifty chapters about the architecture of a Basilica explaining the symbolic meaning, religious and social functions of its atrium, portals, nave, altar, baptistery, and sacristy from an historical perspective. Drawing from ancient sources Sarnelli suggests how in a ship-like church the bishop is the captain of the sanctuary while the priests are its sailors and worshippers. Three main front doors allow for separate entrances by males and females.

When considering Sarnelli as a polygraph and polyglot, it becomes clear that alongside and within the very large number of ecclesiastic writings one finds a genuine passion for linguistic and literary endeavors. Sarnelli loved languages and practiced them in his translations, from his early version of a French rendering of the stories of Fortunato to the translation from Latin of *Chirofisonomia*. He cherished the plurilingualism he encountered in Naples and became a steadfast admirer and advocate of Neapolitan language and literature. His literary and didactic ecclesiastic Italian writings are frequently in the form of dialogues. He had a deep interest in ancient history and art history, as seen in *Basilicografia* and in the two *Guide de' forestieri*.

THE *POSILECHEATA*

***Posilecheata*: Capsule summaries**
Masillo Reppone to the Virtuous Readers
In his Preface, Masillo Reppone justifies writing fairytales as a recreation and literary experimentation in Neapolitan, a language he considers superior to both Tuscan Standard and Lombard dialects. Inspired by Giambattista Basile's *Cunti*, he promises to write more than one hundred *Posilecheatas*, fairy tales that fathers may read to their numerous children in summer and winter to make them fall asleep, thus saving dinner.

Introduction

Masillo pays a visit to his friend Petruccio in Posillipo on July 26, 1684. He arrives just in time for lunch and is welcomed by Petruccio and the maid, Cianna. As food is being served Marchionno drops in, an uninvited doctor who treats Petruccio at the baths in Ischia. The gluttonous doctor lectures the hosts about numbers and symbols while gorging on all the food. At the end of the banquet Cianna's four daughters Cecca, Tolla, Popa, and Ciulletella sing and prepare to tell a story each.

Cunto I   La Piatà Remmonerata / Pity Rewarded

Ciulletella narrates the story of Pacecca and Cocchiarone. Pacecca shows empathy for the poor, giving away her clothes, naively trusting her husband to get new ones. Cocchiarone laughs at her and abandons her in a forest. While waiting for her husband to return, Pacecca saves a dove from the claws of a giant bird by throwing a stone and causing it to drop the dove on a patch of grass. The fairy dove offers her the blades of grass that will save her from future trouble. It takes Pacecca to a luxurious palace where she finds a murdered prince and dead knights. The dove resuscitates the prince who proposes to Pacecca, but she decides to wait. As she begins to live the life of a queen, she agrees

Illustration of Posillipo, second edition of *Guida de' forestieri curiosi di vedere ed intendere le cose più notabili della real città di Napoli* (1688) with a dedication to Fulvia Pico (p. 413). www.memofonte.it.

to take care of Renzullo, the king's youngest child. When Cocchiarone hears about Pacecca's fortunes, he offers his services as a cook at the court. Pacecca recognizes him and treats him well despite the abuse she suffered. While bringing her a meal Cocchiarone kills Renzullo, who lies in bed with her, then he alerts the court, accusing his wife of the crime. Pacecca is imprisoned and threatened to be burned at the stake. To prove her innocence, she revives Renzullo with the grass. The child testifies to having been killed by the cook. Pacecca asks the king to forgive Cocchiarone despite his evil actions. As the truth is revealed, Cocchiarone runs to hide in the kitchen but falls into an icy pond and dies. Pacecca gets married to the prince, and a statue of Cocchiarone with a punishing inscription is placed in front of a sewer in Naples.

Cunto II   La Vajassa Fedele / The Loyal Maid

Poppa tells the story of Pomponiella, the daughter of Queen Jacova of the Kingdom of Greenland. Pomponiella is blessed at birth by six fairies but is given an evil spell by the seventh fairy, who is angry because of a foot injury caused by chestnut scraps. The spell will transform Pomponiella into a serpent when entering her husband's bed on their wedding night, staying like that for three years, months, days, hours, minutes, and forever unless she finds a loyal maid with two ugly sisters who is the daughter of a mother without mother and father, grandfather, and male children, looking just like her. Before dying Jacova shares this secret predicament with Pomponiella, who searches the land and finds the perfect maid, Petruccia, fitting all of the spell's requirements. When she marries the King of Redland, she asks Petruccia to help her with the serpent transformation and to look after her while exiled in the garden. As she takes on Pomponiella's role, the loyal maid asks the king to wait for three years and four months without sleeping with her. She eventually helps the serpent back into human shape and altruistically lets Pomponiella marry the prince. As a reward for her loyalty, she becomes a queen by marrying the King of Shadowland, the king's brother, who takes the marble statue of Medusa's head to Naples placing it at the Serpent Fountain with an epitaph celebrating loyalty.

Cunto III   La 'ngannatrice 'ngannata / A Deceiver Deceived
Tolla features the story of Minec'Aniello and his three daughters Lella, Cilla, and Cicia. Minec'Aniello asks his friend Marcone to watch over his daughters after his death by keeping them locked up with their embroidering. On a hunting expedition, the King of Monterotondo hears the daughters talk about their marriage fantasies. He meets all of them, takes Cicia as his wife, and arranges Lella's and Cilla's weddings. When Cicia gives birth to two lovely children, the king's hateful and resentful stepmother, Pascaddozia, replaces them with two pups and orders a page to kill the babies, while Cecca is imprisoned. The page tricks Pascaddozia by keeping the tots alive and abandoning them in the countryside. A miller's wife finds Jannuzzo and Ninella and takes care of them together with her own son, Rienzo. When a fight breaks out between the youngsters, Jannuzzo and Ninella decide to leave and wander across the world in search of their true parents. After settling near the king's palace, a companion lady of Pascaddozia challenges Ninella, prompting her to find a singing apple, dancing water, and a speaking bird to enhance her beauty. Ninella obliges Jannuzzo, who undertakes the searches with help and advice from an old man. However, when reaching for the speaking bird in a field filled with statues of people and animals punished for their crimes, he turns himself into a statue. Ninella eventually finds Jannuzzo, who is revived by the speaking bird as a favor to the siblings' family. After returning to the Palace the speaking bird tells the true story of Cicia and evil Pascaddozia at a sumptuous banquet in honor of the King. The King threatens Pascaddozia, yet Cicia asks him for for-

giveness. The singing bird then turns Pascaddozia into a statue that is donated to the King of Naples and is placed in front of the university.

Cunto IV   La Gallenella / The Little Chicken

Cecca tells the story of Sole and Luna, the children of Peppone and Zezolla, later called Mineco and Cecca. Zezolla has Cenza, from Grumo, breastfeed her children. Unable to look after them she abandons them in a *basso*, where a woman from a neighboring mansion finds them and takes care for them. She gives Cecca an egg that will hatch and yield a pretty hen companion that one day flies up to a window, trying to kill a lizard. Cecca saves the fairy lizard which rewards her with a spell and shows her a hidden warehouse with a bronze horse full of precious coins. The fairy lizard instructs Cecca to let her brother Mineco enter the warehouse only after reaching good judgment, to ask him to marry a poor woman and keep her tattered clothes, and to use milk when in trouble. Mineco marries poor Belluccia who despises Cecca and deceives her by getting her fattened to look pregnant. To save his honor, Mineco abandons Cecca in a ravine. A wealthy merchant saves and marries her, after curing her from the little serpents in her belly by teasing them out with milk. When the happy merchant family visits Mineco later on, they instruct their daughter Liviella to keep asking for a story during dinner. Liviella complies, and Cecca tells the story of her life and the misdeeds perpetrated by Belluccia and her companion lady, Colospizia Papara. As the true story unfolds, stunned Belluccia breaks her neck while Colospizia runs to hide in the bronze horse but is found by the lizard and burned to death. The bronze horse is sold and melted down. Evil Belluccia's tombstone displays an epitaph disparaging social climbing.

Cunto V   La Capo e la Coda / Head and Tail

Cianna, the elderly mother and maid of Petruccio, tells the final story of Nunziella, the daughter of stingy Rosecachiuove, who kicks her out of the house because she gave a poor woman the head and tail of a sardine prepared for her mother. A fairy disguised as a beggar places a spell on Nunziella, rewarding her empathy with a precious ring. Nunziella sells the ring to a merchant who marries her. When they run into disagreements the fairy offers them a palace with a head and tail code to open the gate, defying Lo Gigante from blocking their access. The fairy tests newly rich Nunziella to see if her wealth spoiled her kindness. Nunziella wins the test, defending the fairy dressed up as a pleading beggar from an abusive disparaging gentry in front of the palace, throwing back at them her own litany of insults. Nunziella eventually saves a drowning old woman who turns out to be Rosecachiuove, inviting her to the palace. Unable to enjoy life, the stingy mother stubbornly pursues her miserliness, prompting the sardine fairy to transform her into a toad.

Conclusion

Masillo, Petruccio and Marchionno board a boat to witness and enjoy a great feast at sea honoring the Spanish viceroy on the evening of July 26, ending Masillo's visit to Posillipo. The grandiose scenery with its spectacular attractions and fireworks for the Neapolitan people serves to exalt the "Golden Age" of Naples and its kingdom. Mythological references to the topography of the Gulf of Naples enrich the fantastic summer spectacle.

Features Shared by the Tales of the *Posilecheata*

The five tales share some core themes and features. Empathy for the weak and poor is found in the first and fifth stories, with Pacecca and Nunziella giving away their meager belongings. They will suffer for their generosity but be vindicated through the help of fairies. Empathy is also present in the third and fourth stories, "The Little Chicken" and "A Deceiver Deceived," in which two women save abandoned children who will prosper in their lives. Despite being repeatedly victims of their husbands' or lady companions' evil actions in the first and third *cunti*, Pacecca and Cicia do not seek revenge, asking the king to forgive Cocchiarone and Pascaddozia. Magical rewards for virtuous deeds crisscross the stories thanks to the spells and actions of bird, reptile, and sardine fairies and fairies disguised as beggars: Pacecca has access to a royal palace; Petruccia's sustained love and unceasing loyalty to Pomponiella is requited with her marriage to the young king of Shadowland; by saving the fairy lizard from an aggressive chicken Cecca is led to a room with a bronze horse filled with riches; Nunziella's unwavering moral integrity is recompensed with a happy life in a palace. Conversely, betrayal and treachery are eventually punished: the cook Cocchiarone drowns accidentally in a pond; Pascaddozia is turned into stone; Belluccia breaks her neck and dies; Colospizia burns to death; and Nunziella's stingy mother Rosecachiuove is transformed into an earth-eating toad. Transformations and social mobility from rags to riches are present in most stories, as abandoned women turn into prosperous individuals. The impossible becomes possible thanks to the fairies' use of magic in the search for a loyal maid in the second story who must fulfill a hyperbolic set of highly complex requirements. Contrasts and inequality between the lowest and highest social orders are highlighted similarly, through rich illustrations of fashion in the first story and spectacular banquets and feasts in the frame story and in "A Deceiver Deceived." The weak are vindicated in all stories, as moral values of social justice are promoted throughout Sarnelli's writings.

The protagonists celebrated in the *Posilecheata* are notably women: Pacecca in "Pity Rewarded," Pomponiella and Petruccia in "The Loyal Maid," Cicia and Ninella in "A Deceiver Deceived," Cecca in "The Little Chicken," and Nunziella and Roseca-chiuove in "Head and Tail." The storytellers of the frame story are female and so are the fairies, with their power to transform and to entertain. The lambasting of curses against a woman beggar in the fifth and final tale may be perceived as misogynistic, consistent with some statements in Sarnelli's religious writings, yet Nunziella's stunning defense of the beggar with her own strong curses flung at the gentry shows courage and steadfast strength of character reminiscent of women celebrated in Boccaccio's *Decameron*. The list of curses also reminds us of Sarnelli's fascination and philological endeavors with the Neapolitan language and its expressive potentials.

Among the many features shared in *Posilecheata* are the author's strong interest in Naples and the arts, particularly sculptures, statues and architecture described in his guides for foreign visitors. References to Naples and the kingdom described in the 1685 *Guida de' forestieri* of Naples appear throughout the fairytales, especially in *cunto* III, where Reppone's narrative refers to Mergellina and its pier with the *Lanternone*, to Chiaja and Chiatamone, the Sebeto river, the Sellaria and Santa Lucia fountains, to Mount Vesuvius, and to the islands of Capri, Ischia, and Nisida. Intertextuality between the *Posilecheata* and the Neapolitan guide is also noted in *cunto* IV and *cunto* V.[xxvi]

Sarnelli's love of history, mythology, and magic are visible throughout the *Posilecheata*, as statues conclude each tale as reminders of negative or positive human behavior: Cocchiarone's statue bears an inscription in *cunto* I; a symbolic relief left in front of Pomponiella's royal garden is taken to Naples in *cunto* II; a shaming statue of Pascaddozia is placed in front of the university in *cunto* III; a statue of hateful Belluccia is taken to Naples in *cunto* IV; and a statue of Lo Gigante is present in *cunto* V. A passage opening the story of "The Little Chicken" evokes the horrors of the plague as a reminder of one of the deadliest scourges devastating the city in 1656, killing about half the population.[xxvii]

Last but not least one notes the play with names: Masillo as the humble visitor of his friend Petruccio and author of the fairytale collection, Marchionno as the Baroque character of the frame story, a hyperbolic glutton and smart entertaining intellectual. Petruccia's name in the second story is reminiscent of Petruccio's, and the name of the storyteller Cecca reappears in the fourth story. Numerology is displayed by Marchionno in the frame story and in the fairy's curse thrown at Pomponiella in the second tale. Among perhaps the most modern stories, "La Vajassa Fedele" stands out with the complex, gendered love relationship between Pomponiella and Petruccia, and between the two women and their royal suitors. All tales are framed from beginning to end by a proverb or saying to secure their internal unity.

The Language of the Posilecheata

The *Posilecheata* stands out among Sarnelli's works as a *summa* of his aspirations: in it we find morality, playfully entertaining inventions, the search for the bizarre, ethical values, erudition, and the Neapolitan backdrop and ambiance. The story collection celebrates empathy for the downtrodden and humility but also harbors a covert admiration for the ruling aristocratic class and for wealth. During the two centuries of Spanish rule Naples underwent a formidable demographic transformation due to immigration from the provinces of southern Italy, the Spanish presence, and its prestige as a great European cultural capital. Its population doubled within few decades, reaching some 350,000 inhabitants by the mid-seventeenth century. The crowded, multicultural city was made up of diverse social classes speaking different varieties of Italian and Neapolitan. In his early seventeenth century chronicles Giulio Cesare Capaccio addresses the city's internal divisions between the nobility, the bourgeois and business community, and the lowest popular strata. Capaccio discusses linguistic varieties used in Naples, such as the nobility's "parlar polito," a regulated standard variety of Italian comparable to the *lingua cortigiana*, a variety used also by some merchants in the business community side by side with the dialectal or popular Italian variety, suggested in Giulio Cesare Cortese's *Vaiasseide*. The "parlar impolito" or dialects with their internal diatopic stratifications were instead used by a large plebeian population.[xxviii]

The second century of the Spanish rule is also the period in which Neapolitan dialect literature flourished with Giambattista Basile and Giulio Cesare Cortese, two authors who nurtured Sarnelli's passion for the Neapolitan language and culture and his proficiency in the written dialect. These writers focus their attention on popular culture and its linguistic expressions by collecting and sometimes inventing Neapolitan words and idioms for their masterpieces and Baroque experimentalism, highlighted by Basile's fairytale collection, *Lo cunto de li cunti*, considered by critics the most beautiful book of the Italian Baroque age. In both Basile and Sarnelli, one finds a taste for accumulation and synonyms with catalogues of terms from specific semantic areas such as food and fashion. These authors celebrate the superiority of the Neapolitan language over other dialects and sometimes distance themselves from the growing hegemony of the Tuscan literary language, which they use abundantly, however, in their works.

The native Apulian and adoptive Neapolitan's literary dialect is a language that combines spoken popular speech with some erudite lexicon aimed at creating a cultivated written variety of the language. As noted by Vincenzo Valente, Sarnelli's language lacks traces of his native dialect. His relatively homogenous balanced style[xxix] between popular and learned features, with some interference from standard Italian in the vocabulary and syntax, results from careful study of the language, idioms and proverbs in Neapolitan literary texts.

The Editions

The first edition of 1684, with its dedication to Ignazio De Vives, was reprinted and edited throughout the twentieth century. It gained the attention of important critics such as Benedetto Croce and Vittorio Imbriani, and more recently Enrico Malato. In addition to a 1751 reprint, Chiachieppo Boezio prepared an edition in the late seventeenth or eighteenth century which he dedicated to "Sua Autezza Lo Geante de Palazzo," with numerous changes to Sarnelli's 1684 edition,[xxx] owing mainly to orthographic uncertainties of transcribing a literary dialect. Ten years after a critical study of *Il gran Basile*, the Neapolitan Vittorio Imbriani published in 1885 shortly before his death a sixth edition of the *Posilecheata*, following closely Sarnelli's original version and adding a plethora of more than 100 pages of "Illustrazioni," detailed comparative historical and philological notes about specific passages, some of them written by Rinaldo Köhler. In his introduction, Imbriani praises Sarnelli as "tra [i] più colti ed operosi ingegni del suo secolo e del suo paese" (among the most learned and industrious minds of his century and his country),[xxxi] before providing a description of the previous five editions (1685 through 1761) of the *Posilecheata*. Almost a century later, Enrico Malato prepared an edition of the *Posilecheata* with an introduction and Italian translation in 1962, followed by a slightly revised new edition in 1986.

Note on translation

This first full-length translation of *Posilecheata* is based on the 1986 edition by Enrico Malato. The Neapolitan and English versions appear on opposite pages, inviting a comparative reading and enjoyment of the language of the fairytales composed in the Neapolitan dialect. As to the translation criteria, an attempt was made to remain closely to the Neapolitan original text while aiming at a colloquial English version. Altamura's and Rocco's Neapolitan dictionaries, and the notes and Italian translations of Malato's 1986 edition were of significant help. The Neapolitan forms of names have been preserved, while some toponyms are rendered in English. The translation is intended as a bridge to reading the original Neapolitan fairytale collection. Endnotes were kept to a minimum.

Acknowledgments

Ever since publishing a panorama of Italy's rich literary dialects (*The Other Italy*, University of Toronto Press, 1999) I have been intrigued by the scarcity of narrative dialect prose throughout the canon and fascinated by its unique wealth in Neapolitan thanks to Giambattista Basile's superb Baroque masterpiece *Lo Cunto de li cunti* and Pompeo Sarnelli's *Posilecheata*. My translation of the *Posilecheata* aims at getting the work better known among Anglophone readers and letting them enjoy the Neapolitan literary language that Sarnelli cultivated and cherished throughout his life.

My thanks go to Luigi Ballerini and Gianluca Rizzo for welcoming my book in the Opuntia series and for their editorial work at Agincourt Press. I am indebted to Enrico Malato for the use of the Neapolitan text of his edition, to Nicoletta Maraschio and the Fondazione Memofonte in Florence and the editors of the Neapolitan *Guide*, to the Biblioteca Nazionale Centrale of Florence for the reproductions of the frontispieces of Sarnelli's first edition of the *Posilecheata* and of his edition of Basile's *Cunto*. I thank Massimo Fanfani and Antonio Vinciguerra for reading the Introduction and making invaluable suggestions. I am indebted to Gianpiero Doebler for editing the English texts, and to Clara Ramazzotti for keyboarding the Neapolitan text and proofreading it. I thank Charles Traub and Malik Clement for their assistance in preparing all illustrations. And I thank the staff at the Biblioteca Nazionale of Florence and the New York Public Library for their tireless research assistance.

Endnotes

i For an overview of Italian dialect literature and the scarcity of literary prose in dialect, see Hermann W. Haller, *The Other Italy. The Literary Canon in Dialect.* Toronto-Buffalo-London: University of Toronto Press, 1999; Enrico Malato (ed.), *Lingua e dialetto nella tradizione letteraria italiana.* Rome: Salerno Editrice, 1996.

ii According to Giovanni Muto ("Urban Structures and Population," in Tommaso Astarita (ed.), *A companion to early modern Naples.* Leiden-Boston: Brill, 2013, 35-61), the city had 300,000 residents by 1630 and about 186,000 residents in 1688 due to the devastating plague of 1657.

iii For a historical overview of literary fairytales see Jack Zipes, "Towards a definition of the literary fairytale," in id. (ed.), *The Oxford Companion to Fairy Tales.* Oxford-New York: Oxford University Press, 2000, xv-xxxii.

iv After working as a clerk at the San Biagio bookstore for two years, Antonio Bulifon (1649-1707) began his own editorial and publishing enterprise. He shared with Sarnelli a keen interest in historiography and literature, publishing sixteenth-century women's poetry, works such as Summonte's *Historia della città e regno di Napoli* (1675), and several of Sarnelli's works, becoming a very successful publisher with an international network. His bookstore served as a hub for intellectual exchange by writers, jurists, and scientists. See Gaspare De Caro, "Antonio Bulifon," *Dizionario biografico degli Italiani* vol.15, 1972, 57-61.

v The Dominican priest Pierfrancesco Orsini (1650-1730) took the name Vincenzo Maria when he became cardinal at age twenty-two. He was appointed bishop of Siponto three years later, of Cesena in 1680, and of Benevento in 1686. Known for his religious fervor and efforts to reform the church he became Pope Benedict XIII in 1724. See Gaspare De Caro, "Benedetto XIII," *Dizionario biografico degli Italiani*, vol. 8, 1966, 384-393.

vi Angelo Custodero, *Un diario inedito (1690-1718) di Pompeo Sarnelli.* Trani: Tip. V. Vecchi, 1907. Custodero narrates Sarnelli's *Vita* from 1690 to 1718, translating Latin diary notes on his ecclesiastic career and on daily events in his Pugliese diocese that include Turkish incursions and skirmishes with slave rescues. The incomplete diary pages seem to confirm the very prolific summer of 1684 spent at the convent of S. Brigida de' Padri Domenicani, where Sarnelli supposedly wrote the *Posilecheata*, the Naples and Pozzuoli guides, and a volume of *Lettere Ecclesiastiche*.

vii For a translation of the foreword, see Nancy L. Canepa in Ruth B. Bottigheimer, *Fairy Tales Framed. Early Forewords, Afterwords, and Critical Words.* Albany: SUNY Press, 2012, 72-75.

viii Pompeo Sarnelli's edition of Basile's *Cunto de li cunti*, titled *Il Pentamerone del cavalier Giovan Battista Basile, overo Lo cunto de li cunte, trattenemiento de li peccerille, di Gian Alessio Abbattutis nuovamente restampato, co tutte le zeremonie corrietto* was published by Bulifon in Naples in 1674. The illustration of changes noted here is between this edition of 1674 and the 1637 edition published in Naples by Ottavio Beltrano. For a detailed description of editions of Basile's fairy tales, see Carolina Stromboli (ed.), *Lo cunto de li cunti di Giovan Battista Basile.* Rome: Salerno Editrice, 2013, vol. 2, 987 ff.

ix In Canto I of his *Viaggio di Parnaso* (1621), Giulio Cesare Cortese (1575-1627) celebrates *vuce chiantute de la maglia vecchia, / c'hanno gran forza, ed énchieno l'aurecchia* (robust [Neapolitan] words made of ancient mesh that have great fortitude and fill our ears) (v.24). Inspired by Giulio Cesare Caporali's 1582 *Viaggio in Parnaso*, Cortese's popular parody is aimed at introducing Neapolitan literary dialects to the Parnassus, thus freeing them from conventional rules. Sarnelli was familiar with Cortese's works in Neapolitan (Vaiasseide, Micco Passaro 'Nnamorato, Li travagliuse ammure de Ciullo e Perna, etc.).

x For a detailed analysis of this scene and the importance of proverbs in Sarnelli's *Posilecheata*, see Daniela D'Eugenio, *"Lengua che no' la 'ntienne, e tu la caca.* Irony and Hilarity of Neapolitan Paroemias in Pompeo Sarnelli's *Posilecheata* (1684)," *International Studies in Humour* 5(1), 2016, 74-111. For a comprehensive study of proverbs in Sarnelli's *Posilecheata*, see Daniela D'Eugenio, *Paroimia. Brusantino, Florio, Sarnelli and Italian Proverbs From Sixteenth and Seventeenth Centuries.* West Lafayette, IN: Purdue University Press, 2021.

xi Emanuele Rocco, *Vocabolario del dialetto napolitano,* ed. Antonio Vinciguerra. 4 vols., Florence: Accademia della Crusca, 2018. Following the first volume with the introduction, volume 2 consists of a reprint of Rocco's incomplete second edition (Letters A-FELETTO) of 1891. Volumes 3 and 4 are Antonio Vinciguerra's critical edition of the unpublished manuscripts held in the Archives of the Accademia della Crusca (FIGLIASTRO-PROPOSCIA; PROPOSETO-ZZO).

xii In cunto V (*Head and Tail*), Sarnelli seems to lift a broad range of curse words from Basile's correspondence with Cortese. Some twenty-seven of thirty-seven curse words launched at Nunziella by the gentry correspond to Basile's in his Fourth Letter, and twenty-eight of thirty-seven terms reappear verbatim in Nunziella's invective against the abusive gentry. Sarnelli also adds his own creations or imitations from a variety of sources. See Giambattista Basile, *Lo cunto de li cunti overo lo trattenemiento de peccerille, Le Muse Napolitane e Le Lettere,* ed. Mario Petrini, Rome-Bari: Laterza 1976, 590-596. I thank Antonio Vinciguerra for drawing attention to Basile's *Lettere* as a source for Sarnelli's curse words.

xiii For the rich literature on the Italian language debate known as *questione della lingua,* see for example, Claudio Marazzini, "Questione della lingua", *Enciclopedia dell'italiano,* vol.2, ed. Raffaele Simone. Rome: Istituto della Enciclopedia Treccani, 2011, 1207-12; Raffaella Scarpa, *La questione della lingua. Antologia di testi da Dante a oggi.* Rome: Carocci, 2012.

xiv See the elegant edition, *Scuola di Bestie. Bestiarum schola* (Bari: Cacucci Editore, 2008), edited and introduced by Antonio Iurilli with an Italian translation of the Latin work by Damiano De Virgilio and a preface by Francesco Tateo.

xv The citation is from volume 10 of Sarnelli's *Lezioni ecclesiastiche* (4 10-11): "Le favole per lo più contengono cose o istoriche o filosofiche o morali, ma dette di maniera che rechino diletto (…). La favola adunque (…) è una falsa narrazione di cose maravigliose simile al vero" (cited in Francesco Tateo's Preface to Antonio Iurilli's 2008 edition of *Bestiarum Schola*, 11).

xvi For an illustration of a selection of *Lectiones*, see Appendix 1.

xvii Cited in Antonio Bulifon's Preface to the 1685 Neapolitan *Guida*, see *Appendix* 2. Sarnelli may have used additional sources for his Neapolitan *Guida* such as Giulio Cesare Capaccio's *Il forastiero* (1634) and Giovanni Alvina's *Catalogo di tutti gli edifici sacri della città di Napoli e suoi sobborghi* (1643). See the rich section "Guide, descrizioni e appunti di viaggio" with numerous editions of guides to Naples published on the website of the Fondazione Memofonte founded by Paola Barocchi (https://www.memofonte.it/ricerche/napoli).

xviii Perhaps due to an oversight, Sarnelli's 1674 edition of Basile's *Cunto de li cunti* is missing among the works cited.

xix The first edition of 1685 and the second of 1688 of the *Guida de' forestieri* to Naples contained 46 and 55 illustrations, respectively. See the introductions to the various editions of this *Guida* at https://www.memofonte.it/ricerche/napoli/#pompeo-sarnelli.

xx In "La guida de' forestieri per Pozzuolo," *Proculus. Rivista trimestrale della diocesi di Pozzuoli* lxxxvii, n.s., 2012, 101-23, Maria Lenci discusses the various editions of the Phlegrean guide and its success as a bestseller for educated tourists.

xxi See Appendices 2 and 3 for illustrations of selected passages of the two guides.

xxii For a discussion of Sarnelli's religious thought, see Giovanni Pinto, "Il pensiero religioso di Pompeo Sarnelli," *Archivio storico pugliese* xxx, 1977, 229-53, and Francesco Tateo, "Pompeo Sarnelli fra storiografia ed erudizione", ibid., 203-227. The descriptions of Sarnelli's ecclesiastic writings are based on a review of the printed editions examined at the Biblioteca Nazionale Centrale of Florence, Italy and at the New York Public Library. They are limited to a few notes, as they require an in-depth reading and analysis by specialists.

xxiii See Appendix 4 for an excerpt from Sarnelli's *Memorie dell'Insigne Collegio di S. Spirito di Benevento*.

xxiv *Lettere ecclesiastiche* vol.2, 1716. In his writings, Sarnelli uses a large amount of accents (hò goduto / non hò dubbio / hà voluto / fù conceduto / si và studiando / mà / à quel tempo) and apostrophies (un'atto, un'anno, un'Eccclesiastico), as well as latinizing initial h- in various grammatical categories (humanità / haveva, l'havrò, humilmente).

xxv The six letters written by Sarnelli to Antonio Magliabechi (1633-1714) between 1686 and 1688 examined in the *Carteggio Magliabechi* of the Biblioteca Nazionale Centrale in Florence humbly ask the famous librarian for an opinion of his publications. In a letter dated August 22, 1687, Sarnelli explains his preference for writing in Italian instead of Latin for "i miei nazionali", the Italian people who understand him better in their mother tongue.

xxvi References to Naples in the *Posilecheata* coincide with those found in the *Guida de' forestieri* published in the same year: Posillipo (327), Mergellina (331), Sannazaro (335), the Kingdom of Naples (421), the Tarcena (39), the Sebeto river (373, 375), Chiaja (345), Somma or Mount Vesuvius (402). The Neapolitan *Seggi* and the *Cavallo d'avrunzo* (bronze horse) (52 and 71-72, respectively) are mentioned in Cunto IV. Additional references include the *Palazzo Reale* (38), Chiatamone (34), the Lanterna del Molo (38), etc.

xxvii Plagues also struck the city in 1493, 1526 and 1764. See David Gentilcore, "Tempi sì calamitosi: edipemic disease and public health," in Tommaso Astarita (ed.), *A companion volume to early modern Naples*. Leiden-Boston: Brill, 2013, 281-306.

xxviii See Nicola De Blasi's comprehensive linguistic history of Naples, *Storia linguistica di Napoli*. Rome: Carocci, 2012.

xxix Vincenzo Valente aptly describes the "temperanza espressiva" (expressive restraint) of Sarnelli's style and the "festevolezza" of his Neapolitan in his essay "La lingua napoletana di Pompeo Sarnelli," *Archivio storico pugliese* xxx, 1977, 255-265.

xxx Chiachieppo changes numerous transcriptions of Sarnelli's original 1684 edition, trying perhaps to make the text more Neapolitan: *li primme huommene* > *li primm'uommene; non serve* > *nno serve; per non darencella* > *pe nno darencella; quarche recreazione* > *quacche recreazione; che quarche travo rutto no strida* > *che quarche travo siseto no strilla*, etc. (from *A li vertoluse lejeture*, 3).

xxxi Pompeo Sarnelli, *Posilecheata. Ristampa di 250 esemplari curati da Vittorio Imbriani.* 6th ed. Naples: Morano, 1885, xii.

Bibliography

Primary Sources

Posilecheata de Masillo Reppone de Gnanopoli. Al virtuosiss. Signore Il Signor Ignazio de Vives. Naples: presso Giuseppe Roselli, a spese di Antonio Bulifon, Libraro di S.E., 1684.

Posilecheata de Masillo Reppone de Gnanopoli. Naples 1751.

Posilecheata de Masillo Reppone de Gnanopoli adecato da Chiachieppo Boezio. Naples, XVII / XVIII c.

Pompeo Sarnelli, *Posilecheata. Ristampa di 250 esemplari curata da Vittorio Imbriani.* 6th ed., Naples: Domenico Morano, 1885.

Pompeo Sarnelli, *Posilecheata.* Testo, traduzione, introduzione e note di Enrico Malato. Florence: Sansoni, 1962.

Pompeo Sarnelli, *Posilecheata.* A cura di Enrico Malato (*Testi dialettali napoletani no. 7*). Rome: Benincasa, 1986.

Other Works by Pompeo Sarnelli

Pompeo Sarnelli, *Alfabeto greco con grandissima facilità ordinato da Pompeo Sarnelli.* Rome: Mascardi, 1675.

Pompeo Sarnelli (ed.), *Antichità di Pozzuolo et luoghi convicini...* del signor Ferrante Loffredo. Naples: Bulifon, 1675.

Pompeo Sarnelli, *Antica Basilicografia di Pompeo Sarnelli dottor della Santa teologia e delle leggi, dedicata all'eminentissimo Vincenzo Maria Cardinale Orsini Arcivescovo di Benevento.* Naples: Bulifon, 1686.

Pompeo Sarnelli, *Bestiarium schola ad homines erudiendos ab ipsa rerum natura provide instituta.* Cesena: presso Pietro Tipografo Episcopale, 1680.

Pompeo, Sarnelli, *Bestiarum schola, ossia Delle favole di Mons. Pompeo Sarnelli fra i più eruditi e moderni del '600.* Vito de Donato (ed.). Putignano: Vito Radio, 2007.

Pompeo Sarnelli Aesopus Primnellius, *Scuola di bestie = Bestiarum Schola.* A cura di Antonio Iurilli, traduzione di Damiano De Virgilio, prefazione di Francesco Tateo. Bari: Cacucci, 2008.

Pompeo Sarnelli, *Cronologia de' vescovi et arcivescovi sipontini colle notitie histori-che di molte notabili cose ne' loro tempi avvenute tanto nella vecchia e nuova Siponto quanto in altri luoghi della Puglia*. Manfredonia: nella Stamperia Arcivescovale, 1680; Bologna: Forni, 1986 (rist. anast.).

Degli avvenimenti di Fortunato e de' suoi figli: historia comica tradotta dal francese et ampliata da Masillo Reppone de Gnanopoli. Libri due. Naples: Antonio Bulifon, 1676.

Della magia naturale del signor Gio. Battista della Porta Napolitano Libri xx. Tradotti da latino in volgare, o dall'istesso Autore accresciuti, sotto nome di Gio. De Rosa (...). Accresciuta d'un Indice copiosissimo, e del Trattato della Chirofisonomia non ancora stampato. Tradotto da un Manoscritto latino dal Signor Pompeo Sarnelli. Naples: Bulifon, 1677.

Pompeo Sarnelli, *Dello specchio del clero secolare*. Naples: Bulifon, 1678.

Pompeo Sarnelli, *Donato distrutto, rinnovato con i versi di Catone in altrettanti versi italiani trasportati*. Naples: Novello De Bonis, 1675.

Pompeo Sarnelli, *Filalete dialogo delle cose spirituali, ed invisibili. Opera non solo utile, ma necessaria ad ogni Cristiano di Monsignor P.S. Vescovo di Biseglia*. Venice: Appresso Antonio Bortoli, 1708.

Pompeo Sarnelli, *Guida de' Forestieri curiosi di vedere ed intendere le cose più notabili della regal città di Napoli e del suo amenissimo distretto, ritrovata colla lettura de' buoni scrittori e colla propria diligenza dall'Abate Pompeo Sarnelli*. Naples: Bulifon, 1685; bilingual Italian-French edition, 1702.

Pompeo Sarnelli, *Guida de' forestieri curiosi di vedere e d'intendere le cose più notabili della regal città di Napoli e del suo amenissimo distretto*. Naples 1685, Giuseppina Acerbo (ed.), 2008; 2nd ed., Naples 1688, Federica De Rosa, Alessandra Rullo and Simona Starita (eds.), 2014; 4th ed., Naples 1697, Manuela Altruda (ed.), 2019; 5th ed., Naples 1708-1713, Lucio Oriani and Mariano Saggiomo (eds.), 2015; 6th ed., Naples 1752, Sara Concilio and Lorenzo Galasso (eds.), 2016. https://www.memofonte.it/ricerche/napoli/#pompeo-sarnelli.

Pompeo Sarnelli, *Guida de' Forestieri curiosi di vedere, e considerare le cose notabili di Pozzoli, Baja, Miseno, Cuma, ed altri luoghi circonvicini. Ritrovata colla lettura de' buoni Scrittori, e colla propria diligenza dall'Abate Pompeo Sarnelli*. Naples: Bulifon, 1685 (1691, 1769, etc.).

Pompeo Sarnelli, *La guida dei forestieri di Pozzuoli (1734)*. Prefazione di Carlo De Frede. Ristampa anastatica. Bologna: Forni, 2002.

Pompeo Sarnelli, *La guide des etrangers curieux de voir, & de connoitre les choses les plus memorables de Poussol, Bayes, Cumes, Misene, Gaete, et autres lieux des environs. Expliquée à l'aide des bons auteurs, & par la propre recherche de l'Abbé Pompeo Sarnelli. Traduite en François par Antoine Bulifon*. Naples: Bulifon, 1700.

Pompeo Sarnelli, *La guide des etrangers curieux de voir, & de connoitre les choses les plus memorables de Poussol, Bayes, Cumes, Misene, Gaete, et autres lieux des environs. Expliquée à l'aide des bons auteurs, & par la propre recherche de Monseigneur l'evèque de Biseglia, Pompee Sarnelli; et enrichie par Antoine Bulifon de plusieurs figures en taille douce, & augmentee de quelques particularitez tres curieuses.* Naples: Aux Dépenses de X. Rossi, 1769.

Pompeo Sarnelli, *Il clero secolare nel suo splendore o vero della vita comune chericale Trattato di Pompeo Sarnelli.* Rome: Nella Stamperia della Reverenda Camera Apostolica, 1688.

Pompeo Sarnelli, *L'Arca del testamento in Biseglia.* Venice: Andrea Poletti, 1694. Ristampa anastatica. Bisceglie: Antonio Cortese, 2008.

Pompeo Sarnelli, *Il vero Tesoro de' Santi Corpi de' gloriosi martiri Mauro Vescovo, Pantaleone e Sergio Cavalieri Romani ritrovato a' x di Maggio 1167 nel villaggio di Sagina, operetta villareggia di M. Epompo Narsellu, Primo Ministro di detti Santi.* Naples 1709; Bisceglie: Antonio Cortese, 2010.

Pompeo Sarnelli, *Lettere ecclesiastiche di monsignor Pompeo Sarnelli vescovo di Bisceglia.* 10 vols. Naples: Antonio Bulifon, 1686-1696; Naples: nella Stamperia di Felice Mosca, 1686-1716; 9 tomi, Venice: appresso Antonio Bortoli, 1716-1718.

Pompeo Sarnelli, *Lezioni scritturali alla mente, ed al cuore sopra l'uno, e l'Altro Testamento secondo le Interpretazioni del celebre Pietro Comestore Maestro della Storia Scolastica.* Venice: Appresso Antonio Bortoli, 1705.

Pompeo Sarnelli, *Lume a' Principianti nello studio delle Materie Ecclesiastiche, e scritturali.* Naples: Nella Stamperia di Felice Mosca, 1723.

Pompeo Sarnelli, *Memorie cronologiche de' Vescovi ed Arcivescovi della S. Chiesa di Benevento.* Naples: Bulifon, 1677. Bologna: Forni, 1976.

Pompeo Sarnelli, *Memorie dell'Insigne Collegio di S. Spirito della città di Benevento.* Naples: Bulifon, 1688.

Pompeo Sarnelli, *Memorie de' Vescovi di Biseglia, e della stessa città. Ricercate dal vescovo P.S.* Naples: Bulifon, 1677.

Pompeo Sarnelli, *Ordinario grammaticale, utilissimo ad ogni studioso della lingua latina.* Naples: presso Giuseppe Roselli, 1691.

Pompeo Sarnelli (ed.), *Il Pentamerone del cavalier Giovan Battista Basile, overo Lo cunto de li cunte. Trattenemiento de li Peccerille, di Gian Alessio Abbatutis. Nuovamente restampato, e co' tutte le zeremonie corrietto.* Naples: Bulifon, 1674.

Pompeo Sarnelli, *Specchio del clero secolare overo vite de' SS. Cherici secolari.* Naples: Bulifon, 1678.

Translations

Pompeo Sarnelli, *Posilecheata*. Salzburg: Internationale Arbeitsgemeinschaft für Forschung zum Romanischen Volksbuch, 1982.

Pompeo Sarnelli, *Die fünf Märchen vom Gastmahl in Neapel*. Frankfurt a. Main: Insel Verlag, 1988.

Pompeo Sarnelli, *Les contes napolitains*. Trans. Claude Perrus. Belfort: Circé, 2000.

Pompeo Sarnelli, Foreword to *An Outing to Posillipo*, translated by Nancy L. Canepa in Ruth B. Bottigheimer (ed.), *Fairy Tales Framed*. Albany: SUNY Press, 2012, 76-79; "The Little Hen," translated by Nancy L. Canepa, in ead., (ed.), *The Enchanted Boot. Italian Folktales & Their Tellers*. Detroit: Wayne State University Press, 2023, 151-167.

Secondary Sources

Acerbo, Giuseppina, "L'abate Pompeo Sarnelli e la sua Guida di Napoli". *Equipéco* 6, 2007, n.11, 102-104.

Allasia, Clara, "La Posilecheata, una still-life fiabesca." In *I novellieri italiani e la loro presenza nella cultura europea: rizoni e palinsesti rinascimentali,* eds. Guillermo Carrascón – Chiara Simbolotti. Turin: Accademia University Press 2015, 255-267.

Altamura, Antonio, *Il dialetto napoletano*. Naples: F. Fiorentino, 1961.

Altamura, Antonio, *Dizionario dialettale napoletano*. Naples: F. Fiorentino, 1968.

Arienzo, Donato, *Saggio sulla Posilecheata di mons. Pompeo Sarnelli*. Bari: M. Cavalli, 1960.

Astarita, Tommaso (ed.), *A Companion to early modern Naples*. Leiden-Boston: Brill, 2013.

Basile, Giambattista, *Lo cunto de li cunti overo lo trattenemiento de peccerille, Le Muse Napolitane e Le Lettere,* Mario Petrini (ed.), Rome-Bari: Laterza, 1976.

Basile, Giovan Battista, *Lo cunto de li cunti overo Lo trattenemiento de' peccerille,* Caterina Stromboli (ed.), 2 vols., Rome: Salerno, 2013.

Basile Bonsante Mariella, "Appunti su Pompeo Sarnelli moralista e scrittore d'arte." *Atti del Congresso Internazionale di studi sull'età del Viceregno*. Eds. Francesco De Robertis and Mauro Spagnoletti. Bari: Grafica Bigiemme, 1977, 242-256.

Bellucci, Ermanno, "Le guide di Napoli come prodotti editoriali dal XVI al XIX secolo", in Francesco Amirante et al. (eds.), *Libri per vedere. Le guide storico-artistiche della città di Napoli: fonti testimonianze del gusto immagini di una città*. Naples: Edizioni scientifiche italiane, 1995, 333-357.

Bernardi, C., "Basile Cortese Sgruttendio: Che passione!" *Belfagor* 40/4, 1985, 429-447.

Bianchi, Patricia, De Blasi Nicola, Librandi Rita, *Storia della lingua a Napoli e in Campania*. Naples: Pironti, 1993.

Bondi, Fabrizio, "Il 'cunto' dello Scontento. Proposte su Imbriani e la fiaba". *Annali dell'università Suor Orsola Benincasa* 14/2, 2021, 257-283.

Bottigheimer, Ruth B. (ed.), *Fairy Tales Framed. Early Forewords, Afterwords, and Critical Words.* Albany: SUNY Press, 2012.

Bronzini, Giovanni Battista, "Italien". *Enzyklopädie des Märchens. Handwörterbuch zur historischen und vergleichenden Erzählsforschung.* Hrsg. Von Rolf Wilhelm Brednich, Bd.7/1, Berlin-New York: De Gruyter 1991, 336-370.

Calvino, Italo, *Sulla fiaba.* Milan: Mondadori, 1996.

Canepa, Nany, "Sarnelli, Pompeo (1649-1724)." *The Greenwood Encyclopedia of Folktales and Fairy Tales.* Ed. Donald Haase. Westport, CT: Greenwood Press, 2008.

Canepa, Nancy, "Literary Culture in Naples, 1500-1800", in Tommaso Astarita (ed.), *A Companion to Early Modern Naples.* Leiden-Boston: Brill, 2013, 427-451.

Capasso, B., *"Napoli descritta ne' principi del secolo XVII da Giulio Cesare Capaccio",* *Archivio storico per le province napoletane* 7, 1882, 68-103, 531-554, 776-797.

Capozzoli, Raffaele, *Grammatica del dialetto napoletano.* Naples: Chiurazzi, 1889.

Caputi, Pasquale, *L'attività pastorale di Pompeo Sarnelli vescovo di Bisceglie (1692-1724).* Bisceglie: Eurografica, 2006.

Cefalo, Dora, "Glossari del primer cunto de la Posilecheata de P. Sarnelli", *Quaderns d'Italià* 23, 2018, 161-178. Accessed 4/6/2022. https://raco.cat/index.php/QuadernsItalia/article/view/344272

Cherchi, Paolo, "The Seicento. Poetry, Philosophy, and Science", in Peter Brand and Lino Pertile (eds.), *The Cambridge History of Italian Literature.* New York: Cambridge University Press, 1999, 301-317.

Chirofisonomia del Sig. Gio. Battista Della Porta Napolitano Tradotta dal Sig. Pompeo Sarnelli. In Giovan Battista Della Porta, *De ea naturalis physiognmoniae parte quae ad Manuum lineas spectat libri duo, e in appendice Chirofisonomia.* Oreste Trabucco (ed.), Naples: Edizioni Scientifiche Italiane, 2003, 75-142.

Cortese, Giulio Cesare, *Viaggio di Parnaso,* Enrico Malato (ed.), Naples: Fausto Fiorentino, 1963.

Crane, Thomas Frederick, *Italian Popular Tales,* Jack Zipes (ed.). Oxford-New York: Oxford University Press, 2003.

Croce, Benedetto, *Nuovi saggi sulla letteratura italiana del Seicento.* Bari: Laterza, 1968.

Custodero Angelo, *Un diario inedito (1690-1718) di Pompeo Sarnelli.* Trani: Tip. V. Vecchi, 1907.

D'Ascoli, Francesco, *Nuovo vocabolario dialettale napoletano.* Naples: Gallina, 1993.

De Blasi, Nicola, "Notizie sulla variazione diastratica a Napoli tra il '500 e il 2000." *Bollettino Linguistico Campano* 1, 2002, 89-129.

De Blasi, Nicola, *Storia linguistica di Napoli.* Rome: Carocci, 2012.

De Blasi, Nicola, and Alberto Varvaro, "Napoli e l'Italia meridionale." *Letteratura italiana,* Alberto Asor Rosa (ed.), vol.7. Turin: Einaudi, 1988, 235-325.

De Donato, Nicola, *L'erudito Monsignor Pompeo Sarnelli fra i più moderni del Seicento (Vescovo di Bisceglie)*. Bitonto: Garofalo, 1906; Bari: Levante, 1983.

D'Eugenio, Daniela, "*Lengua che no' la 'ntienne, e tu la caca.* Irony and Hilarity of Neapolitan Paroemias in Pompeo Sarnelli's *Posilecheata* (1684)", *International Studies in Humour* 5(1), 2016, 74-111.

D'Eugenio, Daniela, *Paroimia. Brusantino, Florio, Sarnelli and Italian proverbs from the Sixteenth and Seventeenth centuries*. West Lafayette, IN: Purdue University Press, 2021.

Di Leo, Giuseppina, "Pompeo Sarnelli tra edificazione religiosa e letteratura", *Odegitria* 13, 2006, 167-244.

Dizionario biografico degli italiani. Rome: Treccani.

Duggan, Anne E. and Donald Haase with Helen J. Callow, *Folktales and Fairytales*. Vols. 1-4, *Traditions and Texts from around the World*. Santa Barbara: CA – Denver, CO, 2016.

Ferraro, Luca, "Dal *Pentamerone* alla *Posilecheata*: il ruolo di Pompeo Sarnelli nell'impresa tipografica di Antonio Bulifon." *Generi. Rivista internazionale di letteratura italiana* 3, 2025, 123-133.

Fierro, Aurelio, *Grammatica della lingua napoletana*. Milan: Rusconi, 1989.

Franzese, Rosa, "Luoghi favolosi nella *Posilecheata* di Sarnelli." *Napoli Nobilissima* 23, 1984, 114-123.

Fulco, Giorgio, "La letteratura dialettale napoletana. Giulio Cesare Cortese, e Giovan Battista Basile, Pompeo Sarnelli," in Enrico Malato (ed.), *Storia della letteratura italiana*, vol.5, *La fine del Cinquecento e il Seicento*, Rome: Salerno Editrice, 1998, 813-867.

Galiani, Ferdinando, *Del dialetto napoletano*. Ed. Enrico Malato, Rome, Bulzoni, 1970.

Getto, Giovanni, *Il Barocco letterario in Italia. Barocco in prosa e poesia*. Milan: Mondadori, 2000.

Giglio, Raffaele, "Il cunto 'dotto' di Pompeo Sarnelli."*La tradizione del "cunto" da Giovan Battista Basile a Domenico Rea*. Ed. Caterina De Caprio. Naples: Edizioni Libreria Dante & Descartes, 2007, 141-156.

Gimma, Giacinto, *Elogj Accademici della società degli spensierati di Rossano*. Naples: Carlo Troise, 1703.

GDLI *Grande dizionario della lingua italiana*. Turin: UTET.

Haase, Donald, *The Greenwood Encyclopedia of folktales and fairytales*. Westport, CT, Greenwood Press, 2008.

Haller, Hermann W., *The Other Italy. The Literary Canon in Dialect*. Toronto-Buffalo-London: University of Toronto Press, 1999.

Imbriani, Vittorio, "Il gran Basile: studio biografico e bibliografico". *Giornale napoletano di filosofia e lettere, scienze morali e politiche* 1-2, 1875.

Iurilli, Antonio, "Paremìa e favola. La *Bestiarium schola* di Pompeo Sarnelli". In Temistocle Franceschi (ed.), *Ragionamenti intorno al proverbio. Atti del II Con-

gresso internazionale dell'Atlante paremiologico italiano. Andria 21-24 aprile 2010. Alessandria: Edizioni dell'Orso, 2011, 315-328.

Klotz, Volker, *Das europäische Kunstmärchen. Fünfundzwanzig Kapitel seiner Geschichte von der Renaissance bis zur Moderne*. Stuttgart: Metzler, 1985.

Ledgeway, Adam, "Understanding Dialect: Some Neapolitan Examples", in id., Anna Laura Lepschy (eds.), *Didattica della lingua italiana. Testo e contesto*. Perugia: Guerra, 2008, 99-115.

Ledgeway, Adam, *Grammatica diacronica del napoletano. Beihefte zur romanischen Philologie 350*. Tübingen: Niemeyer, 2009.

Lenci, Maria, "*La guida de' forestieri per Pozzuolo* di Pompeo Sarnelli". *Proculus* 87, 2012, n.s., fasc. n.1-4, 101-206.

Malato, Enrico, "La letteratura dialettale campana." *Lingua e dialetto nella tradizione letteraria italiana. Atti del Convegno di Salerno, 5-6 novembre 1993*. Rome: Salerno Editrice, 1996, 255-272.

Marino, John A., "Constructing the Past of Early Modern Naples: Sources and Historiographies", in Tommaso Astarita (ed.), cit., 11-34.

Martorana, Pietro, *Notizie biografiche e bibliografiche degli scrittori del dialetto napoletano*. Naples: Chiurazzi, 1874.

Mauriello, Adriana, "I 'cunti' di Basile e i 'cunticielli' di Sarnelli: da *Lo cunto de li cunti* alla *Posilecheata*." *Esperienze letterarie* 49, 2024, 9-27.

Moro, Anna, *Aspects of Old Neapolitan: The Language of Basile's "Lo cunto de li cunti"*. Munich: Lincom Europa, 2003.

Nicolini, Fausto, "Pompeo Sarnelli". *Enciclopedia Italiana* vol.30, Rome: Istituto dell'Enciclopedia Italiana, 1936.

Nigro, Salvatore, "Il regno di Napoli". *Letteratura italiana. Storia e geografia. II. L'età moderna*. Turin: Einaudi, 1988, 1147-1192.

Nigro, Salvatore, "*Lo cunto de li cunti* di Giovan Battista Basile." *Letteratura italiana*, Alberto Asor Rosa (ed.). vol. 2, Turin: Einaudi, 1993, 867-891.

Paccagnella, Ivano, "*Uso letterario dei dialetti*". In Serianni, Luca and Trifone, Pietro (eds.), *Storia della lingua italiana*, vol. 3. Turin: Einaudi, 1994, 495-539.

Pinto, Giovanni, "Il pensiero religioso di Pompeo Sarnelli", *Archivio storico pugliese* 30, 1977, 229-253.

Pinto, Valter, *Racconti di opere e racconti di uomini: la storiografia artistica a Napoli tra periegesi e biografia, 1685-1700*. Prefazione di Andrea Emiliani. Naples: Paparo, 1997.

Pironti, Pasquale, *Bulifon, Raillard, Granier, ediori francesi a Napoli*. Naples: Lucio Pironti, 1982.

Pompeo Sarnelli: un vescovo meridionale nel solco della controriforma (1692-1724). Bisceglie: Antonio Cortese 2011.

Preziosa, Vittori, *Pompeo Sarnelli, Un vescovo pugliese fra Sei e Settecento. Produzione letteraria, attività pastorale e committenza artistica*. Lecce: Edizioni del Grifo, 2002.

Quondam, Amadeo, "Dal Barocco all'Arcadia", *Storia di Napoli,* vol.6, 1970, 809-1094.

Radtke, Edgar, "La questione della lingua e la letteratura dialettale a Napoli nel Seicento". In *Italica e Romanica: Festschrift für Max Pfister zum 65. Geburtstag.* Band 3, *Dialektologie und Soziolinguistik: Onomastik. Literatur und Kulturgeschichte. Wissenschaftsgeschichte.* Tübingen: Niemeyer, 1997, 75-86.

Rak, Michele, *Napoli gentile: la letteratura in 'lingua napoletana' nella cultura barocca (1596-1632).* Bologna: Il Mulino, 1994.

Ragazzini, Giuseppe, *Dizionario inglese italiano italiano inglese.* Bologna: Zanichelli.

Rasy, Elisabetta, *Posillipo.* Milan: Mondadori, 1997.

Rocco, Emmanuele, *Vocabolario del dialetto napolitano. A-FEL.* Naples: Chiurazzi, 1882-1891.

Rocco, Emmanuele, *Vocabolario del dialetto napolitano.* Ed. Antonio Vinciguerra. 4 vols., Florence: Accademia della Crusca, 2018.

Rubini, Luisa, "Fortunatus in Italy. A History Between Translations, Chapbooks and Fairy Tales". *Fabula* 44/1, 2003, 25-54.

Sammartino, Alberto, "Polemica letteraria antitoscana e produzione dialettale a Napoli nel tardo '600." *Annali della Facoltà di Lettere e Filosofia dell'Università di Napoli* 20, 1977-1978, 215-235.

Spera, Lucinda et al., *La novella barocca, con un repertorio bibliografico.* Naples: Liguori, 2001.

Stromboli, Carolina, "La lingua de *Lo Cunto de li cunti* di Giambattista Basile". Tesi di Dottorato, Università degli Studi di Napoli Federico II, Naples 2005.

Stromboli, Carolina, "La lingua de 'Lo cunto de li cunti' tra fiaba e realtà", in *La tradizione del "cunto" da Giovan Battista Basile a Domenico Rea.,* ed. C. De Caprio. Naples: Dante & Descartes, 2007, 67-91.

Stromboli, Carolina (ed.), *Lo cunto de li cunti di Giovan Battista Basile.* 2 vols., Rome: Salerno Editrice, 2013.

Stromboli, Carolina, *Le parole del Cunto. Indagini sul lessico napoletano del Seicento.* Florence: Cesati, 2017.

Tateo, Francesco, "Pompeo Sarnelli fra storiografia de erudizione", *Archivio storico pugliese* 30/1-4, 1977, 203-227.

Tateo, Francesco, "'*Humana Historia*' di Pompeo Sarnelli", in id., *I miti della storiografia umanistica,* Rome: Bulzoni, 1990, 137-179.

Valente, Vincenzo, "La lingua napoletana di Pompeo Sarnelli." *Archivio storico pugliese* 30, 1977, 255-265.

Valente, Vincenzo, "Per una migliore intelligenza del napoletano di G. Basile." *Lingua Nostra* 40, 1979, 43-49.

Valente, Vincenzo, *Puglia. Profilo dei dialetti taliani,* ed. Manlio Cortelazzo. Pisa: Pacini, 1975.

Vecchio, Paola, "Storia linguistica e letteratura dialettale riflessa: il caso dei pronomi personali in napoletano". Naples: Liguori, 2006, 97-142.

Vocabolario degli Accademici della Crusca, 1612.

Würl, Paul-Wolfgang, "Das Gastmahl auf dem Posilipp: ein katholischer Kirchenfürst als Märchenerzähler", *Märchenspiegel* 27/4, 2016.

Zipes, Jack (ed.), *The Oxford Companion to Fairy Tales*. Oxford-New York: Oxford University Press, 2000.

POSILECHEATA
DE MASILLO REPPONE

THE POSILECHEATA
A DAY TRIP TO POSILLIPO

Neapolitan version of Malato's edition of Sarnelli's *Posilecheata*

A LI VERTOLUSE LEJETURE
MASILLO REPPONE

[1] È na pazzia marcia chella de ciert'uommene, che puro mostano d'avere jodizio, li quale se credono de fare livre accossì agghiostate che nesciuno nce aggia a rapire vocca, e tutte, co na belledissima lleverenzia, l'aggiano a levare lo cappiello. [2] Pocca li primme uommene de lo munno porzí songo state cenzorate, essenno 'mpossibbele che quarche travo rutto no' strida e che quarche strenga rotta non se metta 'n dozzana: anze, trattannose de livre, vide pe nfi' a li strunze (parlanno co lleverenzia de le facce voste) che diceno: *Nos coque pomma natamus*. [3] Pe la quale cosa no cierto pennarulo, vedennome a cert'ore de lo juorno scrivere sto passatiempo, me decette: «E non se vregogna no paro tujo perdere lo tiempo a ste bagattelle? Haje scritto tant'opere grave e de considerazione, e mo scacàrete co sti cunte dell'uorco? E po' a lo mmacaro avisse scritto 'n lengua toscanese o 'n quarch'auto lenguaggio, pocca veramente la lengua napoletana non serve che pe li boffune de le commeddie». [4] Io, mo, che ste sonate le tengo sotta coscia, e n'aggio 'ntiso tanta de st'asenetate, puro pe non darencélla pe benta le responnette: Chi è chillo che me pò negare che l'ommo studiuso non s'aggia da pigliare quarche recreazione leceta ed onesta? Ma qual auta è la recreazione de lo vertoluso, se no' spezzare quarche bota li studie grave e spassarese co chille che songo alliegre? [5] Otra che lo scrivere cunte n'è cosa de verrille. Pocca, comme decette chillo Pico che cantava meglio de no rescegnuolo, non ce vò manco studio a fare na stàtola de creta che n'auta de oro e d'argiento. Anze, pe fare cheste abbesogna sapere fare lo modiello de chella. [6] E po' co sta lengua toscana avite frusciato lo tafanàrio a miezo munno! Vale cchiú na parola napoletana chiantuta che tutte li vocabole de la Crusca: e qual auto lenguaggio se le pò mettere 'mparagone? [7] Chi decerrà che lo parlare latino n'è no gran parlare? E puro Pompeo Magno, venuto a Napole e 'nnammoratose de sto parlare nuosto, lassaje lo latino; e quanno Cicerone ne le fece na lavatella de capo senza sapone, isso responnette ca non sapeva chello che se deceva, pocca si avesse prattecato a Napole

MASILLO REPPONE
TO THE VIRTUOUS READERS

(1) What a darn shame it is that certain people, even though reasonable, set out to write books no one understands but that everyone ought to admire and hold in high esteem. (2) Indeed, even the earliest folks on earth have been censured, since it is impossible for a broken beam not to squeak and for a dozen laces not to have a broken one.[i] And while we are talking about books, remember how even feces (speaking respectfully to your faces) claim: "We can swim too."[ii] So much so that seeing me write leisurely in the middle of the day, a scribbler told me: "Aren't you ashamed wasting time with these trifles? You wrote so many serious books, and now you are putting out these foul ogre tales? If you had at least used Tuscan or some other language, considering that Neapolitan is good only for clowns in comedies." (4) Being familiar with such tunes, and having often heard such stupidity, not to give in I retorted, "Who on earth can deny a scholar well-deserved, honest leisure? And what other leisure is there for the virtuous than to interrupt serious study from time to time and have fun with merry tales, (5) keeping in mind that writing tales is not a kids' game? As noted by that Pico[iii] who sang better than a nightingale, it is just as hard to make a statue of clay than one of gold and silver. In fact, to build the latter, you have to make a mold with the former. (6) Also, with this Tuscan language, you're screwing half the world! A strong Neapolitan word is worth more than all the words of the Crusca dictionary:[iv] what other language can equal it?! (7) Who would deny that Latin is a great language? Even Pompey the Great, on his visit to Naples, fell in love with our language and gave up Latin. And when Cicero scolded him, he replied that he didn't understand what he meant—had he lived in Naples, he too would have given up Latin for Neapolitan, which was but a mixture of Greek and Latin, a nice alloy to sweeten the mouth, palate, and throat. (8) Our very own Summonte, glory of Naples, declares in Book One, chapter six of his famous history to have read this in Cicero's *Epistles* to Atticus.

avarria lassato isso porzí lo parlare latino pe lo napoletano: lo quale auto non era che na mmesca de grieco e de latino, che faceva na bella lega p'addoci' la vocca, palataro e cannaruozzolo. [8] Accossí dice d'avere lejuto a le *Pístole* de Cecerone ad Atteco lo Sommonte nuesto, grolia de Napole, a lo cap. 6 de lo lib. I, de la storia soja tanto fammosa.

[9] E po', che 'mpertenenzia è chesta: dicere che lo parlare napoletano serve sulo pe li boffune de le commeddie? Chesto tutto soccede perché li frostiere che lo diceno non fanno studio a le parole noste, perché vedarriano quanto songo belle cheste e brutte le lloro. [10] Na vota, cammenanno no cierto felosofo de Posileco pe la Lommardia, perché parlava napoletano chiantuto e majàteco, tutte se ne redevano. Isso, mo, pe farele toccare la coda co le mmano, decette ad uno che faceva lo protaquamquam: — Vedimmo no poco, de 'razia, si songo meglio le parole voste o le noste! [11] Nuje decimmo *Capo*, e buje comme decite? — Nuje decimmo *Co*, respose l'auto. Ed isso: — Nuje decimmo *Casa*, e buje? — *Ca*, decette l'auto. — Nuje decimmo *Io*, e buje? — *Mi*, llebrecaje lo Lommardo. Ora lo felosofo decette accossí: — Di' alla 'mpressa le parole meje a lengua toja: *Io, Casa, Capo*. E lo Lommardo, súbeto: — *Mi Ca-Cò!* — E si te cacò — decette lo Napoletano — te lo mmeretaste! Pocca se dice a lo pajese che non è mio: *Lengua che no' la 'ntienne e tu la caca*. Ora vide chi parla a lo sproposeto, nuje o vuje? —

[12] E pe dire lo vero, non pareno pataccune chelle belle parole accossí grosse e chiatte, che non ce manca na lettera? [13] Non saje chello che se conta de no poverommo de li nuoste, lo quale, partuto da Napole, addove lo pane se chiamma *pane*, arrevaje a n'auto pajese e trovaje che se deceva *pan*; passaje cchiú 'nnanze, e se chiammava *pa*. Tanno decette a lo compagno: — Tornammoncénne, ca se cchiú 'nnanze jammo non trovarrimmo cchiú pane, e nce morarrimmo de famme! —

[14] Ma lassammo ghire sti chiàjete e dica ognuno chello che bòle. Chi ha fatto lo stromiento co li Toscanise de parlare a lengua loro, s'aggia pacienzia: io non ce l'aggio fatto, e perzò voglio parlare a lengua de lo pajese mio. E chi no' lo pò sentire, o s'appila l'aurecchie, o cinco lettere. [15] Spero ca li pajesane mieje l'azzettarranno co gusto, quanno maje ped auto, sulo perché è cosa nova: pocca se bè millanta valentuommene hanno scritto dapo' lo Cortese vierze napoletane, nesciuno dapo' Giannalesio Abbattuto ha scritto cunte. E se pe sciorta sti cuntecielle mieje, che dongo a le stampe pe mosta, piacerranno, voglio fare io porzíne lo livro gruosso, perché pozzo tornare a Posileco quanno voglio, e farence quinnece ciento Posilecheate. [16] Ora se l'Abbattuto scrivet-

(9) And how arrogant it is to say that Neapolitan is only the language of buffoons in comedies? That's just because foreigners who say this do not study our words, they would otherwise see how beautiful they are and how ugly theirs are. (10) When a certain philosopher from Posillipo visited Lombardy, speaking a thick and robust Neapolitan, everyone laughed at him. In order to make his point to a pretentious pedant, he said, "Let us just see, if you do not mind, which words sound better, yours or ours! (11) We say *Capo*, what do you say? – We say *Co*, the other replied. – And he continued: We say *Casa*, how about you? – *Ca*, the other said. – We say *Io*, what about you? – *Mi*, the Lombard replied. Then the philosopher said: Now repeat these words fast in your language: *Io, Casa, Capo*. And the Lombard quipped: *Mi Ca Cò!* – So if you shitted - the Neapolitan said, - you deserved it! Because they say in a foreign land, not in my town, that *A language you do not understand, you shit*.[v] So let's see who is talking out of turn, you or me? -

(12) And to tell the truth, don't those beautiful, big, fat words that do not miss any letter look like medals? (13) Don't you know the story of a poor fellow who left Naples, where bread is called *pane*. When he arrived in another town where it was called *pan*, and further North *pa*,[vi] it prompted him to tell his companion, "Let's return home. If we go on, we won't find any more bread and will be starving!"

(14) But let us forget about this argument, and may everyone say what they please. Whoever made a deal with the Tuscans to speak their language should relax. I have not done it; therefore, I want to speak the language of my town. If you cannot take that, plug your ears or get lost. (15) I hope my compatriots will accept it favorably, if only for its novelty. While thousands have written poems in Neapolitan after Cortese, no one has written tales after Giannalesio Abbattuto.[vii] And if by chance you should like my little tales printed as moral illustrations, I too want to compose a large book, going back to Posillipo whenever I please to write some hundred and fifteen Posillipo tales. (16) If Abbattuto wrote to entertain only children, while also being read by adults, and even more so by foreigners, I hope that my little book will do the same for them. Should all fail, it will be useful to daddies with their numerous children (17) so that reading it at night *al fresco* on the terrace in summer or around the fireplace in winter, the young and old will fall asleep from all the silly stuff, go to bed, skip dinner, and bless the heart of the writer, who kisses your hands if you washed them, giving his own blessings.

te pe trattenemiento sulo de li peccerille e po' ha servuto porzí pe le giúvene e pe li viecchie, e cotte meglio porzí pe li frostiere, spero ca sto livreciello mio non sarrà sgrato a li stisse, e quanno tutto manca jovarrà a li patre de fameglia c'hanno peccerille assaje: [17] pocca la sera, lejennolo o a lo frisco fora la loggia, la 'state, o a lo focolaro, lo vierno, non sulo li peccerille ma li granne s'addormarranno pe lo rencrescemiento de le tanta freddure che nce songo, e facennole mettere tutte a lietto sparagnarranno lo magnare, e benedicerranno l'arma de chi l'ha scritto. Lo quale vasannove le mmano, si ve l'avite lavate, s'arrecommanna.

Endnotes

i This sentence is found in Giulio Cesare Cortese's Introduction *Lo Poeta a Li Leieture* to his *Viaggio in Parnaso*.

ii The Latin expression *Nos quoque poma natamus* is found in one of Aesop's stories, *Poma et sterquilinum* (Malato 1986, 3).

iii Perhaps a reference to the Renaissance philosopher Giovanni Pico della Mirandola (1463-1494).

iv Sarnelli was obviously familiar with the *Vocabolario degli Accademici della Crusca*, published in 1612.

v The parahypotactic phrase, *Lengua che no' la 'ntienne, e tu la caca* conveys Neapolitans' disregard for foreign languages. For a discussion of the phrase, see Daniela D'Eugenio's essay, *"Lengua che no' la 'ntienne, e tu la caca.* Irony and Hilarity of Neapolitan Paroemias in Pompeo Sarnelli's *Posilecheata* (1684)", *International Studies in Humour* 5(1), 2016, 74-111.

vi The comparison between *pane* and *pa* highlights the apocope found in Lombard and other Northern Italian dialects. For a discussion of Sarnelli's claim of superiority of Neapolitan over Tuscan, see Daniela D'Eugenio, *Paroimia. Brusantino, Florio, Sarnelli, and Italian Proverbs From the Sixteenth and Seventeenth Centuries*. West Lafayette, IN: Purdue University Press, 2021, 202-210.

vii Referring to the poetry and prose works of the great writers in Neapolitan dialect Giulio Cesare Cortese (ca. 1570-1624/1627) and Giambattista Basile (1575-1632). Basile's anagram was Giannalesio Abbattuto.

'NTRODUZZIONE
DE LA POSILECHEATA
E COMMITO D'AMMICE FATTO A POSILECO

[1] Na longa vita senza na recreazione, a lo munno, è ghiusto comme a no luongo viaggio senza na taverna pe defrisco, senza n'alloggiamiento pe repuoso. Pe la quale cosa li stisse uommene d'azzò, e che camminano co lo chiummo e lo compasso, de quanno 'n quanno fanno quarche 'sciuta, quarche sferrata fore de lo cafuerchio, pe pegliare àjero e non fetire de 'nchiuso e de peruto. [2] Ora io mone, che se bè non songo de chelle perzune tanto composte che co l'acito lloro pare che bogliano conciare tutte le 'nzalate de le tavole d'autre, e puro aggio na 'ncrinazione casarínola, ca vorria sempe stareme reterato, no juorno appe golío de fareme na Posilecheata, avenno 'ntiso dicere da no cierto studiante che Posileco è parola greca e che vene a spalefecare a lengua nosta *Cojeta-malenconia*. [3] Tanto cchiú che a Posileco nc'era n'ammico mio, pe nomme Petruccio, lo quale era frostiero, e benuto a Napole s'aveva chella 'state scívoto pe stanza na casa passato lo palazzo de Medina, pe potere ghire e benire da Isca, dove pigliava cierte vagne c'avea de besuogno pe la sanetate. [4] Co chisto sio Petruccio èramo state ammice scorporate a lo pajese sujo, na vota che cammenaje lo munno, e súbeto che ghionze a Napole se nne venne a derettura a la casa mia, dove stette tutta la primmavera; la 'state po' se reteraje a Posileco, e sempe me screveva che lo jesse a trovare e stare cod isso quarche juorno. Ma perché la frattaria non troppo me piace, me pegliaje na falluca, e sulo sulillo me consegnaje a lo luoco tòpeco, arrevanno justo justo ad ora de magnare. E chesto fu a li 26 de luglio de s'tanno 1684.

[5] Non porria dicere quant'allegrezza appe l'ammico quanno me vedette: m'abbracciaje, l'abbracciaje, e basannoce tutte duj 'n fronte, co li cinco e cinco a dece, facettemo li solete compremiente. Me disse perzò l'ammico mio che le despiaceva che fosse juto cossí a la 'mprovisa, perché non m'avarria potuto trattare a gusto sujo. Io le disse che fra nuje non ce volevano zeremonie, e ca chello ch'era apparecchiato ped uno poteva vastare porzí pe duje.

[6] Cossì chiacchiarejanno chiacchiarejanno se mese la tavola da na

INTRODUCTION
TO THE POSILECHEATA
AND BANQUET WITH FRIENDS IN POSILLIPO

(1) A long life in this world without any leisure is like a long journey without a tavern to refresh and a place to rest. For this reason, even serious, cautious, and circumspect folks take time out every once a while, stepping out of their den to get some fresh air and not to smell stale and moldy. (2) Despite the fact that I am not one of those dignified people who think they have to season everyone's salad with their vinegar, and despite my homely nature and preference to retreat, one day I felt a desire to take a trip to Posillipo, having heard a certain scholar claim that Posillipo is a Greek word that in our language means, "a cure for melancholy."[i] (3) Moreover, I had a friend in Posillipo named Petruccio, a foreigner who came to Naples that summer and chose a house past the Medina palace so he could go back and forth to Ischia, where he went to the baths that he needed for his health.[ii] (4) Petruccio and I had been intimate friends back in his town, when I was traveling the world. As soon as he arrived in Naples, he naturally came to see me, staying with me throughout the spring. He then moved to Posillipo in the summer and always wrote asking me to visit him for a few days. As I do not like large crowds, I took a little boat, traveling all alone to his place, and I arrived just in time for lunch. This happened on July 26, 1684.

(5) Words could not describe my friend's happiness upon seeing me. We hugged and kissed each other, shook hands, and exchanged the usual compliments. My friend told me he regretted that I had arrived so suddenly and unannounced, because he couldn't treat me as generously as he wished. I told him that there was no need for ceremonies between us, that food for one was going to be enough for two.

(6) While we chatted, an elderly woman named Cianna set the table. She was a native from the mountains and the wife of a wealthy greengrocer who served my friend not out of need but as a good neighbor. She was a courteous, gracious, and pretty woman who, as a young girl, must have been one of the

vecchiarella pe nomme Cianna, nativa de la montagna e mogliere de n'ortola-no ricco, che serveva all'ammico non pe besuogno ma ped essere bona vecina: tanto cortese e graziosa, e de cossí bella 'mmerejana, che mostava essere stata una de le tre Grazie quann'era giovane. E mettenno mettenno la tavola me disse quatto parole, scusannose co la 'mprovesata se mancava quarche cosa da la parte soja.

[7] Posta la tavola, a mala pena nce sedettemo che nce vedimmo ad-duosso no ciert'ommo, co na sottanella nfi' a lo denucchio tutta sbottonata pe la gran panza c'aveva: teneva no paro de spalle che parea vastaso de la Doana, aveva na vocca cossí larga che parea de lupo, e no naso apierto comm'a caval-lo. [8] E co na facce tosta che no' l'avarria sperciata no pontarulo, a mala pena ditto: «Ben trovate!», schiaffannose da miezo a miezo nfra me e l'ammico, 'ncomenza a dicere: «Non sapite vuje, segnorielle mieje, ca a lo 'mmito non deveno essere né manco de le Grazie, né cchiú de le Muse? Azzoè o tre o nove, ma duje è troppo poco. Otra po' che lo numero de lo tre ha cchiú bertute che non hanno tutte le nummere 'n chietta.

[9] «Vuj sapite che tre songo li principie naturale: Materia, Forma e Privazione; tre sogno le sciorte de l'anemale: Vegetativo, Sensetivo e 'Ntel-lettivo; tre le dute prencepale de l'anema de l'ommo: Memmoria, 'Ntelletto e Bolontà; tre cose squatrano ogne cosa: Nummero, Piso e Mesura; tre songo li termene d'ogne ncosa: Prencipio, Miezo e Fine; tre cose non songo stemmate: forze da vastaso, consiglio de poverommo e bellezza de pottana; tre cose son-go 'nsoffribele: ricco avaro, povero soperbio e biecchio 'nnammorato; [10] a tre cose non se deve credere: all'archemista povero, a lo miedeco malato e a lo remito grasso; tre cose stanno male a lo munno: n'auciello 'mmano de no peccerillo, no fiasco 'mmano de no Todisco, na zita giovane 'mmano de no viecchio; tre sciorte de perzune songo patrune de lo munno: pazze, presentuse e sollícete; tre cose non possono stare annascose: le fusa dinto de lo sacco, le femmene 'nchiuse 'n casa e la paglia dintro de le scarpe; tre cose abbesogna tenere a mente: che ammore non vò bellezza, che appetito non vò sàuza e che l'accattare non vò ammecizia. [11] E de cchiú, chi accatta ha da sapere che se deve accattare l'uoglio de coppa, lo vino de miezo e lo mmèle de funno. Tre bote tre unnece cose fanno bella na femmena: azzoè tre cose longhe e tre corte; tre larghe, tre strette e tre grosse; tre sottile, tre retonne, tre piccole, tre ghianche, tre rosse, tre negre: e se le bolite sapere, leíte la *Fràveca de lo Munno*. [12] Ma chi porria mai dicere tutte le bertute de lo tre? Pocca tre so' le cannele che s'allummano quanno se fa no stromiento de notte; tre parme

three Graces. Preparing the table, she spoke a bit with me, apologizing if anything was missing in the improvised meal.

(7) As soon as the table was set and we sat down, we were surprised by a big fellow dressed in a petticoat that reached to his knees and was unbuttoned because of his large belly. His shoulders were broad like those of a customs porter, his mouth large like a wolf's, his nose open like a horse's. (8) With a chutzpah that nothing could have derailed and a bare "Good evening," he plunked down between me and my friend saying, "My dear fellows, don't you know that at a banquet you shouldn't be fewer than the Graces and not more than the Muses? That's three or nine, two are too few. Besides the fact that the number three has more virtues than all numbers combined."

(9) "As you know, three are the natural principles: Matter, Form, and Emptiness. Three are the types of living beings: Vegetative, Sensitive, and Intellective. Three are the main assets of the human soul: Memory, Intellect, and Will. Three things square off everything: Numbers, Weights, and Measures. Three are the boundaries of all things: Principle, Means, and End. Three things are not appreciated: a porter's strength, a poor man's advice, and a harlot's beauty. Three other things are intolerable: the stingy rich, poor proud folks, and old men in love. (10) Don't trust three individuals: a poor alchemist, a sick doctor, and a fat hermit. Three things are not fitting this world: a bird in a child's hand, a wine bottle in a German's hand, and a young girl hugged by an old man. Three kinds of people rule the world: the mad, the brazen, and the busybodies. Three things cannot be hidden: purrs inside a sack, women locked in a house, and straw inside shoes. You must remember three things: love not asking for beauty, a sauce not stirring an appetite, friendship that doesn't matter when buying things. (11) Furthermore, whoever goes shopping must remember to take oil from the top shelf, wine from the middle, and honey from the lower shelves. Three things times eleven make a woman beautiful—that is three long and three short things; three large, tight, and huge things; three thin, round and small things; three white, red and black things. If you want to know them all, read *La Fabbrica del Mondo*.[iii] (12) But who could ever name all the virtues of the number three? You light three candles when you get up to pee at night. A three-foot rope is sufficient to hang a man. Three things chase a man out of the house: smoke, stench, and an evil woman. Three things damage a home: zeppole, warm bread, and macaroni. Three women and a gosling are enough to set up a market. A fish needs three letters *f*: *fritto, freddo, fermo* – fried, cold, and firm. Those in love need three letters *s*: solitary, solicitous,

de funa danno vòta a lo 'mpiso; tre cose cacciano l'ommo da la casa: fummo, fieto e femmena marvasa; tre cose strudeno la casa: zeppole, pane caudo e maccarune; tre femmene e na papara fanno no mercato; tre *fff* vole avere lo pesce: fritto, friddo e futo; tre *sss* besognano a lo 'nnammorato: sulo, sollíceto e secreto; tre *mmm* songo chelle delle quale ognuno n'ha la parte soja: matto, miedeco e museco; tre sciorte de perzune se tene la bonarrobba: smargiasso, bello giovane e corrivo; tre cose arroínano la gioventute: juoco, femmena e taverna; tre cose songo utele a lo cortesciano: fegnemiento, fremma e sciorte; tre cose abbesognano a lo ruffiano: gran core, assai chiacchiare e poca vregogna; tre cose osserva lo miedeco: lo puzo, la faccia e lo càntaro. [13] Ma no' nne sia cchiú! Magnammo, e stammo allegramente!», e cosí decenno, perché non erano ancora venute le vevanne, afferraje no quarto de na palata de pane, ed aprenno chella voccuzza che l'arrivava nfi' all'aurecchie ne fece no voccone, sbotanno l'uocchie comm'a gatta frostèra.

[14] Io che bidde sto negozio restaje ammisso, stoppaſatto e fora de li panne, e ghiéa decenno fra me: «Malatía! Scúmpela! Le schiaffa pepítola!» Quanno Petruccio, fattome zinno, me disse: «Allegramente, sio Masillo mio, pocca stammattina nce faoresce lo Dottore nuosto, che me coverna a li Vagne, e da lo trascurzo te puoje addonare quanto è letterúmmeco e bertoluso. Me despiace sulo che la provesione è scarza, ma dove mancarrà la bona cera de lo pesce comprescerrà la bona cera mia. Vorria che fosse juorno de cammara, azzoché lo sio Dottore potesse avere chille compremiente che mereta».

[15] «Chesto poco 'mporta — responnette Marchionno (ch'accossí se chiammava lo miedeco) —. Non sapite vuje ca è cchiú goliuso lo pesce che la carne? Pe la quale cosa li Rommane de la maglia antica chiammavano l'uommene dellecate *Ichthiophagi*, cioè magna-pisce. Orasússo, Ciannetella mia, porta da lavare».

[16] Venne Cianna co lo voccale e lo vacile, e ntramente che Marchionno se lavava, addomannaje a mene qual era la meglio acqua de lo munno. Io responnette: «Se m'addemmanne dell'acque de Napole, io te lo pozzo dicere: ma de tutto lo munno è troppo». Ed isso: «Volite sapere - lleprecaje - quale è la meglio acqua de lo munno? È chesta che se porta pe lavare le mmano mprimma de magnare, perché fa strata a lo vino».

[17] Assenno nfra de chesto venuta na menesta de pesielle, Marchionno, pecché nc'era vruodo assaje, spetacciata na palata de pane e revotatela dinto de lo piatto, assajato comm'a cane de presa e co la lopa 'n cuorpo, co na carrera che bolava, gliottenno sano, e l'uno voccone n'aspettanno l'autro, 'n quatto

and secret. Everyone shares three letters *m*: the mad, the medical doctor, and the musician. A wicked woman keeps company with three types of people: the brave, handsome youths, and squanderers. Three things ruin young people: games, women, and the tavern. A courtesan needs three things: the ability to pretend, coolness, and luck. A pimp needs three things: a big heart, lots of gossip, and no shame. And a doctor needs to check three things: the pulse, the face, and the stool. (13) But enough of that! Let's eat and rejoice!" Saying this, while the food had not yet been served, he took a quarter of a loaf of bread, opened his mouth, which reached all the way to his ears, and ate it with one bite, opening his eyes wide like a wild cat.

(14) Witnessing this scene, I was surprised, shocked, and stunned, saying to myself, "Shame on you, stop it, hold your sick tongue!" Petruccio said to me with a nod, "My dear Masillo, cheer up. This morning we are honored by our doctor who treats me at the baths. You can tell from his speech how learned and skilled he is. I only regret that there may not be enough food. Should there not be enough fish, I will make up with good cheers. May this be a festive day, honoring the good doctor as he deserves."

(15) "Never mind," Marchionno replied (that was the doctor's name). "Don't you know that fish tastes better than meat? That's why the ancient Romans called delicate people *ichthiophagi,* fish eaters. My Cianna darling, go ahead now, bring the water so we can wash our hands."

(16) Cianna showed up with a mug and a basin, and while Marchionno washed, he asked me where the best water came from. I answered, "If you're asking about water in Naples, I can tell you, but not about the water in the whole wide world." He gave back: "You want to know the world's best water? It's the one you use to wash your hands before eating, because it is followed by drinking wine."

(17) Meanwhile, a pea soup was served, and because there was a lot of broth, Marchionno broke a loaf of bread, stirred it in the dish, and gobbled it down bite after bite in great haste without chewing it, like a rabid dog, hungry like a wolf, finishing the soup in no time. And yet, this was a rich dish in an exceptionally large bowl, but me and my friend were left with just two mouthfuls.

(18) Petruccio then said to the doctor, "How do you like the soup, isn't it good?" "It is good," was the reply, "but it doesn't provide a good foundation. Don't you know the Spanish saying, *Sobre una cosa redonda no se hace buen edificio?*[iv] If that is so," Petruccio said, "it's time for the mullets, my dear Cianna."

pízzeche ne frosciaje la menesta: e puro era no piatto reale, che pareva na scafaréa! De manera che a mene ed all'ammico a mala pena ne toccajeno duje voccune ped uno. [18] Tanno Petruccio disse a lo Dottore: «Che te pare de la menestra? È bona?»

«È bona! — respose isso —. Ma non è cosa da farence fonnamiento. Non sapite ca dice lo Spagnuolo: *Sobre una cosa redonda no se haze buen edificio?*»

«S'è cosí — disse Petruccio —, Cianna mia, porta chille ciefare».

[19] «Buono! — dice lo Dottore —. Cèfaro 'n grieco vò dire capo, e da chisso se deve 'ncommenzare. Ma mprimma ed antemonia portate da vevere».

«Vecco ccà lo carrafone — disse Petruccio —. Pigliate lo becchiero, ca te servarraggio io. Ma mettimmoce mprimma no poco d'acqua, pecché è bino gagliardo».

[20] «Che acqua?! — rispose lo Dottore —. Non saje ca lo vino adacquato fa l'ommo scialacquato? Io perzò, pe te servire, pocca l'acqua non se deve nommenare, voglio che se nommene la fontana: pruójeme ccà lo carrafone, ca voglio fare la fontanella»: e pigliatose lo carrafone, a suono de lo *cròcrò* ne scese cchiú de la mmetate, che bò dicere tre carrafe e mezza. E bíppeto: «Accossí — decette — se vene a correjere l'umedetate de lo pesce».

[21] Ed io: «Ccà besogna correjere lo Dottore, che n'ha ancora accomenzato a magnare pesce ed ha paura de l'omedetate».

«O bona! — responnette isso —. E non sapite ca *Prossimo accignendo habeto ped accinto*? Ma, a lo remmedio»: ed accossí ditto deze na granfata a no cefaro, che ne lo scese comm'a beluocciolo d'uovo; e co la scusa ca na spina se l'era 'ntraverzata 'ncanna cercaje da vevere, e ne scese lo riesto de lo carrafone.

«Bello remmedio — dicette io — pe cacciare le spine da la canna! Auto ca chillo de masto Grillo!»

[22] Venne appriesso no gran piatto de porpette fatte de sardelle, co no vrodillo che l'addore se sentea no miglio, e le gatte ne facevano no giúbelo da stordire co lo *gnao-gnao*: quanno lo gattemenaro de Marchionno (da dove viene? da lo molino!) accommenza a menare le mmano comm'a sonatore de pífaro: e scésene na mano de porpette, comme se carreccasse quarche farconetto o cannone, le mannava a bascio a scapillacuozzo. [23] E chino lo stefano quanno nuje a mala pena avéamo ontato li diente: «O che bella cosa! — decette —. Cheste songo le bere palle da cannoniare la famme, azzò stia arrasso da nuje. Vaga chi vòle a la guerra pe farese sperciare e smafarare la panza da le

(19) "Fine," the doctor said. "*Cèfaro* in Greek means head—that's what you've got to start with. But before and above all, bring something to drink." "Here's a large pitcher," Petruccio said. "Take your glass, I will serve you. But first, let's pour some water into it—this wine is strong."

(20) "What water?!" the Doctor said. "Don't you know that watered-down wine wastes you? To serve you, since water shouldn't be mentioned, let's talk about a fountain. Hand me the pitcher, so I can make a little fountain. He grabbed the pitcher and drank more than half of it to the sound of *glu glu*—the equivalent of three and a half small pitchers—saying, "That's how you fix the moisture of the fish."

(21) I quipped, "Here we must challenge the doctor. He hasn't even begun to eat fish and is already concerned with its moisture."

"Great!" was the answer. "Don't you know the saying, *It is best to consider done that which will happen soon?*[v] But let's make up for that," and he grabbed a mullet and swallowed it like an egg yolk. With the excuse of a bone stuck in his throat, he asked for a drink and emptied the rest of the pitcher.

"Nice job," I said, "the way to get rid of bones in your throat—better than Doctor Grillo's cure!"[vi]

(22) A dish with sardine balls followed, with a broth whose fragrance you could smell a mile away, making the cats rot and meow, as that wolf cat of Marchionno began to move his hands quickly like a fife player, grabbing a handful of fish balls—as if charging some falcon or cannon—and eating them up like a daredevil. (23) We had barely whetted our teeth, when after filling his gut, he said, "Oh great. These are the bullets you need to gun down the hunger and make it stay away from us. May those who wish go to war to get their bellies pierced and opened by lead bullets—instead, this is the true battle! A battle that brings life, while the other one brings death. In fact, to better preserve life, give me some grape juice," and saying this, he grabbed the other pitcher with the white wine.

(24) Petruccio then asked, "How do you like this wine?" He replied: "I think it is like a good horse's tail." I said, "In truth, for the war with fish balls, there was no need for another horse. I only regret that by drinking, more horse or a tail will be left." And the doctor: "Good," he said, "no more bullets, no more wars."

(25) Meanwhile, a dish of fried sole arrived at the table, and the quick-witted doctor noted, "To fight the bullets back, these soles are all you need. Elsewhere, they are called *lenguátele*, so let's join them with our

palle de chiummo: chesta è la vera battaglia! Pocca chella dà la morte e chesta la vita. Anze, pe meglio mantenere sta vita, dateme no poco de zuco de vite», e cossí decenno deze de mano all'auto carrafone, ch'era de vino janco.

[24] «E che te pare de sto vino?», decette tanno Petruccio. Ed isso: «Me pare na bona coda de cavallo». Ed io: «Veramente pe la guerra de le porpette autro cavallo non nce voleva: sulo me despiace ca co n'auta véppeta che faje non nce sarrà cchiú né cavallo né coda». E lo Dottore: «Bene! — decette —. Scompute le palle, scomputa la guerra».

[25] Ntratanto fu portato a tavola no piatto de palaje fritte, e lo Dottore, lesto co li mutte: «Pe rebattere — decette — le palle, non ce volevano che cheste *pale*. Ad autre paise le chiammano *Lenguàtele*, e perrò facimmole aonire co la lengua»: e cosí decenno scommenza a 'nchire li vuoffole e scopare lo paese, de manera che 'n quatto menate de mano se vedde la pétena de lo piatto; e dato de mano a lo carrafone, lo sciosciaje, zorlaje e scotolaje tutto a no sciato, fi' che se vedde lo funno.

[26] Ed io: «Che te pare, sio Dottore, non è no bello pesce la palaja?»

«Bellissemo! — responnette —. E co ragione autre la chiammano *sfuoglio*, perché se sfoglia comme a cappiello de pasticcio; autre la chiammano *sòla*, perché sola nfra li pisce treonfa; autre la vozero chiammare la *pernice de lo maro*, pocca no poco de zuco de cetrangolo le vasta pe qualesevoglia sàuza».

[27] Pe retopasto venne no piatto cupo chino de fragaglie fritte: e lo Dottore accommenza a pigliarele ad uno ad uno pe la coda, e co la capo ad accostare mprimma a la vocca, e po' a l'aurecchia. Chisse gieste nce fecero maravegliaire: pe la quale cosa, curiuse, l'addemannajemo che ne spalefecasse lo secreto. [28] Ed isso: «Sacciate — decette — ca la bonarma de pàtremo, Dio l'aggia 'n grolia e 'n sanetate nosta, morette annegato, de manera che lo catavero sujo non s'asciaje maje. Io perzò aggio addemannato a sti pescitielle se l'avessero maje visto, ed isse m'hanno arrespuosto ca essenno nate iere non ne sanno niente, ma che addemannasse a chillo gruongo gruosso che sta 'n cocina» (pocca lo sio Delluvio n'avea sentuto l'addore, anze ca da la tavola vedeva quanto se faceva 'n cocina). [29] Ma Petruccio, pe darele cottura e ped annozzarele lo muorzo 'n canna, responnette: «Io no' approvo chillo proverbejo: *Carne giovane e pesce viecchio*, pocca sti pescetielle me piaceno. E cosí, sio Dottore mio, haje sbagliato, o coll'uocchie o co lo naso: e perzò se te piaceno ste fragaglie, magnale, e se no' vengano li frutte».

[30] Quanno lo Dottore sentette sta nova, senza responnere auto, comm'a n'aseno che magnasse paglia, se cannarejaje chillo piatto, ch'era zippo zippo:

tongues." Saying this, he began to fill his jaws and to clean the slate, so that after four handfuls, you could see the gloss of the plate. Picking up the pitcher, he blew into it and shook it, emptying it in just one breath.

(26) "What do you think, doctor, isn't the sole a great fish?" I asked. It's fantastic!" was the reply. "Others call it rightfully *sfuoglio*, because you can scale it like a pastry crust; still others call it *sòla*, because it stands out among all fish; still others prefer the name *pernice de lo mare* (partridge of the sea) because you need just a bit of cucumber juice for any sauce.

(27) As dessert, they served a dish full of tiny fish. The doctor began to grab them one by one by their tail and to move their head to the mouth and then to the ear. These moves surprised us, so we asked him out of curiosity to explain his secret moves. (28) "You must know that the good soul of my father, may God bless him and protect our health, died by drowning, and his corpse was never recovered. Therefore, I asked the little fish if they had ever seen him. They answered that they were born only yesterday and couldn't know anything about him, but that they would ask the fat conger waiting in the kitchen (Mr. Deluge smelled its fragrance and saw from the table what they were preparing in the kitchen). (29) To challenge him and to make him choke on a morsel, Petruccio answered, "I do not agree with the proverb, *Carne giovane e pesce viecchio* (young meat and old fish), because I like these small fish. Therefore, you are mistaken, my dear doctor, with your eyes or with your nose. If you like these tiny fish, go ahead and eat them; if not, let them serve fruit."

(30) When the doctor heard this, without uttering a word he devoured that dish filled to the brim like a straw-eating donkey. He mentioned the conger not because he disliked the small fish but for them not to forget about it, as he enjoyed quantity more than quality, without ever forgetting his drinks, emptying one glass after the other.

(31) After the small fish were gone, Petruccio asked Cianna to bring the fruit and more bread, because the doctor had cleaned up everything on the table. Cianna, who was aware of it, brought small loaves of dark bread, saying there was no white bread left, that they had eaten as much bread this morning as the master of the house would eat in one week. (32) When the doctor saw this bread, he said, "I fear the baker died, and this bread serves to mourn him. These are no small loaves of bread, only shadows of bread. Please, Cianna, don't bring any more, otherwise we'll have to light the candles."

pocca n'avea citato lo gruongo perché li piscitielle no' le piacessero, ma perché non se ne scordassero, addelettannose veramente cchiú de la quantetate che de la qualetate. Né scordannose maje de zucare lo tútaro, devacanno becchiere.

[31] Scompute le fragaglie, decette Petruccio che Cianna portasse li frutte ed autro pane, pocca lo Dottore n'aveva arresediato quanto nc'era 'n tavola. Cianna, che stea 'ntesa, portaje na mano de palatelle negre, decenno ca pane janco non ce n'era cchiúne: pocca chella matina se n'era consomato tanto, quanto lo patrone ne potea strudere na semmana. [32] Quanno lo Dottore se vedde chillo pane 'nnante: «Aggio paura — decette — che lo fornaro sia muorto e che sto pane ne porta lo lutto. Cheste non songo palatelle, ma ombre de palatelle. De 'razia, Ciannetella, non ne portare cchiúne, ca se none abbesognarrà fare venire le cannele».

[33] Venne ntratanto lo caso e li frutte a tavola, e lo Dottore, afferrata na palatella negra, decette: «Aggio 'ntiso dicere ca lo pane nigro èje appetetuso: lo boglio provare, mmaretannolo co sto casillo e dannole pe dote sto piro». Ma chesta fu la dote, che no piro tiranno l'auto, comm'a le cerase, priesto lo pane e lo caso e li frutte sparettero. [34] E lo Dottore auza la voce: «Dapo' lo crudo lo puro!», ed eccote Cianna che porta da vevere; ma lo Dottore sgregnanno lo musso, se bè lo bevette, addemannaje: «E che bino è chisto? Songo io fuorze quacche cannone che non saccia terare diece cuorpe l'uno appriesso a l'autro senza essere lavato co l'acito?»

[35] «Comme co l'acito?», dicette Petruccio. E chiammata Ciannetella l'addemannaje che bino era chillo.

E Cianna: «Songo scompute — dicette — li dudece fiasche che erano fore: lo vino che l'aggio dato è chillo che ce remmase iere».

«Haje ragione — dicette Petruccio —. Ma pocca non chiove, ca delluvia, vèccote la chiave de l'autra cantenetta 'n grazia de lo sio Dottore».

[36] «Compiatite — dicette Marchionno —, ca iere non magnaje (accossí soleno dicere li mangiune). Otra che sapite ca lo moto è cchiú biolento 'mmierzo la fine: e de 'razia non me 'mpedite, ca la rota, quanno è 'n furio, se quarcuno la tocca torna da capo. Ma dimme — secotaje —, sio Petruccio mio! Stammo a Posileco e n'avimmo magnato fico?»

[37] «Vuje nce corpate! — responnette isso —. Ca pe la pressa de magnare c'avive Cianna se n'era scordata»: ed accossí decenno ordenaje che Cianna portasse 'n tavola le ffico.

«Mo va buono — dicette lo Dottore —, pocca se se fa l'arrore a l'ordene, non se fa ne la sostanza de la facenna». [38] Ed abbistato cierte ffico che

(33) By now, cheese and fruit were brought to the table. The doctor grabbed a loaf of black bread and said, "I heard people say that black bread is tasty. I want to try some, marrying it with this delicious cheese and adding this pear as dowry." Such was the dowry that one pear followed another, just like the cherries, so the bread and cheese and fruit disappeared in no time. (34) The doctor raised his voice: "After raw food, pure tastes!" So Cianna brought wine, but the doctor twisted his muzzle while drinking and asked, "What wine is this? Am I perhaps some cannon that doesn't know how to shoot ten blows without being washed with vinegar?"

(35) "What vinegar are you talking about?" Petruccio asked. He called Cianna, asking about the wine she had served. Cianna replied, "The twelve bottles that were outside are finished; the wine I served was a leftover from yesterday."

"You are right", Petruccio said. "But since it does not rain but pours, take the key to the other cellar, for the doctor's sake."

(36) "Excuse me," Marchionno said, "I haven't eaten since yesterday (that's what gourmands claim). Besides, as you know, hunger is stronger towards the end of dinner, so please do not slow me down. Once it is turning, the wheel starts all over if someone tries to stop it. Tell me, my dear Petruccio!" he continued, "we are in Posillipo and haven't been served any figs?"

(37) "You do us wrong!" Petruccio replied. "You ate so fast that Cianna forgot," and with this, he ordered Cianna to bring figs to the table.

"Fine," the doctor said, "a slip in the order does not mean a slip in substance." (38) Noticing some figs all torn like the rags of a beggar with a hanged neck and tears of a woman about to trick, he stretched out his hands, picking them with a fork and asked, "What figs are these?" "Trojan figs," I answered. And he rebutted, "They really look like the Trojan horse with an army made of crickets inside and with the only difference that to enter Troy, you needed to tear down the walls, but not here. That's what caused Troy to burn, and these figs warm the stomach."

(39) But because the doctor was eating as if he had just begun, I asked him why our ancestors called the cheese and fruit and other similar dishes *seconna tavola*. "You know why?" he replied. "Because they ate so much, and when it was time to eat cheese and fruit, they seemed to start all over again. So you tell me now: what dish do guests dislike the most?" We gave different answers, and he said: "Cheese is the worst dish, because it is not followed by more dishes."

stevano co la veste tutta stracciata comm'a 'pezzente, co lo cuollo de 'mpiso e co le lacreme de femmena che vò gabbare, nce deze de mano, e 'ngorfútole, addemannaje: «Che ffico so' cheste?»

«Fico trojane», diss'io.

Ed isso: «Veramente pareno lo cavallo trojano, e l'arílle l'asèrzeto che nc'era donto: co chesta deverzetate, che pe far entrare chillo dinto Troja abbesognaje rompere le mmura, e ccà no. Chillo fu causa che s'ardesse Troja, e cheste me scarfano lo stommaco».

[39] Ma perché lo Dottore magnava come se tanno accommenzasse, io l'addomannaje perché l'antiche lo caso e li frutte ed autre cose simmele le chiammavano *seconna tavola*.

«Sapite perché? — responnette —. Perché l'antiche magnavano assaje, e quanno venevano lo caso e li frutte pareva che tornassero da capo. Ora mo deciteme vuje: quale è chillo civo che cchiú despiace a le commetate?» Responnettemo chi na cosa e chi n'auta; ed isso: «Lo peo civo — decette — è lo caso, perché appriesso a isso non vèneno cchiú vevanne».

[40] E Petruccio: «Voglio — decette — che sta vota lo caso non ce perda de repotazione: su, Ciannetella, porta chillo pesce arrostuto»; ed ecco che Ciannetella portaje lo gruongo.

[41] Tanno lo Dottore decette: «Vedite mo che io deceva buono quanno venettero le fragaglie».

Responnette Petruccio: «Tu, V.S., deciste ch'era no gruongo, ma nuje a lo pajese nuosto no' lo chiammammo accossí».

«Chesta — lleprecaje lo Dottore — è costejone de nomme, che li filuosofe non ne fanno cunto: perché abbesogna attenere a la sostanza de le cose, comme faccio io»: e cossí decenno, comme se nfi' a tanno n'avesse magnato, menaje li cliente e dette lo portante a le mascelle co tanta furia, che lo povero gruongo sparette comme se fosse stato 'ncantato. [42] Accossí Marchionno, stracquo sí, ma non sazio ancora: «Abbesogna — decette — segellare lo stommaco», e co chesta rasa arresediaje quante tozze erano rommase 'n tavola, de manera che Cianna non avette auta fatica che de levare le brocche.

[43] E primma che se auzasse lo mesale lo Dottore decette: «Se nce fosse da sciacquare, n'averria besuogno».

E Petruccio: «Sta vota — decette — te voglio dare a bevere chillo vino che cchiú te piace: tu scrive, ed io me fermo».

[44] E Marchionno: «L'*Asprinio* — accomenzaje a dicere — non me piace, perché l'asprezza che porta a lo nomme la lassa a lo palato. La *Raspata*,

(40) Petruccio said, "I do not want cheese to get a bad reputation. Go ahead, Cianna, bring the roasted fish." So Cianna brought the conger.

(41) The doctor then said, "See, I told you the truth when the small fish were served."

And Petruccio: "You, sir, said it was a conger, but in our town, it has a different name."

"That's a question of names," the doctor replied, "which the philosophers don't consider, because you must pay attention to the substance of things, as I do." Saying this, he moved his teeth and jaws with such fury that the poor conger disappeared as if it were entranced.

(42) Marchionno was tired by now but not satiated yet. "I've got to seal my stomach," he said, and with a brush, he wiped off all breadcrumbs left on the table, so that all Cianna had to do was to pick up the mugs.

(43) Before the tablecloth was taken off, the doctor said, "If there is anything to wash down, send it over here." And Petruccio: "This time I'll serve you the wine you like best, I guarantee."

(44) Marchionno began, saying, "I do not like the *Asprinio,* the bitterness of the name sticks to the palate. The *Raspata* scratches you where it shouldn't, the *Mazzacane* gets to your head like a stone, the *Mangiaguerra* is good as it lightens warring bad thoughts. The *Lacrima* too, as it makes you cry from happiness. Please pour me a glass of the latter, I want to make a toast to my friends."

(45) "Cianna," Petruccio called out, "bring the bottle with the *Lagreme de li Galitte* and serve the doctor." When the *Lagreme* arrived and they filled a huge glass resembling a lamp, Marchionno began to sing: (46) *"To your health / my dearest Petruccio and Masillo! / May God give you prosperity and health. / Whatever you wish for / may it accrue smoothly for you, just like the wine flows into my gut."*

(47) We laughed at the last verse of the song, and after the banquet, we went out to the terrace above the sea, while Cianna called her four daughters: Cecca, Tolla, Popa and Ciulatella. The first two played two tambourines, the third castanets, and the fourth sang in a slowly changing scene between singing and playing instruments. But who could now repeat their beautiful songs?

1. These were Cecca's songs.

te raspe a dove non te prode; lo *Mazzacano* dà 'n capo comme na savorra; la *Mangiaguerra* è bona, che se mangia la guerra de li pensiere fastidiuse; la *Lagrema* porzíne, che te fa lagremare de l'allegrezza, e de chesta, non te sia 'n commannamiento, dammene no becchiere, ca ve voglio fare no brinnese 'n chietta».

[45] «Cianna — dicette Petruccio —, porta chillo fiasco de *Lagrema de li Galitte* e sierve lo sio Dottore».

Venuta la *Lagrema*, e chino no gruosso becchiero, che parea na lampa, accossí 'mprovisaje lo sio Marchionno:

[46] «*A la salute vosta,*

O Petruccio, o Masillo mieje garbate!

Che Dio ve dia bene e sanetate.

Quanto addesiderate

Ve cola bene, a chiummo ed a ciammiello,

Comm'a sto vino dinto a lo vodiello».

[47] Rísemo a la bella chiusa de la canzone: e levata la tavola ascettemo a na loggia 'ncoppa a lo maro, addove Cianna fece venire quattro figliole ch'aveva, una de le quale se chiammava Cecca, l'auta Tolla, la terza Popa e la quarta Ciulletella: le primme doje avevano duje tammorrielle, l'auta le castagnelle e la quarta cantava; e accossí de mano 'n mano mutanno scena, cantava l'auta e l'aute sonavano. Ma chi pò dicere mo le belle canzune che decettero?

1. — Chelle de Cecca fujeno cheste:

I

[48] *O quanta vote, la sera, a lo tardo,*

Ghievamo a spasso co tanta zitelle

'Ncoppa lo scuoglio de messè Lonardo!

E là facéamo spuonole e patelle!

II

[49] *Chi t'ha fatto ste belle scarpette?*

E no' l'haje pagate, no?

Da dereto me senco chiammare:

— Vòtate, vòtate, e pagale, mo!

Tríncole e míncole!

I (48) "How many times did we go for a walk late in the evening / with many girls / above Mr. Leonardo's rock! / And there we ate oysters and limpets."

II (49) "Who made these pretty shoes for you? / You didn't pay for them, right? / I hear them calling me from behind: / Turn around, turn around, pay them now! / Pendants and frills! / Laces and brooches! / Spindles and ladles from Mercogliano! / What is my woman up to that she doesn't join us?"

This one was incredibly beautiful, and so is the following:

III (50) "Open up, my love, we are seven, / and the seven of us don't have a penny. Join us, Beppe, come with us!"

2. With a siren voice, Tolla recited this other song:

IV (51) "My love, where did / this rusty young fellow come from? / Is he sharp or is he dumb / Is he serious or is he joking? / Is he from Naples or from abroad? / He says he is a baron / but no one believes him, / because you can obviously see / he is a poor lad. / How unfortunate, go to hell! / Say something that's credible! / You know what he did the other day? / To kill a pig / he used a sword and a small wheel."

And these other ones:

(52) V "How many flowers, how many bells, etc."

VI "My little red apple, my little red apple, etc."

VII "My sweet little singer, / Do you want to sing with me? / Watch out, I'll win the hat! / Tomorrow is a holiday, time to wear it."

3. Popa, who did not want to fall behind her sisters, recited this one:

VIII (53) "Who wants to see the hen spin, / and the little chicks comb

> *Lazze e spíngole!*
> *Fuse e cocchiare de Mercogliano!*
> *Che fa la donna mia che non compare?*

Chesta veramente fu bella. E chest'auta:

III

> [50] *Apreme, bene mio, ca simmo sette,*
> *E tutte sette n'avimmo sei rana!*
> *'Nchiana, Peppo! Peppo, 'nchiana!*

2. — E Tolla co na vocella de Serena decette chest'aute:

IV

> [51] *Bene mio, da do' nne è 'sciuto*
> *Sto sio giovane arroggiuto?*
> *Dà de chiatto, o dà de ponta?*
> *Fa abborlanno, o fa da vero?*
> *È de Napole, o frostiero?*
> *Isso dice, ch'è Barone,*
> *Ma nesciuno nce lo crede:*
> *Perché a l'utemo se vede*
> *Ch'è no povero guarzone.*
> *O sciaurato, che sia 'mpiso!*
> *Di' quarcosa che sia criso!*
> *L'auto juorno sa che fice?*
> *Pe scannare na porcella*
> *Nce pigliaje spata e rotella.*

[52] E chest'aute:

V

> *O quanta sciure, o quanta campanelle, ecc.*

VI

> *Russo melillo mio, russo melillo, ecc.*

the linen? / Who wants to see the tavernkeeper Cicco / pour wine without measuring it with a pitcher?"

IX (54) "How beautifully the lark sings / in the morning, an hour before sunrise! / And how beautifully the little sheep eats fresh grass / without walking around!"

4. Ciulletella, the most gracious of all, sang these beautiful songs:

X (55) "The old woman, losing her spindle, / goes around looking for it all Monday, / on Tuesday, she finds it broken, / she fixes it on Wednesday, / on Thursday, she combs the distaff, / on Friday, she prepares the spindle, on Saturday, she washes her head, / on Sunday, she doesn't spin, it's a holiday."

XI (56) "The other night, at the party / I took a hoe and went out to sow. / I found a bush of hazelnuts, / how many of those grenadines did I pick! / The owner of the peaches then arrived: / 'Watch out, don't eat those peaches!' The donkey, going after cherries, / to pick some figs / fell on the ground and broke its nose. / The wolves broke out in laughter. / The children stole the cheese / from the fox who made the macaroni. / The cat was patching up the sheets, / the mice swept the house with a broom. / A large mosquito comes out of a barrel, / picking up a sword and going to the court: / 'Oh chief, do me a favor! / Grab the mosquito and jail it! / The mosquito went out through the gate. / A poor blind man found a loaf of bread!"

(57) The four singers' music was very lovely, following the mountain tradition, but because the sound of the tambourines and castanets was piercing and began to crack eardrums, since we were not used to it, Petruccio said, "I have been told, dear Cianna, that the tales in your language are so extraordinary that as soon as a book with them is in print, there's no one—not even a foreigner speaking another language—who doesn't try to get it because of its plot, bizarre concepts, and the graceful language. Therefore, I would like to ask you to please tell us a story you know, since we do not have that book at hand." [vii]

VII

Cantatoriello mio, cantatoriello,
Co mico te vuoje mettere a cantare?
Vì ca te lo venco lo cappiello!
Craje è la festa, e non haje che portare.

3. — Popa, che no' la cedeva a le sore, disse accossí:

VIII

[53] *Chi vò vede' la vòccola filare,*
Li pollecine pettena' lo llino?
Chi vò vedere Cicco tavernaro
Senza carrafa mesurà lo vino?

IX

[54] *Bello canta' che fa la calantrella*
Un'ora 'nnante juorno, la matina!
Bello magna' che fa la pecorella
Che trova l'erva fresca e non cammina!

4. — Ciulletella, ch'era cchiú graziosa dell'aute, cantaje cheste belle canzune:

X

[55] *La vecchia, quanno perde la conocchia,*
Tutto lo lunedí la va cercanno
Lo martedí la trova tutta rotta,
Tutto lo miercodí la va concianno;
Lo juovedí se pettena la stoppa,
Lo viernadí la vace 'nconocchianno;
Lo sapato se lava po' la testa,
Non fila la dommeneca, ch'è festa.

XI

[56] *E l'auta sera, quanno fuje la festa,*
Pigliaje la ronca e ghiette a semmenare.
Trovaje no sammuco de nocelle:
Quanta ne còuze de chelle granate!

(58) "This is our craft", Cianna said. "If you wish, my daughters will each tell a story. But you must bear with us if they do not measure up to the very refined tales of the mentioned book. We will tell our stories in a rustic manner, the way we heard them told by our ancestors."

(59) "We will enjoy them so much more!" Petruccio said. Sitting outside on the terrace, with the men on one side and the women on the other, Ciulletella, the youngest, after tidying her apron, cleared her throat and with the hands resting on her knees, blushing lightly, she began her story graciously.

Endnotes

i In his *Guida de' forestieri curiosi di vedere e d'intendere le cose più notabili della regal città di Napoli e del suo amenissimo distretto* (Naples 1685), Sarnelli explains the etymology for the Greek toponym PAUSILIPUM with Latin *MOERORIS CESSATIO,* 'the cure for melancholy,' owing to the astounding beauty of the town (Book III, ch. 1.1, 327). Sarnelli shows an interest in etymologies also in his *Lettere ecclesiastiche* (see, for example, ECCLESIA in the first volume).

ii In his *Guida de' forestieri curiosi di vedere e considerare le cose notabili di Pozzoli, Baja, Miseno, Cuma ed altri luoghi convicini* (Naples 1685), Sarnelli introduces visitors to the thermal baths of the area surrounding Naples and their health benefits for numerous diseases, particularly in chapters 10 (Averno) and 14 (Baja) (see Appendix 3).

iii The dictionary, *La Fabrica del mondo*, by Francesco Alunno (1485-1556) was published in Venice in 1546-1548. It is divided into volumes on different topics (God, Heaven, World, Elements, Soul, Body, Man, Quality, Quantity, Hell).

iv Spanish proverb meaning, "You cannot build a house on top of a round foundation".

v Translation of Marchionno's hybrid Latin-Italian saying, *Prossimo accignendo habeto ped accinto.* For the rich proverbs used in Sarnelli's *Posilecheata*, see Daniela D'Eugenio, *Paroimia. Brusantino, Florio, Sarnelli, and Italian Proverbs from Sixteenth and Seventeenth Centuries.* West Lafayette, Purdue University Press, 2021, 195-252.

vi *Masto Grillo* was a talented popular Neapolitan physician, noted for having helped the king's daughter remove a herringbone from her throat by massaging her buttocks to make her laugh.

vii Giambattista Basile's, *Cunto de li cunti,* of which Sarnelli prepared an edition with the title, *Pentamerone*, that was published in 1674.

> *E benne lo patrone de le pèrzeche:*
> *— E bì che non te magne ste percòca! —*
> *L'aseno, che saglieva a lo ceraso*
> *Pe cogliere no túmmolo de fico,*
> *Cadette 'n terra, e se rompíjo lo naso:*
> *Li lupe se schiattavano de riso.*
> *La vorpe, che facéa li maccarune,*
> *Li figlie le grattavano lo caso;*
> *La gatta repezzava le lenzóla,*
> *Li súrece scopavano la casa.*
> *Esce no zampaglione da la votta,*
> *Piglia la spata, e se ne va a la corte:*
> *— Sio Capetano, famme no faore:*
> *Piglia la mosca, e miettela 'mpresone! —*
> *La mosca se n'ascíje pe la cancella...*
> *No povero cecato, na panella...*

[57] Gostosissima fuje la museca de ste quatto cantatrice, all'uso de la montagna: ma perché lo suono de li tammorrielle e de le castagnelle era troppo strepetuso e nce accommenzava a rompere le chiocche, perché no' nc'èramo aosate, disse Petruccio: «Io aggio 'ntiso, o Cianna, ca li cunte a lengua vosta so' accossí curiuse, che asciutone da le stampe no livro, no' nc'è ommo, se bè frostiero e d'auto lenguaggio, che no' aggia gusto d'averelo: e pe la 'mmenzione de la tessetura, e pe la vezzarria de li conciette, e pe la grazia de le parole. Perzò vorria, e non te sia 'n commanno, che pocca non avimmo chillo livro, se nne saje quarcheduno non te 'ncresca contarencéllo».

[58] «Chesta è arte nosta! — disse Cianna —. Anze ste fegliole, s'accossí ve piace, ne decerranno porzíne uno ped uno: avarranno perzò pacienzia se non saranno comme a chille de lo livro, che songo cose stodiate, ma nuje le decimmo a la foretana, accossí comme l'avimmo 'ntiso contare da l'antecestune nuoste».

[59] «Tanto cchiú l'avarrimmo a gusto!», disse Petruccio. E sedutoce fora a la loggia, addove stevano l'uommene da na banna e le femmene dall'auta, Ciulletella, ch'era la cchiú piccola, acconciatose lo mantesino, fatta na rascata, e co le mmano stese 'ncoppa le denocchia, co na grazia granne, cresciutale cchiú da lo farese rossolella, accossí commenzaje a dicere:

LA PIATÀ REMMONERATA

CUNTO PRIMMO

[1] Veramente disse buono, e non potea dicere meglio, chillo che decette: *Fa bene e scordaténne*. Pocca quanno manco l'ommo se lo penza trova lo contracàmmio, se non dall'aute uommene, da lo Cielo stisso. E pe lo contrario: *Chi fa male, male aspetta*: che non è possibile semmenare grano e cogliere ardiche, o puro chiantare ardiche e cogliere vruoccole, pocca chello che se semmena s'arracoglie, comme ve farraggio vedere co lo cunto che secoteja, se chiudarrite la vocca e raprarrite l'aurecchie.

[2] Dice ch'era na vota na magna femmena foretana pe nomme Pacecca, tanto bona che n'avarria saputo 'ntrovolare l'acqua: no piezzo de pane, na pasta de mele, ummele comme a l'agniento, e tanta compassionevole co li poverielle (comme soleno essere le gente de ssi casale) che non se potea dicere cchiú: s'avarria levato lo pane da la vocca pe non vedere stennerire de la famme no povero figlio de mamma.

[3] 'Ntraveníje mo, che stanno sta bona femmena a tiempo de pegliare marito, 'mmattette 'mmano de no cuoco lo cchiú sciauratone che se trovasse sotto la cappa de lo sole, cannarone, pierde-jornata, sacco-scosuto, canna de chiaveca, che lo chiammavano pe soprannomme masto Cocchiarone. — Ma che nce farisse 'n questo? —, disse chella bona cepolla, che sguegliaje pe lo cannaruozzolo appiso a na perteca. [4] Non 'ncappa maje a rezza né a biscate farcone o sproviero, ma sulo li povere marvizze e li 'nnoziente reviezze. Accossí sta povera penta palomma 'ncappaje a la rezza de sto male juorno ed a le biscate de sto guzzo forfante, che da buono cuoco, isso se 'ngorfeva le bone morzella, e la mogliere la pasceva de fummo. [5] 'Ntanto che no juorno le disse la poverella: «Ah, marito mio! ed è impossibele che da lo fummo de lo pegnato de le miserie meje, che me volle e male coce, non se scommoveno ss'uocchie tuoje a quarche compassione? Tu vide ca fatico da la matina a la sera, e sempe vago scàuza comme a la gallina: àggene piatate, ed a lo mmacaro famme no paro de scarpe. Io non te cerco, comm'a l'aute mogliere, lo mantic-

CUNTO PRIMMO

PITY REWARDED

(1) Whoever said, *"Do a good deed, then forget about it,"* was on target and could not have said it better. In fact, when you least expect it, you get a reward from someone else, or even from Heaven. And the opposite: *"Whoever sows evil should expect evil,"* also works, because you cannot sow wheat and reap nettles, or plant nettles and reap broccoli.[i] You reap what you sow, as I will show you with the following tale if you keep quiet and listen carefully.

(2) There was once upon a time a fine country woman named Pacecca, so good-natured that she could not muddy the water: happy with a piece of bread or honey cake, humble as ointment, and so compassionate with poor folks (as are the people from around Naples) that you couldn't find a better one. She would have sacrificed her meals to save a kid from starving.

(3) It so happened that when the good woman was about to get married, she fell for a cook, the most wretched fellow you could find under the sun: a greedy, lazy, spendthrift glutton surnamed Master Cocchiarone. "What are you going to do with this one?" the sweet sprouting onion said, hanging from a perch. (4) You cannot catch a falcon or a sparrow hawk with a net; it works only for the poor, miserable thrush and harmless chaffinch. So this poor dove ended up in the net on a sad day and in the birdlime of this gluttonous scoundrel who, as a good cook, gorged on the best morsels while feeding his wife with smoke. (5) One day, the poor broad told him, "My dear husband, isn't it possible that the smoke from the pot of my miseries that's boiling and barely cooking could move your eyes to a bit of compassion? You see how I toil all day long, always barefoot like a hen. Have pity, make me at least a pair of shoes. I am not asking like other women for a scarf, gloves, a coat, necklaces, earrings, and other useless frippery. I am begging you to provide just what I need."

(6) "Yes," Master Cocchiarone replied, "they'll be ready tomorrow." "May God bless you, my dear husband, now and forever!" Pacecca replied.

co, li guante, lo manechitto, le cannacche, li scioccaglie e tant'aute 'mbroglie, ma te cerco e t'addemmanno sulo chello ch'è necessario».

[6] «Sí, mogliere mia! — responnette masto Cocchiarone —. Pe craje so' leste».

«Lo Cielo te lo renna, marito mio — disse Pacecca —, e 'a ccà a cient'anne!» [7] Ma non s'addonava la scura ca lo marito la 'nfenocchiava, e decea chelle parole pe darele la quatra. Pe la quale cosa steva allegramente, e passanno na poverella, che pe mostare quant'avea secotata la fortuna soja, che cchiú de na cerva le jeva 'nnante fojenno, jea co li piede scauze e stroppiate, a mala pena chesta raprette la vocca e cercaje lemmosena, che Pacecca, mossese a piatate, le deze le scarpe soje, cossí becchie comm'erano, co speranza che lo marito le portasse l'aute.

[8] Ma longa se vedde, corta se trovaje: pocca venuto lo marito, e bedutola scauza, le decette: «E bè, ched haje quarche callo a li piede che non puoje ghire cauzata?». «Gnorenone — decette essa —, l'aggio dato a na poverella che ghieva scauza e co li piede tutte 'nchiajate, ca stongo secura ca tu me portarraje le nnove».

[9] Ed isso redennose de la mogliere, e stemannola bestejale, le disse: «Sí, mogliere mia, dàlle le cauze porzí, ca te le boglio portare nove sciammante!»

«Sia beneditto! — responnette Pacecca —. Lo Cielo te pozza 'mprofecare, ca saccio che non me farraje mancare lo latto d'aucielle, se vuoje!»

«D'aucielle de notte!», responnette lo marito, e redenno se ne jeze pe lo fatto sujo.

[10] Ed essa, passanno no pezzente, che pe mostare quant'era la lava de le desgrazie che passava jeva co le gamme nnude, lo chiammaje decenno: «Tè, poveriello mio, pigliate ste cauzette».

«Lo Cielo l'aggia azzietto!», responnette lo pezzente, e pigliatese le cauze súbeto le bennette, ca creo che no' le jevano bone.

[11] Tornato po' lo marito a la casa súbeto l'addemannaje le cauze e le scarpe, e decennole lo marito: «Che n'haje fatto de le toje?», respose: «L'aggio date a lo poveriello».

«E che faje — llebrecaje Cocchiarone — che no' le daje perzí la gonnella? Ca mo vene no vasciello de panne de Sciannena e te la voglio fare co lo rechippo!»

«Oh, che Dio te dia bene e sanetate! — decette Pacecca —. Accossí vonn'essere li marite».

[12] E bèccote che da llà a n'auto poco passaje na scura femmena, che

(7) But the unfortunate woman did not realize that the husband fooled her and made fun of her with his words. She was so happy to show off her pending good fortune run away faster than a deer to a poor passing woman with bare and wrecked feet. As soon as she opened her mouth asking for alms, Pacecca, filled with compassion, gave away her broken old shoes, hoping she would get new ones from her husband.

(8) But there's the rub: when the husband saw her barefoot, he told her: "What's the matter, do you have some callus on your feet that you cannot wear shoes?" "No sir," she replied. "I gave them to a poor broad who was barefoot with injured feet, because I know you are going to give me new shoes."

(9) Laughing at the woman and considering her stupid like an animal, he said, "Yes, my dear, give away your stockings too, I'll get you brand new ones." "Bless you," Pacecca answered, "may Heaven reward you. I know you would give me anything, even bird's milk, if I asked for it." "For sure, even nightingale's milk," the husband said, laughing and going about his business.

(10) When a beggar passed, walking with naked legs to show off his runaway misfortunes, she called out to him: "Here, poor lad, take these stockings!" "May Heaven smile on you," the beggar replied, taking them and selling them right away, as I believe they did not fit him.

(11) When the husband returned, Pacecca inquired at once about the stockings and shoes, and the husband asked, "What did you do with yours?" to which she answered that she gave them to a poor fellow. Cocchiarone retorted, "What are you waiting for; why don't you give away your skirt too? A garment ship from Flanders will arrive soon; I'll get you a plissé skirt." "May God give you wealth and health," Pacecca said, "that's how husbands should be!"

(12) A little later, a miserable woman walked by, an incarnation of beggary. Her rag of a skirt was so ripped and battered that she looked like a fish pulled from a sea of plenty wrapped in a net of poverty and splashed with unpleasant vinegar on top of the grill of misery. (13) The good-hearted, compassionate Pacecca told her she wanted to give her alms, so she threw her skirt from the window and sent her on her way.

(14) When Master Cocchiarone saw her dressed in a shirt, he thought she was laundering the skirt and said, "What's the matter, my dear wife, are you too hot walking around the house like this?" "Well, my dear husband, I am waiting for the new skirt, stockings, and shoes." "And what have you done with the old skirt?" "I gave it to a poor woman who needed it badly."

(15) "Well done, since you are rich!" Cocchiarone gave back. "You

pareva lo retratto de la pezzenteria: pocca chillo poco de straccio de gonnella che portava era tanto rutto e brenzoluso, che essa pareva no pesce cacciato da lo mare de la recchezza ed arravogliato dinto na rezza de povertate, ped essere sguazzariato co l'acito de li desguste 'ncoppa la gratiglia de la meseria.

[13] E la bona Pacecca co n'affrezzione granne le decette ca le voleva fare la lemmosena, e projennole da no fenestriello la gonnella soja, la mannaje connio.

[14] Venuto masto Cocchiarone, e bedennola 'n cammisa, se credeva che se facesse lo scaudatiello a la gonnella, e le disse: «Ched è, mogliere mia, haje caudo sopierchio che baje accossí pe la casa?»

«Ah, marito mio! — dicette Pacecca —. Stongo aspettanno la gonnella nova, le cauze e le scarpe».

«E de la toja — disse lo masto —, che n'haje fatto?»

«L'aggio data a na poverella che n'avea propio abbesuogno».

[15] «Sí, ca tu sì ricca! — llebrecaje Cocchiarone —. Sa' che buoje fare? Da' la cammisa porzí, se te pare, ca de sta manera te 'ncegnarraje tutta de nuovo».

«Gnoressí, marito mio, ma fà priesto chello c'haje da fare, ca mo restarraggio a la nnuda».

«Volanno, volanno te servo!», disse lo marito, e botato carena vrocioliaje pe le grade pensanno che male 'mmatteto avea fatto, piglianno co male fèle chello che la scura mogliere facea pe troppo nzemprecetate.

[16] E accossí, spianno Pacecca pe no pertuso de lo fenestriello se passava pezzente, vedette na poverella che pe fare toccare co mmano quant'era antica la casa soja 'mpezzenteria, jea mostanno li quarte. E mentre che pe lo vico jea decenno: «Pane, pane a na poverella morta de friddo e de famme! Quacche cammisa vecchia, ped amore de lo Cielo!», Pacecca le decette: «Aspetta, aspetta!», e spogliatase nuda, pe non fare a bedere le braccia soje spogliate le cacciaje co na mazzarella la cammisa.

[17] Restata la poverella accossí a la nnuda, vèccote che sente lo marito tozzoliare a la porta: ed essa, pe non se fare a bedere de chella manera, s'arravogliaje co no farrajuolo viecchio de lo marito, e n'avea core de raprire. [18] Cocchiarone dàlle ca tozzoliava e scampanejava a grolia, ed essa responneva: «Non posso raprire!»

«E perché?», decea Cocchiarone.

Ed essa: «M'haje portato le scarpe nove, le cauze, la gonnella e la cammisa? Ca io stongo a la nnuda, justo comme me fice màmmama!»

know what you should do? Give away your shirt too, if you like, so you'll start all over with new clothes." "Fine, dear husband, but hurry and do what you promised, because I will now end up naked." "I will serve you right away," the husband said, turning around and running down the stairs. He thought about the bad deal he had made, stewing from his wife's deeds and simplemindedness.

(16) Looking through the crack of a window to see if any beggar passed by, Pacecca saw a poor broad showing off her longstanding beggary and her naked body. As she went through the neighborhood shouting, "Give some bread to a poor freezing starving woman, please! Give me an old shirt, for Heaven's sake!" Pacecca called out, "Wait, wait!" She got undressed and, to hide her naked arms, she used a small stick to throw her shirt down.

(17) Stark naked by now, she heard the husband knock at the door. To avoid being seen like this, she wrapped herself with one of her husband's old capes but hesitated to open. (18) Cocchiarone continued to knock and appeal loudly, and she replied, "I cannot open." "How come?" he asked. And Pacecca: "Did you bring my new shoes, stockings, skirt, and shirt? I am naked, buck naked!"

(19) When the husband heard this lovely news, he got so angry that he would have killed her, clutching her neck in his rage. But the lucky broad was safe.

(20) As the sky began to darken like a chimney stack, after burning the earth's leaves with the sun's rays and extinguishing those rays and throwing them like embers westward, Master Cocchiarone knocked again at the door: "Open up, Pacecca, enough is enough!" "Did you bring the clothes?" Pacecca asked. "Don't worry, put something on and come with me. I bought the clothes, but the tailor needs to take measurements; he cannot come here."

(21) Naively believing Cocchiarone's big words, she opened the door and walked with her husband wrapped in that rag of a cloak that made her look like a peeled quail in a net.

(22) After a short walk to the tailor's shop, which wasn't there any longer, they arrived at a distant farm around midnight when the stars begin to move to the other half of the sky like golden hazelnuts, among houses looking more ancient than envy from a distant time, described by that Tuscan poet as: *"Everything ends up being covered by sand and grass."* [ii]

(23) The grass had grown so tall on those steep mountains, resembling a forest. Darling Cocchiarone left her there in a remote cavern, like putting a

[19] Quanno lo marito 'ntese sta bella 'mmasciata, le venne tant'arraggia che l'averria scannata, se l'avesse potuto avere le granfe 'ncuollo 'n chella furia: ma essa, — sepponta, Vecenza — stea 'n securo.

[20] Ntramente lo sio Cocchiarone, vedenno ca lo cielo, dapo' d'avere cotte le foglie de la terra co li ragge de lo sole, astotato lo fuoco de chille ragge co farelo sbauzare comm'a tezzone a chella banna de l'occasso, s'accommenzava a fare negro comm'a cemmenèra, tornaje a tozzolejare, decenno: «Rapre, Pacecca, su! No' nne sia cchiúne!»

«Haje portato li vestite?», responnette Pacecca.

«No' 'mporta — decette isso —. Arravògliate quarcosa e biene co mmico, ca se bè aggio accattato la robba nce manca che lo masto te piglia la mesura, pocca isso non po' venire».

[21] Essa ch'era na nzemprece, credenno a lo chiacchiarone de Cocchiarone, raprette la porta e s'abbejaje co lo marito accossí comme steva, arravogliata co chella straccia de farrajuolo che pareva quaglia pelata dinto na rezzetella.

[22] Ma dapo' d'avere cammenato no buono piezzo, chest'era la poteca de lo masto, che non s'asciava cchiúne: quanno, mmiero la meza notte, a chell'ora justo che le stelle, comm'a nocelle 'nnaurate, accommenzavano a rocioliare all'auta metate de lo cielo, arrevajeno a na certa massaria lontana lontana, addove nc'era no scarrupo de case vecchie, cchiú antiche de la 'mmidia, che parevano le case de lo Tiempo: de le quale potea dicere chillo poeta toscanese:

Il tutto cuopre al fin l'arena e l'erba

[23] Pocca era tanto cresciuta l'erva, pe chelle montagne scarropate, che parevano no vosco. Lloco te la consegnaje lo buono Cocchiarone, lassannola a no recuoncolo comme s'avesse 'nfornato no pastone, e decennole ca «Mo mo torno co li vestite», auzaje lo fierro, e dàlle ca tallonejaje. [24] Ma la povera Pacecca aspetta aspetta, e no' bedenno cchiú lo marito, c'aveva fatto la juta de lo cuorvo, se bè vegliaje tutta chella notte, se 'nzonnaje co tutto chesto lo male juorno. [25] E non sapenno che luoco fosse chillo, né da chi abetato, se ne chiarette la matina, pocca appena ascette l'Arba a dire: — Banno e commannamiento da parte de masto Chiommiento che tutte l'aucielle, uommene ed anemale escano a salotare lo Sole, che mo se ne vene —, che súbeto se vedde ascire e zompare da ccà n'urzo, da llà no gatto maimone, da na banna no vozzacchio, da n'auta n'auciello grefone: li quale pe grazia de lo Cielo, che maje se scorda de l'abbannonate, no' le fecero niente, perché se la nasconnette sotto l'ascelle la 'nnocenzia soja. [26] E fuorze chill'anemale àppero compas-

large loaf of bread in the oven, telling her, "I'll be right back with the clothes." He then took off, running away fast. (24) Poor Pacecca kept waiting. Not seeing her husband who had left for good, despite being awake all night long, she dreamt about her unlucky fate that day. (25) While she didn't know what place this was and who its residents were, the morning cleared everything as soon as Dawn came out to announce: "On behalf of Master Chiommiento, I am ordering that all birds, people, and animals come out to greet the rising sun." At once, you could see a bear come out and jump around over here, a big cat, a buzzard, and a griffon over there. They left her unharmed because of her innocence, thank Heaven which never forgets the forsaken. (26) Perhaps those animals felt pity for the unfortunate woman whose boundless compassion for others had reduced her to misery, while saving their teeth and claws for ungrateful and cruel creatures.

(27) The miserable abandoned woman did not know what to do and where to turn, and she did not take any step without stumbling on those cliffs. At daybreak, she saw a nearby palace. Thinking that perhaps a gentleman lived there, she went to knock at the door, asking for alms. (28) Knock as long as you like; no one answered. But the knocks made a door hatch fall down, making so much noise that a lovely dove came out of a nest in a hole of the courtyard, all terrified and confused. (29) Suddenly, a big, bad bird flew out from the cliffs, attacking it and tattering it with its claws. Out of compassion, Pacecca threw a stone that luckily hit the buzzard and caused it to drop the dove from its claws. It fell on a patch of grass, tumbled as soon as it hit the ground, rolled around, and flew away as if it had never been tattered.

(30) Pacecca ran to catch the dove and saw how the large patch of grass touched by the dove had withered. Thinking that the grass might bring the dead back to life, she took a handful placing it on her chest saying: "May I never need it! Virtue is always a good thing!"

(31) Now that she could enter the palace after the lock fell off, she lost no time and entered into an exceptionally large courtyard surrounded by porphyry columns. Two royal staircases led on both sides to four apartments, with windows that opened to four balconies surrounding the palace. (32) Pacecca began to ascend the stairs to the right. She was afraid, as she didn't hear or see a living soul. She began to shout, "Have mercy and pity!" to see if anyone answered her call for alms. But after yelling for a whole hour at the magpies, she took heart and went up.

(33) In the first apartment, she came across a huge, endless lounge.

sione de na sfortonata, che ped avere avuto troppo compassione dell'aute era arredotta a chella meseria, stepannose li diente e le granfe pe chille che songo sgrate e crodele.

[27] Ma la scura, vedennose chiantata, non sapeva a che s'arresorvere né addove dare de pietto, se bè non deva passo senza 'ntoppare pe chille scarrupe: quanno, fatto juorno chiaro, s'addonaje ca nc'era no palazzo llà becino. E credennose ca fosse abetato da quarche segnore, ce jette a tozzolejare pe cercare na lemmosena. [28] Ma tózzola che te vuoje, ca no' responneva nesciuno; ed a lo tanto vattere e tozzolejare cadette no portiello de lo portone, che fice no fracasso accossí granne che na povera palommella, che steva a no pertuso de lo cortiglio, addove s'avea fatto lo nido, ascette tutta sorrèsseta e sbaottuta. [29] E bèccote che da chille scarrupe addove era stata Pacecca ascette súbeto no brutto auciello, che dannole de pietto, co le granfe la spetacciava; e Pacecca pe compassione menaje na savorra sopramano, e pe bona fortuna cogliette lo vozzacchio e le fece cadere la palommella da le granfe: la quale, caduta 'ncoppa na troffa d'erva, a mala pena la toccaje che súbeto, fatte quatto capotròmmola e brociolejata no poco 'n terra, se ne tornaje a bolare bella e bona comme se maje fosse stata scannarozzata.

[30] Pacecca, ch'era córzeta pe pigliare la palommella, veduto lo negozio tennemente a chell'erva, e bedde che la troffa era grossa e che chella che la palomma avea toccato s'era ammosciata; da la quale cosa pensaje che chell'erva avesse vertute de resorzetare li muorte co la morte soja, e còutane na bona vranca se la mese 'mpietto, e decenno: «Non pozza maje servire! La vertú sempre è bona!»

[31] Accossí potenno trasire a lo palazzo, perché era caduto lo portiello, no' nce fece auto: trasette dinto, e bedde no cortiglio grandissemo, tutto attorniato de colonne de porfeto. Da na banna e dall'auta nc'erano doje gradeate reale, pe le quale se jeva a quatto appartamiente, tutte co le feneste ch'ascevano a quatto balaostrate che ghievano attuorno a lo palazzo. [32] Pacecca pe le grade che stevano a mano ritta accommenzaje a saglire, ma appe paura, non sentenno né bedennoce anema nata. Tanno se mese a strillare: «Meserecordia e piatà!», azzò co l'occasione de cercare la lemmosena, se nc'era quarcuno responnesse. Ma dapo' d'avere strellato a le ciàvole n'ora tosta, fece de la trippa corazzone e sagliette 'ncoppa.

[33] Ed a lo primmo appartamiento trovaje no grannissemo salone, che no' nne vedive la fine; da llà passaje a na cammara, e po' a n'auta cammara, e po' a doj'aute cammare, e po' a quatt'aute cammare, ed a no cammarone fore

From there, she went to one room, then to another, then to two and four other rooms, and in another unusual room, she found a beautiful walnut closet loaded to the brim with shoes of all kinds: cordovan, cowhide, Moroccan, shoes with white and red soles, sprouted in the French fashion with fisherman-style high heels, closed Spanish style shoes, cleaved shoes with crocheted laces, and embroidered slippers. (34) Next to it was another pear wood closet, packed with the best wool and knitted and woven silk stockings: English, Neapolitan, and Roman stockings, their heels reinforced with silk and gold of all sorts— amazing things. (35) In front of it there was another closet, loaded with precious clothes, skirts, dresses, petticoats, shirts, bodices, jackets, gabardines, vests, soutanes, and fashionable open clothes, overcoats, and farthingales. (36) Next to it was still another closet with drawers filled to the brim with shirts made of *soffia-che-vola* cloth; Flanders, Dutch, Orleans, Cambrai fabrics, and fabrics from Cava dei Tirreni; some thirty-two-thread fabrics; balm cloth embroidered, back-point sewed three or four times, with fringes; laces looking like dog teeth and cat claws yet embroidered red with silk and gold that would have even ladies exclaim: "Oh, mother of mine, this is too much!"

(37) So the poor buck-naked child Pacecca (the way she came out of her mother's knee), upon seeing all these beautiful things, could not just stay there without providing for herself, since in the end, when facing extraordinary needs, everyone acts the same. That's what she did, taking only a few things to remedy her needs without giving in to vanity. (38) Newly dressed, after passing through other chambers, she arrived at a parlor adorned with mosaic-shaped arabesques, tiltable desks, shrines, silver amphoras with flowers, and other things suited for a crowned king. (39) And there was indeed a king's son. Noticing a beautiful canopy, she approached it and found a very handsome young man who had been killed—God forbid!—with a wound on his chest. Next to him were several knights and princes, all lying strewn about the room.

(40) Seeing this horrible scene, poor Pacecca panicked and began to scream desperately. Her screams resounded through those rooms with echoes; it seemed to her that there were one hundred screaming voices. Stunned, frightened, shocked, and terrified, the poor woman raced through the rooms and downstairs so fast that when she was in the courtyard, she couldn't remember how she got there.

(41) Hearing all the noise and screams, the dove flew from her nest and, seeing Pacecca's pale face, said to her: "Don't be afraid, my dear Pacecca, I

de l'úrdene trovaje no bello stipo de noce chino chino, zippo zippo e barro varro de scarpe d'ogne sciorte, de cordovana, de vacchetta, de marrocchino, co le sòle janche, co le sòle rosse, spontate a la franzesa, co lo tallonetto a la pisciavina, scarpe chiuse a la spagnola, sgavigliate, co li cairielle, chianielle e scarpe arragamate pe dinto li chianielle. [34] Appriesso nc'era n'auto stipo de piro, curmo curmo, e co l'accoppatura, de cauzette de filo e de seta, fatte co li fierre ed a lo telaro, all'angresa, a la napoletana, a la romana, co li cugne lavorate de seta e d'oro e di tutte le sciorte, ch'era cosa da stordire. [35] Faccefronte a chisto nc'era n'auto stipo chino a carcapede de vestite preziuse: ccà nc'erano gonnelle, rrobbe, sottanielle, cammesole, corpiette, sciammerghe, cavardine, jeppune, faudiglie ed abete apierte all'osanza, longarine e porzí guardanfante. [36] Appriesso a chisto nc'era n'autro stipo a tirature chino nfi' 'ncoppa de cammise de tela sciósciala-ca-vola, de tela de Sciannena, d'Olanda, d'Orletta, de Crambaja; de tela de la Cava, tela 'n trentadoje, tela cetranella, lavorate co cartiglie, cosute a retopunte, co la doja e la tre, co sfilatielle, co pezzille fatte a la rocca, a dente de cane ed a granfe de gatta, e porzí arragamate de seta e d'oro, che cchiú d'una, se bè segnora, avarria ditto: «Eh mamma, ca moro!»

[37] Ora mo Pacecca, poverella, ch'era 'nfante e nuda comme era 'sciuta da lo denucchio de la mamma, vedenno tanta belle mobele, non potette stare co lo core accossí stabele che non se provedesse: pocca a la fina fatta, a tiempo de 'strema necessetate ogne ncosa è commone. Chesto sí: che la scuressa se pegliaje le cose de cchiú bascia mano, volenno sopprire a la necessetate, e non dare pasto a la baggianaria. [38] Cossí bestuta, passate ciert'aute cammare, arrevaje a na stanzia tutta aparata de contrataglie a la mosaica, de screttorie, scaravatte, de giarre d'argiento co sciure e co tant'aute belle cose, che nce potea stare no Re de corona. [39] E de fatto nc'era lo figlio de no Re: pocca avenno visto no bello bardacchino, s'accostaje, e nce trovaje sotta no bellissemo giovane, ch'era stato acciso, arrasso sia, co na feruta 'mpietto, ed appriesso nc'erano na mano de Cavaliere e Princepe tutte scannarozzate, chi caduto da na banna e chi da n'auta.

[40] Quanno la povera Pacecca vedde sto strevèrio, appe tanta paura che se mese a strellare comme a na speretata, li quale strille de tale manera 'ntronajeno pe chelle cammere che nce fecero l'ecco, e le parze comme se ciento vuce strillassero. Pe la quale cosa la poverella, meza storduta, agghiajata, sorrèsseta e schiantata, passate 'n quatto sàute tutte chelle cammare, vrocioliaje pe le grada abbascio, de muodo e de manera che quanno fu a lo cortiglio non s'allecordava manco pe do' nne era scesa.

am here for you through thick and thin, wherever you go. (42) You must know that your goodness brought you here to be a queen. I am the dove you saved from the buzzard's claws; falling on that grass, I came back to life. I now want to reward you for your virtuous deeds. (43) I am the fairy of the handsome slain young man you saw, for your benefit. He is the son of the king of Campochiaro, who was going to marry the queen of Montaguzzo, at that time one of the most beautiful and wealthy women whose father promised her to the son of the king of Pierdesinno. The two came to a duel, and Campochiaro injured Pierdesinno. (44) Revengeful Pierdesinno knew that Campochiaro was visiting the palace and had him finished off by his assassins the way you found him. Out of despair, the father closed the palace and did not want anyone to get close to it. (45) But as his fairy, I preserved him so that his body and those of the knights and princes serving him would not decompose and someone would eventually come to bring him back to life for his poor father, who by now is decrepit and blind with only a young son, as his wife bore only girls after the prince's murder, giving birth recently to a young boy. (46) The time has now come for you to win the beautiful prize by touching him with a bit of the grass that revived me and will bring him and his knights and princes back to life. Be careful though, the grass dries as soon as you touch it. Save it; keep four blades for future needs. (47) Run now, don't waste any time, make death spiteful. And since you are in such miserable shape, I am going to bless you with all my magic. May you be more beautiful than Cocetrigna, may good fortune smile on you, may you overcome any misfortune that may happen to you!"

(48) With these words, the dove began to fly ahead of her. Walking beside her, she arrived at the room with the clothes. The dove stopped and said, "Go ahead and get dressed in the best clothes; you will soon be the mistress. And bless you for your fine manners, having chosen only the worst dresses; another dishonest broad would have taken seven of the best skirts, loading her chest, pockets, and sleeves as much as possible."

(49) After dolling herself up like a queen, Pacecca went to the king's son and touched his wound with four blades of grass. As soon as the grass dried up, the young man opened his eyes as if waking from sleep. Seeing the young woman in front of him and realizing she had given him his life back, he kneeled in front of her, believing she was a fairy. (50) The dove then said, "Get up, King, because I am the fairy. This woman will be your wife, because she gave life to me and to you. And you, Pacecca, to make the celebration more splendid, go ahead and bring back to life these other princes and knights."

[41] A lo remmore ed a lo strellatorio ascíje da lo nido la palommella, e beduta Pacecca co na facce che parea 'nzolarcata, accossí le disse: «N'avere paura, Pacecca mia, ca stongo io ccà pe tene, a barda e a sella, a pede e a cavallo, pe mare e pe terra. [42] Sacce ca lo buono essere tujo t'ha portato a sto luoco, ad essere Regina. Io so' chella palomma che tu haje fatto cadere da le granfe de lo vozzacchio, che caduta 'ncoppa chell'erva songo resorzetata. Mo te ne voglio rennere lo buono miereto. [43] Io songo la Fata de lo bello giovane c'haje visto acciso, 'n sanetate toja: chisto è lo figlio de lo Re de Campochiaro, lo quale pretennenno lo matremmonio de la Regina de Montaguzzo, ch'era na segnora la cchiú bella e la cchiú ricca che se trovava a tiempo sujo, che da lo patre era stata 'mprommettuta a lo figlio de lo Re de Pierdesinno, venne co chisto a doviello, e Capochiaro ferette Pierdesinno. [44] Pierdesinno, volennose mennecare, avenno saputo che Campochiaro era venuto a spasso a sto palazzo sujo, co na mano d'assassinie l'arreddusse a lo termene che l'haje trovato, e lo patre pe desperazione fece chiudere lo palazzo, e non voze che nesciuno cchiú nce accostasse. [45] Ma io che so' la Fata soja l'aggio conzervato, che non se 'nfracetasse lo cuorpo né d'isso né de li Cavaliere e Princepe che lo servevano: azzò co lo tiempo venesse chi, co resorzetare lo muorto, desse la vita ad isso ed a lo povero patre, c'oramaje è biecchio 'n terra e non ha auto che no fegliulo peccerillo, pocca la mogliere dapo' l'acciso n'ha fatto auto che figlie femmene, ed all'útemo ha fatto lo peccerillo. [46] Ora sússo, lo tiempo è benuto, e tu sì chella che t'haje da guadagnare sto bello palio, pocca toccannolo co no poco de chell'erva che sorzetaje a mene, sorzetarraje ad isso porzíne, ed a li Cavaliere e Princepe suoje. Ma sta 'n cellevriello, ca l'erva comme tocca se secca: sparàgnala, e stipatenne quatto fila pe quarch'auto abbesuogno. [47] Curre, addonca, e non ce perdere tiempo, ca restarrà corriva la morte. E perché staje male arreddotta, vèccote che te dongo tutte le bone fataziune meje: che singhe bella cchiú de Cocetrigna, ed agge bona sciorte, e puozz'ascire da tutte li travaglie che maje te ponno abbenire!»

[48] Cossí decenno la palommella l'accommenzaje a bolare 'nnanze, ed essa, cammenannole appriesso, arrevaje a la cammera de li vestite. E la palomma, fremmatase, le decette: «Tornate a bestire de li meglio vestite che nce songo, pocca sarraje tu la patrona, e singhe benedetta pe la bona crianza c'haje avuta co pigliarete le peo robbe, che n'auta pettolella se sarria puesto sette gonnelle de le meglio che nce songo, e s'avarria chino lo pietto, le sacche e le mmaneche quanto cchiú fosse stato possibele».

[49] 'Nciricciatase addonca Pacecca comm'a na Regina, se ne jeze ad-

Dividing the grass so that some was left according to the dove's advice, she brought back to life those other folks, defying death.

(51) Seeing all the good received from Pacecca's touch, they kneeled in front of her to thank her, swore with one hand on top of the other that they would always serve her, and began a miraculous feast. (52) To make the party even more joyful, they sent the good news to the king of Campochiaro, the prince's father, who was still alive. The king arrived with his young son, brother of the revived prince, accompanied by his court, with carriages drawn by six horses, coaches with stretchers, and carts and chests filled with gold coins. After hand kisses and hugs, he wanted to know from beginning to end what had happened. Hearing all of Pacecca's charitable deeds, he ordered the prince to marry her. (53) However, Pacecca asked the lords to be patient and wait for a few months, saying that she may not be able to comply unless there was a certain stellar constellation. (54) The dove told the king that it would not take long, so he readily agreed to wait, but he asked Pacecca to take care of his youngest brother, named Renzullo, as his sister-in-law. She accepted with immense pleasure.

(55) By now, after all these events, Master Cocchiarone remembered his wife and went back to the place where he left her to see if she had died, so that he could take another wife as he pleased. He arrived at the cliffs but didn't find those crumbling houses and the grassy forest. (56) Everything was neat like the palm of a hand. A gorgeous fountain had been placed in front of the palace next to other statues. In the middle, there was a naked girl giving with one hand shoes and stockings to a poor woman, with the other, a skirt and a shirt to a beggar. A dove sat on her head, donning with its beak a royal mantle that partly covered the statue's nudity in picturesque fashion.

(57) Seeing all of this, Cocchiarone became suspicious. He asked the neighbors (as the court had rebuilt all crumbling houses) when the statue had been made and what it meant. They told him Pacecca's well-known story and how she became a queen. (58) In his despair, Master Cocchiarone thought of revenge. He went to see the butler and offered his services. Asked about his profession, he said he was a cook and that no one in the whole world knew better how to prepare a pork stew, a tripe, a beef loin in a reduced broth, a delicate cabbage soup with chopped lard, a pot of dried fresh beans, a stuffed frittata, a dish of blood with aromatic herbs, a bran pizza infused with honey, tasty morsels, dainty treats, and much else. (59) "It is the work and not the words that prove a master," the butler said. "Let's test you with the melons! Come with

dove steva lo figlio de lo Re, e pigliato quatto fila dell'erva soja le toccaje la feruta: ed appena se seccaje l'erva che lo giovane, comme si se fosse scetato da no suonno, raprette l'uocchie, e bedennose chella segnorella 'nnante, e canoscenno ca da le mmano soje receveva la vita, se l'addenocchiaje 'nnante credennose che fosse quarche Fata. [50] Quanno la palommella sparaje a dicere: «Auzate, Re, ca io songo la Fata, e chesta ha da essere la mogliere toja, perché essa ha dato la vita a me ed a te. E tu, Pacecca, azzò la festa sia cchiú comprita, resórzeta st'aute Principe e Cavaliere», ed essa scompartenno l'erva de manera che nce ne restasse no poccorillo, secunno lo consiglio de la palommella, recchiammaje a la vita tutta chella gente a la varva de la morte.

[51] Li quale vedenno avere avuto tanto bene da le mmano de Pacecca, subbeto s'addenocchiajeno a li piede suoje, e dengraziatala, joranno co na mano 'ncoppa a l'auta de volerela sempe servire, accommenzaro na festa da stordire. [52] E pe compremiento de l'allegrezza mannaro la nova a lo Re de Campochiaro, che era lo patre de lo Prencepe, ancora vivo: lo quale, venuto e portatose lo fegliulo peccerillo fratiello de lo resorzetato, accompagnato da tanta segnure, co carrozze a sei e co galesse, co lettiche, co carriagge e co casce de doppiune, dapo' li vasamano e l'abbracciamiente voze sapere da l'*A* pe nfi' a lo *Rummo* quant'era socciesso: ed avenno 'ntiso che Pacecca avea fatto tanto bene, ordenaje che lo Prencepe se la pigliasse pe mogliere. [53] Ma Pacecca pregaje sti segnure che se contentassero aspettare quarche mese, decenno che se non passava no cierto 'nfruscio de stelle non poteva connescennere. [54] Lo Re, avvisato da la palommella ca sto tiempo sarria priesto venuto, decette c'averria de bona voglia aspettato, e che ntratanto Pacecca se contentasse d'avere pensiero, comme cajenata, de lo fratiello peccerillo de lo Re, che se chiammava Renzullo. Ed essa l'azzettaje co no gusto grannissemo.

[55] Ora mo, essenno passato quanto s'è ditto, masto Cocchiarone s'allecordaje de la mogliera, e ghiuto a lo luoco dove l'avea lassata pe bedere s'era morta cessa, azzò se ne potesse pigliare n'autra a gusto sujo, venette a dove erano li scarrupe: ma non ce trovaje cchiú chelle fraveche cadute e chillo vosco d'erve. [56] Anze ch'era tutto annettato comm'a chianta de mano, e nc'era stata fatta na bellissima fontana, perché era faccefronte a lo palazzo, addove nc'erano cchiú statue: ma 'mmiezo nc'era na femmena a la nnuda, che deva a no poveriello, co na mano, scarpe e cauzette, ed a na pezzente, coll'autra, gonnella e cammisa, e 'n capo tenea na palommella che co lo pizzo le spannea sopra no manto riale, che co muodo pittorisco veneva a coprire parte de la nudetate de la stàtola.

me, prove your talents, you won't regret it." (60) After Master Cocchiarone became the king's cook, Pacecca realized that it was her husband. Convinced that he had not recognized her, she treated him very kindly, getting on familiar terms with him more so than with the other courtiers, hoping to eventually introduce him to the king and the prince, and getting him back as her husband. Pacecca was so good-natured that she did not care what he had done to her, as she preferred to be married to a poor cook and live the way she had been treated than to be a queen, contrary to faith and the laws of matrimony.

(61) Since it wanted her to be the queen and to reward her for all her virtuous deeds, as every good deed always gets rewarded, Heaven let Cocchiarone find out that the prince's brother Renzullo slept with Pacecca. One night when all was quiet and he had to bring some cake to Pacecca, who wasn't feeling well and had asked for him to deliver it, he found her asleep and decided to kill the child and to put the knife in her hand. (62) Renzullo, who was awake and saw him come, kept quiet as always without any malicious thought. Cocchiarone quietly stuck a knife in the boy's throat, slaughtering him like a little lamb, then put the knife in Pacecca's hand. He then went out and began to scream, "Help, help, Pacecca killed the prince's little brother, the king's son!" The entire court woke up at this commotion, and the king and prince went to Pacecca's room finding her with a knife in her hand and Renzullo slain.

(63) You can imagine the rage of the prince and the father unloaded on poor Pacecca, who was unaware of what had happened. Seeing the slain child beside her, she froze, clutching herself in fear and turning immobile like a mummy. Meanwhile, the lords placed guards in front of her room, and without any counsel ordered to prepare a big fire the next morning before dawn to burn Pacecca alive. (64) That's what happened: everyone congregated at the planned site—first of all the cook, who stirred the wood with a three-pronged iron for a speedy demise of his wife. The king had the gate shut out of fear of a revolt by the neighbors who all loved Pacecca, as she never let anyone down and helped all of them and their daughters.

(65) After they locked the gate, Pacecca was led down and tied up with a rope like a winch. Kneeling in front of the king, she said, "Your Most Serene Highness, as I am completely devastated by today's horrible incident, I swear on my grandmother's soul, since I am unable to swear with my hands tied with handcuffs, that I am innocent. Had I committed this crime, I would have killed myself with the same knife to prevent me from turning into ash before dust, as shame is worse than death for honorable women. (66) But should a woman's

[57] Cocchiarone che vedde sta cosa 'ntraje 'n sospetto, ed addemmannanno a le becine (mente attuorno a lo palazzo s'erano refatte tutte le case scarrupate che nc'erano, pe servizio de la corte) quant'era che s'era fatta chella fontana e che 'gnefecava, le fu contata tutta la storia de Pacecca, che già s'era sprubbecata, e comme già era deventata Regina. [58] Pe la quale cosa masto Cocchiarone, venuto 'n desperazione, pensaje de farene mennetta, e ghiutosenne a lo majardommo l'addemannaje si avea besuogno de servetore. Chillo le decette che professione era la soja, ed isso responnette che sapea fare lo cuoco, e che no' la cedeva a lo primm'ommo de lo munno a fare no 'ngrattenato de no campanaro de puorco, no ciento-fegliole, idest na cajonza co lo vruodo conciato, no pegnato de torza spinose co lo lardo adacciato, na ciaulella di fave 'ngongole, no sciosciello, no piatto de sango co l'aruta, na pizza de rerita 'nfosa a lo mele, muorze gliutte, voccune cannarute, e ba' scorrenno. [59] «Opera lauda lo masto, e non parole! — decette lo majardommo —. Li mellune se pigliano 'mprova! Vienetenne, e portate buono, ca non te farraggio lamentare».

[60] Trasuto masto Cocchiarone pe cuoco de lo Re, Pacecca s'addonaje ca chisto era lo marito, e credennose che essa non era canosciuta da isso le facea mille cortesie, dannole confendenzia cchiú dell'autre cortesciane, speranno co lo tiempo de farelo canoscere a lo Re ed a lo Prencepe, e tornare a pigliaresillo pe marito: tanto la bona Pacecca era de buono core, non curannose de chello che isso l'avea fatto, contentannose cchiú priesto essere mogliere de no povero cuoco comm'era tenuta, che essere Regina contra la fede e la legge de lo matremmonio.

[61] Ma lo Cielo, che la volea Regina e che le voleva rennere tutte l'opere bone ch'avea fatte, che maje nesciuna opera bona non fu premmiata, fece soccedere che Cocchiarone avenno abbistato ca Renzullo, fratiello de lo Prencepe, dormeva 'nsieme co Pacecca, na sera che bedde lo munno muto cojeto e c'avea da portare na certa torta a Pacecca, che stea poco bona e bolea che nce la portasse isso, trovaje che s'era addormuta: pe la quale cosa fece pensiero d'accidere lo figliulo, e mettere lo cortiello 'mmano a Pacecca che dormeva. [62] Renzullo, che stea scetato, lo vedde, e credenno che benesse comm'era soleto, senza penzare a malizia se stea zitto: e lo sio Cocchiarone bello nfra uocchie ed uocchie le 'mpizzaje no cortiello 'ncanna e lo scannarozzaje comm'a no pecoriello, mettenno lo cortiello 'mmano a Pacecca. Ed asciuto fore accommenzaje ad auzare la voce, decenno: «Currite, currite, ca Pacecca have acciso lo fratiello de lo Prencepe, lo figliulo de lo Rre!» Tutta la corte a sto vesbiglio se scetaje, e ghiuto lo Rre e lo Prencepe 'mperzona trovajeno Pacecca co lo cortiello 'mmano e Renzullo scannato.

oath be worthless, how can you think even for a moment that I would kill this beautiful child who didn't do me any harm? When I gave life back to the prince and all the knights assembled here without anyone asking me to do so, while instead I could have left them slaughtered, plundered and robbed them, and run away with all their belongings! (67) Without considering that I was to become the prince's wife, how could I have been a stepmother before being a mother, taking the life of this child, ruining the vines whose wine was going to cheer me up all my life? But if you do not hear my pitiful pleading, do me at least a favor and let the truth be told by the child. Bring him here in front of me and untie my hands."

(68) The prince and the king did as Pacecca requested. With the dead boy present and her hands untied, Pacecca took the few remaining blades of grass from her chest, thanking the dove for its good advice. She placed them on the child's wounds, and Renzullo woke up as if from deep sleep, running to embrace Pacecca as if she were his sweet mom. (69) Then the poor woman took heart and said to Renzullo, "Tell me, dear boy, who killed you? Because these gentlemen accuse me of being the evil murderer." The king and the prince asked the same question—one hugging his son, the other his brother.

(70) Renzullo replied, "It is the cook who killed me." The king then ordered the cook to be apprehended right away and thrown into the burning flames, while everyone present shouted: "Down with that wolf, kill him, burn that dog!"

(71) But good-hearted Pacecca, kneeling in front of the king and the prince, begged them for the life of Renzullo to forgive Master Cocchiarone, because he was her lawful husband. If the devil blinded him to commit that crime, he did not do it to offend the king but to spite her, to get her burnt alive. Since she had to make good a dreadful thing, she was asking for forgiveness, because a husband was still a husband.

(72) The king recognized Pacecca's good heart and began to shed tears out of tenderness and to scream, "May Heaven grant to find at least one such woman in every town! For this kind of woman has vanished, and it is the husbands who, in our days, do not love their wives enough!" To please her, he ordered not to burn Master Cocchiarone but to imprison him and to punish him for his error, so that he would come to understand the meaning of a good wife. (73) But what happened then and there? When the cook heard the boy mention his name, he fled with his spear to the kitchen to hide, out of his own bad conscience. He was blinded so much by fright that he fell into a tank left open

[63] Ora ccà te vediste a chelle primme furie lo Prencepe e lo patre fare fuorfece fuorfece contra la scura Pacecca: la quale non sapenno che l'era soccieso, e bedennose co chillo fegliulo accossí scannarozzato rente, deventaje no pezzechillo, restaje attassata, tutta de no piezzo, e comm'a na mmummia. Li segnure nfradechesto mettettero le guardie a chella cammara, e senz'autro consiglio ordenajeno che la matina, primma ch'ascesse l'arba, se facesse no gran focarone dinto a lo cortiglio e nce abbrosciassero Pacecca. [64] Accossí fu fatto: e benute tutte a lo luoco che s'è ditto, e mprimma d'ogn'autro lo cuoco, che co na forcina de fierro co tre diente 'mmano attezzava le legna, che dessero priesto fine a la mogliere, lo Re fece serrare lo portone avenno paura de quarche revota de li vecine, ch'erano tutte affezzionate a Pacecca, che non facea partire nesciuna scontenta da la casa soja, pocca facea bene a tutte e conzolava tutte le figlie de mamma.

[65] Serrato lo portone, fu portata a bascio Pacecca attorniata de fune commme a no manganiello, la quale addenocchiatese 'nnante a lo Re, accossí decette: «Serenissima Autezza, nfi' 'ncoppa a l'àstreco oje 'ntrovolata pe lo nigro azzedente, te juro pe l'arma de vava, pocca non pozzo jurare co na mano 'ncoppa a l'autra, trovannomele strénte da le manette, che io songo 'nnozente de sto chiàjeto: pocca se io avesse fatto sto male, io stessa co lo cortiello c'a-veva 'mmano me sarria scannata pe non vedereme deventare primmo cennera che porva: pocca èje a le femmene 'norate de cchiú pena la vregogna che la morte. [66] Ma quanno juramiente de femmena non avessero fede, comme ve pò passare manco pe la capo che io avesse acciso sto bello fegliulo che non m'ha fatto niente? Quanno io aggio dato la vita a lo sio Prencepe ed a tanta Cavaliere ccà presente senza che nesciuno me nn'avesse pregato, anze, quanno poteva farele restare accossí scannarozzate comme stevano, ed io zeppoliarene, cottearene, arravogliarene, azzimmarene, granciarene e scorcogliarene quan-to nc'era! [67] Otra po' ca se io era 'mpromessa pe mogliere a lo Prencepe, comme voleva fare da matreja primma d'essere mamma, e co tagliare la vita de sto peccerillo schiantare tutta la vigna che me dovea dare vino d'allegrezza pe tutta la vita mia? E se avite appilate l'aurecchie a ste piatose vuce meje, faciteme no piacere, ca ve farraggio confessare la veretà da lo stisso fegliulo: facitemello portare ccà 'nnanze, e lassate che me siano sciòute le mmano».

[68] Lo Rre e lo Prencepe fecero quanto decette Pacecca: fatto venire lo muorto, e sciòvete le mmano ad essa, Pacecca pegliaje da 'mpietto chelle poco foglietelle d'erva che l'erano rommase, dengrazianno la palommella che le avea dato st'aviso: e puostole sopra la feruta de lo fegliuolo, Renzullo se

in the haste to witness Pacecca's death. He froze, more due to his fault than to the freezing water, drowning and holding the spear so tightly that it stuck to his hand. (74) Pulled from the pond, stiff like plaster, they brought him to the king, holding him upright. The dove started to fly around his head, shitting on it three times, and the corpse turned into marble with the spear in his hand, as I told you. With tears in her eyes, Pacecca would have liked to bring him back to life, but she ran out of grass blades and could not do anything about it.

(75) The dove then said, "Let's move on. The one who had to be chastised was duly punished. If he escaped from the fire—which serves the cook—he could not escape from water. May the reward go to those who deserve it! And you, my Lord King, let the prince marry Pacecca, since the dark vibes are gone by now. Be assured that he will have the best wife in the whole world, without fear to have but the crown of the kingdom that he will inherit. Move that frozen statue in front of a giant sewer so that it is scented with the stench it deserves."

(76) The dove then flew away, and Pacecca married the prince with a great feast. A few days later, she was taken with carriages and coaches to Campochiaro, where Cocchiarone's statue was also taken. (77) But few years later, the statue was moved from Campochiaro to Naples and placed above the fountain in front of Castle Square, close to a giant sewer, since that is its fate, even though many claim that it is Neptune's statue, and that Master Cocchiarone's story is just a fairy tale.

(78) But it isn't so, because in Campochiaro, above the Square's sewer where the statue stood, you can still read these verses:

This is the burial place / of a cook named Master Cocchiarone. / Whoever passes by must not pray for his peace, / the rascal was always trouble. / He even endeavored to ruin his good and decent wife. / But she became a queen, living in glory, / whereas he just stares at a giant sewer.

(79) But let the writers say whatever they please, what matters more is the belief that

Those who seek to damage others do no good to themselves, / and those doing good deeds always find rewards.

(80) Everyone liked Ciulletella's story, as no one chatted from beginning to end. Instead, they were all left with their mouths open, looking like statues, and when the story ended, everyone applauded, some praising its graceful-

scetaje, comme da no suonno, e súbeto corze ad abbracciare Pacecca comme se fosse la mammarella soja. [69] Tanno la poverella, pigliato armo, decette a Renzullo: «Di', fegliulo mio, chi t'have acciso? Pocca sti segnure teneno a mene pe mala fèle e ped accedetara». Lo stisso addemmannajeno lo Rre e lo Prencepe, che corzero l'uno ad abbracciare lo figlio, l'auto lo fratre. [70] E Renzullo: «Chillo che me have acciso è stato lo cuoco». Tanno lo Rre commannaje che de zeppa e de pésole fosse pigliato lo cuoco e ghiettato dinto a chelle bampe allommate, e tutte li chille che nc'erano presiente facevano: «A lo lupo! A lo lupo!», decenne e strellanno: «Acceditelo, abbrosciatelo sso cano!»

[71] Ma la bona Pacecca, addenocchiatase a li piede de lo Re e de lo Prencepe, le pregaje che pe la vita de Renzullo perdonassero a masto Cocchiarone, pocca chillo era lo marito sujo. E se lo diàschence l'avea cecato a fare chillo sproposeto, no' l'aveva fatto pe despietto de lo Re ma pe despietto sujo, azzò che essa fosse abbrosciata: ma perché essa aveva da rennere bene pe male, pocca lo marito era sempe marito, le cercava sta grazia.

[72] Lo Rre, vedenno lo buono core de Pacecca, se mese a chiagnere pe tenerezza e gredaje: «Piacesse a lo Cielo che de sse femmene se ne trovasse a lo mmanco una pe pajese! Pocca se nn'è perduta la razza, se lo manco che ammano oje le ffemmene songo li marite!» E perzò, pe darele gusto, commannaje che non s'abbrosciasse masto Cocchiarone, ma che se mettesse 'mpresone e fosse 'mparte castecato de l'arrore, azzò che benga a canoscere che bò dicere bona mogliere. [73] Ma che soccesse? Quanno lo cuoco se 'ntese nommenare da lo fegliulo, vottato da la propria coscienzia, se nne fojette co la forcina 'mmano dinto la cocina pe s'annasconnere: e tanto jeze cecato de la paura che cadette dinto a na cesterna 'n chiana terra, ch'isso avea lassata aperta pe la pressa de venire a bedere morta Pacecca. E ghielato, cchiú da l'arrore che dall'acqua, ch'era freddissema, nce s'annegaje, e tanto stregnette la forcina che nce le restaje 'mmano. [74] Cacciato fora da li pozzàre, tíseco comme se fosse de stucco, fu portato 'nnanze a lo Rre, che lo tenevano accossí, deritto deritto. La palommella accommenzaje a bolare 'ntuorno a la capo, 'ncoppa la quale avenno cacato tre bote, lo catavero deventaje de màrmora, restannole, comme v'aggio ditto, la forcina 'mmano.

Pacecca avarria co le lagreme all'uocchie volutolo resorzetare, ma l'erva era scomputa, e pe chesto non ce potte fare auto.

[75] Tanno la palommella decette: «Orasússo, scompímmola: chi aveva d'avere lo castico già l'ha avuto, che se scappaje da lo ffuoco, che ajuta lo cuoco, non ha potuto sarvarese da l'acqua. Aggia mo lo premmio chillo a chi

ness, others the fine memory or something else.[iii] (81) Meanwhile Popa got ready for her story, a bit overwhelmed by the praise her sister received. She choked a bit, then began her tale after brushing her lips with a new handkerchief made of soft cloth, beginning this way:

Endnotes

i For the multiple meanings of this term and an analysis of selected words used in Basile's *Cunto* and also in Sarnelli's *Posilecheata*, see Carolina Stromboli, *Le parole del cunto. Indagini sul lessico napoletano del Seicento.* Florence: Cesati, 2017 (see, for example *vruoccole* p. 63, *cetrulo* p. 42, *cotecune* p.118, *maccarune* p.49, *marvizze* p.96, *vava de parasacco* p.132).

ii The Italian poet Torquato Tasso (1544-1595) whose poem *Jerusalem Delivered* (1591) depicts an imaginative version of the siege of Jerusalem and the combats between Christians and Muslims at the end of the first Crusade.

iii Note the frequent Neapolitan hyperboles and Baroque metaphors such as the following: *lo fummo de lo pegnato de le miserie meje* (the smoke from the pot of my miseries); *lo cielo, dapo' d'avere cotte le foglie de la terra co li ragge de lo sole... saccommenzava a fare negro comm'a cemmenèra* (the sky began to darken like a chimney stack, after burning the earth's leaves with the sun rays); *mmiero la mezanote, a chell'ora justo che le stelle, comm'a nocelle 'nnaurate, accommenzavano a rocioliare all'auta metate de lo Cielo* (around midnight when the stars begin to move to the other half of the sky like golden hazelnuts), etc.

tocca! E buje, segnore Rre, date pe marito lo Prencepe a Pacecca, ca già è passato lo nigro 'nfruscio, e stia securo c'avarrà na mogliere che non se ne trova la para a lo munno, senza paura d'avere auta corona che chella de lo Regno, che le tocca pe 'redetate. E chella statola jelata facitela mettere 'nnante na chiaveca maesta, azzò sia 'ncenziata co li spreffumme che mmereta».

[76] Ed accossí ditto la palommella se ne volaje, e Pacecca co festa granne se 'nguadiaje co lo Prencepe, e dapo' na mano de juorne fu co carrozze e galesse portata a Campochiaro, dinto la quale cetate porzí portajeno la statola de Cocchiarone. [77] Ma dapo' na mano e mano d'anne chesta statola fu straportata da Campochiaro a Napole, e messa 'ncoppa la fontana 'nnanze lo Làrego de lo Castiello, vecino la chiaveca maesta, pocca accossí è lo destino sujo: se bè mute vonno che chella sia la statola de Nettunno, e sto cunto de masto Cocchiarone lo teneno pe favola.

[78] E puro n'è lo vero: pocca a Campochiaro, 'ncoppa la chiaveca de la chiazza, addove steva la statola se leggeno ancora sti vierze:

Sebbetura e catavero, ccà stace
No cuoco ditto masto Cocchiarone.
Non sia chi passa che le prega pace,
Ca sempe guerra fece lo guittone:
E la mogliere soja, bona e garbata,
Precoraje de vede' tarrafinata.
Ma chella fu Regina, e steze 'n festa,
Isso guarda na chiaveca maesta.

[79] Ma dicano puro chello che bonno li scretture, che chello che cchiú 'mporta è sacrederese che

Chi vò male ped aute a sé non jova,
E chi fa bene, sempe bene trova.

[80] Piacette tanto lo cunto de Ciulletella a tutta la commertazione, che da che accommenzaje pe nfi' ca fenette non se vedette nesciuno pepetare. Anze, stanno tutte cann'apierte, parevamo tanta statole, e quanno po' scompette ognuno de nuje le facette n'apprauso, chi lodannone la grazia, chi la mamoria, e chi na cosa e chi n'auta. [81] Ntrattanto erase apparecchiata Popa pe dicere lo sujo, e meza annozzata pe la gran lauda data a la sora, sprugaje no piezzo, ed a la fine, stojatose lo musso co no moccaturo nuovo de cànnavo fino, accossí deze prencipio:

LA VAJASSA FEDELE

CUNTO SECUNNO

[1] Vorria che fosse vivo chillo Sanzaro de Mergoglino, tanto stemmato da li pojete, che jette a dicere chille vierze accossí scostommate:

> *Ne l'onda solca e nell'arena semina*
> *E i vaghi venti cerca in rete accogliere*
> *Chi sue speranze fonda in cor di femina.*

[2] Pocca le vorria dare na mentita pe la gola, essennose trovate e trovannose de le femmene che non sulo manteneno la fede e le parole, ma fanno tanto de cchiúne de chello c'hanno mprommisso, comme ve farraggio toccare co mmano co lo cunto che ve songo pe dicere.

[3] Era na vota a lo Regno de Terraverde na Regina chiammata Jacova, la quale trovannose grossa prena, venuta l'ora de lo pàrtoro 'scette a luce, e fatta na bella squacquara la chiammaje Pomponia: pocca da lo primmo juorno mostrava che avea da essere la pompa d'ammore, e pe dicerela 'n cincociente parole pareva fatta co lo penniello, e non se ce asciava no piecco, pocca pareva na puca d'oro.

[4] A chille tiempe s'aosava che quanno na Regina avea figliato, s'aparava tutto lo palazzo, comme se nce avesse a benire no 'Mperatore, e facennone ire fora tutta la gente de casa, venevano le Fate a fatare la creatura: e nesciuno poteva sentire che cosa decevano se no' la mamma, la quale, serrata co le cortine de lo lietto, spiava pe na senghetella.

[5] Aparato addonca lo palazzo, e scopato comm'a na chianta de mano, soccedette che no paggio tentillo, magnannose certe nocelle, s'avea fatto cadere le scorze 'mmiezo a l'antecammara. [6] Ntramente vennero le Fate, che fujono sette, e cammenanno pe la casa co li piede scauze, a l'uso de la Fataria, la sesta Fata se chiavaje na scorza de chelle a lo pede: lo quale ped essere troppo tiennero se rompíje subeto a sango, e co n'arraggia de lo diàschence trasíje co le compagne a la cammara addove steva la nennella. [7] Ora mo, 'ncommenzanno le Fate a dare le fataziune lloro, la primma, che bedde ca la creatura

CUNTO SECUNNO

THE LOYAL MAID

I wish that highly revered poet Sannazaro from Mergellina[i] were still alive, the
author of these dreadful verses:

> *Whoever places hope in female hearts*
> *plows waves in the sea, sows in the sand,*
> *trying to catch faint winds with a net.*

(2) I would tell him that he lied through his teeth, since there have always been women who are not only faithful and keep their promises but go beyond what they promised, as you will see first-hand and realize in the following tale.

(3) There was once upon a time in the kingdom of Greenland a queen named Jacova who was highly pregnant. When the time arrived, she gave birth to a beautiful little girl she named Pomponia, who from the first day on showed to be love's splendor. To say it in five hundred words, she seemed painted with a brush, flawless, like a little angel.

(4) Back in those times, when a queen gave birth, the palace was adorned all over like for an Emperor's visit. Everyone had to leave when the fairies arrived to bless the child, and no one was allowed to hear what was being said except for the mother, who was hidden behind the bed's drapes, spying through a tiny crack.

(5) After the palace was prepared and scrubbed spotless like the palm of a hand, it so happened that a careless page ate some nuts, dropping the shells in the middle of the antechamber. (6) When the seven fairies arrived, walking barefoot through the palace as fairies do, the sixth of them stepped on one of the shells, injuring her tender foot, making it bleed, which is why she entered the baby's room with her companions filled with a devilish rage. (7) As the fairies began to make their magic spells, the first, noticing the child's picture-like perfection, said: "May you turn into the most beautiful woman on earth in your lifetime, and may no smallpox blisters or other diseases ever

era na pentata cosa, le decette: «Va, che puozz'essere la cchiú bella femmena che s'aggia a trovare a lo munno a tiempo tujo, e che né le bòne, né auto male te pozza guastare ssa bella faccella: te deventano li capille oro filato, sia ssa facce na luna 'n quinquagesema, chiss'uocchie doje stelle che te parleno, ssa canna sempe mellese, sso pietto ceniero, ssa mano pastosa!»

[8] «Va, che puozz'essere — disse la seconna — lo sciore de le belle, lo spanto de le femmene, lo schiecco e lo cuccopinto de Vennere, e cchiú saputa de Sanzone!»

Disse la terza: «Va, che tu singhe la cchiú bemmoluta de lo munno, auta comm'a no confalone, e spettacolo da strasecolare!»

Secotaje la quarta: «Va, che tutte le felicetate e le contentizze de lo munno te vengano a colare a chiummo ed a ciammiello!»

E la quinta: «Va, che non nce sia Regina accossí ricca che se pozza mettere 'mpretennenzia co tico!»

[9] La sesta, arraggiata e 'nforiata pe lo dolore ch'aveva a lo pede, le disse: «Va, che la primma notte che borraje stare co maríteto, 'n toccanno lo lietto puozze arreventare serpa, e cossí puozze stare tre anne, tre mise, tre juorne, tre ore e tre momiente! E se, passato sto tiempo, non trovarraje na vajassa fedele, c'aggia doje sore cotecune, e sia figlia de na mamma che non aggia né mamma, né patre, né bavo, né figlie mascole, e che la facce de la vajassa fedele arresemmeglia tutta a la toja, nce puozze stare pe sempe!»

[10] Ma la settema, mosseta a piatate de chella scura peccerella, che non corpava niente a lo mmale de lo pede de la sesta e che aveva da fare la penetenzia ped auto, le decette: «Va, che puozz'asciare tutto chello che cercarraje, azzò che puozze ascire da tutte guaje!» E accossí decenno se ne jezero pede catapede e chiano chianillo, de manera che non se senteva no minemo sfruscio de piede: e sarriano jute pe coppa no campo de grano sicco senza farene cotolejare na spica. Ma la lava de lo sango de la Fata ancora scorre pe llà 'n terra.

[11] La scura mamma, che sentette lo 'mbruoglio, se lo stepaje dinto a lo core sujo. Ed essenno la figlia cresciuta a parmo, comme la mal'erva, deventaje bella, saputa, graziosa, benvoluta, secunno le fataziune de l'aute Fate: ma la Regina, sempe che la vedeva, le 'scevano doje pescerícole dall'uocchie, penzanno che male chiòppeta aveva da guastare la bella colata de chella facce spasa a lo sole de tutte le grazie, che brutto cravone dovea cadere a lo meglio vullo de chillo pegnato d'ammore, che male juorno avea da portare na brutta notte a chillo cielo de bellezzetuddene cosa.

damage your pretty little face. May your hair turn into golden yarn, may your face look like a full moon, your eyes be two shining stars, your throat always be silky and endearing, your chest soft and your hands gracefully delicate!"

(8) "Yes," said the second, "may you be the fairest flower, the amazement among women, the mirror and Cupid of Venus, wiser than Samson!"

The third said: "May you be the world's most cherished woman, tall like a banner, a stunning spectacle!"

And the fourth: "May all the world's happiness and satisfactions cautiously and wisely besiege you!"

And the fifth: "May there be no queen so wealthy as to be able to compete with you!"

(9) Enraged and angry because of her foot's injury, the sixth said: "May you turn into a serpent on the first night with your husband when touching the bed, and may you stay like that three years, three months, three days, three hours, and three minutes! And forever unless you find a truly loyal maid who has two boorish sisters, is the daughter of a mother without a mother, a father, a grandfather and sons, with a face just like yours!"

(10) The seventh fairy, moved to pity for that poor child who had no fault for the sixth fairy's foot injury and had to pay penance for someone else, said: "May you find everything you need to always get out of trouble!" After that, they walked away very slowly, setting one foot after the other so that you could not hear the slightest swish of feet, as if walking on a field of dry wheat without moving a blade. Yet the fairy's hot blood continued to flow there on the ground.

(11) The unfortunate mother heard the predicament and kept it inside her heart. Growing taller than weed, the child turned pretty, wise, graceful, and well-liked, according to the fairies' infatuations. But whenever the queen saw her, she shed some tears thinking about the horrible rainstorm that was going to ruin that beautiful sun-blessed face and about the ugly carbon that was going to damage the best part of that love vessel on the wretched day that would dump an ugly night on that heavenly beauty.

(12) Poor Pomponia, noticing her mother pale whenever she saw her, pressed her to tell the reason, without success, as the mother did not want to sadden the poor child so soon with the dark secret, since it is a fact that most of the time one worries more about the fear of an impending disaster than about the disaster itself when it strikes. (13) But with time healing things, when—due perhaps to melancholy—the hour approached for the queen to pay Death

[12] Pomponia scura, che sempe che bedeva la mamma la vedeva mutare de colore, la jea scauzanno pe cacciarene lo costrutto: ma non poteva, perché la mamma non avea core d'annegrecare co sto scuro penziero la negra figlia tanto tiempo mprimma: pocca è berissemo ca lo cchiú de le bote è de cchiú consederazione l'apprensione de lo male c'ha da venire, che non è lo male quann'è benuto. [13] Ma perché lo tiempo fa gran cose, venuta fuerze pe la malanconia chell'ora che la Regina dovea pagare lo cienzo a la morte, pe la casa de lo cuorpo che tanto tiempo s'avea goduto, co pagarene a mala pena le terze de quacche poco de frève o de na doglia de capo, se chiammaje la fegliola, decennole: [14] «Pomponiella mia, figlia mia benedetta, ecco ca io songo vecina a serrare l'uocchie pe la porvera che sparpagliano pe l'ajero le rote de lo carro de la morte. Abbesogna che da oje 'nnante le rapre tune, pocca songo forzata de te dicere chello che tanta vote t'aggio negato. [15] Haje da sapere la qualemente cosa: quanno io te fice dare la fatazione, che tu stive dinto la cònnola 'n fasciolla, na Fata, pe certe scorze de nocelle che t'hanno a nocere tanto, figlia mia, se rompíje no pede a sango, e ped arraggia, te jastemmaje che la primma notte che tu toccasse lo lietto de maríteto, arreventasse serpa, arrasso sia!, e accossí avisse da stare tre anne, tre mise, tre juorne, tre ore e tre momiente: e se, passato sto tiempo, non trovasse na vajassa fedele che tutta t'arresemegliasse, c'avesse doje sore cotecune, e fosse figlia de na mamma che n'avesse né mamma, né patre, né bavo, né figlie mascole, tu nce avisse da stare pe tutte tiempe. [16] Io mo non te l'aggio voluto dicere mprimma azzò lo schianto che io te deva non fosse stato no serpe che, mozzecannote lo core, non avesse acciso a te pe la paura, a me pe lo dolore: ma pocca dico *bonanotte*, non pozzo non darete la nova de sto male juorno, lo quale non te porrà non cogliere se tu no' lassaraje de pegliare marito». [17] E accossí decenno scappaje a chiagnere, e co la lava de lo chianto l'arma poverella sciuliaje fora de lo cuorpo, quanno la scura Pomponiella dinto chella lava non trovava auto che chiuove de dolore che le perciavano lo core.

[18] Ad ogne muodo, comme che li dolure de li pariente muorte songo comme a le tozzate de gúveto, che doleno assaje ma durano poco, subbeto che fece lo remmedio che li modierne hanno accacciato a la morte, azzoè atterrare la mammarella soja, Pomponiella accommenzaje a pensare a lo fatto sujo, ca chillo de la mamma era scomputo: ca se bè portava lo lutto co na coda de ciento parme, non era tant'asena, pe la fatazione avuta, che se fosse sbavottuta pe le parole che le decette la mamma. Ma perché sapeva lo cunto sujo, votava l'argatella de lo pensiero na bona matassa che le servesse pe filo da 'scire da lo labrodinto ne lo quale s'asciava.

the mortgage for the body's home she had enjoyed so long, barely paying interest with some slight fever or headache, she called her daughter and said, (14) "My sweet blessed little Pomponia, I am about to shut my eyes because of the dust strewn in the air by the wheels of Death's carriage. Henceforth, you must keep your eyes wide open, because I must share with you what I denied you for so long. (15) You must know a little secret. When I had you blessed in your cradle and swaddling clothes, a fairy, my dear—because of some nut-shells that will hurt you very badly—injured her foot and flung a curse at you filled with rage: that on the first night you touch your husband's bed, you will turn into a snake—may that time be far off!—for three years, three months, three days, three hours, and three minutes, and that you'll stay like that forever unless you find a loyal maid who looks just like you, has two boorish sisters, is the daughter of a mother without a mother, father, grandfather, and sons. (16) I did not want to tell you earlier, so that the shock I caused you would not turn into a serpent that, biting your heart, would kill you from fear and kill me from suffering. But as I must soon say good night, I cannot spare you from telling you about this curse, which will be unavoidable unless you renounce marriage." (17) She then burst into tears, and with the flow of hot tears, her poor soul slid out of her body, as the miserable Pomponiella found in that river only painful nails that pierced her heart.

(18) In any event, as mourning the death of relatives is like a kick in the elbow that hurts a lot but lasts only for a short while, following her sweet mother's burial as a remedy for death invented by modern society, Pompo-niella began to think about her own fate, since her mother's had ended. Al-though she mourned her mother for quite some time, she wasn't so stupid as to be scared by her mother's story of the fairy's spell. Knowing her fate, she wrapped skin around the spinning wheel of her thinking to escape the laby-rinth in which she found herself.

(19) It so happened that few months later, the king, Pomponiella's fa-ther, received the visit of ambassadors of the king of Redland, a young ul-tra-wealthy man, the most valorous and graceful you could find in those times. They reported that having heard famously about Pomponiella's great accom-plishments and beauty, their lord asked her to be his wife and mistress. They also reported that he wanted to marry her very soon, because without Pom-poniella, he couldn't care less about the pomp and prosperity of his kingdom.

(20) The king of Greenland realized how much he valued this relation-ship, that he wouldn't have found any better even when searching with a little

[19] Soccedette mo, 'n capo de poche mise, che vennero a lo Rre patre de Pomponiella cierte Ammasciature de lo Rre de Terrarossa, ch'era no gioveniello ricco comm'a lo maro, e lo cchiú baloruso ed aggraziato che s'asciasse a chille tiempe, decennole ca lo segnore lloro, avenno sentute sprobeccare da la fama lo gran sapere e la gran bellezza de Pomponiella, la voleva pe mogliere e pe patrona. E decettero de cchiú ca nce la cercava co tanta premmura, che senza sta Pomponiella isso no' stemmava no líppolo tutte le pompe e recchezze de lo Regno sujo.

[20] Lo Rre de Terraverde, vedenno ca sto parentato le 'mportava assaje, e che se l'avesse cercato co lo sprocchetiello no' l'avarria potuto asciare meglio, e che a la figlia le cadeva lo vruoccolo dinto lo lardo, lo maccarone dinto lo ccaso: ca co fare sto matremmonio faceva lo buono juorno, la 'nzertava a milo sciuoccolo, le veneva colata e le resceva a pilo, nce dava a lo pizzo e la 'nnevenava; tanto cchiú che lo Regno de Terraverde e chillo de Terrarossa erano confenante e stavano da lo naso a la vocca, se chiammaje la fegliola e le decette: [21] «Io saccio, fegliola mia, ca tu farraje sempre tutto chello che bòle lo tataruozzolo tujo, e ca io scrivo e tu te firme, ca accossí fanno le bone fegliole: e perzò, essenno tu cresciuta comm'a bruoccolo specato, e pare no confalone, già è tiempo de pigliare marito, azzò primma de la morte mia me pozza vedere li belle nepotielle. Otra po' che lo marito che lo Cielo t'ha mannato è cosí bello, ricco e baloruso, che ogn'autra Regina non se farria a pregare. Su, che nne dice, fegliola mia, che singhe benedetta? Non vuoi fare comme te dico io?»

[22] «Gnore mio — responnette Pomponiella —, vuje sapite ca io non me songo maje partuta da le commannamiente vuoste, ed aggio sempre puosto la lengua addove vuje avite puoste li piede: ma perché lo matremmonio è na cosa che ha da dorare pe tutta la vita, abesogna pensarece buono. [23] E se bè saccio ca se lo partito non fosse buono vuje non me l'averrissevo puesto 'nnante, puro vorria na grazia che spero non me la negarrite: azzoè che non avenno io cchiú de dudece anne, sso segnore che me vole se contentasse d'aspettare n'aute tre anne, e le potite dare parola ca io non pegliarraggio auto ca isso».

[24] Lo patre, se bè le pareva che st'addemmanna fosse a lo spreposeto, puro pe non desgostare la figlia, ca le voleva bene, mannaje pe l'Ammasciature sta resposta a lo Rre de Terrarossa. Lo quale, perché era fegliulo isso porzí, e perché veramente se n'era 'ncrapicciato, avuta sta 'mprommessa se contentaje.

[25] Ntrattanto Pomponiella, pe remmediare a lo male che necessariamente dovea soccedere, co no core 'ntréppete, pocca pietto forte vence mala sciorte, chiammatose no cammariero le disse che cammenasse pe tutto lo Re-

twig, and how lucky his daughter was with everything working out beautifully, just like broccoli dropping into lard and macaroni into cheese. This marriage would make for a good day as a match that suited him perfectly, even more so since the kingdoms of Greenland and Redland bordered each other neck to neck. He called his daughter and said to her, (21) "My dear child, I know that you will always do anything your darling daddy asks you to do, with me writing down and you signing, as good daughters do. Therefore, after growing up like a perfect beauty, tall like a banner, the time has come for you to get married, so that I can enjoy beautiful grandchildren before my death without even considering that Heaven sent you such a handsome, wealthy, and valiant husband that no other queen would refuse. So what do you think, my dear child, aren't you blessed? Don't you want to do as I say?"

(22) "My Lord," Pomponiella replied, "you know that I never opposed your orders, and that I always kissed the ground touched by your feet, but since marriage must last a lifetime, one must consider it carefully. (23) Although I know that you would never propose a bad deal, I would nonetheless like to ask for a favor I hope you won't deny me. Since I am only twelve years old, the man who asks to marry me should agree to wait for three years, with my pledge that I will marry no one else."

(24) The father, although considering the request inappropriate, sent this reply through his ambassadors to the king of Redland, in order not to disappoint the daughter he loved dearly. The king, himself a young boy and persisting in the marriage, was satisfied with the answer.

(25) Meanwhile Pomponiella, to remedy the impending disaster with a fearless heart, since courage defeats bad luck, called for a servant, asking him to crisscross the kingdom and to find a mother who had no mother, father, grandfather, and no sons but three daughters, with one of the girls resembling her.

(26) Even though the task seemed hopeless, as not to contradict his mistress (aware of the custom among courtiers to oblige a lord's requests by saying that they are easy to carry out, even if it was some stupidity that couldn't be done) the servant complied, saying he would do everything by speeding through the kingdom, as in fact he did. (27) As the seventh fairy confirmed that she would find anything to help her get out of trouble, the servant arrived at a hamlet in Villanova, where against any expectation, he found an old woman who had three daughters and no sons and fulfilled all requirements. The daughters were named Livia, Zeza, and Petruccia, and after asking the old

gno sujo e bedesse de asciare quacche mamma che non avesse né mamma, né patre, né bavo, ma tre figlie femmene, senza mascole, e che una de le figlie femmene arresemigliasse ad essa.

[26] Lo cammariero, se bè sta 'mmasciata le parze no spreposeto, pe no' lebrecare a la patrona (sapenno ll'uso de li cortesciane, che tutto chello che dice lo patrone soleno dire ch'è buono e ch'è facele a fare, quanno sarrà quarche asenetate ed averrà de lo 'mpossibele) decette c'avarria fatto tutto, e ca sarria juto volanno, comme 'nfatto jeze. [27] E pecché la Fata settema aveva ditto che potesse asciare tutto chello che cercava ped ascire da tutte guaje, arrevato lo cammariero a lo casale de Villanova, addove manco se lo credeva asciatte na vecchiarella c'aveva tre figliole femmene, senza mascole, co tutte le connizziune ch'abbesognavano. Le quale fegliole se chiammavano Livia, Zeza e Petruccia, ed avenno ditto a la vecchiarella ca le volea vedere, vedutole, trovaje che Petruccia arresemegliava tutta a Pomponiella. Pe la quale cosa lo cammariero a la 'ncorrenno tornaje da la patrona, e le disse quanto l'era 'ntravenuto.

[28] Ora la Prencepessa, volenno vedere se le doje primme sore erano cotecune (ch'era una de le connezziune ch'abbesognavano) se mannaje a chiammare Livia, ch'era la cchiú granne. Ma perché ste scure figliole erano accossí pezziente e stracciate che le carne lloro, comm'a povere carcerate, affacciatose da le fenestre de le gonnelle cercavano lemmosena de compassione da l'uocchie che pe llà passavano, Livia pocosinno se ne jeze da la Prencepessa accossí comme se trovava.

[29] Pomponiella, fattele mille carizze, le disse: «Tè, figlia mia, tèccote sta decina de lino: pettenamélla bona, e fammela trovare filata pe dimane», e accossí decenno la 'nzerraje dinto na cammara.

[30] Livia pegliato lo lino, e co no musso che parea porciello, senza manco fare na lleverenzia a la segnora se 'nzerraje: e facenno cierte file che parevano fonecielle de varca, attenneva a sbregarese, credenno che li pasticce avessero a benire pe l'ajero e li pastune le sarriano portate a cuofane. [31] Ma scomputa la facenna venne Pomponiella, e fattole quatto carizze peluse le decette: «Tè, non te voglio fa' perdere le fatiche toje, piglia ccà sta noce e batte' connio». Dapo' votatase a lo cammariero sujo, decette: «Va l'accompagna, e siente chello che dice».

[32] La scura Livia, vedennose accossí trattata, per l'arraggia deventaje tutta gialla, e mettenno la lengua 'n mota accommenzaje a ghiastemmare la Prencepessa, comme femmena senza descrezzione, e comme ca lo sazio non

woman to see them, he found Petruccia to resemble Pomponiella perfectly. So the servant ran back to his mistress, telling her what he found.

(28) The princess wanted to find out if the first two sisters were boorish (one of the requirements), so she sent for Livia the elder. But the poor girls being such tramps, with rags and bodies like those of women prisoners looking through the windows and asking passing eyes for pitiful alms, dimwit Livia went to the princess without changing.

(29) Pomponiella caressed her over and over again and said, "Good girl, take these linen rolls, comb them well, and bring them back tomorrow." She then locked her inside a room.

(30) Livia took the linen with a piglike face and locked herself in the room without any reverence to the lady. She made threads that resembled ropes for a ship and worked hurriedly, waiting for goodies to arrive through the air in copious quantities. (31) After she finished, Pomponiella arrived and said, after some fake caress, "I don't want to waste your time; take this nut and beat it." She then turned to the servant, "Go follow her and listen to what she says."

(32) Seeing the way she was treated, poor Livia turned yellow from rage and began to move her tongue, cursing the princess as an insensitive woman, sated and unable to see anyone starving, with a heavy crown that impacted her eyes so that she couldn't see straight. And she uttered many other nursery rhymes that even a poet couldn't have come up with.

(33) On his return, the servant reported the story word-for-word to the mistress, who sent for Zeza the following day. Thinking she would have better luck, she went on her way but behaved worse than her sister, with even less discretion. She was given ten and a half linen rolls to comb and thread that same day. (34) Enraged, Zeza said she had been wronged by being asked to take on heavier tasks in less time than her older sister. But the princess caressed her and took her to a room where Zeza locked herself in without a word of thanks. (35) After the work was done, God knows how, you couldn't tell if it was threads or grass, Pomponiella praised her lavishly, sending her away with the servant like the other one and gave her a chestnut. Unhappy with the way she was treated, sullen Zeza began to grumble from the palace stairs with so many insults that the poor servant could not report half of them.

(36) The next day, the princess sent for Petruccia. As her clothes looked more tattered than her sister's, she borrowed some apron from her mother, as it seemed like bad manners to show up in rags. With a headscarf, she went to the palace, and there she paid her due respect to the lady, so that everyone was

crede lo dejuno, e ca lo piso de la corona fa calare tal'ommore all'uocchie che non vedeno lo deritto, e tant'aute felastòccole che non le avarria ditto manco no poeta.

[33] Tornato lo cammariero, referette tutto lo neozio, parola pe parola, a la segnora, la quale lo juorno appriesso mannaje a chiammare Zeza: chesta, credennose de ce avere meglio fortuna, s'abbiaje, ma portatose cchiú bellanamente de la sore, pocca nn'avea quatto jédeta a lo sottile, ebbe 'mparte soja na decina e mezza de lino, co commannamiento che pe chillo juorno stisso la pettanasse e felasse. [34] Zeza, 'ngottata, decette ca l'era fatto tuorto, pocca essenno cchiú peccerella de la sore, veneva cchiú carrecata de fatica e l'era dato manco tiempo: ma la Prencepessa facennole carizze l'accompagnaje dinto la cammara, ed essa senza dicere *a gran merzé* se 'nzerraje. [35] Scomputo lo staglio Dio sa comme, che non se sapea s'era filo o travo, Pomponiella, fattole cierte compremiente sarvateche, ne la mannaje, comm'a l'autra, co lo cammariero, co averele data na castagna. Zeza negrecata, vedennose trattata de sta manera accommenzaje a tatanejare da le grade de lo palazzo, e tanta ne disse che lo scuro cammariero no' nne potette referire la mmetate.

[36] L'autro juorno la Prencepessa se mannatte a chiammare Petruccia, ed essa che cchiú brenzolosa de le sore se retrovava, parennole mala creanza ire da la segnora accossí spetacciata, se fece 'mprestare da la mamma no cierto mantesino c'aveva. E céntase co chillo, co na magnosa 'n capo, se la abbejaje sommiero a lo palazzo: addove arrevata fece tante belle creanze a la segnora, che tutte se maravegliajeno comme na foretanella sapesse tanto. [37] E Pomponiella pe provarela le deze doje decine de lino, decennole: «Bella fegliola mia, ped oje sto lino ha da essere pettenato, filato, e po' lassa fare a mene».

[38] Petruccia, vasata la mano a la segnora, se pegliaje lo llino e decette: «A gran merzé!» E 'nchiusase dint'a na cammara, fatecanno comm'a cane, tanto fece, tanto s'ajutaje, che pe la sera fece trovare lo lino filato accossí sottile ch'era na bellezza a bederelo. [39] E la Prencepessa, veduto lo filato, le decette: «Me pare troppo grossariello, ma non perrò non voglio che ne rieste scontenta: tèccote sta nocella».

[40] «Compiatisceme — respose Petruccia —, bella segnora mia. Non t'aggio servuto comme mierete pocca n'aggio saputo cchiú, e te rengrazio de lo favore che m'haje fatto, pocca tengo cchiú cara sta nocella ca se m'avisse dato no tresoro. Vasta che sia venuta da le mmano voste: e pe sta bella grazia toja te vorria servire a barda e sella, senz'auto salario che de potereme chiammare vajassa toja».

surprised how a country woman had such refinement. (37) To test her, Pomponiella gave her twenty linen rolls with these words: "My beautiful child, this linen has to be brushed and threaded by the end of the day, I will then take care of the rest."

(38) Petruccia kissed the lady's hand, took the linen, thanked her profusely, and locked herself inside the room. Toiling like a dog, she made such efforts that the linen was threaded so thin by the end of the day that it was beautiful to look at. (39) When she saw the linen, the princess said, "It looks a bit too rough, but I don't want you to feel bad—here, take this nut."

(40) "Forgive me, my beautiful lady," Petruccia said. "I haven't served you as you deserved, since I couldn't do any better. I thank you for doing me a favor, because I cherish this nut more than if you had given me a treasure. Because it was given to me by your own hand as a graceful gesture, I want to serve you in every which way, without any compensation save for being able to be called your loyal maid."

(41) The princess saw Petruccia's good nature and asked if she wanted to stay with her, and the girl accepted gratefully. Pomponiella continued by saying, "Listen, Petruccia dear, I will tell your mother that you died from too much labor and send her some minor change to keep her quiet. As to you (and for me to find out if you would truly do for me anything you say you'd do) you will have to stay locked in your room as long as I please. What do you think, are you up to it?"

(42) Petruccia answered, "Not only will I be content for the love of yours when people say I died, but if necessary while serving you, I'll be more than happy to die a real death not once but a hundred thousand times. I will not only stay locked inside a room for as long as you wish, but inside a grave forever if you so demand, because where you love, you die."

(43) "May Heaven reward you, my dear child," the princess said. "Cheer up, you won't have any regrets." After hearing the lie about Petruccia, the miserable old woman swallowed the nonsense, burying the little money in a hole—without it, she might have died.

(44) Shrewd Pomponiella locked Petruccia inside a room, getting her dressed in her own clothes. Observing themselves in a large mirror inside, the two women looked so similar that you could not tell one from the other, so that the princess began to show her great affection, even more so as Petruccia's manners were those of a queen. (45) No one in the palace knew about the princess's plan, and no one entered Petruccia's room except Pomponiella,

[41] La Prencepessa, vedenno lo buon'essere de Petruccia, le decette se bolea stare cod essa, e la fegliola azzettaje de bona voglia lo partito. Llebrecaje Pomponiella: «Siente, Petruccella mia, io mannarraggio a dicere a màmmata ca tu pe la troppo fatica, sì morta, e le voglio mannare na mano de tornesielle perché se stenga zitto. Tu poje (perché io voglio vedere se veramente farrisse pe mene tutto chello che dice) haje da stare 'nchiusa dinto a na cammara pe tutto lo tiempo che piacerrà a mene. Che dice, lo buoje fare?»

[42] E Petruccia: «Io non sulo — decette — me contento che pe l'ammore tujo se dica ca so' morta, ma s'abbesogna, pe te servire, so' contentissima de morire da vero, non una ma cientomilia vote. E non sulo me starraggio 'nchiusa dint'a na cammara pe nfì' che piace a tene, ma dinto na sebetura, pe sempre, s'accossí commanne, pocca dove se vò bene llà se more».

[43] «Che lo Cielo te pozza 'mprofecare, bella figlia mia! — decette la Prencepessa —. Statte allegramente, ca non te ne pentarraje». Ed accossí, mannato a dicere a la mamma de Petruccia la 'mmenzione, chella scuressa se gliottette la paparocchia, e co chille tornise, ch'erano na mano de docate, appilaje quarche pertuso, senza li quale sarria stata 'mpizzo 'mpizzo d'esserele appilate le pertosa co la vammace.

[44] Ora mo Pomponiella, che sapeva lo conteciello sujo, 'nserraje dinto na cammara Petruccia e la vestette de li vestite suoje. E tenennose mente tutte doje a no schiecco granne che nc'era llà dinto, erano tanto simmele che non se potea descernere l'una dall'auta: pe la quale cosa la Prencepessa le pigliaje n'affrezzione granne, tanto cchiú ca li costumme de Petruccia erano propio de Regina. [45] Ma chesta 'mmenzione che fece la Prencepessa nesciuno de lo palazzo la sapeva, ed a chella cammara non ce traseva anema nata, sulo che Pomponiella, la quale covernava la cammarata soja a latte d'auciello e la facea dormire 'nsieme cod essa: de manera che pe la semmeletuddene e pe l'ammore parevano n'anema 'n duje cuorpe. E chello che cchiú 'mporta, erano tutte doje de n'ajtate, e crescevano comm'a doje puche d'oro.

[46] Duraje sta doce commertazione tre anne. Quanno, venuto lo tiempo che lo Rre de Terrarossa se ne veneva pe fare lo matremmonio co Pomponiella, essa, avennone avuto nova, na sera abbraccianno ed accarezzanno cchiú de lo soleto Petruccia, le decette: [47] «Sore mia (ca pe tale t'aggio sempe tenuta!), da lo bene che te voglio e che t'aggio voluto tu puoje canoscere ca io non t'aggio tenuto 'nchiusa ccà dinto pe despietto, ma pe necessetate. La quale è de sta manera: sacce ca songo tre anne che io songo stata 'mprommesa pe mogliere a lo Rre de Terrarossa, giovane bello, valoruso e ricco, lo quale già è 'n viaggio

who fed her companion with the finest delicacies and had her sleep with her, so that they seemed one soul in two bodies for their resemblance and their mutual affection. And what's more important, both had the same age and grew like two angels.

(46) This sweet intimacy lasted three years. When the time approached for the king of Redland to arrive for the marriage, Pomponiella, who had heard the news, hugged and kissed Petruccia more than usual and said to her, (47) "My dear sister (that is what I always considered you to be!), my love for you now and forever should make you understand that I locked you inside not out of spite but out of necessity. You must know that three years ago, I was to become the wife of the king of Redland, a handsome, valiant, and wealthy young man, who is now on his way here to marry me. But this marriage won't happen because of a fairy's curse, that when touching my husband's bed I will turn into a serpent, and I will stay inside that dark skin for three years, three months, three days, three hours, and three minutes. (48) Since you resemble me so much, and for the husband to have his way and for you to be rightfully rewarded for the love you showed me, I want you to be the queen. On the night of the wedding, we will leave the door to the garden open, you will stay under the bed, so that after I turn into a serpent, you will take my place in the bed. (49) I only ask you for the love of mine to visit me once in a while in the garden, and to help me climb out of the ugly skin after the three years, three months, three days, three hours, and three minutes have passed. I will count the days and call for help; you will grab my skin so that I can return to the way I am now."

(50) When Petruccia heard her companion's dreadful story, she felt like dying right there, since she never wanted to be separated from her. But because you cannot undo a spell and the wedding had to happen, Petruccia cheered up and promised to do what Pomponiella had asked of her. On his arrival at Greenland, the groom was welcomed with immense joy by all the barons and princes of that land and by the king himself, who wanted the wedding to take place at once, after seeing the groom's great qualities and the patience he had shown waiting for such a long time.

(51) On the wedding night, Petruccia hid under the bed, as had been agreed. After all the members of the court had left, Pomponiella and the king of Redland went into the bedroom, and the groom told his wife to enter the bed. She replied, "No, my dear husband, you go first, while I am saying my prayers."

pe venirese a 'nguadiare co mico. Ma sto matremmonio non potarrà rescire, pocca pe jastemma de na Fata, súbeto che toccarraggio lo lietto de marítemo deventarraggio na serpa, e dinto a chillo nigro scuorzo aggio da stare tre anne, tre mise, tre juorne, tre ore e tre momiente.

[48] Ora perché tu arresemmiglie tutta a mene, azzò lo zito aggia lo 'ntiento sujo e tu lo buono miereto de l'ammore che m'haje portato, io me contento che tu singhe Regina. E perzò la notte de lo matremmonio lassarrimmo aperta la porta che ba a lo ciardino, e tu te starraje sotta a lo lietto, azzò quanno io sarraggio deventata serpa, tu pe scagno mio puozze trasire dinto lo lietto. [49] Sulo t'arrecommanno che pe l'ammore che t'aggio portato da quanno 'n quanno me vienghe a besetare dinto a lo ciardino, e quanno sarranno passate li tre anne, tre mise, tre juorne, tre ora e tre momiente, me vienghe a cacciare fora da lo nigro scuorzo c'avarraggio 'ncuollo: pocca io, tenenno bene a mente li juorne che passarranno, chiammarraggio ajuto, e tu quanno affierre a la pella, ca io me n'escarraggio fora accossí comme songo mone».

[50] Quanno Petruccia sentette sto malo annunzio de la cammarata soja appe a morire de schianto, pocca n'avarria maje voluto scrastarese da essa: ma perché la fatazione non se potea sfuire, e lo matremmonio abbesognava che soccedesse, fattose armo, Petruccia 'mprommese de fare quanto Pomponiella l'avea ditto. Ed essenno già venuto a Terraverde lo zito noviello, fu recevuto co n'allegrezza granne da tutte li Barune e Princepe de chillo pajese, e da lo Rre medesimo: lo quale vedenno le granne qualetà de lo zito, e la bontate che aveva avuto d'aspettare tanto tiempo, voze che súbeto se facesse lo matremmonio.

[51] Venuta la notte che se aveano da accocchiare 'nsémmora li zite, Petruccia se mettette sotta lo lietto, comm'era l'appontamiento. E Pomponiella e lo Rre de Terrarossa, trasenno dinto la cammara e lecenziata tutta la corte, decette lo zito a la mogliere che se corcasse. Ed essa: «No, marito mio, corcateve 'nnanze vuje, quanto ca io me dico cierte 'graziune».

[52] Se corcaje lo zito, e Pomponiella, stutata la cannela, se levaje tutte li panne e le 'nzerraje dinto na cascia: dapo' accostatase a lo lietto de lo marito, 'n toccare la travacca deventaje no serpe, e se l'abbiaje pe la vota de lo ciardino.

[53] Petruccia, avenno 'ntiso lo sfrúscio, ascíje da sotta lo lietto, e lo zito, che 'ntese isso porzí lo remmore, decette: «Pomponiella, che sfruscio è stato chisto?»

E Petruccia: «E che bò essere? — responnette —. Quant'è buono a dicere le 'graziune! Pocca ntramente che io deceva cierte devuziune meje m'è

(52) The husband lied down in the bed, and after extinguishing the candle, Pomponiella took off all her clothes, placing them in a dresser. When approaching the husband's bed and touching the canopy, she turned into a serpent and started out toward the garden.

(53) When she heard the swish, Petruccia came out from under the bed, and the husband, who heard it too, asked, "Pomponiella, what noise was that?" Petruccia replied: "What could it be? What blessing it is to say grace! As I recited certain prayers, my mother's soul appeared to me—may God keep her in glory and health—saying: 'My dear child, what are you doing? Don't you see that you are going to die when you think you are going to bring to life more people? You must know that you were cursed by a fairy and will die at once if, after the wedding, you do not stay away from your husband for three years, three months, three days, three hours, and three minutes— may this never happen!' She then disappeared and made the swishing noise you heard. Therefore, my dear husband, if you want me alive, since you waited for such a long time, you should wait three more years and months, so that afterwards we can live happily and in peace forever."

(54) The poor groom swallowed this story like a pill, and because he genuinely loved the woman, he agreed to wait three more years. Thus, Petruccia went to sleep in another bed, staying separate for the entire period agreed upon, one of them keeping the promise made to Pomponiella, the other nurturing hope, since the good and bad come to a happy end. Meanwhile, they treated each other like husband and wife.

(55) Remembering her mistress, Petruccia went every day to the garden, where she dug a hole for the serpent to rest, adorning it and covering it with a pretty little mattress. She treated her to sugar pastries, holding her in her lap all day long, giving her the finest delicacies. (56) To protect the serpent from any accident, she ordered that no one of any rank be allowed to enter the garden under the threat of the death penalty. To please his presumed wife, the king, who was a learned man, had a marble block placed at the garden entrance, with an engraved Medusa head, a beautiful face with snake hair threatening the transformation of humans into stones, as if to say that whoever violated the order by entering would be better off being petrified than facing endless punishments. And just maybe his heart told him to make a snake ornament or hieroglyph.

(57) Thus, Petruccia continued to look after the serpent, holding it in her lap to keep it cool in the summer, dressing it with warm clothes during the

appàrzeto l'arma de màmmama, Dio l'aggia 'n grolia e 'n sanetate vosta, decennome: "Ah, figlia mia, e che faje? Non vide ca tu vaje a la morte quanno te cride de morteprecare gente che bengano a la vita? Sacce ca tu haje avuto na jastemma da na Fata, che se, dapo' fatto lo 'nguadiamiento, pe tre anne, tre mise, tre juorne, tre ore e tre momiente no' staje lontana da maríteto, morarraje de súbeto, arrasso sia!", e accossí decenno è sparuta, ed ha fatto chillo sfrúscio c'hai 'ntiso. Perzò, marito mio, se mme vuoje viva, pocca haje aspettato tanto, aspetta st'aute tre anne e tre mise, azzò dapo' campammo cchiú contiente e consolate».

[54] Lo povero zito se gliottette comm'a pínolo sta 'mmenzione, e perché le portava veramente affrezzione se contentaje aspettare st'aute tre anne. E accossí Petruccia se jeze a corcare a n'auto lietto, e secotaje sto separamiento pe tutto lo tiempo stabeluto, una pascennose co lo mantenimiento de la data fede a Pomponiella, l'auto co la speranza, pocca male e bene a fina vene. E nfratanto se trattavano comm'a marito e mogliera.

[55] Petruccia, mo, arrecordannose de la patrona, ogne juorno se ne jeva a lo ciardino, addove avea fatto no pertuso quanto nce capeva la serpe, e l'aveva aparato tutto de contrataglie a l'antica, co no bello matarazziello, e se la covernava co le pastetelle de zuccaro, tenennosella tutto lo juorno 'n sino, senza farele mancare latte d'aucielle. [56] E perché la serpe stesse cchiú secura da quarche desgrazia, fece fare ordene che sotto pena de la vita nesciuno, de qualesevoglia connizione, fosse trasuto a chillo ciardino. E lo Rre, ch'era letterúmmeco, pe dare gusto a la creduta mogliere voze che se mettesse a la porta de lo stisso ciardino na preta marmora addove era 'ntagliata la capo de Medusa, azzoè na bella facce co li capille de sierpe, ca dice ca chella faceva arreventare l'uommene de preta: quase volesse dicere che chi rompesse lo mannato e nce trasesse, meglio ped isso se reventasse de preta, tanta castiche le volea dare. E fuorze fuorze lo core le parlaje a fare no cerefuoglio o ceroglifeco de sierpe.

[57] Accossí Petruccia secotaje a covernare la serpe, tenennosella la 'state 'n sino, a la frescura, e lo vierno facennole panne caude: e la serpa se l'arravogliava 'ntuorno, leccannola ed accarezzannola pe rengraziamiento de l'ammorosanza che le portava.

[58] Ma lo diàschence che fece? Non ce volevano cchiú d'otto juorne a fornire lo tiempo destenato che Pomponiella aveva da lassare la spoglia (vedite comme songo le cose de lo munno!), ch'essenno venuto no Prencepe a besetare lo Rre de Terrarossa, stanno tutta la corte 'ntrecata a fare li solete

winter. The serpent twisted around, licking and caressing her to thank her for her loving care.

(58) But what was the devil up to? Barely eight days before Pomponiella was to shed her snakeskin (see how things turn out in this world!) a prince came to visit the king of Redland, and while the entire court paid the usual respects, the pages and foreign staff who kept an eye on the garden saw the serpent, which had come out to enjoy the sun. (59) To show off their prowess they climbed the garden wall and went after the snake, which began to flee, but not quickly enough to avoid a wound on her side from the blow of a sword, which would have killed her from pain had she not been blessed by a fairy.

(60) When Petruccia heard the news of that dreadful attack, she lost consciousness for a while, as if the house had fallen on top of her. When she came to, she acted not like a woman but like a wild cat, accusing them of having ruined her house, because that serpent was the fairy that had provided all her wealth. To calm her down, the king tried to find the perpetrator, but as always, no one knew about anything. The culprit was rumored to be a little page; he received a good beating. (61) Without wasting any time, Petruccia called for a healer to cure the serpent with natural remedies, and thanks to the king of serpents and the fairies' blessing, it recovered after four days.

(62) When the three years, three months, three days, three hours, and three minutes ended, the king told Petruccia that he was pleased the stars' bad influence had been waning, and that if she agreed, it was time to sign the marriage contract in front of ready witnesses. (63) Petruccia replied that she was agreeable, but that she only asked for the entire court to be sent away from the palace for three hours and three minutes, and some additional hours, and for him not to come back before two in the morning, since she had to wash from top to bottom and to perform some other ceremonies that were conducted in those days. The king did as his wife said. To satisfy her again, he left with the entire court. (64) Petruccia then went down to the garden and heard these words come out of the serpent's hole:

> *Good faith, good faith!*
> *May I keep my good faith!*
> *Now that you are the queen,*
> *What are you going to do with me?*

(65) On hearing these words, without saying a word, Petruccia quietly approached the hole, and as the serpent came out as always, she grabbed its tail

compremiente, stanno li pagge e li settepanella frostiere a teneremente a lo ciardino, abbistajeno la serpe, ch'era 'sciuta a lo sole. [59] Isse, credennose de fare prova, scravaccajeno lo muro de lo ciardino e dezero 'ncuollo a la serpe, la quale, se bè se mettette a foire, non fu accossí lesta che no' restasse feruta a no scianco co na botta de spata, de muodo e de manera che se non fosse stata affatata sarria morta de spasemo.

[60] Quanno Petruccia sentíje sto negozio e sto brutto schiuoppo, comme se le fosse caduta 'ncuollo la casa, stette no buono piezzo ascevoluta: e quanno potte dare a la voce, non fice cosa de femmena ma de gatta scatenata, decenno c'avevano arroinata la casa soja, pocca chella serpa era la Fata da la quale veneva tutto lo bene sujo. Lo Rre pe cojetare fece cercare chi era stato lo malefattore, e decenno ognuno, comm'è lo soleto, ca non ne sapeva niente, lo remmore jeze a fenire a no paggiotto che nce guadagnaje na bona spogliatura. [61] Petruccia, senza perdere tiempo, fece chiammare no 'nciarmatore, e fatta mmedecare la serpe co cierte remmedeje sarvateche, pe grazia de lo Rre de li sierpe, e pe la fatazione che la serpe aveva, 'n quatto juorne se sanaje.

[62] Venuto po' lo termene de li tre anne, tre mise, tre juorne, tre ore e tre momiente, lo Rre a l'utemo juorno decette a Petruccia che se rallegrava ch'era passato lo 'nfruscio de le stelle, e che, se se contentava, era tiempo chella sera de fermare lo stromiento, pocca li testemmonie erano leste. [63] Responnette Petruccia che non ce aveva niente 'n contrario: sulo lo pregava che pe tre ore e tre momiente, e quarch'autra ora de cchiú, lecenziasse da lo palazzo tutta la corte, ed isso porzí non tornasse a la casa se non fossero le doje ore de notte, pocca s'aveva lavare tutta e fare cert'autre zeremonie che se aosavano a chille tiempe. Lo Rre fece quanto decette la mogliere, pe darele st'auta 'sfazzione, e co tutta la corte se reteraje. [64] Tanno Petruccia scese a lo ciardino, e da lo pertuso addove stava la serpe sentíje ste parole:

> *Bona fede, bona fede!*
> *Bona fede me puozze tenere!*
> *Mo che sì Regina*
> *Che ne vuoje fare de mene?*

[65] Petruccia, sentuta sta cosa, zitta e mutta s'accostaje a lo pertuso, ed essenno asciuta fora la serpe, comm'era soleto, l'afferraje pe la coda e tiraje forte la spoglia: la quale restatele 'mmano comme a fodero de spada, ne 'scíje da dinto Pomponiella, assai cchiú bella che non era primma. E Petruccia, che s'avea portato cod essa li vestite de la patrona, subeto la vestette, e poje s'ab-

and pulled the skin, which stayed in her hand like a sword's sheath and from which Pomponiella emerged, prettier than ever. Petruccia had brought along the clothes of her mistress, got her dressed quickly, then they hugged and kissed each other in such a way that they looked like an elm tree and its vine. (66) But who could repeat the words they exchanged? Pomponiella thanked Petruccia for all the good she had done, taking such good care of her, healing her deadly wound, and freeing her from her serpentine prison. Petruccia asked her for forgiveness if she had not treated her as she deserved, that the accident was not her fault, and that what she had done was her debt and obligation[ii] to her.

(67) With no time to waste with words, as the night was falling, the two of them went up to the king's room, where Pomponiella said to her companion, "This is the time, my dear Petruccia, for you to give back to me what I have done for you. You've got to keep me locked up where I kept you, treating me the same way I treated you, until that time when Heaven will let me out with my honor intact."

(68) "I will do anything you wish," Petruccia said. "But tonight, while the king is away, you must honor my bed. Lie down right away, you need a rest, while I am preparing a meal for you. And tonight, I will sleep with you." Pomponiella did as Petruccia asked, and after eating, she fell asleep.

(69) When it was two in the morning, which had felt like an eternity, the king came back with the court and found Pomponiella asleep, thinking she was the other woman. When he joined her in bed, she woke up. The king hugged her and said, "Finally, the three years, three months, three hours, and three minutes are over—they felt like three centuries! The nasty stars' influence that almost killed me is gone. You are mine now, may Heaven keep you for me!"

(70) Half dazed from sleep Pomponiella, thought she spoke with Petruccia and answered, "Thank you for your faithfulness. Without it, I would still be inside that miserable serpent skin. In fact, I would be dead had you not healed me from that wound."

(71) "What skin, what wound?" the king asked. "I do not remember any of those things." "I know," Pomponiella replied, "you are talking like this because out of your goodness you do not want to be thanked for all the favors you did for me. But be assured that they are inscribed in my heart with golden letters, and I thank my good fortune, which left a sign when I came back as a woman so that nothing could blind me and make me forget your virtuous deeds, my beautiful Petruccia." "What Petruccia?" the king asked. "Tell me, sweetheart, are you awake or asleep? Are you dreaming, or are you teasing me?"

bracciajeno tanto e de tale manera che parevano l'urmo e la vite. [66] Ma chi pò dicere le parole che se decettero l'una co l'auta? Pomponiella rengraziava Petruccia de li tante beneficie che l'avea fatte, cod averela covernata accossí bona, averele sanata la feruta mortale ed averela leberata da chella carcere serpentina. Petruccia se scusava se no' l'aveva trattata comme se mmeretava, e che la desgrazia non era socceduta pe corpa soja, e ca chello che aveva fatto era stato debbeto ed obrecazione.

[67] Ma non essenno tiempo da perdere 'mparole, pocca già se faceva notte, tutte doje se ne sagliettero 'ncoppa a la cammara de lo Rre zito, addove Pomponiella decette a la compagna: «Orsú, Petruccia mia, ora maje è tiempo che tu me rienne chello che t'aggio fatto io: tu me haje a tenere 'nchiusa dinto a chella cammara dove io aggio tenuto a tene, e trattareme de la stessa manera che fice co tico, pe nfí' che a lo Cielo piacerrà che n'esca co lo 'nore mio».

[68] «Farraggio tutto chello che bolite — decette Petruccia —. Ma pe sta sera, pocca lo Rre è juto fora, haje da fare 'nore a lo lietto mio. E cóccate, non ce perdere tiempo, ca n'haje de besuogno, ca io mo mo t'apparecchio na colazione. E da poi stanotte dormerraggio co tico». Fece Pomponiella quanto decette Petruccia, e dapo' d'avere fatto colazione s'addormette.

[69] Nfrattanto, sonate le doje ore de notte, che a lo Rre parzero duje anne, tornaje co la corte a la casa, e trovata addormuta Pomponiella, che se credeva chell'autra, 'n corcarese isso porzí, chesta se scetaje. E lo Re, abbracciatola, le decette: «Ecco scompute già sti tre anne, tre mise, tre juorne, tre ore, tre momiente, che me so' pàrzete tre secole! Ecco passato lo nigro 'nfruscio che poco nce voleva e me ne frosciava! Già sì la mia, lo Cielo me te guarde!»

[70] Pomponiella, mezza storduta da lo suonno, credennose che fosse Petruccia responnette: «Gran merzé a la bona fede toja, ca se no' ancora starria dinto a chillo nigro scuorzo. Anze, sarria morta cessa, se tu non me sanave da chella feruta».

[71] «Che scuorzo, e che feruta? — decette lo Rre —. Non m'allecordo ste cose».

«Saccio — llebrecaje Pomponiella — ca dice accossí pocca pe la bontate toja non vorrisse manco essere rengraziata de li piacire che m'haje fatto. Ma tiene pe cierto ch'a lettere d'oro me l'aggio scritte a sto core, e rengrazio la sciorte mia che, porzí tornata femmena, ha boluto che me ne resta lo 'nzegnale, azzò non sia cecata da qualesevoglia cosa a scordareme de li beneficie tuoje, bella Petruccia mia».

(72) Realizing she spoke with someone else, Pomponiella said: "Move away, don't touch me! Who are you?" "I am the king; I am your sweet husband! Don't you recognize me, my dear Pomponiella? And what are you saying, what are you telling me? I have been waiting for three years to marry you, and three more years, months, days, hours, and minutes after the marriage in order to pluck these fruits, and now it looks as if I have become a thief caught by his master!"

(73) "What other three years?" Pomponiella asked, as she understood what was happening. The husband said: "Didn't you tell me that you had to stay away from me three years, months, days, hours, and minutes because of who knows what stars' influence? And I waited because of my love for you— another might not have done this—while displeasing my people, who did not see the young queen flourish and season the cheerful wine they would have tasted seeing the heir of my kingdom, while now you pretend to be naïve and dazed?"

(74) With her heart soft like a lung, Pomponiella hugged her husband, crying from joy and said, "You are right, my love! But you must know that I am not the woman you saw this morning, that was not Pomponiella but Petruccia, as I turned into a serpent on the first wedding night, I believe you heard the swish when I left. Knowing I had to live in that miserable skin for three years, months, days, hours, and minutes, in order not to make you unhappy, I had Petruccia replace me as your wife, with her face and manners so similar to mine, worthy of a queen, with the understanding that she would get me out of that false skin when the time was up, since I would have stayed a serpent forever if idling just for a few minutes. Only she could help me with that spell. (75) But this woman, may God bless her, has not only been faithful to me, taking care of me and keeping me alive, she also wanted to save me for you, my dear, when she could have been the queen and let me be a serpent forever, when she could have ascended the throne and have me crawl on earth. She could have eaten sweets and me dirt, she could have married the best of men, and myself stay a big ugly snake. (76) Therefore, dear husband, let's not think of anything else tonight but to give her a great reward for her unwavering loyalty, and even though no prize will be big enough, let the world at least know that we have not been ungrateful." Pomponiella almost fainted saying these sweet words, as did the other from contentedness, and so they fell asleep.

(77) The following morning, at the crack of dawn, Petruccia appeared with fresh eggs to please the newlyweds. Pomponiella threw her arms around

«Che Petruccia? — decette lo Rre —. Dimme, core mio, duorme o sì scetata? Te 'nsuonne o me daje la quatra?»

[72] Pomponiella, accortase ca parlava co n'auto, le decette:· «Arrassate, non me toccare! Chi sì tu?»

«Songo lo Rre, songo lo maritiello tujo! — decetto isso —. No' mme canusce, Pomponiella mia? E che termene so' chisse, che parole songo cheste che me dice? Aggio aspettato primma de 'nguadiarete tre anne, e dapo' sposata aute e tre anne, tre mise, tre juorne, tre ore e tre momiente pe cogliere sti frutte, e mo pare che sia deventato mariuolo e nce sia stato cuoto da lo patrone!»

[73] «Comme, tre autr'anne?», dicette Pomponiella che trasette 'n malizia.

E lo zito: «No' me deciste tu — llebrecaje — ca non saccio pe che 'nfruscio de stelle abbesognava che stasse lontana da me tre anne, tre mise, tre juorne, tre ore e tre momiente? Ed io pe lo bene che t'aggio voluto, che fuorze n'auto no' l'averria fatto, aggio aspettato, co desgusto de li puopole mieje, che non vedeano sciorire sta pempenella, che co li rammoscielle suoje connisce lo vino de l'allegrezza ch'isse avarriano provato vedenno l'arede de lo Regno mio, e mo me faje la 'nsemprece e la storduta?»

[74] Tanno Pomponiella, c'aveva lo core tiennero comm'a premmone, abbracciato lo marito e chiagnenno pe l'allegrezza, le decette: «Hai ragione, marito mio! Ma sacce ca io non songo chella de stammatina, ca chella non era Pomponiella, ma Petruccia: pocca io la primma notte che me sposaje deventaje serpe, e creo ca ne sentiste lo sfrúscio quanno me partíje. E perché sapeva ca doveva stare io dinto a chillo nigro scuorzo tre anne, tre mise, tre juorne, tre ore e tre momiente, pe non te fare restare sconsolato faciette che Petruccia, tutta simmele a mene, e de faccia e de costume, degna d'essere Regina, fosse scagno mio mogliere toja: co chisto patto, che benuto lo tiempo me cacciasse da chella pella posticcia, pocca se passavano chille sule momiente no momento de cchiúne io sarria stata serpe pe sempre. Né auta che essa me potea fare sto servizio, comm'era la fatazione. [75] Ma essa, la benedetta da Dio, non sulo m'è stata fedele, co covernareme e conservareme la vita, ma de cchiú ha voluto conservareme a te, marito mio, quanno essa se poteva fare Regina e a me lassareme serpe 'n sempeterno: essa auzarese sopra lo truono e a me fareme ire ventre pe terra, essa magnare cose de zuccaro ed io terreno, essa maretarese co lo schiecco de l'uommene ed io co no cervone. [76] Perzò, marito mio, non penzammo ad auto sta notte che a rennerele lo buono miereto de tanta bona fede: e se bè non c'è premmio vastante, a lo mmacaro canosca lo munno ca non simmo state sgrate». Ed accossí decenno Pomponiella quase ascevolette

her neck, kissing her over and over, thanking her for her great loyalty and her good deeds. Petruccia bathed Pomponiella's face with joyful tears, saying she had done only little, that it was all her duty, that this was what faithful servants had to do for their mistresses.

(78) "What servant!" the groom said. "You should be a queen against your destiny. I have a younger brother who is the king of Shadowland, who today happens to visit the king of Naples—he should become your husband. What better wife than you could one find, even when crisscrossing the entire world? There is no more precious jewel than loyalty and honor. You are the one who, unlike all other women, have set an example that will travel among people as long as the world lasts.

(79) That's what the groom said, and he kept the king's promise, sending for his brother in Naples, getting him married to Petruccia, and arranging jousts and tournaments that were out of this world. He then commissioned a sensational musical composition based on this story, thus spreading it throughout the globe.

(80) The king of Shadowland was pleased with his great fortune and returned to Naples with his wife, taking along the marble plate from the garden entrance as a happy memory. (81) Back in Naples, he told the full story to the king of Naples. With his permission, he had Medusa's head placed on the wall of a public square. On the top of it, he had a sculpture added that resembled Petruccia dressed in the fashion of those times with the following epitaph:

> *To Petruccia,*
> *Women's glory,*
> *Whose loyalty as a maid*
> *Turned her into a queen*
> *This memorial is made by three crowned kings*
> *Of Greenland, Redland, and Shadowland*
> *In the Year...*

(82) And in truth, until today you can find Medusa's head at the *Fontana de li Sierpe* (Serpent Fountain). Petruccia's bust was taken to a square at the beginning of an alley near the Market Gate, and the people call it the *Capo de Napole* (Head of Naples). There is no record of the epitaph except in some ancient books without year of publication. This beautiful story shows the world that *Loyal servants will be rewarded.*

pe la tennerezza, e l'auto simelmente pe la contentezza, e 'n chesta manera s'addormettero. [77] La matina, appena fatto juorno, vèccote Petruccia co l'ova fresche a confortare le zite: quanno Pomponiella, jettate le vraccia 'n cuollo a Petruccia, non se ne saziaje de vasarela, rengraziannola de tanta fede che le aveva asservato e de tanta beneficie che l'aveva fatto. E Petruccia lavanno a Pomponiella la facce co le lagreme che l'ascevano pe l'allegrezza, deceva che quanto avea fatto era poco, e che tutto era obbrecazione, accossí dovenno fare co le patrune le bajasse fedele.

[78] «Che bajassa! — disse allora lo zito —. Haje ad essere Regina a despietto de la fortuna, pocca aggio io n'auto fratiello cchiú giovane de mene, ch'è lo Rre de Terra-d'Ombra, che oje se trova 'nsémmora co lo Rre de Napole: chillo ha da essere lo marito tujo. Che mogliere meglio de tene non è possibele asciare se cammenasse tutto lo munno: pocca se non se trova gioja cchiú preziosa de la fede e de lo 'nore, tu sì chella ch'a le garge de tutte l'aute femmene n'haje fatto e dato n'assempio che ghiarrà pe le bucche de l'uommene pe nfi' che dura lo munno».

[79] Accossí decette lo zito, e le mantenne la parola da Rre: pocca mannato a chiammare da Napole lo fratiello, le fece 'nguadiare Petruccia, e fece fare giostre e torneje che fujeno cose fora de li fore. E po' fece fare na bellissima opera 'n museca addove se rappresentaje tutta sta storia, e de sta manera se sprobbecaje pe lo reverzo munno.

[80] Alliegro, lo Rre de Terra-d'Ombra, d'avere fatto sto buono 'mmàtteto, se ne tornaje a Napole co la zita, e se portaje la preta marmora che steva 'ncoppa la porta de lo ciardino pe mammoria. [81] Venuto a Napole, contaje tutto lo fatto a lo Rre de li Napoletane, e co lecienzia soja fece mettere e fravecare a no muro de la chiazza prubbeca la capo de Medusa, 'ncoppa a la quale nce fece fare no miezo fusto che arressemmegliava a Petruccia, vestuta a l'uso de chille tiempe, co no spetaffio de la manera che secoteja:

A PETRUCCIA
GROLIA DE LE FEMMENE
CHE PE LA FEDELETATE SOJA
DA VAJASSA DEVENTAJE REGINA
PONETTERO STA MAMMORIA
TRE RRI DE CORONA
TERRAVERDE, TERRAROSSA, TERRA-D'OMBRA
L'ANNO ...

(83) We all greatly loved Popa's beautiful tale, especially Petruccio, since the faithful woman bore his name, and he was known to be a loyal friend, which in fact he was. I can vouch for him, having seen in person how he would kill himself for a friend, and how his loyalty had no equal. Fortunate are those who had him as a friend! The love between Pilate and Orest, Damon and Pizia, Patroclus and Achilles, Eurilus and Nisus, Mark and Fiorella[iii] was none compared to his.

(84) Since Popa was praised no less than Ciulletella, Tolla began to get ready to arrange her thoughts, and among the many tales she remembered, she chose the following, convinced that it was the best she ever heard from the first day she had ears to today.[iv]

Endnotes

i Jacopo Sannazaro (1456-1530), a poet known for his Latin and Italian works, among them *Arcadia*, a pastoral romance. He is celebrated in Sarnelli's Neapolitan *Guida de' forestieri* as the poet from Mergellina. Part three of the *Guida* includes a Latin poem and an image of Sannazaro's sepulchre (332 ff.).

ii Note Sarnelli's Neapolitanizations of abstract Italian terms and learned words such as *obrecazione* (obbligazione), *connizione* (cognizione), *commodetate* (comodità), *osanza* (usanza).

iii The list of loyal friends is taken from Giulio Cesare Cortese's *Li travagliuse ammure de Ciullo e de Perna* (Malato 1986, 94).

iv Several Baroque metaphors and similes enrich the style of the fairytale: *la Regina dovea pagare lo cienzo a la morte, pe la casa de lo cuorpo che tanto tiempo s'avea goduto* (the queen [had] to pay Death the mortgage for the body's home she had enjoyed so long); [la Regina] *scappaie a chiagnere, e co la lava de lo chianto l'arma poverella sciuliaje fora de lo cuorpo* ([the queen] burst into tears, and with the flow of hot tears, her poor soul slid out of her body); *comme che li dolure de li pariente muorte songo comme a le tozzate de gúveto, che doleno assaie ma durano poco* (as mourning the death of relatives is like a kick in the elbow that hurts a lot but lasts only for a short while); *no gioveniello ricco comm'a lo mare* (a young ultra-wealthy man), etc.

[82] E chesto è tanto vero che nfi' a lo juorno d'oje, addove steva e stace puro la capo de Medusa, se chiamma la *Fontana de li Sierpe*. Lo miezo fusto de Petruccia fu trasportato a la chiazza che fa capo a no vico vicino a la porta ch'esce a lo Mercato, e la gente la chiammano la *Capo de Napole*; de lo spetaffio non ce nn'è mammoria, se no' a cierte livre viecchie, e nce manca l'anno. Ed accossí, co sto bello cunto, se vene a fare chiara mosta a lo munno che

> *Chi serve fedele aspetta premmio.*

[83] Àppemo tutte no gusto 'ndecibele de lo bello cunto ditto da Popa, ma cchiú d'ogn'auto Petruccio n'appe no sfizio granne, pocca la femmena fedele aveva nomme comm'ad isso: tanto cchiú ca isso faceva professione d'essere buon ammico, comm'era 'n fatto. Ed io lo pozzo dicere, che l'aveva spremmentato ca pe n'ammico se sarria fatto fare tonnina, e 'n cunto de fedeletate non aveva paro a lo munno. Felice chi lo poteva avere ped ammico! Pocca l'ammore che fu tra Pilade ed Oreste, tra Dammone e Pizia, tra Patruoco ed Achille, tra Eurialo e Niso, e tra Marco e Sciorella era na scentella, posta a la preta paragone de lo sujo.

[84] Ma perché Popa non fu manco laudata de Ciulletella, accommenzaje Tolla a mettere lo cellevriello a signo, e ntra li mute cunte che le jevano pe la mente sceuze chillo che secoteja, credennolo pe lo meglio c'avesse 'ntiso da lo primmo juorno che le servíjeno l'aurecchie pe nfi' a lo juorno d'oje.

LA 'NGANNATRICE 'NGANNATA

CUNTO TIERZO

[1] Non c'è peo morte, a lo jodizio mio, che chella de lo marvizzo, pocca isso se caca lo bisco co lo quale è 'ncappato. Chell'aquela de Jasuopo de nesciun'auta cosa, morenno frezzejata, se dolette tanto, quanto che la frezza avea volato co le penne soje. E la ragione è che tutte le desgrazie songo degne de compassejone, fore de chelle che l'ommo da se stisso se procaccia: pocca ogn'uno le dice: — Nce lo bòle. Accossí soccesse a n'arraggiata vecchia, che morette 'nfamma ped avere procurato de fare morire de famme na scura 'nnozente, comme sentarrite co lo cunto mio.

[2] Dice ch'era na vota a lo Regno de Monterotunno no gentelommo chiammato Minec'Aniello: lo quale, essennole morta la mogliere, era restato co tre figlie femmene, che se chiammavano Lella, Cilla e Cicia. [3] Ed essenno vecino lo tiempo che le spiche ammature dell'anne de lo scuro Minec'Aniello porzíne fossero metute da la fauce de la morte, ped essere poste dinto la fossa, chiammaje no compare sujo, decennole: «Marcone mio! (ca accossí se chiammava lo compare), a l'abbesuogne se canosceno l'ammice, e comme lo buono vino è sempre buono pe nfi' a la feccia, cosí lo buono ammico dura porzí dapo' la morte. Ecco ca io fore me nne chiammo da le tempeste de la vita, e se bè sto pe pigliare puorto, non esce contenta st'arma da la varchetta de sto cuorpo se tu, compare mio, non me daje parola d'essere cchiú ca patre a ste fegliole meje. [4] Nc'èje, pe grazia de lo Cielo, agresta pe conciare sse fragaglie, e le lasso co quarche commodetate; sulo voglio da te, ch'essenno loro accossí belle (lo Cielo le guarde) me le 'nchiude a lo palazzo c'aggio fore a la massaria, e llà lassale fatecare, perché sanno arragamare e fare pezzille de Sciannena ch'è no stopore: ca se bè non hanno abbesuogno de campare a la jornata, la fatica sempre è bona, perché l'ozio e lo stare co lo ventre a lo sole songo causa de mute guaje. E buje, fegliole meje benedette, abbedite a lo compare, ca chisto sarrà lo patre vuostro».

[5] A ste parole non se pottero tenere che non se mettessero a chiagnere:

CUNTO TIERZO

A DECEIVER DECEIVED

(1) There is no worse death in my opinion than death from thrush, as you try to get rid of the birdlime from which you caught it. In Aesop's tale,[i] the eagle who died of an arrow shot complained mostly about the arrow having flown with its own feathers. That's because all misfortunes deserve compassion except those that people procure themselves, the reason why everyone is saying that you asked for it. This is what happened to an angry old woman who died infamously after trying to starve a poor innocent girl to death, as my tale will show you.

(2) There was once upon a time, in the kingdom of Monterotondo, a gentleman called Minec'Aniello who, after his wife's death, was left with three daughters: Lella, Cilla, and Cicia.

(3) As the time approached when poor Minec'Aniello's ripe annual harvest was about to be reaped by the sickle of Death and placed into a ditch, he called one of his buddies and told him, "My dear Marcone! you get to know your friends when you are in need. Just as good wine is always great down to the lees, a good friend lasts beyond one's death. Life's tempests are already behind me, and as I am about to dock in the harbor, my soul cannot happily leave the small vessel of my body unless you promise, my dear friend, to be more than a father to my daughters. (4) Thank heavens there is some dough to take care of them, and I am leaving them some goods. Because they are so beautiful—may Heaven watch over them—all I am asking of you is to lock them inside the mansion I own at the farm and to let them work there, as they are great at embroidering and making amazing Flanders laces. They do not need to earn money, but work is always a blessing, as leisure and idleness cause much trouble. And you, my blessed daughters, do obey my friend; he will be your father." (5) Hearing these words, they all could not hold back their tears, the father for his tender feelings, the daughters for their sorrow, the friend for his compassion. Vines do not weep as much at the pruner's cuts as the girls did for Death cutting their father's life, unraveling their lives.

lo patre pe tenerezza, le fegliole pe dolore, e lo compare pe compassione. Né chiagneno tanto le bite pe lo taglio de lo potaturo, quanto chiagnevano chiste pe lo taglio che la morte dava a la vita de lo patre, facennone sautare le magliolle de chelle scure fegliole.

[6] Accossí, muorto lo patre, bon'arma, lo compare asservaje pontualemente quanto Minec'Aniello aveva ditto, e 'nchiuse le fegliole a lo palazzo le deva da fatecare e le covernava comme se commeneva a lo grado loro. [7] Ntramente lo Rre de Monteretunno, ch'era no bello omore e no cellevriello coriuso, essenno juto a caccia nce fo cuoto da lo miezo juorno, e non potenno zoffrire li ragge de lo sole, che parevano frezze, se reteraje a l'ombra de na prèvola che steva sopra la porta de lo cortiglio de chillo palazzo; ed era isso sulo, lontano da l'aute cacciature. E sentenno vervesejare dinto lo cortiglio, pe na senga de lo portone vedde le tre fegliole che stevano a ragamare a lo frisco, e co l'arecche pésole voze sentire chello che tataneavano.

[8] Le fegliole, che oramaje fetevano de 'nchiuso e de peruto, una a l'auta decevano: «Io (era Lella, la granne, che parlava) pe no' stare cchiú dinto sta carcere vorria essere mogliere de lo cammariero de lo Rre, ca jarria bello a spasso, sarria servuta, e bedarria tutte le giostre e li torneje che se fanno 'nnante Palazzo».

[9] «Ed io — decea Cilla — vorria essere mogliera de lo segretario, ca sarria cchiú stemmata, avarria cchiú spasse, e no' starria cchiú 'nchiusa ccà dinto, ch'adesa nce songo pegliata de grànceto».

[10] Cicia, ch'era la cchiú peccerella, ma la cchiú bella e cchiú provéceta de l'aute, decette: «E comme site ciucciarelle, perdonateme! Lo patre nuesto n'è stato tanto vile che se fosse vivo averriamo 'mmidia a sti cortescianielle: ca puro simmo state a la casa nosta da Regine! Se io m'avesse a trovare no marito me vorria pegliare lo Rre, che tanto è squetato: pocca se s'have a morire de caduta, è meglio cadere da auto che da vascio».

[11] Accossí ste fegliole facevano lo cunto senza lo tavernaro. Quanno lo Rre, avenno 'ntiso sto trascurzo, e piaciutole la grazia de Cicia, notaje lo palazzo e se ne jeze pe li fattecielle suoje.

[12] Lo juorno appriesso, quanno l'arba pe la fatica che fa de schianare la via a lo carro de lo sole, tutta rossa, suda de manera che ne vagna li sciure e l'erve tennerelle, isso se mannaje a chiammare le tre fegliole. Lo scuro compare, non sapenno che l'era socciesso, l'addemannaje se canoscevano nesciuno a Palazzo: responnettero ca non sapevano niente, ma che se mettevano 'mmano de lo Cielo, che sempre ajuta la 'nnocenzia.

(6) After the good soul of a father died, his friend did exactly what Minec'Aniello had asked for, locking the girls inside the mansion, putting them to work, and looking after them suitably. (7) Meanwhile, the king of Monterotondo, a handsome man with an inquisitive mind, while hunting at midday under scorching sunrays that felt like arrows, took refuge in the shadow of a pergola above the entrance to the courtyard of that mansion all by himself, far from the other hunters. He heard whispers in the courtyard and saw through the door's crack the three girls embroidering outdoors. He pointed his ears to hear what they chatted about.

(8) Sick by now and tired of being locked up and watched, the girls said to each other, "I (Lella, the oldest) would like to be the wife of the king's chamberlain, to get out of this prison, so I could go happily for a walk, be served, and see all the jousts and tournaments in front of the palace."

(9) And Cilla said, "I would like to be his secretary's wife, so I would be honored, have more fun, and be no longer locked in here. I am fed up."

(10) Cicia, the youngest, prettiest, and most forward of all said, "How stupid you are, I'm sorry! Our dad wasn't so evil; were he still alive, we would be the envy of all the little courtesans. After all, we lived like queens in our house! Had I to find a husband, I would choose the king, who is a bachelor. If you must die from a fall, it's better to plunge from high above than from lower altitudes."

(11) So the girls did their math without the tavernkeeper. Hearing this talk, and appreciating Cicia's gracefulness, the king took note of the mansion and went about his business.

(12) Next day, when the dawn got tired from paving the road for the sun's deeply red sweaty carriage bathing the flowers and delicate grass, the king sent for the three girls. Unaware of what was going on, their *compare* asked if they knew anyone at the palace. They replied they didn't but that they would let Heaven protect them—it always sided with the innocent.

(13) They set out towards the palace. When they arrived with their *compare* they curtsied graciously in the king's presence. The king said, "What did you say in your courtyard yesterday at noon while you were embroidering?"

(14) Lella, the oldest and most gullible, answered, "I said I wanted to be your chamberlain's spouse." "Good choice," the king said, calling the chamberlain and handing her over to him, to their *compare*'s satisfaction, even though he could have done nothing about it, since lords' requests and considerations are orders. (15) He then asked Cilla, the second girl, and she answered that

[13] S'abbejajeno addo' nn'era la via de Palazzo, ed arrevate co lo compare a la presenzia de lo Rre le fecero na belledissema lleverenzia. E lo Rre le decette: «Che cosa decívevo aiere a miezo juorno dinto a lo cortiglio vuosto, quanno stívevo arragamanno?»

[14] Lella, ch'era la cchiú granne e la cchiú nsemprecona, responnette: «Io deceva ca vorria essere mogliere de lo cammariero vuesto».

«Muto de bona voglia!», responnette lo Rre, e chiammato lo cammariero nce la conzegnaje, essennone contento lo compare: se puro non fu ca no' nne potette fare de manco, ca le pregarie e le creanze de li Segnure songo commannamiente.

[15] Addemannata la seconna, azzoè Cilla, disse ca voleva essere mogliere de lo secretario; e lo Rre 'mprubbeco e 'nnanz'a tutta la corte fece fare lo matremmonio. [16] La terza, azzoè Cicia, addemmannata, jeze sfojenno de dire lo vero, ma llebrecanno lo Rre ca l'aveva 'ntiso isso co l'arecchie soje, responnette ca essenno lízeto ad ognuno de fare li castielle 'nn ajero, perché non se pagava lo cienzo de lo suolo a nesciuno, pocca ognuna se facea lo marito a gusto sujo, essa se nn'avea fatto uno buono, co dire ca voleva lo Rre pe marito. [17] «Accossí sia! — disse lo Rre —. Chi se fa la sciorta isso, e non se la fa bona, guaje ped isso: arma toja, maneca toja!» E accossí decenno, tanno pe tanno se la 'nguadiaje, co no gusto granne de tutta la corte. Sulo a la matrèja de lo Rre, che se chiammava Pascaddozia, l'annozzaje 'ncanna sto muorzo, e no' nne poteva scennere lo zuccaro tanto ne restaje 'ngottata: se bè ca a lo fegliastro non ne fece a canoscere niente, covanno 'n cuorpo lo venino, comme fanno li sierpe. Non perrò la scura Cicia, che cchiú o manco s'era addonata a la ponta de lo naso de sto triunfo, jea traccheggianno a lo mmeglio che poteva.

[18] Né passaje troppo che stanno Cicia pe figliare, essenno grossa prena, lo Rre, che patea de frate malenconece, era juto ped àjero a na massaria soja ch'era lontana. E scompute li nove mise, Cicia, comme se fosse vecchia a l'arte, a la primma sciosciata d'agliariello scarrecaje duje fegliule, no mascolo e na femmena, accossí belle ch'erano duje puche d'oro: e nfra l'auto aveano na catenella ped uno de carne appesa 'n canna, de colore d'argiento accossí sbrannente, c'avarriano 'ncatenate li core de chi avesse visto chille belle nennille, se la perra Pascaddozia, cchiú crodele de Medea, pe mennecarese de l'azzione de lo fegliastro e pe l'odio che portava a Cicia non ce l'avesse levato, súbeto fegliata, e pe scagno de li nennille non avesse puosto dinto la cònnola duje cacciottielle.

[19] Quanno la povera mamma vedde che li figlie suoje co le catene

she wanted to be the secretary's wife, so the king arranged a public wedding in front of the entire court. (16) When asked, Cicia tried to dodge telling the truth. After the king repeated what he had heard with his very ears, she replied that it was everyone's right to build castles in the air, that no tax was due for the land, that everyone was free to choose their own husband, that she had picked a good one by saying that she wanted to marry the king. (17) "Perfect!" said the king. "Whoever chooses their own fate without choosing well will end up in trouble, *arma toja, maneca toja!*[ii] Saying this, he then married her with the entire court's immense joy, except for the king's stepmother, Pascaddozia, who got this bite stuck in her throat and was so annoyed that she could not swallow the sweet event. She was breeding the poison in her body like a serpent without letting her stepson know. Aware of her triumph, Cicia kept it in check as best as she could.

(18) Soon thereafter, when Cicia was big pregnant and about to give birth, the king, who suffered from flatulence, went for a walk to one of his distant farmhouses. After nine months and the first blow into the flask,[iii] as if used to this art, Cicia delivered two gorgeous babies, a male and a female, true jewels. They wore a small fleshy silvery chain around their neck that was shining so strongly that they would have enchanted the hearts of those who saw the beautiful babies, if only merciless Pascaddozia, crueler than Medea, had not taken them at birth and replaced them with two pups in the cradle, as a revenge for her stepson's actions and out of her hatred for Cicia.

(19) When the poor mother saw how her newborn babies with their silver necklaces had turned into dogs to be kept on an iron leash because of the maliciousness of darned Pascaddozia, who had always hated her, she felt like dying on the spot, as there was no time to verify this predicament after that bitch of Pascaddozia alerted everyone at the palace that Cicia had given birth to two pups. (20) Meanwhile, Pascaddozia called a trustworthy courtier, ordering him to kill the two babies in the countryside and bring back, as proof, a flask of blood. She also sent a letter to the king at once, in which she reported her fake story of the birth. (21) The king, who was waiting to hear the good news of the birth of a successor to the kingdom, when reading that two little dogs had been born, went back to the city, enraged as if they had bitten his heart, and without seeing or hearing his innocent wife, had her locked up in a dark chamber with seven bolts and only a small hole through which she was given a slice of bread and a glass of water each day, so that she would die quickly and he could get remarried.

d'argiento erano deventate cane da mettere a la catena de fierro, pe malizia de la mmardetta Pascaddozia, che sempre se l'avea trovata contraria, appe a morire de schianto, tanto cchiú che non fo a tiempo de chiarirese de lo 'mbruoglio; pocca la cana de Pascaddozia, chiammate tutte le gente de lo palazzo, sprobbecaje ca Cicia aveva figliato ed avea fatto duje cacciottielle. [20] Ntrattanto, chiammatose no cortesciano confedente, le commannaje che pegliate li duje nennille le ghiesse ad accidere 'n campagna e l'atterrasse, e che pe signo de lo servizio fatto ne le portasse na carrafella de sango; dall'auta banna mannaje subeto na lettera a lo Rre, addove le contava lo pàrtoro a gusto sujo. [21] Lo Rre, ch'aspettava de sentire che le fosse nato n'arede de lo Regno, lejenno che l'erano nate duje cacciottielle, comme se chille l'avessero mozzecato lo core, arraggiato tornaje a la cetate, e senza né bedere né sentire la 'nnozente mogliere la fece 'nchiudere dinto a na cammara scura, co sette cattenacce, lassannoce sulo no pertosillo pe do' nne le facea calare na fella de pane e no becchiero de acqua lo juorno. Azzò moresse cessa ed isso se tornasse a 'nzorare.

[22] Ma lo cortesciano c'aveva portato li nennille ad accidere, muosseto a compassione de chille scure paciunielle, che te l'avarrisse víppeto dinto a no becchiero de venino, le lassaje vive accanto a no sciummo, anchienno la garrafella de lo sango de no pecoriello che s'accattaje da no pecoraro, e la portaje a la patrona. E lassannola contenta e gabbata, dapo' cierte mise se lecenziaje da chella casa, non potenno zoffrire de vedere chella facce d'Arpia.

[23] Ma lo Cielo, che non se scorda maje d'ajutare li 'nnoziente, anze tanno cchiú l'ajuta quanno songo abbannonate, fece che avenno fegliato na mogliere de no molenaro che stava vecino a chillo sciummo, ed essennole muorto lo fegliulo, non sapeva comme fare pe scarrecarese le zizze chiene de latto; e cammenanno pe la ripa sentíje le bocelle de chille nennille. [24] Essa subeto nce corze, e bedenno doje creature accossí belle, che parevano pintate, accossí decette nfra se stessa: «E quale core de cana ha comportato levarese de tuorno sta bella parte de le bísciole soje senza sentirese ascire le bísole? Ma che dico, core de cane: non ponn'essere, sti belle nennille, figlie de mamma c'aggia mala fèle, perché me pareno tutte zuccaro. Da la pétena io canosco ca non songo piatte de creta rosteca, ma de la cchiú fina Faenza che stia dinto a li repuoste reale. Abesogna che siano de quarche bona jenimma», ed accossí decenno se le pigliaje 'mbraccia e se l'allattaje co no gusto granne, jovanno a se stessa ed a li fegliule, e facenno no viaggio e duje servizie.

[25] Recreate le creaturelle, se le portaje a lo molino, e contanno lo socciesso a lo molenaro, isso che non aveva figlie voze che la mogliere le cre-

(22) The courtier who had taken the babies to kill them in the countryside was moved to compassion for the two unfortunate little creatures that you could have swallowed in a paper cup. So he left them unharmed near a river, filled the flask with the blood of a sheep he bought from a shepherd, and brought it to his mistress. He left her tricked and satisfied but quit his job several months later, as he couldn't bear any longer to look at the harpy's face.

(23) But Heaven, which never forgets to help the innocent and even more so the forsaken, arranged for a miller's wife near that river, who had given birth to a son who died, to find a way to get rid of her breast milk. While walking along the river, she heard the little voices of those babies. (24) She ran there at once and saw the two gorgeous creatures that looked like a painting, saying to herself, "What beastly heart could have abandoned these lovely fruits of the belly without their pupils jutting out? What am I saying, a beastly heart? These beautiful babies cannot be born from an evil mother, they look so sweet. From their appearance, I can tell that they are not made from rough clay but of faience found on the cupboards of royal households. They must come from a good family." Saying this, she took them in her arms and breastfed them with intense pleasure, pleasing herself and the babies, carrying out a double service in one trip.

(25) She then took the happy babies to the mill, telling the miller what had happened. Since they had no children, he wanted his wife to grow them like his own, naming the male Jannuzzo and the female, Ninella. (26) One year later, the miller's wife gave birth to a son named Renzullo. When he was getting older, she brought him up with the other two. (27) After they had grown older and were ready to know each other's story, the miller told them one day what had happened and that only Renzullo was his natural child, while they had found Jannuzzo and Ninella along the river. When the two young boys played together, one day, for an unknown reason, Jannuzzo slapped Renzullo, who reacted not with his hands but with his tongue, insulting him and calling him a mule.

(28) This was not just a word but a dagger into Jannuzzo's heart. He felt deeply hurt and left the game. He called his sister, went to the miller, and said, "We owe you so much, Daddy dear, that we could never express it in words. We will remember it as long as we live, and with Heaven's support, we hope never to be ungrateful to you and your wife. (29) But we no longer want to live with that bug in the head of being treated like mules. Let us crisscross the world until we get news about our parents. That is all; that is what we have decided.

scesse comm'a fegliule suoje, mettenno nomme a lo mascolo Jannuzzo ed a la femmena Ninella. [26] Da llà a n'anno tornaje a fegliare la molenara, e fece no fegliulo che chiammaje Renzullo, e fatto granneciello lo faceva crescere 'nsémmora coll'aute duje. [27] Ma essenno ora maje granne, che ognuno potea sapere lo fatteciello sujo, no juorno lo molinaro contaje tutto lo negozio comme jeva: e ca sulo Renzullo era vero figlio sujo, ma Jannuzzo e Ninella l'aveva asciato a la ripa de lo sciummo. Tanto che no juorno che stevano joquanno 'nsémmora tutte duje li giuvane, Jannuzzo pe non saccio che refferenzia deze na scoppola a Renzullo, e chisto non potenno co le mmano s'ajutaje co la lengua, e 'nciuriannolo, nfra l'aute cose lo chiammaje: «Mulo».

[28] Chesta non fu parola, ma stoccata catalana a lo core de Jannuzzo, lo quale sentennose toccato a lo bivo s'auzaje da lo juoco, e chiammatose la sora se ne jette a lo molenaro e le decette: «L'obbrecazione che nuje t'avimmo, tataruozzolo nuesto, è tanto granne che non te la saparriamo spalefecare, e pe nfi' ca lo spireto anemarrà sti cuorpe nce ne allecordarrimmo; e sperammo, [che] se lo Cielo nce darrà fortuna, de non essere sgrate né a buje, né a la mogliere vosta. [29] D'ogne manera nuje non volimmo stare co sto verme 'n capo d'avere ad essere tenute pe mule: contentate che ghiammo cammenanno pe sto munno pe nfi' a tanto c'avimmo nova de lo patre e de la mamma nosta. Accossí simmo arresolute, e non ce vò auto».

[30] Lo molenaro, che avea manco jodizio de la mula de lo molino, o puro che penzava cchiú a lo figlio sujo che a chille d'aute (co tutto che la mogliere decesse none, ca veramente volea bene a chille giuvene) le deze lecienzia, ed isse s'abbejajeno addove li piede le portavano, non sapenno veramente addove dare de pietto.

[31] Venuta la sera, arrevajeno a no puorto de maro, e ccà, trovato no pagliaro, s'arreposajeno. La matina, quanno l'arba accommenzaje a 'nnargentare lo maro, 'scettero fora, ed a la ripa trovajeno no viecchio c'avea na varva che le copreva tutto lo pietto, e steva stiso 'n terra tutto a la nnuda, ed era de statura cchiú dell'ordenario. [32] Jannuzzo e Ninella lo salutajeno, ed isso rennenno lo saluto le decette che ghievano facenno. Li duje giuvane le contajeno tutta la vita lloro comme l'avevano 'ntiso da lo molenaro, decenno de cchiú ca jevano cammenanno lo munno pe trovare chi era lo patre e la mamma lloro. [33] Tanno le decette lo viecchio: «Sacciate ca io songo no viecchio de marmora, che stongo a Napole a la fontana quanno se scenne da Palazzo primma che s'arriva a la marina, e proprio a lo pontone de la Tàrcena. Io era mprimma no marenaro, lo quale pe no despietto che fice a na Fata, a la vecchiezza deventaje de

(30) The miller, who knew less about mules than about mills or cared more about his own son than the others (unlike his wife, who really loved those kids), let them go, and the two began their journey, not really knowing where to head.

(31) They arrived at a seaport in the evening, where they found a straw mat and rested. In the morning, when the dawn began to silver the sea, they went outside and ran into an unusually tall old man lying naked on the shore, with a beard that covered his entire chest. (32) Jannuzzo and Ninella greeted him. He greeted them back and asked what they were up to. They told him their story as the miller had told them and that they were walking across the world in search of their parents. (33) So the old man said, "You should know that I am an old fellow made of marble. My place is in Naples at a fountain you'll find walking from the palace down to the marina, at the corner of the dock. I used to be a sailor, but I offended a fairy and turned into a marble statue in old age, left on the shore, covered by sand and shitted upon by all those passing by. (34) But one of your ancestors (whose name I cannot tell you at this time, as it is not up to me but up to a certain bird) freed me from that crappy site and built an attractive niche with fishes from the sea, below a canopy from which I can see all the passing ladies and gentlemen of Naples. I am very obliged to your family. (35) You should know that your mom is alive. She would be dead, God forbid, had not a bird brought her food and cared for her like her own daughter. Go to the town of Monterotondo, settle in a house in front of the royal palace, have faith in Heaven, and you will find everything that you are looking for in no time. (36) I know that you need money: go ahead and dig up the mattress you slept on last night; it belongs to some roguish sailors who hid copious amounts of silver coins in it. Scrape them up—Heaven sends them to you—then come see me.

(37) That's what they did. They found clothes and money, took a good amount, and went back to the old man, asking what they could do for him. He showed them his broken leg and begged them to write to Naples to get it fixed at the city's expense, since no one bothered. (38) Jannuzzo promised to do what the old man asked for, but having always lived at the mill and not being worldly, he asked the old man to explain him how men turn into statues.

(39) "I am sorry, you will have to try that out yourself," the old man replied, "but it will only last for a short time. You must realize that there are no rules in this, since things in the world happen at Heaven's discretion. No one

marmora e restaje a no pizzo de la chiaja tutto copierto d'arena, addove tutte li passaggiere me venevano a scarrecare lo ventre adduosso. [34] Ma perché uno de l'antecestune vuoste (che mo non ve lo pozzo dicere, ca non è tiempo ancora: né tocca a mene, ma a no cierto auciello) me levaje da chelle schefienzie e me fece no bellissemo nicchio, co tanta pisce de maro, mettennome comme sott'a no vardacchino da dove veo tutto lo passiggio de le sdamme e de li cavaliere de Napole, io songo muto obbrecato a la casa vosta. [35] E sacciate ca la mammarella vosta è biva, e sarria morta, arrasso sia, se l'auciello no' l'avesse portato da magnare e covernatela comme na figlia soja. Vuje perzò jatevenne a la cetà de Monterotunno e pegliateve llà na casa, faccefronte a lo Palazzo Riale: e lassate fare a lo Cielo, ca trovarrite tutto chello che ghiate cercanno nfra no poco de tiempo. [36] E perché saccio c'avite abbesuogno de frísole, jate e scavate dinto a lo pagliaro addove site state sta notte, ca chillo è de cierte marenare marranchine, li quale nce hanno atterrato na quantetate de fellusse: jate e scervecchiatennille, ca lo Cielo ve le destina, e po' venite a trovareme».

[37] Accossí facettero, e trovate vestite e denare se provedettero de bona manera. Tornato po' Jannuzzo co la sore a lo viecchio, le decettero che cosa potevano fare pe lo servire; ed isso, mostrannole na gamma tutta rotta, decette che screvessero a Napole e nce la facessero acconciare a spese lloro, pocca non nc'era nesciuno che se nne pegliasse fastidio. [38] 'Mprommettette Jannuzzo de fare quanto lo viecchio addemmannaje; ma perché era stato sempe a lo molino e non sapea le cose de lo munno, decette a lo viecchio, che no' le fosse 'n commannamiento, de dicerele no poco comm'era sta cosa che l'uommene deventavano statole.

[39] Responnette lo viecchio: «Me despiace ca tu stisso l'haje da provare: è bero perrò ca durarrà poco. Ora sacce ca chesta è na cosa che non se ce pò dare regola, pocca le cose de lo munno soccedono comme vole lo Cielo, e nesciuno se pò fare masto e dicere: *Pe chesta via non passo!* Se vaje a Napole mio, ch'è lo sciare de 'Talia, lo schiecco d'Auropa, la preta preziosa de l'aniello de lo munno, ne vedarraje tanta mammorie, de ste straformaziune, che restarraje ammisso e tutto de no piezzo.

[40] «Vedarraje mprimma Posileco, che oje è na montagna sempre allegra, sempre verde, che tene no pede 'n terra e l'auto a maro, e tene pe la mano na bella Serena, che l'antiche chiammavano Partenope: 'ncoppa d'isso non c'è auto che ciardine e palazze, e tutta la ripa è semmenata de case dove abetano lo spasso e la contentezza. [41] Chillo maro che le vasa lo pede è sempe chino de falluche de segnure, che co musece e suone se nne vanno la sera pe lo ffrisco,

can decide and say, 'I will not go through here!' If you go to my beloved Naples—which is Italy's flower, Europe's mirror, a precious jewel in the world's ring—you will see plenty of records about these transformations so that you will be completely amazed.

(40) "First, you will see Posillipo, an evergreen, cheerful mountain with one foot on land and the other at sea, holding the hand of a beautiful siren that the ancients called Partenope. On top of it, you'll find gardens and palaces. The entire shore is lined up with houses where fun and happiness live. (41) The sea that bathes its feet is always full of boats belonging to gentlemen sailing in the evening's fresh air at the sound of music, enjoying the sweet climate. There is no corner or hidden inlet without people eating and having fun. (42) Posillipo was a very handsome young man without equals in the entire city, his bad luck was to fall in love with Niseta, an ungrateful and rude countrywoman who never cared for him and avoided him. Posillipo's despair and Niseta's peevishness were so great that he turned into a mountain, and she became an island that still remembers the past and out of spite stays at a distance.

(43) "Below, you will see the Somma mountain, named Vesuvius in the past. This was a Neapolitan gentleman who too fell in love with a woman of the Capra family from the Sieggio clan. The relatives did not get along. The more the two loved each other, the more their plans were challenged. The woman was sent to Capo Minerva, where she could no longer see her lover, so one day on a boat ride, she threw herself into the sea, turning into an island that is called Capri up to our days. (44) Vesuvius heard the news and began to throw out sighs of fire, turning slowly into the mountain called Somma. Because he can see his beloved woman, the mountain is always burning and throwing out fire. When it gets angry, it makes Naples tremble and repent for not giving him the woman he loved.

(45) "And that beautiful Sebeto river was but a young man who was married to Megara, a very attractive lady he sent one evening on a boat ride. When the sailors tried a maneuver in front of Pizzofalcone, the boat capsized and the lady drowned, turning into a rock at the site of today's Castello dell'Uovo. (46). Poor Sebeto heard the news and began to cry when seeing from afar his wife turn into a rock. He cried so hard that he became a beautiful river that cheers up every garden it passes, arriving at the sea where it looks for the wife he still loves.

(47) "Old folks will tell you about a fisherman who lived above Posillipo. When he saw a siren pass by singing with a violin in her hands, he fell in

pascennose de chell'aria 'nzoccarata. Non c'è pontone né recuoncolo addove non bide la gente darese spasso e mettere sott'a lo naso. [42] Ora chisso era no giovane tanto bello che non aveva simmele 'n tutta la cetate, e pe mala sciorta soja se 'nnammoraje de na foretana chiammata Niseta, la quale, sgrata e scortese, non se le voze maje atteccolejare attuorno, anze sempe lo fojeva; e tanto fuje la desperazione de Posileco e la coteconaria de Niseta, che chillo deventaje na montagna e chesta è n' isola, ch'ancora s'allecorda de le cose passate, e pe despietto se nne stace arrasso.

[43] «Vedarraje appriesso la montagna de Somma, che mprimma se chiammava Vesuvio: chisto era no gentelommo de Napole che se 'nnammoraje porzí de na segnora de casa Crapa, che a chille tiempe era casata de Sieggio. E perché li pariente non ce vozero acconsentire, quanto cchiú isse s'ammavano tanto cchiú se vedevano rutte li designe lloro; anze li pariente mannajeno la segnora a starese a lo Capo de Menerva, addove non potenno essa vedere l'ammante sujo, no juorno che ghieva a spasso dinto na falluca se jettaje a maro, e deventaje n'isola, che pe nfi' a lo juorno d'oje se chiamma Crapa. [44] Vesuvio, avutone la nova, accommenzaje a ghiettare sospire de fuoco, ed a poco a poco arreventaje na montagna, che se chiamma de Somma: e perché bede sempe la 'nnammorata soja, montagna e bona sempe arde e sempe jetta fuoco: e quanno se mette 'n collera fa tremmare la cetà de Napole che se pente, ma senz'utele, de non averele dato chella che desederava.

[45] «E chillo bello sciummo Sebeto che auto fu che no giovane lo quale, a mala pena s'appe 'nguadiata Megara, ch'era na belledissema segnora, che avennola mannata na sera a spasso pe maro, quanno arrevaje faccefronte a Pizzofarcone, volenno li marenare fare lo caro, se revotaje la falluca ed essa s'annegaje, deventanno no scuoglio: che oje, essennocese fatto no castiello, se chiamma lo castiello dell'Uovo? [46] Sebeto, lo povero giovane, avennone avuto la nova, e bedenno da lontano la mogliere soja fatta no scuoglio, se mese a chiagnere, e tanto chiagnette che deventaje no sciummo: lo quale pe nfi' a lo juorno d'oje mosta quant'era bello, pocca isso rallegra tutte l'uorte pe dove passa, e sboccanno a maro pe sott'acqua va a trovare la mogliere soja, ch'ancora l'amma.

[47] «Sentarraje contare da li viecchie comme no cierto pescatore che steva 'ncoppa Posileco, vedenno passare la Serena che co no violino 'mmano jeva cantanno, isso tanto se 'nnammoraje de chillo suono e de chillo canto che pe la pressa de scennere da la montagna cadette a maro e fece lo papariello. E dapo' d'essere sagliuto e sciso tre bote, comme se pe gusto sommozzasse, all'utemo deventaje no scuoglio, che accostatose a la montagna pare tutt'uno:

love so badly with that melody and song that he ran down the mountain so fast that he fell into the sea with a great dive. After surfacing three times as if swimming below the water for fun, he ended up as a rock that joined the mountain and looked united. To remember this event, they named it Mergellina. (48) The heartbroken siren rewarded him with a magic spell, so that all the gentlemen of Naples in their street carriages and all the knights in their boats at sea would honor him, a ritual observed every summer.[iv]

(49) "Not to hold you back any longer, I will not speak about Pietrabianca, a lady admired for her white skin which gave her the name, and I won't speak about the two sisters named Ischia and Procida, one angry with her bowels filled with fire, the other sweet, making everyone happy with its green pastures and beauty. And I won't talk about Antignano, Amalfi, Sorrento, Pozzuoli and Baja, which once were men and women and for one reason or another became what they are today. (50) But as I have fed your curiosity, go on, dear Jannuzzo, together with Ninella, and do as I told you. I will always be there for you in case of need. I am now leaving you." Saying this, he disappeared from their sight like a flash.[v]

(51) Jannuzzo and Ninella thanked Heaven for looking after them by letting them meet that good old man. They went on their way to the city of Monterotondo, where they settled in a house in front of the royal palace. Dressed in the beautiful clothes they had found and spending all their money, they looked like gentry served by waiters and a fine lady companion of Ninella, who had become the most beautiful woman of the region.

(52) It then happened that one day, when Ninella stayed at the window, a bridesmaid of the king of Monterotondo's stepmother noticed her, like those folks who always meddle in other people's affairs, and said, "How pretty you are, my child! / But you would be even prettier / if you carried a singing apple in your hand!"

(53) On hearing this, Ninella told her brother what had happened. Out of his deep love for her, he promised to walk until he would find that apple. (54) After walking for some forty miles, he arrived at a plain with a tree in its center that was so full of those apples that it seemed about to crash. You could feel, in that surrounding, a harmony that would have caused a monstruous bird to drop stones from their claws and make you fall asleep. (55) But try to grab one! All sorts of dangerous animals surrounded it: bears, lions, panthers, leopards, crocodiles, scorpions, snakes, dragons, and so many other small animals that would have scared Rodomonte.

e pe mammoria de lo caso socciesso lo chiammajeno Mergoglino. [48] La Serena, che n'appe desgusto, le deze na fatazione: che tutte li Segnure de Napole co le carrozze lo corteggiassero pe terra e li Cavaliere co le falluche pe mmaro, la quale cosa s'asserva ogn'anno pe tutta la 'state.

[49] «Ma pe no' ve 'ntrattenere cchiú lasso de parlare de Pretajanca, ch'era na segnora tanto stemmata pe la janchezze soja, ch'ancora ne porta lo nommo; d'Ischia e de Proceta, ch'erano doje sore, un'arraggiata, ch'ancora ha le bísciole chiene de fuoco, l'auta galante, che nfi' ad oje te rallegra lo core co la verdura e la bellezze soja. E accossí d'Antegnano, Amarfa, Sorriento, Pezzulo e Baja, che tutte mprimma erano uommene femmene, e chi pe na cosa e chi pe n'auta deventajeno chello che lo juorno d'oje se vede. [50] Ma pocca aggio dato pasto a la coriosetate toja, vavattenne, Jannuzzo mio, co Nennella toja, e facite quanto v'aggio ditto, ch'a le besuogne vuoste sarraggio sempe lesto, e m'arrequaquiglio»; e accossí decenno sparette da l'uocchie loro, comme se fosse stato no lampo.

[51] Jannuzzo e Nennella, rengraziato lo Cielo che s'avea pegliato pensiero de loro, facennole 'ncontrare chillo buono viecchio, s'abbiajero a la cetate de Monteretunno, dove s'allogajeno na casa faccefronte a lo Palazzo Riale: e bestutose de chille belle vestite c'aveano asciato, e spennenno chille denare, comparevano da segnure, servute da staffiere e da na bona donna de compagna che se steva co Nennella, la quale era deventata la cchiú bella segnora che fosse pe chille contuorne.

[52] Ora mo soccesse che no juorno, stanno Ninella a la fenesta, na sdammecella de la matrèja de lo Rre de Monteretunno che la vedette, comme ca sta razza de gente vonno sempe mettere lo sale a li pegnate de l'aute, le decette:

«Quanto sì bella, fegliola mia!
Ma cchiú bella sarrisse
Se lo milo che canta 'mmano avisse!»

[53] Ninella che 'ntese chesto, venuto lo fratiello, le contaje la cosa comm'era passata: e lo fratiello, che le voleva no bene svisciolato, le 'mprommese de cammenare tanto pe nfi' che trovasse sto milo. [54] E dapo' d'avere cammenato na mano de quarantena de miglia, arrevaje a na chianura 'mmiezo de la quale nc'era n'arvolo tanto carreco de ste mela che pareva che se rompesse e se senteva pe chillo conturno n'armonia c'avarria fatto scappare le prete da le granfe de li gruoje, tant'era lo suonno che facea venire. [55] Ma che? Quant'ar-

(56) Seeing those wild animals, Jannuzzo got so scared that he turned around and left, fearing an early death and ending up in some animal's belly because of his sister's beastly whim. (57) He took refuge in a den, wondering if he should leave or stay. As he remembered the good old man, he called upon him, as he had asked the city of Naples to fix his broken leg. He showed up towards evening accompanied by four other elderly, sad-looking fellows. (58) Taking heart, Jannuzzo greeted the old man and his companions, and out of curiosity and caring more about others' fate than his own, he asked who the four were. The old man answered, (59) "The four fellows were once fishermen at the pier. They used to take people all day long with a boat to Ischia for its healing hot waters and sand, or for a walk to Posillipo. At night, after returning from their trips, they would go for water at the Lanternone with pitchers.

(60) "One evening, when they went later than usual, they had barely filled their pitchers when a sailboat arrived and Turks landed on the pier for a looting. The four old men heard the noise and, out of fear, crouched down with the pitchers between their legs, shoulder to shoulder, in order to avoid being attacked from behind, as they thought them to be sailors. (61) But when they heard them speak Turkish, they froze and were scared silly, begging Neptune not to let them die at the hands of the Turks. So they turned at once into marble with their pitchers, and when the Turks attacked them, they could not harm them. (62) Having turned into fountain statues at the end of the pier, the poor fellows, who used to serve the Neapolitan people, continued this custom, throwing water from their pitchers to help folks cool off. People remembered them, calling them out as if they were their fathers. If someone asked, 'Who's paying?' they would reply, 'The four fellows from the Pier.' (63) After staying happily at the pier, the poor fellows were asked to leave the area like bad women or troublemaking students and move to the river where the Sun hides at night; that's why they are so sad. As a good friend living close by, I accompanied them all the way here. (64) But you, my dear Jannuzzo, why do you look for other people's troubles when you have enough of your own up to your neck? What are you doing here?"

"I came here," he said, "to get one of those apples for my sister who broke my balls about them. But there are so many wild animals that I fear they might devour me."

"Don't be afraid," the old man said, "let a champion handle this." (65) So what did he do? He ordered the four men from the pier to make, together, a fountain with their pitchers. Without ever having seen water, those animals riva e 'mpizza! Era l'arvolo attorniato da tutte sciorte d'anemale velenuse: llà nc'erano urze, leune, pantere, gatteparde, coccetriglie, scorpiune, scorzune, dragune, e tant'aute frúscole che avarriano fatto sorrejere no Rodamonte.

[56] Quanno Jannuzzo vedde chelle fere appe tanto jajo che fece chilleto arreto e s'arrassaje, avenno paura de non avere pe sebetura quarche bentre d'anemale primma de lo tiempo sujo, pe no crapiccio bestiale de la sore. [57] E puostose a no recuoncolo accommenzaje a pensare se dovea tornaresenne o fremmarese, quanno, allecordatose de lo viecchio, se nce arrecommannaje de core, tanto cchiú ch'avea scritto a Napole che le fosse acconciata la gamma rotta: e bèccote che 'mmiero la sera lo vedde spontare, co quatt'aute viecchie che jevano muto malanconeche. [58] Tanno Jannuzzo, fatt'armo, salutaje lo viecchio co la compagnia, e perché era coriuso, pensanno cchiú a li fatte d'aute ch'a li suoje, l'addemmannaje chi erano chill'aute quatto. E lo viecchio accossí decette: [59] «Chiste quatto erano mprimma quatto pescature de lo Muolo, li quale jevano tutto lo juorno co na falluca, portanno la gente mo ad Ischia, pe li remmedie de li vagne, e de stufe, e de la rena, e mo a spasso a Posileco; e la sera, tornate da li viagge, se nne jevano co cierte tenielle a pigliare acqua vicino la fontana de lo Lanternone. [60] Soccesse na sera che essenno jute cchiú tarde de lo soleto, a mala pena avevano chino li tenielle che, benuta na tartana, sbarcajeno na mano de Turche a lo Muolo pe fare presa: 'ntesero sti quatto lo rommore e pe la paura, puostese li tenielle nfra le cosce, s'agguattajeno, tenenno l'uno le spalle votate all'auto pe non essere cuovete da dereto, credennose che fossero puro marenare. [61] Ma quanno accommenzajeno a sentire parlare torchisco s'agghiajajeno, ed àppero tanto la cacavessa e lo tremmoliccio che s'arrecommannajeno a Nettuno, che le facesse fare qualesevoglia morte fore che pe mano de Turche: ed eccote ne n'attemo che tutte quatto, co tutte li tenielle, deventajeno de preta marmola, e quanno li Turche le posero le mano adduosso se trovajeno co no parmo de naso. [62] Ora mo sti poverielle, restate statole de la fontana 'mponta a lo Muolo, perché erano solete de fare servizie a le gente de Napole, secotajeno sta osanza, e da chille tenielle cacciajeno sempre acqua pe defrisco de li cetatine: li quale pe bona mammoria ad ogne parola l'annomenavano, comme se fossero li patre loro, ed accossí se uno deceva: — Ed a me chi me paga? —, responnevano: — Li Quatto de lo Muolo! —, e ba scorrenno. [63] Ora mo sti poverielle, dapo' d'essere state co tanto gusto loro a lo Muolo, hanno avuto no mannato che sfrattano, comme a femmene marvase o comme a stodiante fastediuse, e che vagano a chillo sciummo addove la sera s'annasconne lo sole: e perzò stanno accossí malenconeche. Ed io che stongo

would run for it so Jannuzzo would be free to pick an apple with his own hands. (66) That's what they did. The animals all ran to drink, Jannuzzo picked the apple, said goodbye, and left, and the old men also went on his way.

(67) Jannuzzo returned to his sister after a long journey and, full of joy, gave her the desired apple. Ninella couldn't wait to see the bridesmaid at the palace. As soon as she saw her, she showed her the apple. But the lady said to her, "Now you are much prettier! / But you would be even prettier / if you held in your hand the dancing water."

(68) Ninella realized how much her brother loved her and that he would have sacrificed his life for her, so she asked him for this new favor in order not to become the most unfortunate woman on earth. It's enough to speak about getting prettier, but for a woman, there is nothing worse than being called old and ugly.

(69) To please his sister, the loving brother went on his way at once, and after passing mountains, plains, rivers, and the sea, arrived at a cave with the dancing water. But there was this banging door, and there were so many dead men lying around who had been killed by the unstoppable door—a truly astounding scene. (70) Facing this danger, poor Jannuzzo called upon the old man and took shelter in a nearby den, so he wouldn't be stunned by the banging. (71) The old man reappeared, accompanied by a beautiful young girl who came running. They greeted Jannuzzo, who asked about the girl. (72) "This girl was honored in Naples for her beauty, given the surname of Venus, but deep down, she continues to be chaste Diana as the daughter of one of the old men you met. The other three are her relatives. (73) She lived at the Largo del Castello in front of a fountain above the wall of the ditch, resembling an arch or small bridge, and because she suffered from the intense heat and having an ardent nature, she went every night to wash at that fountain. (74) One night, when she didn't find water, she went to sleep below the arch, but the humidity made her sleep throughout the morning. People passed by as she was still asleep lying there buck naked, and because she was so beautiful, everyone stopped to look at her. (75) When she woke up and saw all those people, she felt such shame that she begged Diana to take her away from that crowd, at the risk of her life. Moved by the request of that honorable girl, Diana turned her into a marble statue, known as Venus up to our days. (76) When hearing that some misfortune had happened to her father and some relatives, the good girl received permission from a gentleman to visit them. To prevent anyone from noticing, he had a replacement made for that fountain, as different as an owl

poco lontano d'addove stevano lloro, comme buono ammico l'aggio accompagnate nfino a chisto luoco. [64] Ma tu, Jannuzzo mio, che baje cercanno li guaje d'aute e creo ca ne staje chino nfi' 'n canna, che faje lloco?»

«Songo venuto — decette isso — ped avere uno de cheste mela e portarelo a sòrema, che me nn'ha rutto le chiocche. Ma nce songo tanta de st'anemale sarvateche c'aggio paura che non me magneno».

«N'avere paura — decette lo viecchio —, lassa fare a sto fusto». [65] E che fece? Ordenaje a li Quatto de lo Muolo che aunite 'nsémmora facessero co li tenielle lloro na fontana, pocca chill'anemale, che non avevano maje visto acqua, nce sarriano curze: e Jannuzzo trovato campo franco s'avarria potuto co le mmano soje cogliere lo milo. [66] Accossí se fece, ed essenno tutte l'anemale jute a bevere, Jannuzzo se còuze lo milo, e lecenziato, che se ne jesse tanno pe tanno, li viecchie puro se nne jettero pe lo fatto lloro.

[67] Jannuzzo, addonca, dapo' luongo viaggio tornato a la sore, tutto alliegro le consegnaje lo milo tanto addesedderato. E Ninella le parze mill'anne de vedere la sdammecella, pocca a mala pena nce parlaje che subeto le mostaje lo milo. Ma chella le decette:

«Mo sì cchiú bella assaje!
Ma muto cchiú bella sarrisse
Se chell'acqua ch'abballa 'mmano avisse».

[68] Ninella ca bedde che lo frate le voleva bene veramente, e che avarria puosto la vita ped essa, lo pregaje de st'auto piacere, ch'autamente se sarria tenuta la cchiú sbentorata de lo munno. Vasta che se parlava d'essere cchiú bella, ch'è quanto se pò dicere a na femmena che non ha peo d'essere chiammata o brutta o vecchia.

[69] Lo frate, che n'era cuocolo, pe consolare la sore súbeto se mese 'n cammino, e dapo' d'avere passato e munte, e balle, e chiane, e sciumme, e maro, arrevaje a na grotta addove scorreva st'acqua: ma nc'era na porta che sempe sbatteva, e nce stevano tanta uommene muorte, che l'aveva accise chella porta, pocca nesciuno la poteva fremmare, ch'era na cosa de stopore. [70] Jannuzzo, pover'ommo, vedennose a sto pericolo, s'arrecommannaje a lo zi' viecchio sujo, e pe non essere storduto da chillo sbattetorio se reteraje a no cafuorchio da llà becino. [71] Quann'eccote che le compare n'auta vota lo viecchio, che facea la guida a na bellissema giovenella che beneva a carrera stesa, ed arrevate addove steva Jannuzzo lo salutajeno. Ed isso appena rennuto lo saluto addommannaje chi era chella zitella, e lo viecchio: [72] «Chesta —

and a phoenix. (77) These are the misfortunes of this poor girl. But let's hear now about your own troubles; you came to this place that no one visits unless prompted by some adversity."

"I am here," Jannuzzo said, "because of my unreasonable sister and her continuous temptations by a bridesmaid of the king of Monterotondo's step-mother, who put this crazy request into her head to get a carafe of dancing water. But I do not dare grab it, because that banging door would do to me what it did to all the dead lying around, aside from the fear that the water could make me dance too, taking my hand and making me slam with a somersault like a billy goat into one of those stones, leaving an ugly memory."

(78) "Come on now, don't be afraid," the old man said, "I will change into marble, puncture the door, and this girl who is used to staying in the danc-ing water will fill the carafe for you." (79) That's what they did. Everything worked out fine, Jannuzzo thanked the statues, and he headed back to Mon-terotondo. On his arrival, he handed the carafe to his sister, telling her all that happened to him. (80) Ninella was very appreciative and showed the carafe as soon as she could to the bridesmaid who said, "Do you realize how more beautiful you'd be if you had a speaking bird in your hand?"

(81) As this new unspeakable request sank in, Ninella told her brother that all he had done amounted to nothing if he did not get her the speaking bird, that her soul would get wings and fly out of her body if she did not get that bird. (82) Accustomed by now to these expeditions, Jannuzzo set out for this new task. After ruining three pairs of shoes on his peregrinations across the world, he arrived at a mountain that looked like a sculpture shop. Here you could see a human marble statue, over there a horse made of stone, elsewhere a woman made of magma. All over the mountain, men and animals turned into statues that would fill all of the princes' galleries with the most authentic stat-ues they could ever dream of. The only thing they lacked was speech. Indeed, they turned everyone speechless from amazement by looking at them, unable to tell who was more a statue, the living or the dead.

(83) On top of the mountain was the tree with the speaking bird. Who-ever heard it speak would turn into a statue. (84) Jannuzzo didn't know about this. Thinking to act smartly by not calling the old man for help, he waited until the evening to catch the bird after it fell asleep. But the fairy bird knew right away that there was going to be some ambush. (85) At night, when all the birds go to sleep, the speaking bird pretended to sleep. Jannuzzo approached it and was about to raise his hand to catch it when the bird said, "Get lost, scoundrel!"

responnette — era na giovene 'norata e tanto bella ch'a Napole pe sopranomme la chiammavano Vennere; ma a lo core era sempre la casta Diana, ed era figlia d'uno de chille viecchie che bediste l'auta vota, e chill'aute tre le songo pariente. [73] Ora chesta steva de casa a lo Largo de lo Castiello, faccefronte a na fontana 'ncoppa lo muro de lo fuosso, ch'èje a semeletudene de n'arco o de no ponteciello, e perché essa pateva de gran caudo, essenno de natura focosa, se nne jeva ogne notte a chella fontana a lavarese. [74] Na notte non ce trovaje acqua e se mettette a dormire sott'a l'arco, ma tanto suonno le deze chell'ommedetate che se fece juorno: passavano la gente ed essa ancora dormeva accossí a la nnuda, comme la fece la mamma, e perché era bellissema tutte se fermavano a tenerelemente. [75] Quanno essa se scetaje, e vedutase spettacolo de tanta gente, fu tanta la vregogna che n'appe che pregaje Diana che le levasse chella confusione, co tutto che nce perdesse la vita. Diana, mòsseta a la pregaria de sta 'norata fegliola, la fece deventare statola de preta marmora, che nfi' ad oje lo juorno se chiamma Vennere. [76] Ora sta bona fegliola, avenno saputo ca lo patre e li pariente hanno passato non saccio che desgrazia, have avuto lecienzia da no segnore granne de ghirele a trovare; e chillo segnore pe no' nne fare addonare la gente nce ha puosto a chella fontana lo scagno, ma tanto deverzo quanto è na coccovaja da na fenice. Chiste songo li guaje de sta povera fegliola. [77] Ora dimme no poco li tuoje, pocca sì benuto a sto pajese addove ommo non arriva se non portato da quacche mala sciagura».

«Io songo ccà — decette Jannuzzo — pe lo poco cellevriello de sòrema e pe na tentazione de na sdammecella de la matrèja de lo Rre de Monteretunno, che le mette 'n capo ste pazzie, pocca vorria na carafella de chest'acqua ch'aballa. Ma io non me confido de pegliarela, pocca chella porta che sempe sbatte me farria chello c'ha fatto a tante che stanno muorte llà 'nnante, otra che aggio paura che l'acqua non faccia abballare a mene porzí, pegliannome co la mano e facennome co na crapiola tozzare comm'a caperrone a na preta de chelle, e lassarence la brutta mammoria».

[78] «Orsú, n'avere paura — decette lo viecchio —. Io tornanno marmora, comme songo, pontellarraggio la porta, e sta fegliola, ch'è pratteca a stare dinto a li balle de l'acqua, te n'enchiarrà la carrafella». [79] Accossí facettero, e socceduto tutto co gusto, Jannuzzo, rengraziate le statole, votaje carena vierzo Monteretunno, addove dapo' quarche tiempo arrevato, consegnaje la carrafella a la sore, decennole quanto l'era socciesso. [80] Ninella, tutta prejata, a la primma accasione che le venne mostaje la carrafella a la sdammecella, la quale vedutala le decette:

Hearing this, Jannuzzo felt something like ice run through his veins. He turned into a statue at once, with his right hand raised as if ready to catch the bird.

(86) Not seeing her brother return after three years and with money about to run out, Ninella decided to dress as a pilgrim and roam all alone, trying to find him. She crossed many cities, towns, and forests and arrived at that mountain. Seeing all those statues, she stopped, spellbound. As she arrived in the evening, she was afraid walking among those stony folks. Without knowing what to do, she remembered the favors her brother had received from the old man and began to call on him with a trembling voice that could move you to pity. (87) The old man appeared at once in front of her and said, "You were smart to call me, my dear child, because the speaking bird is on top of this mountain. Whoever hears even only just a word turns into marble. I am sorry that your brother fell into the trap by not calling me; he wanted to be a hunter but ended up hunted himself."

(88) When Ninella heard the news about her brother, she burst into tears and beat her chest, because she was the reason for his misfortune. (89) But the old man said to her, "Calm down, my dear child. Don't be afraid; I am here for you. You should know that this bird is a friend of your family, because your dear mother, while living in a farmhouse, prepared nets to catch birds, and this one flying around ended up in her nets. When it spoke to find help, the net turned into stone. If your mother had been not quick breaking the marble with a hammer, it would have died. Since then, the bird asked Jupiter to let things turn into stone not through speech, but through willpower, which he granted graciously. (90) The bird was so grateful to your family that whenever there was a need, it would come for help. You should know that your mother has been in prison ever since you were born. Without the bird, she would have starved to death. (91) Remember to speak before it speaks and start screaming as soon as you approach the statues (since its voice reaches all the way to the top), saying the following, "Blessed bird! / I am Cicia's daughter. / She saved you from the stony nets / when you were in trouble!"

(92) After saying this, the old man melted away like snow in the sun and disappeared like smoke in the wind. Ninella wished the old man had not disappeared, so she could ask him to tell her once and for all who her mother was. But she remembered that the old man told her once that the bird asked her to leave that question behind and to worry about present troubles. Following this advice, she began to recite the song as soon as she arrived at the first statue, screaming at the top of her lungs. (93) The bird appeared right away

«Saje tu quanto cchiú bella sarrisse
Se l'auciello che parla 'mmano avisse?»

[81] Ninella, 'mprenatase de st'auta comme-se-chiamma, accommenzaje a dicere a lo fratiello ca quanto aveva fatto era zuba se non jeva a pegliare l'auciello che parla, e che se essa non aveva st'auciello l'arma soja metteva l'ascelle e se ne volava fore de lo cuorpo. [82] Jannuzzo, che s'era aosato a li viagge, se mese a st'auta 'mpresa, e dapo' d'avere strutto tre para de scarpe cammenanno pe lo munno, arrevaje a no monte che pareva na poteca de scolture: pocca da ccà vedive n'ommo de marmora, da llà no cavallo de preta, a n'auta banna na femmena de pepierno, ed accossí pe tutto lo monte uommene ed anemale deventate statole, de manera che se nne potevano arrecchire tutte le gallarie de li Princepe, che statole cchiú natorale de chelle non avarriano maje potuto avere. Pocca no' le mancava auto che la parola, anze facevano mancare la parola pe lo stopore a chi le bedeva, che non sapive chi era cchiú statola, lo vivo o lo muorto.

[83] Ora 'n cimma a sto monte era l'arvolo addove steva l'auciello che parlava, pe lo quale ogn'ommo che lo senteva parlare statola deventava. [84] Jannuzzo, che de chesto no' nn'era 'nformato, credennose de 'nfelare perne a lo junco, senza chiammare l'ajuto de lo viecchio aspettaje la sera, pe 'ncappare l'auciello quann'avesse appapagnato l'uocchie: ma l'auciello, ch'era affatato, sapeva subeto se nc'era quarche agguàito. [85] Venuta la sera, quanno tutte l'aucielle s'ammasonano, l'auciello che parla fegnette de dormire e Jannuzzo, accostatose, tanno voleva auzare la mano ed afferrarelo, quanno disse l'auciello: «Addio, mariuolo!», e Jannuzzo sentenno cheste parole se sentíje correre comme no jaccio pe le bene, e 'nnitto 'nfatto na statola deventaje, co la mano deritta auzata comme se bolesse acciaffare.

[86] Ora Ninella: non bedenno cchiú tornare lo frate (ed erano già passate tre anne, e li tornise fornute, pocca le casce mostavano lo funno), se resorvette de vestirese da pellegrina e ghire sperta e demerta trovannolo; e tanta cammenaje cetate, passaje paise ed arrevotaje vuosche, ch'arrevaje a chillo monte, e biste tanta statole se nce fremmaje comme 'ncantata. E perché st'arrivo fu berso la sera appe paura de cammenare fra chillo puopolo de prete, e non sapenno a che se resorvere, allecordannose de li favure che lo viecchio avea fatto a lo fratiello, l'accommenzaje a chiammare co na vocella tremmante che te facea compassione. [87] Ed eccote nne n'attemo lo viecchio comparirele 'nnante, decennole: «Gran jodizio haje avuto, fegliola mia, a chiammareme, pocca 'ncoppa a sto monte nc'è l'auciello che parla, e chi nne sente, vasta na

with its golden head, purple neck, fleshy wings, yellow tail, and greenish chest and shoulders, greeting Ninella and asking her not to be afraid, to climb that mountain together and say what she needed, and that she would be served like a queen, because the bird owed a debt of gratitude to her family.

(94) To find her brother's statue, Ninella asked the bird to tell her their names, if this were possible. The bird replied, "There are two kinds of statues. Some are due to punishments for some crimes, others to misfortunes, they are imprisoned in the marble for a limited time only. The first are on the left, the others on the right side. (95) Therefore, if you want to identify someone among those on the left side, it will take more than a year, while those on the right side are of no interest. But I am going to oblige you, and I will let you know how to proceed.

(96) Do you see that porter over there carrying a bundle that looks like a ball? He was a thief who stole a poor woman's laundry in the Lavenaro district. When he thought he was on his way home, they took him to this place and, hearing me speak, he turned into a marble statue, as you can see. This statue must go back to Naples on top of the Sellaria fountain. To relinquish its infamous laundry thief reputation, people will say that it is Atlas carrying the world on his shoulder.

(97) Come now with me further up and look at those two: a man and a woman, both buck naked. They lived at Chiaja and were so stingy that their daughters had to walk naked on the beach; walking on the sand in the summer they got burned by the sun, looking like Africans. (98) Due to this nasty punishing custom, even though handsome and young, they were sent to this mountain, where they arrived buck naked after a long journey, and hearing me speak, they turned into statues. They too will go back to Naples on the Chiaia fountain before arriving at Chiatamone.

(99) The marble statue further up of a woman lying on the ground, looking at an owl or barn owl through a branch hanging from her head, was a witch from Benevento who scared the families' children with this owl. When she came to Naples to continue to carry out her evil task, she lived near the house of a philosopher who couldn't sleep at night because of the owl's singing and crying. (100) Realizing that this kind of nuisance was owed to this woman, he told her to go to a mountain, which is famous the world over, to find a feather of the speaking bird, as this would enhance her art. She arrived here through a spell to get flour, but she left the bag here, because she and the owl turned into volcanic rock. They too will go back to Naples to the fountain in the center of

parola, súbeto preta marmola deventa: e me despiace ca nc'è 'ncappato lo fratiello tujo pe non avere avuto jodizio de chiammareme, credennose de fare da cacciatore, ed è stato cacciato».

[88] Quanno Ninella sentette sta nova de lo fratiello, scappaje a chiagnere ed a pesarese lo pietto, pocca essa era stata causa de sta desgrazia. [89] Ma lo viecchio le decette: «Sta zitto, figliola mia, ca songo io pe tene, e non avere paura: sacce ca chisto auciello è ammico de la casa vosta, pocca la mammarella toja, mente che steva a na massaria soja, avenno aparate le rezze pe 'ncappare l'aucielle, chisto che jeva pe cierte negozie suoje 'ncappaje a le rezze: ed avenno parlato pe cercar'ajuto la rezza deventaje de preta, e se la mammarella toja non era lesta a rompere co no martiello chillo marmoro filato, isso nce moreva. Da tanno st'auciello pregaje Giove che non sempre che parlava, ma sempre che boleva le cose deventassero de preta, ed appe la grazia. [90] E restaje accossí obbrecato a la casa vosta che sempe che n'ha avuto quarche nova de li besuogne accorrente isso è accurzo ad ajutare: e sacce ca màmmata sta 'mpresone, tant'anne songo quanto n'avite vuje, e se non fosse stato st'auciello se sarria morta de famme. [91] Ora, mprimma che isso parla, e tu parlale, ed accommenza a gredare subeto che t'accuoste a le statole (ca nfi' llà arriva la voce soja e fa l'affetto) e di' accossí:

"Auciello felice!
Io songo la figlia de Cice,
Che quanno avive guaje
Da la rezza de preta te sarvaje!"».

[92] Ed avenno accossí ditto lo viecchio squagliaje comme neve a lo sole e sparette comme fummo a lo viento. Avarria voluto Ninella che lo viecchio non fosse sparuto, pe pregarelo che le decesse na vota chi era sta mamma soja: ma allecordatase che lo viecchio n'auta vota le decette che l'auciello l'avarria ditto, lassaje sto pensiero ed attese a li guaje presente, e postase a la 'mpresa, subbeto ch'arrevaje a la primma statola accommenzaje a recetare la canzona, gredanno co quanta voce aveva. [93] Ed eccote che l'auciello (lo quale aveva la capo d'oro, lo cuollo paonazzo, l'ascelle 'ncarnatine, la coda gialla, e lo pietto e le spalle verdevaje) se nne venette, e salutata Ninella le decette che n'avesse paura, ma che sagliesse cod isso chillo monte e le decesse zò che l'abbesognava, ca l'avarria servuta da Regina, pocca era obbrecato a la casa soja.

[94] Ora Ninella, pe trovare quale de chelle statole era lo fratiello, pregaje l'auciello che le spalefecasse chi fossero chelle statole, s'era lízeto a sa-

Porto, and the poets of that town will invent a story so that nobody will know that she was a witch. (101) To tell you the stories of all these statues one by one, I wouldn't finish by tomorrow, the day after tomorrow, and the day after. Suffice it to say that all the statues in the galleries and gardens of Rome, Naples, Milan, Venice, and the other famous cities will come from this mountain. Now tell me what you are up to."

(102) "You must know," Ninella said, "that a bridesmaid of the king of Monterotondo's stepmother told me that I would be happy if I had you with me, so I sent my only brother who came here and turned into a statue, not telling you who he was. I would like to ask a favor of you: first to give me back my brother alive and then to accompany me for my needs. You may buy us as chained slaves.

(103) The bird replied, "Cheer up, my dear child, I'm going to comfort you. But tell me, would you recognize your brother?"

(104) "Yes, of course!" replied Ninella. As she walked along the right side, getting close to the tree, she saw her brother with his hand raised towards the bird's nest. (105) Ninella ran to hug him, kissing that cold marble as if to try to make him come alive with her sighs and bathing him with her tears. But the bird told her, "The water of your tears won't revive the statues; you need a different kind of water." (106) The bird flew to wet its feathers at a certain fountain, sprinkling them over the statue, which opened its eyes at once, moved its legs and arms, and turned into Jannuzzo, the man he was before. He hugged his sister, overjoyed, cheering her and remembering what the old man had told him, that he too would be a statue for a while. He thanked the bird and the sister for freeing him from that tomb, for which he didn't care, even though it was made of marble. Then he took a few steps to see if he remembered how to walk.

(107) Delicate Ninella, on seeing all those miserable folks on the right side of the mountain look like pestles, asked the bird to do them a favor as well. (108) "Bless your good heart, my dear Ninella!" the bird said. "May they all be revived for the love of yours!" Saying this and wetting its feathers again, the bird flew over the statues, squirting water over their faces. (109) In an instant, you could hear a horse neigh over here and a donkey bray over there, yawns of humans waking up on one side, a yawning woman on the other side. Astonishing everyone, it seemed to be the age of Deucalion and Pyrrhus. (110) The bird made a beautiful speech like a field captain, saying that it brought everyone back to life for the love of Ninella and Jannuzzo, to whom it was obliged, that

perelo. E l'auciello responnette: «Sacce ca de doje sciorte songo ste statole. Aute songo accossí deventate 'n pena de quarche delitto, aute pe desgrazia, li quale stanno pe quarche tiempo solamente carcerate dinto a chille marmore: li primme stanno a mano manca, l'aute a mmano deritta. [95] Se vuoje perzò saperene quarcheduno di chille de mano manca, ca de tutte non nce vastarria n'anno, e ca de chille de mano deritta non serve, io te voglio dare sto gusto: anze, te voglio dicere de cchiúne chello che se n'ha da fare.

[96] «Vide llà chillo vastaso, che stace co no fardiello 'ncuollo che pare na palla? Sacce ca chillo era no mariuolo, lo quale avenno fatto n'arravoglia cuosemo de na colata de na poverella a lo Lavenaro, quanno se credeva de tornaresenne de notte a la casa, fu straportato a sto luoco, e 'n sentireme parlare deventaje marmola, comme lo vide. Ora chesta statola ha da essere n'auta vota portata a Napole e posta 'ncoppa la fontana de la Sellaria, ed azzò che no' le resta sta 'nfammia d'arrobba-colata dicerranno ch'èje Atlante che tene lo munno 'ncuollo.

[97] «Viene mo cchiú 'ncoppa e bide chille duje, un ommo e na femmena, nude comme le fece la mamma: ora chisse erano de Chiaja, ed accossí avare che facevano ghire li fegliule a la nnuda, che la 'state, cuotte da lo sole, mentre cammenavano pe chell'arene parevano gente de l'Afreca. [98] Ora perché isse accacciajeno sta brutta osanza, pe castico, se bè erano belle giuvane, fujeno mannate a sto monte, addove pe lo luongo viaggio arrevate tutte nude, 'n sentennome parlare deventajeno doje statole: le quale porzí saranno n'auta vota mannate a Napole e poste a la fontana de Chiaja, primma d'arrevare a lo Sciatamone.

[99] «Chella statola che sta cchiú 'ncoppa, ch'è de na femmena stesa 'n terra, e che 'ncoppa a no rammosciello che le penne 'n capo vede na cevettola o coccovaja, porzí de marmola, era na janara de Veneviento, che co chesta cevettola facea mille male a li figlie de mamma: e benuta a Napole a fare sto sarzízio, se mese de casa vecino a no felosofo, lo quale non potea dormire la notte pe lo frusciamiento che le facea lo canto o chianto de la coccovaja. [100] Pe la quale cosa, sapenno che sta jenimma de vordiello nn'era la patrona, le decette che benesse a sto monte, ch'è famuso pe tutto lo munno, ad avere na penna de l'auciello che parla, che accossí sarria stata cchiú balente ne l'arte soja: ed essa co 'ncantiseme se fece ccà straportare, addove venne pe la farina e nce lassaje lo sacco, pocca deventaje pepierno, ed essa e la cevettola: li quale porzí sarranno mannate a Napole, pe la fontana de miezo Puorto, e nce accacciarranno li pojete de chillo paese na favola, pe non fare a sapere ch'era

everyone should rejoice and serve them enthusiastically for just fifteen days, and that there would be no regrets. (111) They all replied, "We would like to serve not only for fifteen days, but for fifteen years!" Then everyone took their horse or donkey and followed the bird to Monterotondo, where it had a very beautiful palace spring up with fancy rooms, antechambers, bathrooms, stables, cellars, cabinets, and so many apartments where crowned kings could live.

(112) A few days later, when the king of Monterotondo was hunting in the lands of his kingdom looking for more preys, the night caught him outside his borders. Seeing the beautiful palace, he sent word asking the owner to let him spend the night. (113) Jannuzzo, who was in great shape, went downstairs accompanied by gentlemen and pages who all looked like princes and offered the palace to the king with everything inside. (114) The king thanked him for his kindness and their gracious welcome. He went upstairs and found a table generously set up with endless goodies. You could see porridge, ravioli, puffs, meat snacks, frittatas, meatballs, black pudding, sausages, zeppole, stews, pies, veal stews, chicken liver, offals, kneaded capons, delicious treats, strangolapreti, macaroni, lasagne, ingannamarito eggs, omelettes, struffoli, gilded liver, gelatine, small millinfanti pasta, tripes, chitterlings, crushed beans, roasted chickpeas, and so many other concoctions that would have fed Xerxes's entire army.

The king was stunned like a statue when seeing the sumptuously laid table. After he ate and drank, Jannuzzo presented the apple for musical entertainment. (116) Seeing this, the king asked, "What is this apple good for? We ate so much corn, celeries, artichokes, onions, radishes, turnips, quince peaches, apples, pear apples, different types of dark and red grapes, fleshy dark cherries, sour cherries, hazelnuts, pears, peaches, and so much more that I think I witnessed all seasons together at the same time, and now you come up with a little apple?"

(117) "Doesn't Your Most Illustrious Majesty know," Jannuzzo replied, "that this apple can sing beautifully?" "What singing?" the king asked. "You're going to hear it now," Jannuzzo said. And there, a beautiful, harmonious voice and such sweet sounds came out of the apple that cymbals, spinets, flutes, cornets, bagpipes, *colasciones*, and other instruments would not have sounded better together. (118) The king stood with his mouth open, listening to the music. Jannuzzo then asked Ninella, who was sitting at a table near him, to bring the little pitcher, and she placed it on the table. As soon as it was open, the water began to dance with such pleasant moves that all were amazed. (119)

na janara. [101] Ma se volesse contare le cose de sse statole una ped una no' la scomparria né pe craje, né pe poscraje, né pe pescrigno: vasta che quanta statole sarranno a le gallerie, a li ciardine de Romma, de Napole, de Melano, de Venezia e de l'aute cetà fammose, tutte sarranno pegliate da sto monte. Ora dimme tu porzíne che baje facenno».

[102] «Sacce — decette Ninella — ca na sdammecella de la matrèja de lo Rre de Monteretunno m'ha ditto ca jo sarria felice se avesse a buje co mmico, e perzò io nce mannaje l'uneco fratiello mio, lo quale venuto ccà e non essennose dato a canoscere a vossoria, è deventato statola: ora io vorria che me facisse piacere, primma, de restituireme vivo lo fratiello, e dapo' de venire no poco co mico, pe li besuogne mieje, ca nce accattarraje pe schiave de catena».

[103] Responnette l'auciello: «Sta' allegramente, fegliola mia, ca te voglio consolare. Ma dimme: canoscerrisse tu lo fratiello tujo?»

[104] «Cierto ca sí!», responnette Ninella; e cammenanno pe la mano deritta, comme fu becina all'arvolo vedette lo fratiello, che steva co na mano auzata vierzo lo nido de l'auciello. [105] Tanno Ninella corze ad abbracciarelo, e basanno chella fredda marmora parea che la volesse anemare co li sospire e 'nfonnere co lo chianto; ma le decette l'auciello: «L'acqua de ste lagreme non serve ped anemare le statole, ma nce vole n'aut'acqua»: [106] ed accossí ditto jeze l'auciello a 'nfonnerese le penne a na certa fontana, e scotolannole 'ncoppa la statola súbeto aprette l'uocchie, movette le gamme e le braccia, e deventaje ommo comm'era mprimma, lo si' Jannuzzo: lo quale, vistose la sore 'mbraccia, fece n'allegrezza granne, e s'allecordaje de chello che l'aveva ditto lo viecchio, ca pe poco tiempo sarria stato statola isso porzíne. E rengraziate primma l'auciello, e po' la sore, ca l'aveano leberato da chella sebetura, che se bè era de marmola non se ne corava niente, fece quatto passe pe bedere se s'allecordava de cammenare.

[107] Ma Ninella, ch'era tennerella de premmone, vedenno tant'aute scure che stevano pe la mano deritta de la montagna comm'a pesature, pregaje la bontate de l'auciello che se stava ad isso le facesse la grazia. [108] «Sia benedetta, Ninella mia — decette l'auciello —, pocc'haje sto buono core! Vèccote ca pe l'ammore tujo voglio che resòrzeteno tutte!», ed accossí decenno, vagnatose de nuovo le penne e bolanno pe sopra a chelle statole, stizziava l'acqua a le facce loro: [109] ed eccote, a chillo stante, da llà netrire no cavallo, da ccà arragliare n'aseno, da na banna alare, comme se scetasse n'ommo da n'auta fare li spantevellane na femmena, de muodo e de manera che pareva lo tiempo de Deucalione e Pirra. [110] A li quale l'auciello, comm'a masto de campo,

After that, Jannuzzo said, "Bring the speaking bird." When the bird arrived in all its beauty, after looking it over and admiring it, the king said, "My dear, now speak a little." And the bird replied, "I do not only speak—that's what parrots and parakeets do. I can also guess, which is more important."

(120) "Go ahead and guess something about me," the king said. "I know," the bird replied, "that Your Highness, higher than Bologna's Asinelli Tower, has a wife locked up without any reason inside a room, because your stepmother, a veritable shark, took Cicia's two newborn babies from the cradle, replacing them with two little dogs, because she resented your marriage to a woman she did not approve of and hated. They were a male and female. To recognize them, they wore two silver chains. They are the two handsome youths in front of you, Jannuzzo and Ninella; the mother will recognize them by their chains. (121) My Majesty, you acted badly when you sentenced Cicia to perpetual prison without hearing her story. Your barbarian stepmother did even worse when she reduced the small amount of water and bread given her so that it would not have been enough for a magpie. She did all of that to have her die, as would have happened had I not looked after her as someone who owes its life to Cicia."

(122) When hearing this, the king was dumbfounded. He had Cicia freed from prison at once and ordered the wretched stepmother to appear at any cost. The next day, as Pascaddozia believed that Cicia was going to be burned at the stake, she had her tied up completely like a spindle and watched by many guards who mistreated her like a maid who cleaned out the pantry. (123) When they arrived at the palace and the king saw how run down the poor innocent woman was, he ordered to have her untied, hugging her and asking for forgiveness for all the pain she suffered because of him, and that the fault was not his but his stepmother's, who had deceived him. He then asked her to examine the chest of the young man and his sister. (124) Cicia looked carefully, and when she noticed the two silver chains, she began to cry, saying, "These are my children—not the two little dogs that wretched Pascaddozia put into the cradle!" The king then ordered Pascaddozia and those who maltreated Cicia to be cut up into pieces. (125) But Cicia did not want any retaliation, preferring virtuous deeds, so she knelt in front of the king, begging him not to dirty his hands with blood but to mitigate his rigorous sentence on a joyful day like this, and change his judgment. When the king said that he wanted to get rid of the injustice to make good the damage, the speaking bird stopped all discussion. By addressing Pascaddozia and the cruel women and merciless

fece no belledissemo trascurzo, decennole ca pe ammore de Ninella e de Jannuzzo, a li quale era obbrecato, le aveva dato la vita, e perzò che stessero tutte de bona voglia e li servessero co tutto lo core pe quinnece juorne solamente, ca non ne l'avarria fatto pentire. [111] E lloro: «Non sulo — responnettero — pe quinnece juorne, ma li volimmo servire pe quinnece anne perzí!» E accossí ditto ognuno se pegliaje lo cavallo e l'aseno sujo, e fatta na cavarcata jezero tutte appriesso a l'auciello: lo quale, arrevato a li terretorie de Monteretunno, fece nascere 'nnitto 'nfatto no belledissimo palazzo, co tanta commodetate de sale, antecammere, gabenette, stalle, cantine, despenze, e co tanta appartamiente che nce avarriano potuto stare tre Rri de corona.

[112] Soccedette, passate poche juorne, che lo Rre de Monteretunno, essenno 'sciuto a caccia a chille terretorie de lo Regno sujo, sportato da lo desederio de le prede, le còuze notte fora de li confine, e bisto chillo bello palazzo fece la 'mmasciata che lo patrone le facesse tanta grazia de recettarelo pe chella notte. [113] Jannuzzo, che steva 'n forma probante, scese abbascio, accompagnato da genteluommene e pagge che pareano tanta princepe, e afferze a lo Rre lo palazzo e quanto nc'era. [114] Lo Rre lo rengrazaje de lo buono ammore, e recevuto co granne compremiente sagliette ad auto, e trovaje na tavola accossí bona apparecchiata che non se poteva fare cchiú: llà bedive pastune, pasticce, 'mpanate, piccatiglie, torrise, porpette, sanguinacce, saucicce, zeppole, 'nsottestato, sciadune, spezzatielle, fecatielle e bentrecielle, capune 'mpastate, muorze cannarute, strangolaprievete, maccarune, lasagne, ova 'ngannamarite, frittate, strúffole, fecato 'nnaurato, jelatine, mille-'nfante, trippe, cajonze, fave frante, cícere caliate, e tant'aute 'mbroglie che sarriano vastate a tutto l'asèrzeto de Serse.

[115] Lo Rre restaje comm'a na statola vedenno lo bello apparicchio: e dapo' d'avere dato lo portante a le mascelle e sciosciato lo *crò-crò*, Jannuzzo, pe farele sentire no poco de museca, fece venire lo milo. [116] La quale cosa vista da lo Rre, decette: «A che serve sto milo? Avimmo magnato tanta spogne, acce, cardune, cepolle, rafanielle, rapeste schiavune, percoca, mela diece, mela pera, uva 'nzòleca, uva groja, uva tòstola, uva rosa, cerasa majàteche e tostole, visciole, nocelle, pera, pumma, e tant'aute frúscole che m'è pàrzeto vedere tutte le stasciune aunite 'nzémmora, e mo te nne viene co lo melillo?»

[117] «E non sa Vosta Maestà 'llustrissema — decette Jannuzzo —, ca sto milo sa tanto bello cantare?»

«Comme cantare?», disse lo Rre.

«Mo lo siente», disse Jannuzzo: e bèccote ca da dinto chillo milo nn'a-men who mistreated Cicia, it turned them all into statues, with fear and terror still visible on their faces.

(126) The king was very irritated. He did not want those statues in his house or in his kingdom. To get rid of them, he sent them as a present to the king of Naples, who had them placed in front of the university, where you can still see them today. (127) Cicia thus regained her happiness, and the king his wife and children. Jannuzzo became the heir of the kingdom, and Ninella was married to another prince. As they all remembered the miller and his wife, they gave them so much money that they became the barons of a rural fiefdom. Wrapped in a miserable sheet, the angry, lifeless, frozen Pascaddozia teaches the passersby from her site at the university that

"Deceits befall the deceiver, / even if punishments follow later."[vi]

* * *

(128) Tolla's story was so savory, curious, and gallant that this fairytale alone could be called the tale of tales, as it included all stories of Naples. Neither Petruccio nor the Doctor nor I could hold our tongues, praising the talented storyteller, Tolla. During all the years we lived in Naples, we didn't know anything about its beautiful, ancient history. (129) Cecca, whose turn it was to continue the storytelling, when hearing so much praise for her sister and agreeing that Tolla had outdone the others, did not feel like speaking, as she felt a bit bashful. When everyone asked her to do her part and to keep her promise, she took heart and said:

sceva n'armonia de vuce e no suono tanto soave che l'avarriano ceduto cimmale, spinette, chiuchiére, cornette, cornamuse, calasciune ed aute stromiente. [118] Steva lo Rre vocc'apierto a sentire la museca, quanno Jannuzzo disse a Ninella, che sedeva 'n tavola appriesso ad isso, che facesse venire la carrafella, e benuta la fece mettere 'ncoppa la tavola: ed a mala pena la spilajeno, che asciuta l'acqua fore accommenzaje ad abballare pe coppa la tavola, co tanta belle motanze che tutte restàjeno stoppafatte. [119] Dapo' chesto decette Jannuzzo: «Portate no poco l'auciello che parla». E benuto l'auciello, ch'era la cchiú bella cosa de lo munno, lo Rre, dapo' d'averelo buono considerato, le decette: «Bene mio, parla no poccorillo»; e l'auciello responnette: «Io non sulo parlo, pocca chesso lo fanno porzí li pappagalle e li perocchette, ma chello che cchiú 'mporta, annevíno».

[120] «E annevíname quarcosa a mene», disse lo Rre.

«Io saccio — responnette l'auciello — ca Vosta Autezza, cchiú auta de la Torre d'Asine de Bologna, ha na mogliere 'nchiusa dinto a na cammara senza ragione, pocca la canesca de la matrèja toja, pe despietto tujo, che te pegliaste una che essa non t'aveva consegliato, e ped odio che pe chesto portava a la scura fegliola, quanno partorette Cicia le levaje da la cònnola li duje figlie c'aveva fatto e nce mese duje cacciottielle: li duje figlie fujeno no mascolo e na femmena, che pe segnale avevano doje catenelle d'argiento 'mpietto, e chiste songo sti duje belle giuvene c'avite ccà 'nnante, Jannuzzo e Ninella, comme la povera mamma canosciarrà da li nzegnale. [121] E buje, sio Rre, faciste male quanno connannaste a na carcera perpetua la sia Cicia senza sentirela, e peo ha fatto la varvaresca de matrèjeta, che chello poco d'acqua e de pane destenatole nce l'aveva ammancato, de manera che non sarria vastato a na cola: e tutto chesto ha fatto azzò che moresse, comme sarria socciesso se non l'avesse mantenuta io, che songo obbrecato de la vita a Cicia».

[122] Quanno lo Rre sentette sta cosa appe a strasecolare, ed a chell'ora mannaje a scarcerare Cicia ed ordenaje che benesse la matrèja perra ped ogne muodo. Lo juorno appriesso, credenno Pascaddozia che Cicia pe lo manco dovesse essere abbrosciata, la fece legare tutta attorniata comme a no fuso e nce mese mute 'perzone de guardia che la maletrattajeno comme a na vajassa c'aggia scopata la despenza. [123] Arrevate a sto palazzo, e lo Rre vedenno accossí male arredotta la povera 'nnozente, comannaje che súbeto se sciogliesse, ed abbracciatala le cercaje perdonanza de li travaglie che aveva patuto pe causa soja, pocca non ce corpava isso, ma la matrèja che l'aveva 'ngannato: dapo' le decette che guardasse no poco 'mpietto a chillo giovane ed a la sore de lo

Endnotes

i Aesop, the legendary author of Greek fables. Signing with the pseudonym Aesopus Primnellius, Sarnelli published, a few years before the *Posilecheata,* a collection of one hundred comical-serious animal fables in Latin, the *Bestiarum Schola* (1680). The short, moralistic *Lezioni* stage animals and their features to teach lessons about human behavior observed by its author as a priest in Cesena. For an Italian translation, see the elegant edition, *Scuola di Bestie. Bestiarum Schola,* by Antonio Iurilli with a translation by Damiano De Virgilio and a preface by Francesco Tateo (Bari: Cacucci Editore, 2008). See Appendix 1 for selected illustrations.

ii *Arma toja, maneca toja!* (literally 'Your weapon, your handle!')—i.e. you are responsible for your own choices and actions.

iii The practice by Neapolitan women in the seventeenth century of easing childbirth by blowing into a flask. See the entry *agliariello* in Emmanuele Rocco's *Vocabolario del dialetto napolitano.*

iv Sarnelli's Neapolitan *Guida de' forestieri* (1685) describes the city's numerous palaces, churches, squares, fountains and statues, the Sebeto river, the *Tàrcena,* Chiaia, the University (*Studi Nuovi*), Mt. Vesuvius, the islands of Nisida and Capri, and Posillipo, whose fantastic mythological origins are celebrated in this fairytale. See Appendix 2 for an index and selected texts.

v Pozzuoli and Baja are described in Sarnelli's *Guida de' forestieri curiosi di vedere e considerare le cose notabili di Pozzoli, Baja, Miseno, Cuma ed altri luoghi circonvicini,* published by Bulifon in the same year as the Naples *Guida.* See Appendix 3 for selected illustrations.

vi Metaphors abound in this fairytale: *Né chiagneno tanto le bite pe lo taglio de lo potaturo, quanto chiagnevano chiste pe lo taglio che la morte dava a la vita de lo patre* (Vines do not weep as much at the pruner's cuts as the girls did for death cutting their father's life); *quanno l'arba pe la fatica che fa de schianare la via a lo carro de lo sole, tutta rossa, suda de manera che ne vagna li sciure e l'erve tennerelle* (when the dawn got tired from paving the road for the sun's deeply red sweaty carriage, bathing the flowers and delicate grass); *quanno l'arba commenzaje a 'nnargentare lo mare* (when the dawn began to silver the sea); etc.

mmedesemo. [124] Tenne mente Cicia, e bedenno le doje catenelle d'argiento accommenzaje a chiagnere decenno: «Chiste songo li figlie mieje, e no' li cacciottielle che chella cana de Pascaddozia me mese dinto la cònnola!» Tanno lo Rre ordenaje che tanto Pascaddozia, quanto chille che aveano maletrattata Cicia, fossero tagliate a piezze. [125] Ma Cicia non volenno rennere male pe male, ma cchiú priesto bene, s'addenocchiaje 'nnanze a lo Rre pregannolo che non se sedognesse le mmano de lo sango sujo: ma a no juorno d'allegrezza metegasse lo regore e motasse la settenzia; e decenno lo Rre ca nne voleva cacciare lo fràceto, l'auciello che parlava levaje la defferenzia: pocca parlanno a l'aurecchie de Pascaddozia, de le dammecelle crodele e dell'uommene senza piatate c'avevano maletrattata Cicia, le fice deventare tanta statole, 'n faccia a le quale ancora se vede lo jajo e lo terrore.

[126] Lo Rre, che beramente era 'nzorfato, non voze che chelle statole stassero né 'n casa né a lo Regno sujo, ma pe levareselle da tuorno le mannaje pe regalo a lo Rre de Napole, lo quale le fece mettere a li Studie prubbeche, dove lo juorno d'oje se vedono. [127] Accossí Cicia deventaje felice, lo Rre trovaje mogliere e figlie, Jannuzzo deventaje arede de lo Regno, e Ninella fu mmaretata co n'auto Prencepe: ed allecordannose tutte de lo molenaro e de la molenara, tanta denare le dezero che se fecero Barune de no feudo rusteco, e l'arraggiata Pascaddozia, fredda e jelata, stace arravogliata dinto a no meserabele lenzulo, da lo luoco de li studie 'nsegnanno a chi passa che

> *'Ncoppa a lo 'ngannator cade lo 'nganno,*
> *E se tarda, non manca lo malanno.*

[128] Fu accossí saporito, coriuso e galante lo cunto de Tolla, che chisto cunto sulo se potea chiammare lo cunto de li cunte, avennoce renchiuse tutte le storie de Napole: pe la quale cosa né Petruccio, né lo Dottore, né io no' nne potévamo chiudere vocca, laudannone la sia Tolla che l'avea ditto: pocca pe tant'anne ch'èramo state a Napole non sapévamo niente de tanta belle antechetate. [129] Ma Cecca, a la quale toccava secotare la 'mpresa, sentenno tanta grolie de la sore, e parennole ad essa porzíne che Tolla aveva avanzato l'aute, le mancaje l'armo de parlare, e steva meza vregognosa: quanno pregata da tutte che facesse la parte soja, pe no' mancare a la 'mprommesa, fece de la trippa corazzone ed accossí decette:

LA GALLENELLA

CUNTO QUARTO

[1] No gran Dottore abbesogna che fosse chi decette ca l'ommo comme nasce accossí pasce. E se maje villano fece azzione de galant'ommo, o fu jannizzero o cuorvo janco: pocca da le cevettole non nasceno aquele, né da le ciàvole palumme. E perzò se sole dicere: pratteca co chi è meglio de tene e falle le spese: perché chi meglio nasce, meglio procede, e chi dorme co cane non se nn'àuza senza púllece. Comme ve sacredarrite se sentarrite sto cunto che ve songo pe dicere.

[2] Contava chella bon'arma de Pascarella, ch'era vava de vàvema, na sera che nce arrostevamo quatto castagne sotta la cennere cauda (e me l'allecordo comme se fosse mone, pocca spedetejannose na castagna me jettaje tanta cenise a l'uocchie che m'abbrusciaje meza parpétola) ch'era na vota a Napole no mercante pe nomme Peppone, c'appe da la mogliere soja, che Zezolla se chiammava, no fegliulo e na fegliola tutt'a no ventre: la cchiú pentata cosa che fosse maje asciuta da lo penniello de la Natura, tanto belle che lo patre voze che se chiammassero lo Sole e la Luna. [3] E perché Zezolla era scarza de latte, o puro perché credeva (comme soleno certe femmene) de farese brutta co allattare li figlie, cosa che fa ghire de male 'mpejo le bone jenimme, le deze ad allattare a na mamma de latto chiammata Cenza, che steva a lo casale de Grummo, addove essa se portaje le creature.

[4] Soccedíje che 'n capo de poco mise venne a Napole, che tanno fuje la primma vota, chillo brutto male (che arrasso sia da nuje e 'n funno de maro vaga!), azzoè la pesta: e lloco te vediste restare la cetate netta comm'a bacile de varviero, pocca l'uommene a sellanta la vota sfrattavano da le case de lo cuorpo, senz'aspettare li quatto de maggio. [5] E comme a pesonante cacciate a forza, l'erano jettate le robbe pe le feneste: e la Morte, che aveva li secotorie, scagno de portare appriesso li sbirre co chelle bocche de fuoco che fanno *bú-bú*, li facea legare da li bubune e mettere 'mpresone a no funno de lietto, co li cartielle: *Banno e commannamiento che nesciuno s'accosta sotto pena*

CUNTO QUARTO

THE LITTLE CHICKEN

(1) Whoever said that people turn out to be the way they are born must have been a great scholar. If a peasant ever acted like a gentleman, it must have been a Janissary or a white crow, because eagles are not born to owls, and magpies do not give birth to doves. That's why folks are saying, "Hang out with someone better than yourself and deal with it," since those who are born better get ahead faster, while those who sleep with a dog don't get up without fleas. My tale will persuade you.

(2) The good soul of Pascarella, grandma of my grandma, told us one night as we roasted chestnuts in the hot ashes (I remember it as if it happened now, because an exploding chestnut threw so many sparks in my eyes that it burned half my eyelid) that there was once upon a time a merchant in Naples named Peppone whose wife, Zezolla, gave birth to a twin brother and sister. They were the loveliest things ever drawn by Mother Nature, so beautiful that the father decided to name them Sole and Luna. (3) And because Zezolla did not have much milk of her own or because she thought, like some women, that she would turn ugly from breastfeeding and compromise the future generation, she had them suckled by a wet nurse named Cenza who lived in the Grumo neighborhood. So she took her creatures there.

(4) It so happened that within a few months, Naples was struck for the first time by the plague—that dreadful disease, may we be saved from it, may it be buried at the bottom of the sea. You could witness how the city got cleaned up like a barber's basin, as people kicked the bucket by tens of thousands without anticipating the May fourth rental deadline.[i] (5) And just like renters forced out of their homes, their belongings were thrown from the windows. To avoid bringing along cops with those fiery shouting mouths, Death and its executioners had them tied up with their buboes and detained inside the bed with a sign that read "Notice and order to stay away at the risk of your lives." Many folks did not want to follow those rules, but in the end, everyone abided

de la vita: e mute che non bolevano stare a sti dícome e dísseste, tutte nce 'ncappavano, pocca se lo miedeco toccava lo puzo a lo malato, l'era attaccato lo moccaturo a lo puzo da li sbirre de la Morte ed era portato presone dinto na sebbetura; se lo patre abbracciava lo figlio, la Morte, che stea vicina, co na botta de fauce faceva no viaggio e duje servizie, pocca ne le scervecchiava tutte duje. [6] Vuoje cchiú de la mamma? Che s'allattava li figlie le 'ntossecava, e se no' se le bedea stennerire e morire 'nnante de la famma. Va trova schiattamuorte e sebbeture! Ognuno s'arrassava perché la Morte, comm'a n'auto Cesare, aveva puosto 'n fronte a li súggeche suoje: *Nole me tagnere!*; e perzò co li cruocche afferravano a li scurisse e le sbalanzavano mieze muorte e mieze vive 'ncoppa a li carrettune co li quale treonfava la Morte, servennose pe Campoduoglio de la grotta de li sportegliune. [7] Era deventata la cetate no campo d'ardiche, e addove scorrevano tanta carrozze non se vedevano che carra, varre varre de cuorpe muorte. Quanto tutte li sienze avevano pe chelle bie scialato, tanto patevano 'n chisto 'nfragnente: pocca l'uocchie non vedevano che carne omana strascenata e magnata da puorce e da cane, lo naso ghieva co le pertosa appilate de vammàce 'nfosa a l'acito, pe non sentire lo fieto ch'ammorbava, l'aurecchie non sentevano auto che lamiente de povere agonezzante, la vocca sempe sputava, comme s'avesse magnato agresta, pe lo revotamiento de stommaco, e se metteva paura de se pascere de l'aria pe lo pericolo che no' le facesse perdere 'n tutto lo sciato: e 'nsomma de le somme, chi era restato vivo parea cchiú muorto de li muorte, pe li patemiente e pe la paura.

[8] Ora co tante che ghiettero a l'aute cauzune nce 'ncappajeno porzíne Peppone e Zezolla, e le cetate restaje comm'a casale saccheato, senza gente, e le case pe n'essere abetate se ne accommenzajeno a cadere. Chille poche cetatine che rommasero, non saccio se pe chiagnere li muorte o pe potere contare lo socciesso a chille che sarriano nate appriesso, facettero fravecare chelle case che restajeno 'mpede, azzò che l'erede, se quarcuno ce n'era comme rommasuglia de la peste, non se trovassero senza le carne e senza le robbe porzíne. [9] Ora mone lo Sole e la Luna, che s'allattavano da la notriccia de Grummo, scappajeno sta mala sciorta e se crescettero comme meglio potettero, pocca la scura notriccia, non avenno cchiú lo soccurzo da la cetate, ed essenno lo munno scarzo, pocca no' nc'erano negozie, e chille ch'erano scappate da la peste stezero paricchie anne a tornarece, fece penziero che quanno po' fossero granneciclle l'avarria lecenziate. [10] E de fatto essenno venute a na certa aitate che quarcuno se ne poteva servire pe create, e potevano lloro 'mmezzarese ad abbuscare lo ppane, Cenza co li fegliule se ne ghiette a la cetate; e portatele

by them. If a doctor took a sick person's pulse, Death's cops would wrap his wrist with a handkerchief and bury him. If a father hugged his son, Death—in waiting—took care of killing both with a sickle strike in a single visit. (6) What about mothers? If a mother breastfed children, she would poison them; if she didn't, she would see them wither and starve to death in front of her. And go find gravediggers and graves! Everyone kept away from each other as Death, like a new Caesar, placed a sign in front of its subjects that read: "Don't touch me!", grabbing wretched folks with hooked clubs and throwing them half dead and half alive onto large triumphal death carts, using bat caves as its capitol. (7) The city had turned into a nettle field—all you could see were running carts filled to the brim with dead bodies. Having enjoyed those streets with all your senses, you now suffered the predicament of seeing human flesh dragged around and eaten by pigs and dogs, with your nose plugged with vinegar-drenched cotton balls to prevent smelling the sickening stench, your ears hearing but the poor agonizing folks' relentless lamentations, and your mouth spitting constantly from throwing up, as if you had eaten sour grapes. It was frightening to breathe in the air out of concern of losing one's breath entirely, so that in the end, those who were still alive seemed more dead than the deceased from fear and suffering.

(8) With so many folks going to the other world, Peppone and Zezolla got struck too. The city looked like a pillaged hamlet without people, with abandoned houses that began to crumble. The few citizens who stayed behind, perhaps to mourn the dead or to tell the next generation about the disaster, had their houses fixed so that the heirs, if there were any left after the plague, would not be without home and property. (9) Sole and Luna, who were breast-fed by the wet nurse from Grumo were spared, growing up as best they could. Without support any longer from the city and with few people around and a lack of business—as it took those who had fled several years to return—the poor wet nurse thought she would send the kids away after they grew a bit older. (10) When they reached an age when they could become servants and learn to make a living, Cenza took them to town in front of their father's house, which was nailed up with walled-up doors and windows. She took them to the dilapidated *basso*[ii] and told them: (11) "My sweethearts, I do not know how to take care of you any longer; you are grown-ups now, God bless you. I have almost no food left. I am a poor, starving beggar, God only knows how I was able to raise you. So you are now on your own. May God help you all and may Heaven show you the right path forward." At these words, Sole and Luna

'nnante la casa addove era stato lo patre, la quale trovaje serrata a martiello, e fravecate le porte e le feneste, te le consegnaje a no vascio de la stessa casa, ch'era deventato no scarrupo, e le decette: [11] «Io non saccio, fegliule mieje, comme covernareve cchiúne, pocca vuje site cresciute a parme, Dio ve benedica, e la provisione m'è ammancata a canne. Songo scura pezzente che mme crepo de famme, e Dio sa comme v'aggio cresciute: ognuno ped isso e Dio pe tutte, lo Cielo ve pozza 'nnerezzare a bona via», e accossí decenno lo Sole e la Luna fecero n'aggrisso co lo chianto, e Cenza, chiagnenno essa porzíne, dapo' che l'adacquaje co mute lacreme le chiantaje comm'a cetrule, tornannosenne a lo casale sujo.

[12] Soccedette mo che stanno faccefronte a chillo vascio na certa segnora, sentíje tutta la notte chiagnere sti fegliule, e le parze mill'anne che se facesse juorno pe bedere chi fossero. E benuta l'arba, co li pennielle de li ragge a pegnere li sciure, ch'erano deventate tutte de no colore pe le folinie de la notte, essa se sosette e bedde sti duje sciurille negrecate pe li male patemiente: pe la quale cosa le fece saglire 'ncoppa a lo palazzo, e addemmannatole chi erano, loro, li scure, non seppero spalefecare comme né quanto: pocca la notriccia, ch'era tutta de no piezo, non appe tanto jodizio de direle chi era lo patre e la mamma loro. [13] La bona segnora, che stea co quarche commodetate, se l'avarria tenute comm'a figlie se non avesse avuta essa porzíne na mano de cracace, che comme a sangozuche se l'azzeccolejavano adduosso, zucannole lo sango da la matina a la sera. [14] Co tutto chesto le deze bello a magnare, e fattole mettere no strappontino a chillo vascio, le faceva stare llà la notte, e lo juorno sempe le refonneva quarcosa pe no' le bedere morire accossí sperute; tanto cchiú che la fegliola, sapenno filare, le dava sempe da fatecare ed essa, c'aveva jodizio comme na vecchiarella, s'ajutava la notte e lo juorno; e lo fratiello ghieva pe li servizie, lesto comm'a sorgente, de manera che chella segnora le pigliaje n'affrezzione granne, e no' le faceva male a patere: e pe poterele chiammare le pose nomme Cecca a la fegliola e Mineco a lo fegliulo. [15] No juorno sta bona segnora decette a Cecca: «Ora, Ceccarella mia, io voglio mettere la vòccola, e pe lo bene che te voglio n'uovo ha da essere lo tujo, e chello ch'escerrà, o pollastriello o pollanchella, te lo voglio dare, pocca sì bona fegliola».

[16] Cecca la dengraziaje de lo buono ammore, preganno lo Cielo che le rennesse tutto lo bene che le faceva. Ed accossí 'n capo de vinteduje juorne ascettero li pollecine, e dall'uovo de Cecca ne schiudette na bella gallenella, co no tuppo 'n fronte che pareva na segnorella. [17] Tanno la segnora, chiammata-

began to cry desperately and Cenza, who cried also, after bathing them with her tears dropped them like hot potatoes and went back home.

(12) It so happened that a lady who lived across the street from their *basso* heard the children cry all night long and couldn't wait for the morning to see who they were. At dawn, when the sunrays set out to paint the flowers that had turned ashen-colored from the night, she got up and, seeing how the two little flowers were saddened from their suffering, took them up to her mansion. When asked who they were, the poor kids couldn't give an answer, because the stellar wet nurse didn't bother to tell them who their parents were. (13) The good woman, who was well-off, would have kept them like her own children, if she didn't herself have a bunch of kids who clung to her like leeches sucking her blood from morning to night. (14) She fed them nonetheless, put a mattress in the *basso* at night, and gave them something to eat during the day so they wouldn't die all alone. She gave some work to the girl, who knew how to spin—busying herself day and night like a smart little old lady—while her brother went out for chores, quick like a sergeant, so that the woman became very fond of them, giving them everything they needed. To call them, she named the girl Cecca and the boy, Mineco. (15) One day, the good woman said to Cecca, "My sweet little Cecca, I want the hen to breed. As a token of my love for you, one egg will be yours. When it hatches, I will give you the chicken—male or female—because you are a good girl." (16) Cecca thanked her for the sweet thought, asking Heaven to reward her for all her charitable deeds. After twenty-two days, the eggs hatched, and a pretty little chick came out of Cecca's egg, with a tuft that made her look like a little lady. (17) The woman called Cecca and said, "Here's your little chicken, Cecca darling; it came out of your egg. Make it grow, don't lose it, and watch out for it, my love!" Cecca thanked her profusely, took it to the *basso*, and fed it with crumbs, holding it on her lap all day.

(18) Few months had gone by when, after several rainy days, a pretty, small lizard came out through a hole in the *basso*, which connected to the mansion, to enjoy the sun. Its head was tapped with gold; the paws looked like small silvery hands; its eyes resembled two rubies. (19) When seeing the lizard, the hen ran to kill and eat it, but out of pity, and because she never fed it with the rubbish other chicken eat, Cecca chased it away, calling out, "*Sho sho*, get away!" She clapped her hands and stomped her feet so that the lizard escaped and returned to its hole, and the chicken flew up to the window of the *basso* next to the mansion, to which Cecca never paid attention, as it was full

se Cecca, le decette: «Tèccote, Ceccarella mia, la gallenella toja, ca chesta è 'sciuta: criscetella, e non te la perdere, sa, gioja mia!» Ed essa, decennole: «A mille grazie!», se la portaje a lo vascio e se la crescette a mollechelle, tenennola tutto lo juorno 'nzino.

[18] Passate poco mise, soccedíje che da no pertosillo de lo vascio, che corresponneva a lo palazzo, ascíje a lo sole, c'avea chiuoppeto paricchie juorne, na lacertella tanto bella che non se potea dicere cchiú: avea la capo tutta sghizziata d'oro, le granfetelle pareano manelle d'argiento, e l'uocchietielle erano justo comme a duje rubbine. [19] La gallenella, che bedde sta lacertella, corze pe spetacciarela e magnaresella, ma Cecca avennone compassione, otra ca maje l'avea fatto magnare de ste schifienzie che magnano l'aute galline, la cacciaje decenno: «Sciò, sciò! Fruste là!», e tanto fece, sbattenno le mmano e li piede, che la lacertella, scappata, se ne tornaje dinto a lo pertosillo sujo, e la gallenella volanno se mese dinto a na fenesta de lo vascio, che responneva a lo palazzo, e che Cecca non aveva maje conzederato pocca nc'erano tanta folinie che parea fravecata. [20] Ora avenno la gallenella sperciato chelle rezze de mosche, sautaje a n'auto vascio de lo palazzo, e Ceccarella, fattese 'mprestare na scalella, sagliette a lo fenestiello, e levatone le folinie vedde no vascio accossí buon'acconciato che pareva na gallaria: pe la quale cosa se tiraje la scala, e calatala a chillo vascio nobele nce scese dinto, pigliaje la gallenella, ch'era tutta 'mbrogliata de folinie, e accommenzaje a bedere chella cammera, addove nc'erano na mano de statole, e nfra l'aute no cavallo d'avrunzo cchiú granne de li cavalle ordenarie, da lo cuollo de lo quale penneva no mazzo de chiave: e mente lo conzederava vedde 'n fronte a lo cavallo chella lacertella ch'essa aveva sarvata da la gallina. [21] La quale lacertella, perché era fatata, parlaje e accossí decette: «Luna, bella fegliola mia, sacce ca non sì benuta ccà dinto senza volere de lo Cielo, pocca chisto è lo palazzo de lo patre tujo lo quale morette a tiempo de la pesta, e se chiammava Peppone Stipa, e màmmeta Zezolla Guadagna, che porzí tanno morette: e sto patre tujo era lo cchiú ricco mercante che fosse dinto st'Armiere. [22] Io songo fatata, e perché aggio avuto mute servizie da la casa toja aggio guardato sto palazzo, e t'aggio conservato da le càrole li panne de lo funnaco: se bè songo stata sempe colereca, sapenno c'avea da passare no male 'nfruscio da na gallina, azzò che non me fosse soccessa quarche desgrazia e non avesse potuto soggiovarete. [23] Ora mo, sia laudato lo Cielo, non sulo è passato lo male 'nfruscio, ma ne songo stata sarvata co le manzolle toje. Perzò io, restannote obbrecata, te voglio dare cierte conziglie che te le trovarraje a l'abbesuogne tuoje, e tienele scritte 'n core e non te ne

of soot and seemed walled-up. (20) The chicken passed through the fly nets and jumped into another flat of the mansion. Cecca took a ladder and climbed up to the window. After cleaning the soot, she saw a beautifully adorned room looking like a gallery. She lowered the ladder into that elegant room, picked up the chicken covered with soot and spiderwebs, and began to scrutinize the room with its statues among them: an unusually large bronze horse with a bunch of keys hanging from its neck. While looking around, she noticed on the horse's forehead the small lizard she had saved from the chicken. (21) The fairy lizard began to speak: "Luna, my beautiful child, you must know that you did not enter this room without Heaven's plan. This is the house of your father, who died during the plague. His name was Peppone Stipa, and your mother's, Zezolla Guadagna—she also died at that time. Your father was the richest merchant in the Armiere district. (22) I am a fairy, and because I received many services from your family, I watched over this house and saved the fabrics from the woodworms of the warehouse, even though I was always fretful about the serious danger from a chicken and the misfortunes that could happen to me, so that I wouldn't be able to help you. (23) But thank heavens, the danger has now passed, and I've been saved by your little hands. Since I owe you, I want to give you some advice to use when needed. Write this down in your heart and don't forget it: *Make sure Sole does not enter this room without showing good judgment. Make sure he marries a poor woman. Keep her rags—they will serve you. If you run into trouble, make use of some milk.* (24) Take that bunch of keys—they are for all the rooms and treasure chests of the mansion and warehouse. Remember that this horse is full of money; you can open it between its neck and shoulders. Half of its belly is full of silver coins, the other half has gold coins and sequins.[iii] Know how to use them and take good care."

(25) Goodhearted Cecca, savvy and smart as she was, kept the advice in her memory's drawer first, then wanted to find out how she could open the horse. Not being strong enough because the horse was too large, she took a ladder and placed it up to the horse's neck, lifting it slightly. When she opened it a bit, a handful of ducats fell out, about one hundred. Thinking that they were plenty for now, she took off the ladder quickly, as the horse's neck rejoined the shoulders, drawn by its own heavy weight. (26) She then began to try the keys to the doors and treasure chests, marking them all in order not to have to repeat the task. Every room was richly decorated with superb paintings and silverware galore. The treasure chests were filled to the brim with ironed

scordare: *Non fare che lo Sole trasa a sta casa se non ha sinno. Non dare mogliere a lo Sole se non poverella, e tiene cunto de le stracce soje, ca t'hanno a servire: e trovannote a quarche guaje siervete de lo latte.* [24] Pigliate addonca sto mazzo de chiave, ca songo de tutte le cammare e casce de lo palazzo e de lo funneco, e sacce ca sto cavallo è chino de denare, e se rapre nfra lo cuollo e le spalle: la primma mmetate de lo ventre è chiena de monete d'argiento, e l'auta de zecchine e doppie. Ora sacciatenne servire, e covernamette».

[25] La bona Cecca, che aveva no 'nciegno mellese e ch'era comprennòteca, se stipaje mprimma li conziglie dinto a lo stipo de la mammoria, e dapoje voze vedere comme potea fare pe raprire lo cavallo: e non vastannole le forze, perché la machena era troppo granne, pigliaje la scala, e pontellatela a la canna de lo cavallo fece no poco de leva, e raprennose tantillo ne cadette na mano de docate d'argiento che potevano essere da ciento: e bedenno ca chille erano sopierchie pe tanno, súbeto levaje la scala, e lo cuollo de lo cavallo tornaje ad unirese a le spalle, tirato da lo proprio písemo, ch'era granne. [26] Fatto chesto accommenzaje a provare le chiave a le porte ed a le casce, e sengatele tutte, pe non avere a fare n'auta vota la fatica, asciaje tutte le cammare aparate da segnure, co quatre soperbie e argentaria a botta fascio: tutte le casce zeppe zeppe e chiene chiene, a curmo a curmo ed a carcapede, de biancarie, de drappe, e de tanta robba de mercanzia ch'era no stopore. [27] Avenno addonca veduto e conzederato tutto, tornaje a chiudere e se n'ascette pe lo fenestiello de la gallenella, zitta e mutta, senza dicere niente a nesciuno, avennose chiene le sacche de docate, co li quale destramente ghieva scampolianno, e accattannose quarche cosella ped essa e pe lo fratiello.

[28] Ma essenno passato quase n'anno, e 'n tutto chisto tiempo non avenno ditto niente a Mineco, se bè essa non facea passare semmana che non ghiesse a polizzare lo palazzo, le cammere e le robbe, se pose 'mpenziero se doveva scoprire a lo fratiello ste recchezze: ma allecordatase de le parole de la lacertella, azzoè de non fare che lo Sole trasesse a chella casa se n'aveva sinno, penzaje che pe lo Sole 'ntennesse lo frate, pocca essa porzí l'avea chiammata Luna, ed accossí accommenzaje a scauzare che jodizio se trovava Menechiello, che addesa era deventato Menecone. [29] E na sera, mente stavano a tavola, le decette: «Mineco mio, che ne facimmo de sta gallenella? Vorria sentire lo parere tujo».

Ed isso: «Magnammoncella!», responnette.

[30] «Comme — disse la sore —, l'avimmo cresciuta co tanta stiente e mo nne volimmo cacciare le mmano accossí sciauratamente? Non sarria meglio accattare l'ova e farela vòccola? C'averriamo li pollecine, e chi-

linen, drapes, and so much stuff that it was just astonishing. (27) Having seen it all and studied everything, she closed up and left quietly through the chicken's window, without saying a word to anyone and with her pockets full of ducats, which she used carefully to get by, buying a little thing for herself and her brother.

(28) About one year later, having never said anything to Mineco all this time, even though she cleaned the mansion, its rooms, and the household once a week, she pondered whether she should tell her brother about all this wealth. But she remembered the lizard's words, not to let Sole enter the house without showing good judgment, and by Sole it must have meant her brother, since it addressed her as Luna. So she began to test Menechiello, now grown to a tall Menecone, to see if he had good judgment. (29) One evening during dinner, she said, "My dear Mineco, what should we do with our little chicken? I'd like to hear your opinion." He replied, "Let's eat it!"

(30) "What?!" the sister replied, "We raised it with so much sacrifice, and now we are going to kill it so brutally? Wouldn't it be better to take its egg and breed it? We would have small chicks, and once they turn into hens, we would have a chicken coop that would be the envy of a prince."

(31) "Why wait so long?" Mineco said. "We'll turn to ashes before we see this chicken coop. Don't you know the saying, *'Better a chicken today than an egg tomorrow'?*" Cecca said to herself, "How lucky that I did not spill the beans, Sole would have squandered all the money like melting snow, without even the judgment of a horse."

(32) A year later, she asked him, "Tell me, dear Mineco, if we found a bag of silver coins, what would you do?" "What I'd do?" he replied. "I would go around carrying a sword and show off in the streets, the way even fellows of lower rank do." "It's a good thing Fate made you a beggar, otherwise you would become one anyway, squandering all the money." She then thought to herself, "It's obvious that Sole has still not gained good judgment."

(33) One year later, she asked her brother again, "Tell me, Mineco, what would you do if we got some money?" "What I would do? I would buy a purse and become a porter to earn some money, since I am now a grown adult and broke, without a penny in my pocket, dried up like the pit of a plum. I keep running a hundred miles but earn nothing."

(34) "What if you found a treasure chest?" the sister said, "What would you do with it?" "I would start a business," the brother replied, "we would live honorably, and I would treat you royally."

ste pone deventate galline averriamo no gallenaro de non avere 'mmidia a no prencepe».

[31] «E chi vò aspettare tanto? — decette Mineco —. Primma de vedere sto gallinaro sarriamo cennere. Non saje ca se dice: *È meglio la gallina oje che l'uovo craje?*» E Ceccarella decette nfra se stessa: «Manco male ca non l'aggio ditto niente, pocca sto Sole averria fatto squagliare tutti li denare comm'a neve, avenno manco jodizio de no cavallo».

[32] Da llà a n'aut'anno l'addemmannaje: «Dimme, Menechiello mio, s'asciassemo no sacco de doppiune che nne farrisse?»

«Che nne farria? — responnette —. Me metterria na spata a lato e ghiarria facenno lo bello ammore pe ste chiazze, ca nce songo manco de mene che lo fanno».

«Buono ha fatto la sciorta — decette Ceccarella — che t'ha fatto pezzente, pocca se non te ce avesse fatto essa te nce sarrisse fatto tune, strudennote lo cuotto e lo crudo». E po' decea dinto a lo penziero sujo: «Va, ca lo Sole non ha puosto sinno ancora».

[33] Passato n'aut'anno tornaje a dommannare a lo frate: «Che dice, Mineco, s'avisse quarche denaro, che nne farrisse?»

«Che nne farria? — respose Mineco —. M'accattarria na sporta e farria lo portarroba pe abbuscareme quarche carrino, ch'addesa so' fatto ommo e mme trovo nudo e crudo, senza na crespa 'n crispo a lo crispano, sbriscio senza na maglia, asciutto comm'uosso de pruno, ca corro ciento miglia e no' mme scappa no písciolo».

[34] «E s'asciasse no tresoro — llebrecaje la sore —, che nne farrisse?»

«Me mettarria a negoziare — decette lo frate — e camparríamo 'noratamente, e te farria stare da segnora».

[35] «Ora susso — dicette Cecca -, lo tresoro è lesto, pure che tune vuoglie fare da vero».

«Da vero, e de che manera! — responnette Mineco —. Non ce perdimmo tiempo, ch'a lo tuorno se fanno le stròmmola, te voglio fare a bedere che sa fare sto fusto!» E restate co st'appontamiento, accommenzaje Cecca a penzare comme potesse raprire sto palazzo senza contradizzione, tanto cchiú che abbesognava avere la licenzia de la Corte.

[36] Ora no juorno essenno trasuta dinto a lo palazzo ped arresediare, e portanno appriesso la gallenella, che la secotava comme a cacciottiello, sta gallenella volata 'ncoppa na boffetta, addov'era no screttorio, accommenzaje a terare fora na scrittura pe na senghetella che nc'era: cacciaje Cecca la gallina, azzò

(35) "Well then," Cecca said, "the treasure chest is ready, as long as you are serious." "Really, where is it?" Mineco said. "Let's not waste any time, they are getting ready for the 'stròmmola' games.[iv] I'll show you what a champion can do!" After agreeing with this plan, Cecca began to think how best to open the palace without running into a problem, since she needed to get the court's permission.

(36) One day when she entered the house to tidy up, accompanied by the chicken that followed her like a little dog, the chicken flew up onto a table and pulled a letter through a slot from a casket on top of it. Cecca chased the chicken away to prevent it from tearing the letter apart, drawing it out seamlessly. After cleaning the house, she took the letter and gave it to a student to read, since she did not want to show it to anyone else out of fear that she could get tricked if something valuable was mentioned in it. (37) The student read it—it was a will drafted by the notary Imbrogliacarte [Document Cheater], declaring as universal heir the son from Grumo who was breastfed by Cenza Vozzolosa from the same district. There was also mention of his twin sister who was to receive her portion of ten thousand ducats if she stayed unmarried, or a dowry of fifteen thousand if she was getting married.

(38) Having found the will, Cecca sent for the wet nurse Cenza, and through the lawyer for the poor, contacted the court in Naples. They received permission to open the mansion and to enjoy their father's inheritance based on the straightforward will and the witnesses from Grumo who identified the children of the Neapolitan merchant, Peppone Stipa and Zezolla Guadagna. (39) They set up a warehouse and made plenty of money, not less than the value of the bronze horse, as business was going strong in the city, and the merchandise yielded huge profits.

(40) The time had now arrived for the brother to get married, and he began to walk around with his head above the clouds, planning to enlarge his house and become Knight of Seggio.[v] (41) "Thank God, I have money," he said. "I need nothing else, I will try to become gentry. There are many people with less status and money who moved up—why should I stay behind? Impossible! With a horse like mine, made of bronze and filled with ducats, sequins, and gold coins, you could be a knight for a hundred years. I deserve a title on top of my land, property, and more. I know how to manage!" (42) But his sister, who carefully remembered the lizard's advice, was quick to shut him up by saying, (43) "Stop talking nonsense, dear brother. Keep it to yourself. All that's needed in this house is an honorable poor woman. Although I realize

no' la stracciasse, ed essa la tiraje fora tutta bella e bona. Arresediata la casa, se portaje 'mpietto la scrittura e la mostaje a no scolaro, azzò nce la leggesse, non volennola fare vedere ad aute pe paura che se fosse quarche cosa bona non ce la troffassero. [37] Lejette lo scolaro, e trovaje ch'era lo testamiento fatto da lo parte per mano de Nota' 'Mbrogliacarte, addove deceva che lassava arede generale lo fegliuolo sujo, che stava a Grummo, e lo teneva a lattare Cenza Vozzolosa de lo stisso casale, la quale teneva porzíne la sore, nata tutt'a no partoro, a la quale commannava che se dassero per parte soja diecemilia docate se non se mmaretasse; ma si se mmaretasse fosse la dote soja de quinnecemilia.

[38] Or avenno trovato lo testamiento, mannaje a chiammare da Grummo Cenza la notriccia, e pe miezo de l'Avocato de li povere se 'nnerezzaje a la Vecaria, dove parlanno chiaro lo testamiento, e 'nsammenatese li testemmonie de Grummo comme chisse erano li figlie de Peppone Stipa e de Zezolla Guadagna, mercante de Napole, appero lecienzia de raprire lo palazzo lloro e de gauderese de la 'redetate de lo patre. [39] Accossí accommenzajeno a mettere 'mpede lo funneco, e se facettero no cascione de denare, niente manco de lo cavallo d'avrunzo, pocca erano cresciute li negozie a la cetate e le mercanzie rennevano tresore.

[40] Era venuto mo lo tiempo che lo frate se aveva da 'nzorare, ed accommenzava a ghire co lo cellevriello pe coppa a le cimme de l'arvole, penzanno de 'ngrannire la casa soja e de farese Cavaliero de Sieggio. [41] «Pocca, Dio me le guarde! — diceva isso —, aggio li denare e non ce vò auto, è penziero mio de provare li quarte: nce ne songo state tante peo de mene, che so' passate 'nnanze co manco denare de li mieje, ed io mme voglio restare arreto? Ora chesto non sia pe ditto! Chi avesse no cavallo comme lo mio, d'avrunzo da fora, ma da dinto prieno de docate, de zecchine e de doppie, sarria Cavaliero c'ha cient'anne: no titolo non mme pò mancare 'ncoppa a quarche terra, e ba' scorrenno: io saccio lo cunteciello mio!» [42] Ma la sore, c'aveva a mente l'aviso de la lacertella, steva 'ncoppa la soja, e spezzatole lo parlare 'mmocca le decette: [43] «Appila, fratiello mio, ch'esce feccia! E stipate ssa vocca pe le ffico, ca dinto sta casa non ce voglio auto che na 'norata poverella, ca se bè saccio ch'a respetto de li denare che io t'aggio fatto abbuscare avarrisse la meglio casata de sta cetate, ad ogne muodo te mettarrisse lo fuoco 'nzino, lo pede 'n canna, e te darrisse co l'accetta a le gamme: pigliarrisse patrona e non mogliera, e craje accommenzarrisse co la carrozza, co li pagge, co li staffiere, co chesto e co chell'auto, e quanto ched è, ched è, te trovarrisse netta paletta e 'n chiana terra. [44] Otra che lo matremmonio è comme a no juvo, ed a lo

that with the money earned you could set up the grandest house of the city, you would end up with a fire in your chest, a foot in your mouth, and an axe on your legs. You would end up taking a mistress, not a wife. The day after, you would have a carriage, pages, grooms, this and that, and soon enough you would be with empty pockets, broke, down and out. (44) Without considering that matrimony is like a yoke with two equal oxen underneath, if one is bigger, it destroys the other. Therefore, my dear brother, let's live within our means. Don't mount your head. (45) Take a poor broad, daughter of a good woman, Heaven will like it. She will be your maid, companion, and wife, and we'll both be at peace. I say this for your sake rather than mine, because I could get married and take a large dowry, but I prefer to stay with you and serve you." (46) Cecca's brother saw that his sister's advice would bear some fruit, so he treasured her words. To his sister's great satisfaction, he married a poor, honorable girl who had no companion and brought little or nothing from home, with clothes that were rags falling apart and so worn that you couldn't tell their color. (47) Little Cecca treated her like a sister, primped her from head to toe, and laundered the rags Belluccia (the bride's name) had brought, bundling them up and putting them at the bottom of a chest, as she remembered the lizard's advice to *"Keep her rags, as they will serve you."*

(48) They lived happily for some time. However, true to the old proverbs, whose meaning must be told fully or in part, there is nothing worse than a beggar moving up socially, because the fat gets immediately to their heart, like a well-fed horse that starts kicking. Thus, Belluccia began to hate and loathe Cecca, who behaved like her boss—which in fact she was, subjecting her to her orders. Therefore, she decided to get rid of her, and all day long, her ugly brain turned over and compared precious stones, devising which one would be more valuable. (49) One day, when she was angry and in deep thought, an old woman dropped by who used to sell her cosmetics. (You've got to watch out for certain old women dropping by. They are often like frying pans—as long as they are fine they cook meat on the stove, but when they start to crack and break, they spread fire to the homes of others; they become thieves and rogues, plundering some homes). (50) The old woman said to her, "What's the matter with you, that you are so angry? Your house is filled with goods, Thank God! Your warehouse is like a big sea where all the merchants' rivers of silvery water and golden sand flow in, and you act like an unhappy bride? What's going on? How can I help you? Pay me what I deserve, and I'll take care of it."

(51) "What's going on?" Belluccia replied. "Do you think it is fun to be

juvo li vuoje vonn'essere pare, ca sì uno è granne e l'auto è peccerillo, l'uno scorteca l'auto: perzò, frate mio, stammoce a lo grado nuosto e non ce jammo mettenno 'n case-cavallucce. [45] Pigliate na poverella, figlia de bona mamma, ca farraje na cosa azzetta a lo Cielo, l'avarraje pe bajassa, pe compagna e pe mogliera, e starrimmo tutte duje cojete. E chesto lo dico cchiú pe tene ca pe mene, pocca io mme porria mmaretare e pigliareme la dote mia: ma io aggio cchiú gusto de stareme co ttico e de servirete». [46] Lo frate che bedeva ca li conziglie de la sore le fruttavano quarcosa, fece capetale de ste parole, e co gusto granne de Cecca se 'nguadiaje na povera figlia de mamma, 'norata, sí, ma che non aveva nesciuno ped essa, e poco e niente asceva de casa, pocca li vestite erano accossí arroinate che le cadevano da cuollo, e non se sapeva de che colore fossero state, tant'erano viecchie. [47] Ceccarella se la pigliaje cchiú ca sore, la 'ncerecciaje da la capo a lo pede, ed a chelle brénzole spetacciate che Belluccia (accossí se chiammava la zita) avea portate fece no bello scaudatiello, e fattone n'arravuoglio le mmese a no funno de cascia (allecordannose de le parole de la lacertella: *Tiene cunto de le stracce soje, ca t'hanno da servire*) e 'nchiette de jancaria tutta chella cascia.

[48] De chesta manera se stezero pe quarche tiempo allegramente. Ma perché li proverbie antiche sempe so' resciute, ca non se dice lo mutto se non è miezo o tutto: azzoè ca non c'è peo de pezzente arresagliuto, pocca lo grasso le dà subbeto a lo core, e lo cavallo c'ha uorgio e paglia soperchia tira cauce, Belluccia accommenzaje a pigliare 'nzavuorrio e 'n desagro a Cecca, perché chella faceva la patrona, comm'era veramente, ed essa steva sotto a lo commanno sujo: pe la quale cosa penzava de se la levare da tuorno, e tutto lo juorno a la preta paragona de lo male cellevriello sujo non faceva auto che strecare penziere, pe bedere chi fosse de cchiú carate. [49] E mente no juorno steva accossí penzerosa e colereca, venne na vecchia che la soleva servire de russo e d'argentata (abbesogna stare 'n cellevriello a certe razza de vecchie che prattecano a la casa, ca chesse pe lo cchiú songo comme a li pegnate, azzoè, che pe nfi' ca esse songo bone, còceno la carne a lo focolaro lloro, comme songo sésete o rotte, vanno portanno fuoco a le ccase d'aute e fanno belle trucche e mucche, e cchiú de na casa n'è scaudata). [50] Ora chesta vecchia le decette: «Ched haje, che staje accossí colereca? A la casa toja, lo Cielo te lo guarda, sbromma lo bene: pare lo funneco vuesto no maro addove tutte li sciumme de li negoziante, co l'acque d'argiento e co l'arene d'oro, veneno a sboccare, e buje state comm'a la zita che male nce venne? Che cos'è? A che te pozzo servire? Spienneme pe chello che baglio, e lassa fare a mene».

a wife treated like a maid? My husband's sister is the boss, and I cannot prevail in any which way." "Is that all there is?" the old woman said. "Let me handle this, you'll see her disappear quickly. (52) Here is what you've got to do. I'll bring you some snake eggs—have her eat them. Little snakes will grow in her body and make her belly look as if she were pregnant. You will alert your husband, "Something fishy is going on here!" and he will kick her out like a ball—*festa finita*!

(53) "Thank you, my dear aunt," Belluccia said, giving her some flour and a slice of lard, hidden from her sister-in-law. "Take this for now," she said. "If your plan works, you'll become my companion lady."

(54) With this promise, the old woman set her plan into action with enthusiasm. The following day, as soon as dawn began to eat up the stars, nibbling like hens, she visited Belluccia with those devilish eggs. After Cecca ate them, her belly grew huge like a barrel in just a few days, and she didn't understand what was happening to her. (55) When her brother saw her looking big pregnant, he became suspicious, asking his wife all night long for advice on what to do about it. The malicious, gossipy, and bad-mouthed wife, who was able to set green grass on fire, got into a bad mood, saying, (56) "Come on, how much advice do you really need? You are too naïve, dear husband! Don't you see how your sister's growing belly makes your horns rise honorably up to the moon? Don't let them spill ink and write about your shame; she wants to cuckold you carrying gun powder when you go hunting the deer. Go ahead and load your gun to strike her down. It is better to kick a pig out of the house than to be pointed at like a deer; it is better to tie a noose around her neck than hear people say: *You tie men up at their horns, bulls with words.* She grows your horns; you make a massacre of her flesh. She wants to show you how to make combs—comb her the way she will remember. She wants to make you a field master, so you know how to direct the horns of the army of the shameless. Stick a knife in her chest up to the handle, and make sure it is sturdy handle!"

(57) This was the good advice of the ungrateful, primped-up beggar. Half suspicious and half pressured by his wife, who incited the dogs' lustfulness, the husband one day called his sister, saying, "Come with me; we've got to do an important chore." (58) They walked as far as forty miles from the city to a godforsaken village where there was a deep valley that resembled a burial ground for horses. So many horses and donkeys had been thrown in there that the ground was littered with white bones in a way that would make you smile. (59) The brother left her there, saying, "Wait here for a while, I am

[51] «E che bò essere — llebrecaje Belluccia —, te pare poco essere mogliera e stare pe bajassa? Pocca la sore de marítemo è essa la patrona, ed io non me pozzo prevalere de no tre chialle!»

«Non c'è auto de chesto? — disse la vecchia —. Lassa fare a mene, ca te la faccio scriare da 'nante. [52] Sa' che buoje fare? Vì ca te portarraggio ciert'ova de sierpe, dàncele a magnare, ca le nasceranno li serpetielle 'n cuorpo e se le farrà lo ventre comme se fosse prena; tanno tu di' a maríteto: *Ccà ncè 'mbroglia!*, ca chillo subbeto la sbauzarrà fora comm'a pallone, ed eccote fatta la festa».

[53] «Te rengrazio, zia mia», disse Belluccia, e datole na mappata de farina e na fella de lardo, 'annascuso de la cajenata: «Tèccote chesto pe mone — decette —, ca si lo designo mme resce te voglio pigliare pe donna de compagna».

[54] La vecchia, co sta mprommessa, cchiú de bona voglia se mese a la 'mpresa, e lo juorno appriesso, appena l'arba, pizzolianno comm'a gallina, se magnaje le stelle, che subbeto s'appresentaje a Belluccia coll'ova de lo diascance: le quale, date a magnare a Cecca, chesta poverella 'n capo de poco juorne se asciaje la panza cresciuta quant'a no tummolo, e non sapeva che cosa fosse chello che l'era socciesso. [55] Lo frate vedennola accossí, che pareva grossa prena, accommenzaje a trasire 'n sospetto, e tutta la notte non fece auto che conzigliarese co la mogliere a che se dovea resorvere. La mogliere, 'mmiciata, lengoruta e forcelluta, che avarria puosto fuoco a l'erva verde, accommenzaje a mettere 'ntressía, decennole: [56] «E che? Tanta conziglie nce vonno? Sì troppo semprece, marito mio! Non vide ca comme cresce la panza a sòreta vanno crescenno le corna a la luna de lo 'nore tujo? Non fare che tu dinghe materia de calamare a chille c'hanno da scrivere le bregogne toje: essa te vò dare lo cuorno pe portare la porvera quanno vaje a caccia a crapie, e tu fanne no carreco de scoppetta pe nne messejare ad essa. Meglio che tu te lieve da casa na scrofa ch'essere mostato a dito comm'a ciervo, è meglio che tu lighe no chiappo a lo cannaruozzolo sujo ch'esserete ditto: *L'ommo se lega pe le corna e li vuoje pe le parole*; essa te cresce l'uosso, e tu fa' chianca de la carne soja; essa te vò dare materia de fa' piettene, e tu falle na pettenata che no' la pozza contare; essa te vò 'mmezzare masto de campo, azzocché sacce 'nnerezzare l'uno e l'auto cuorno de l'asèrzeto de li sbregognate, e tu ficcale 'mpietto no cortiello nfi' a la maneca, che sia d'uosso!»

[57] Chist'erano li buone conziglie de la sgrata pezzente arresagliuta. Quanno lo marito, terato parte da lo sospetto, parte vottato da la mogliera,

coming right back." He turned around, leaving her like a squash, and returned to the city, where Belluccia welcomed him back with immense joy, because she didn't see Cecca return. She began to play the boss, thinking her husband had thrown her off a cliff or killed her. (60) She took as her lady companion the old egg woman whose name was Colospizia Papara, spending lots of money, turning the house upside down, and making a stable of the mansion and the *basso* with the bronze horse—which had already been emptied of all the money, deposited with interest in the banks—and whose head was now joining its feet. She filled it with wood and other junk, out of spite for Cecca, who had kept it so clean.

(61) But let's go back to miserable Cecca, without abandoning her the way her brother did. The unfortunate woman waited for Mineco's return, but wait as long as you like, the man never showed up. Knowing that she had done nothing wrong, she did not despair but waited for Heaven to inspire her how to get out of that labyrinth of treacheries, as she started to realize that she had been tricked by her sister-in-law. She had to busy herself among those bones all night long, worse than a dead mare. Thankfully, it was summertime. (62) In the morning, when the dawn's sweeper wipes off the soot from the sky's chimney with a light broom, after the carbons of the stars had been lit up all night long like in a hearth, a merchant from Foggia arrived from the street above, sent by Heaven, passing by, as he had lost his way. He saw the miserable young woman in the deep valley, helped her to get out, and asked what had happened to her. She told him her story, swearing with one hand on top of the other that she had never slept with a man and that she suspected that she suffered from dropsy. (63) The merchant looked her over carefully and said, "Come on, you ate serpent eggs. I know this from the yellow color of your face. You probably have a bunch of little serpents inside your body. I'm afraid they'll eat up your intestine, and like the serpent giving life to others, you'll end up dead."

(64) Realizing her predicament and believing that this was the big trouble the lizard had talked about, when she would need to drink some milk, Cecca said to the merchant, "My dear sir, may Heaven reward you. Take me to a sheep farm—I remember a secret from a woman who loved me; I need to drink some milk." "I understand," the merchant replied. You don't need to drink milk; I know what's to be done. Come with me. Let's hope for inspiration from Heaven." (65) At a nearby farmhouse not far from the deep valley that the merchant had seen on his way, he respectfully said to the sheep farmer's wife,

ch'ajutava li cane a la sagliuta, no juorno se chiammaje la sore, decenno: «Viene co mmico, c'avimmo da fare na cosa che 'mporta». [58] Ed abbiatose, pede catapede se la sfilajeno nfi' a quaranta miglia lontano da la cetate, a no pajese ièrremo addove nc'era no vallone che pareva la sebetura de li cavalle, pocca tutte l'asene e li cavalle muorte li ghievano a derropare a chillo luoco, e tanta nce n'erano state jettate che steva lo suolo tutto 'nselecato d'ossa janche, de manera che te faceano sorrejere. [59] Lloco dinto la lassaje lo frate, decennole: «Aspetta no pocorillo, ca mo vengo»; e botato carena la chiantaje llà 'mmiezo comm'a na cocozza e se la sbignaje a la vota de la cetate, addove fu recevuto da Belluccia co no gusto granne, pocca essa no' bedenno tornare Cecca, e credennose che lo marito sujo l'avesse o derropata o accisa, accommenzaje a fare de la patrona: [60] e fattase donna de compagna la vecchia dell'ova, che se chiammava Colospizia Papara, spenneva e spennava a muodo sujo, revotanno sottasopra tutta la casa e facennone de palazzo stalla, e chillo vascio addove stava lo cavallo d'avrunzo, lo quale aveva già figliato tutti li denare, che s'erano puoste a li banche e a 'nteresse, e ch'era rommaso co la capo a li piede, lo 'nchiette tutto de legna e d'aute scartapelle, pe despietto de Cecca che lo teneva tanto polito.

[61] Ma tornammo a la scura Cecca, pe no' lassarala comme la lassaje lo frate. Aspettava la negrecata che Mineco tornasse, ma aspetta che buoje, chisto fu l'ommo, che non tornaje cchiú. Ora la scuressa, perché sapeva ca non avea 'mbrogliate matasse, non se desperaje, ma aspettaje che lo Cielo le projesse lo filo d'ascire da chillo laborinto de 'nganne, perché cchiú o manco s'addonaje ca la 'mbroglia veneva da la cainata: ad ogne muodo appe che fare, pocca stette 'mmiezo a chell'ossa, peo de na jommenta morta, tutta la notte, e manco male ca fu de 'state. [62] Ma la matina, quanno l'annettacemmenera de l'arba, co la scopa de la luce va levanno le folinie da la cemmenera de lo cielo, addove comm'a focolaro erano state allommate tutta la notte li cravune de le stelle, venette da la via de coppa, portato da lo Cielo, se bè parea de passaggio, no mercante de Foggia c'avea sperduto la via: e bedenno sta scura giovane dinto a chillo vallone la face saglire, e addemmannannole che l'era socciesso, essa le contaje tutto lo fatto, juranno co na mano 'ncoppa a l'auta ca essa non avea maje canosciuto ommo nato, e che sospecava che non fosse retròbbeca. [63] Lo mercante, avennola tenuto mente buono, le disse: «Va, ca tu haje magnato ova de sierpe, e lo canosco a lo giallore de la faccia: ed avarraje no cuofano de serpetielle 'n cuorpo, li quale aggio paura che non te rosecano le bisciole e tu, comm'a la vipara, danno la vita a l'aute non te nne muore».

"Do me a favor. Take whatever you need, fill a large bottle with milk, have this woman stay upside down over the milk, and watch what happens." (66) To help her even more, the good shepherdess hung her upside down with her feet tied, so that her guts moved to her throat. Smelling the milk, the little serpents slid out through her mouth into the bottle, with none left in her body. (67) The shepherdess was dismayed and horrified, telling the merchant what happened. He gave her a nice present. He saw how poor Ceccarella looked much better right away, like a different person. He saw how beautiful she was, although she was worked up, and as compassion turned into love, he asked her that if she wanted to get married, he would take her with just the dowry of her great qualities. (68) She replied that she accepted, that she owed him her life, and that they would discuss the dowry later on, since she would be able to recover fifteen thousand ducats. (69) Pleased with this happy deal, the good merchant decided not to go to Naples but to take her to Foggia, where he treated her like a queen, as he was very wealthy. One year later, she gave birth to a girl who was beautiful like a painting, and they named her Liviella.

(70) It then happened that Rienzo, Cecca's merchant husband, had to go to Naples and stay there for a few months. He told her, "My dear, blessed wife, I have to go to Naples and stay there over a month, as I have to straighten out business with several merchants of that city, most of all with the wealthiest of them, Mineco Stipa. To go there without you would be like going without eyes or a heart, because your goodness to me earned you all my affection. Therefore, I am asking if you would like to accompany me, since I don't want to do anything that displeases you. We'll take Liviella with us; you know that we can afford it, thank heavens." (71) Hearing her brother's name, Cecca liked the news and replied, "My dear husband, I would never disobey your orders, to be with you I would walk barefoot not only to Naples, my city, but all the way to India, as I owe so much to your generosity." (72) After settling this, they packed things up, rented a carriage, and left early. Approaching Naples after traveling three days, Cecca asked Liviella to say this when they were at Mineco's dinner table: "Mommy dearest, tell me a story!" and to continue asking until she would comply. Having tuned up this bagpipe, they arrived safely at the home of Mineco Stipa, who invited them to stay during the first days.

(73) Mineco welcomed them with immense pleasure, both he and Belluccia did not realize that Rienzo's wife was Cecca, convinced as they were that she had been devoured by the wolves or that the little serpents had eaten up her guts. (74) With the dinner table set the night they arrived by the very nasty

[64] Cecca, vedennose a sto 'nfragnente, e pensanno ca chisso fosse lo cchiú gruosso guajo annunziatole da la lacertella, ne lo quale se doveva servire de lo latto, decette a lo mercante: «Bello segnore mio, che lo Cielo te lo pozza rennere, portame a quarche massaria de pecore, ca m'allecordo no cierto segreto che me 'mmezzaje una che me volea bene, quanto me faccio na véppeta de latto».

«T'aggio 'ntiso — responnette lo mercante —: non se veve lo latto, ma sacc'io comme se fa: viene co mico, ca sperammo a lo Cielo de 'nnevenarela». [65] E portatala a na massaria ch'era poco lontana da lo vallone, e che lo mercante avea veduta a lo benire, co na cortesia granne decette a la mogliere de lo pecoraro: «Famme no piacere, e pígliate chello che buoje: ínchieme no caudaro granne de latto, e po' fa stare co li piede aute e co la capo a deritto a lo latto sta segnorella, e bide che nne vene». [66] La bona pecorara, pe farele cchiú servizio, l'appese pe li piede e le fece venire tutte le bodella 'n canna. Li serpetielle, che 'ntesero l'addore de latto, subbeto se n'ascettero pe la vocca e sciuliajeno dinto a chillo caudarone, tanto che no' ce nne restaje uno 'n cuorpo. [67] Ascette la pecorara tutta sbegottuta e sorresseta, e contaje lo negozio a lo mercante: lo quale fece no buono rialo a la pecorara, e trovaje Ceccarella scura nne n'attemo tanto megliorata da chello de primma, che pareva n'auta. E bedenno ch'era muto bella, se bè stava sbattuta, deventata la compassione ammore, le decette si se voleva mmaretare, ca isso se l'avarria pegliata senz'auta dota che de le bone qualetate soje; [68] responnette ca essa se ne contentava, pocca l'era obbrecata de la vita, e ca 'n quanto a la dota n'avarriano parlato appriesso, pocca essa l'avarria fatto recoperare dapo' quarche tiempo quinnece milia ducate. [69] Lo mercante, ch'era n'ommo da bene, contento de sto buono 'mmàtteto lassaje de ghire a Napole pe sta vota e se portaje Cecca a Foggia, addove la trattava da Regina, perché isso era ricco e non aveva abbesuogno; e 'n capo de n'anno nn'appe na fegliola, tanto bella che pareva na pentata cosa, e le mesero nomme Liviella. [70] Soccedette mo, che avenno da ghire a Napole Rienzo (ch'accossí se chiammava lo mercante marito de Cecca), ed avennocese a trattenere pe na mano de mise, decette a Cecca: «Mogliere mia benedetta, io aggio da ghire a Napole ed abbesogna che me nce 'ntrattenga pe cchiú de no mese, pocca aggio d'agghiustare mute 'nteresse mieje co devierze mercante de chella cetate, e cchiú de tutte co Mineco Stipa, ch'è lo cchiú ricco. Che io nce aggia da ghire senza tene sarria lo stesso che ghírece o senz'uocchie o senza core, pocca l'essere tu tanto bona t'ha 'mpossessato de tutto lo bene mio: e perzò vorria sapere s'haje gusto de venire co mmico, pocca non voglio fare

Colaspizia Papara, Belluccia's companion lady, you could hear a commotion in the kitchen as she tried to catch the curly little chicken to kill and roast it. (75) But the chicken flew through the kitchen without being caught, escaped, and went cackling to the room where it saw Cecca. It sat on her lap (being the first to recognize her true mistress), as if looking for help and protection from those harpies. Colaspizia ran to grab it from Cecca's lap, but defending it, Cecca said, "What manner is this to snatch the chicken from my lap? Leave it alone! There's no time to cook it anyway. We will just eat something else instead." She kept the chicken on her lap, petting it. (77) Meanwhile, the food was served at the table with Mineco and Rienzo, Cecca, Liviella, and Belluccia, and they all began to fill their mouths. While they were eating, Liviella asked, "Oh mommy dearest, tell me a story." "What story!" the mother asked, "What has gotten into you—eat and keep quiet." "Why not grant her wish?" Belluccia said. And Cecca: "One must not do everything children ask for. Otherwise, they become brazen." They continued to eat, and Liviella repeated the same litany: "Oh mommy dearest, tell me a story!" "Please stop it," Cecca said. "You are rude and impolite!" (78) The dinner was about to end, and Liviella kept asking, "Oh sweet mommy, tell me a story!" so Belluccia said, "Tell her a story for goodness sake. Do it for me!" And Cecca asked, "What story should I tell her? I only know the tale of the little chicken," (which she still held on her lap). "How about the story of the gosling?" Belluccia said, laughing at Colaspizia who had joined them to hear the story. So Cecca began:

(79) "The story goes that there were once upon a time two siblings named Sole and Luna, the first without rays, the other eclipsed, as both were starving. Until a little chicken like this one, scraping and digging with its feet, found a treasure which made them wealthy, so that Sole turned golden and Luna silvery. (80) The brother got married to a poor beggar he turned into a lady, but she was ungrateful and cruel like a dark bitch, trying to get rid of her husband's sister by ruining her reputation and killing her, so that she alone could be the mistress, although everything she owned belonged to the sister. (81) So what happened? She behaved like a dog barking at the moon, so that all her plotting went up in smoke. To speak more clearly and not to beat around the bush, you Mineco are the Sole, if you remember, and I am Luna. This is the little chicken, and Belluccia is the bitch who had me eat serpent eggs given her by Colaspizia Papara who is here with us. They made my belly grow large like a barrel, and I would be dead if this wonderful man had not saved me. (82) And these are the generous thanks you owe me, Lady

cosa che te sia de desgusto, e nce portarrimmo porzí Liviella nosta, ch'a nuje, comme saje, commodetate non ce nne mancano pe grazia de lo Cielo». [71] Cecca che 'ntese lo nomme de lo frate appe gusto de sta nova, e responnette: «Io, marito mio, non me parterraggio maje da li commannamiente tuoje, e ped esserete sempe a lato venarria a piede scauze non sulo nzi' a Napole, ch'è lo paese mio, ma pe nfi' all'Innia, c'accossì songo obbrecata a la bontate toja». [72] Co chisto appontamiento se mesero 'nn ordene, e co na carrozza 'allo-ghiero s'abbiajeno co la bon'ora: e dapo' tre juorne de viaggio, abbecinannose a Napole, Cecca primma d'arrivare 'mmeziaje a Liviella che quanno sarriano state a tavola de Mineco l'avesse ditto: «O mammagnora, contame no cunto!» E che non scompesse sta canzona pe nfi' ca essa no' le contava lo cunto. Ac-cordata sta zampogna, arrivajeno 'n sarvamiento a la casa de Mineco Stipa, che l'aveva 'mmitato pe chille primme juorne.

[73] Mineco li recevette co gusto granne, e né isso né Belluccia s'ad-donnajeno ca la mogliere de Rienzo era Cecca, perché se credevano che o se l'avessero magnata li lupe, o l'avessero rosecato le biscere li serpetielle. [74] Ora essennose posta la tavola, chella sera ch'arrivajeno, da Colospizia Papara, ch'era fatta donna de compagna, ma sciaurata quanto nce nne capeva, se sen-tíje no fracasso dinto la cocina, ed era che tanno pe tanno volea 'ncappare la gallenella topputa pe acciderela e arrostirela: [75] ma la gallenella volanno pe la cocina non se fece 'ncappare, anze scappata fora e scacateanno ascíje a la sala addove, veduta Cecca, se le jeze a mettere 'nzino (pocca essa fuje la prim-ma a canoscere la vera patrona soja) quase cercannole ajuto e defesa contra de chelle arpie. Corze Colospizia pe sceccarela da lo sino de Cecca, e Cecca defennennola decette: [76] «E che crianza è chesta de sciccareme la gallenella da lo sino mio? Lassela stare! Tanto pe tanto non èje ora d'apparecchiarela, magnarrimmo stammattina quarch'auta cosa pe scagno sujo»; ed accossí se tenne 'nzino la gallenella soja, facennole carizze. [77] Se portaje nfratanto da magnare, sedenno a tavola Mineco e Rienzo, Cecca, Liviella e Belluccia, e saccommenzaje a 'nchire li vuoffole: e ntramente che se magnava accommen-zaje a dicere Liviella: «O mammagnora, contame no cunto!»

«Che cunto! — facea la mamma —. Ente golio che t'è benuto: magna, se vuoje magnare».

«E ched è ca le daje sto gusto?», decette Belluccia.

E Cecca: «Non abbesogna fare tutto chello che diceno ste peccerelle, ca po' se fanno troppo sfacciate». E secotanno a magnare, Liviella llebrecava la stessa canzona: «O mammagnora, contame no cunto!»

Belluccia, for having deloused you and turned your rags into royal drapes. If you do not remember, I do!" Getting up from the table, Cecca opened the large chest where she had placed Belluccia's rags, turning it upside down and saying, "This is the inheritance that you brought to my house. After I raised you to your present state, you treated me like you wouldn't treat your worst enemy. Ungrateful, miserable, wretched little woman! Is this the way you treat my brother's property? Without opening this chest during all these years and without remembering your shameful past." Saying this, she threw the rags into Belluccia's face.

(84) The husband, witnessing it all, and Mineco, recognizing the story, sat there like mummies, and the miserable Belluccia kept changing color, had one of her gout attacks, fell on the floor hitting her head against the marble windowsill, and died. (85) Shocked and repenting his error, the brother went to his sister, asking for forgiveness and telling her that he wanted to make good and treat her better than in the past, that his misdeed was his wretched wife's fault. Making peace between them with good words, Rienzo said that he wanted to give Mineco his sister as his wife, Cecca's very dear friend, and that his entire family was going to move to Naples to enjoy life together.

(86) Mineco accepted the offer, even more so as deceased Belluccia never gave him any children and had pretty much ruined the house. To give Cecca some satisfaction, he asked his servants to find Colospizia Papara. But she had witnessed the outburst and her mistress's death, realizing that she had been found out. Foreseeing a bad day even though it was night, she went to hide in the bronze horse, hoping not to be discovered. (87) As they were all looking for her throughout the house and going down to the *basso* with the headless bronze horse, the lizard on top of the horse's shoulders opened its mouth and said, "Don't look any further, because the bad witch of Colaspina Papara who plotted all the evil suffered by Cecca is in here. Go ahead and take that big bag down there, fill it with straw and stuff it into the horse, then set it on fire. That's how this awful creature—witch, baby-eater, bloodsucker and mother of the devil—deserves to die." (88) So spoke the lizard, and that's what Rienzo and Mineco did, so that pig was overcome by smoke and flames and died like an exploding bladder. Picking up her body they had it thrown into a latrine, walling it up.

(89) Mineco no longer wanted to keep the death machine of that witch in the house. He sold the body of the smoked horse to a merchant at the Campane district, who had canons and other tools made of it. When an important

«E no' la vuoje scompere? — decette Cecca —. Sì proprio sfacciata, presentosa!» [78] Stanno po' 'n fine de la tavola, e llebrecanno Liviella: «O mammagnora, contame no cunto!», e Belluccia: «Contancíllo — decette — previta toja, fallo pe l'ammore mio».

E Cecca: «Che cunto — llebrecaje — le voglio dicere? Non saccio auto cunto che chillo de la gallenella» (e 'ntanto teneva 'nzino la gallenella soja).

«Sia porzí de la papara!», decette Belluccia, redenno 'n faccia a Colospizia ch'era venuta pe sentire lo cunto. E Cecca accommenzaje:

[79] «Dice ch'era na vota no frate e na sora, chiammate lo Sole e la Luna, ma l'uno senza ragge e l'auta aggrissata, pocca se morevano de famme: ora na gallenella, justo comm'a chesta, raspanno e scavanno co li piede asciaje no tresoro co lo quale se fecero ricche, e lo Sole se fece d'oro e la Luna d'argiento. [80] Ora lo frate, 'nzoratose, pegliaje pe mogliera na scura pezzente e la fece segnora, ma chesta, sgrata e scanoscente, anze cchiú crodele de na perra mora, cercaje de cacciare da lo munno, co levarele la repotazione e la vita, la sore de lo marito, pe potere essa sola fare la patrona quanno quant'aveva era de chella. [81] Ma che? Essa fice comme fa lo cane ch'abbaja a la luna: azzoè che tanta màchene soje ghiezero 'n fummo. E per parlare cchiú chiaro, e non tirarela cchiú a luongo: tu, Mineco, sì lo Sole, si te l'allecuorde, ed io songo la Luna; chesta è la gallenella, e Belluccia è la mora che pe tarrafinareme me deze a magnare l'ova de sierpe datole da Colospizia Papara ccà presente, che mme fecero abbottare la panza quanto a no varratummolo, e ne sarria morta si sto buono segnore non m'avesse sarvata. [82] E cheste songo le mille grazie, sia Belluccia, che mme devive, ped averete levato li peducchie da cuollo e fattote deventare le brenzole drappe de Regina: ma se non te l'allecuorde tune me n'allecordo muto bene io!» E sosutase da tavola raprette Cecca lo cascione addove avea puosto le brenzole de Belluccia, e botato sotta lo funno, le decette: [83] «Chesta è l'aredetà c'haje portato a la casa mia: ed avennote io posta a lo stato addove te truove, m'haje trattato de manera che non l'avarrisse fatto a no nnemmico capetale. Sgrata, scanoscente, vrenzolosa, pettolella, scuro cuorpo! Chisto è lo penziero che haje de le robbe de fràtemo? Che 'n tant'anne non avive manco apierto sto cascione e non t'iére abbeduta de le bregogne toje»: e accossí decenno le jettaje le brenzole 'n faccia.

[84] Lo marito, che vedde chesto, e Mineco, che 'ntese lo negozio, restajeno comm'a mummia, e a la negra Belluccia no colore le sceva e n'auto le traseva: tanto che benutole na gotta, ch'essa nne soleva patire, chiavaje de cuorpo 'n terra e deze de capo a lo marmoro de la fenesta, addove nce lassaje

knight passed that street and saw a leg of the horse, he wanted to know how to find the body. (90) The merchant said that he had it melted down. Had he come one week before, he would have found the entire body, although without its head and neck, which were left at the house of Mineco Stipa in the Armieri district. (91) The knight went there out of curiosity, and when he saw the beautiful head, he asked if it was for sale and at what price. Mineco, who did business with the knight's family, furnishing them with drapes, which earned him several thousand ducats, gave it to him as a present. Today, you can find it in the courtyard of a beautiful palace just past the Sieggio de Nido, on the street that leads to the Foro Nostriano. The palace itself took the name of Cavallo d'Avrunzo.[vi]

(92) Coming to the end of the story, Cecca realized the vengeance Heaven had made against Belluccia. She took the dowry of fifteen thousand ducats and enjoyed it with Rienzo. Mineco married Rienzo's sister, a beautiful lady. Colospizia Papara, the one with the serpents' eggs, used poison to poison herself. She died in fire, smoke, and stench. Wretched Belluccia, who never had a brain, still had enough of it to sow its seeds, only to find death. Having been the wife of a rich merchant rewarded her only with a tombstone on top of her grave as a reminder of her perpetual infamy, as it read with big letters:

There's nothing worse than a beggar moving up the social ladder.

(93) Everyone loved Cecca's tale narrated by another Cecca, as the plot was beautiful, well described, and narrated very gracefully. All four sisters felt honored, and none had to feel less valuable than the others. They were now waiting for Cianna to tell her story after a recreation, because the little boats began to head towards Posillipo, which threw the sun behind its shoulders like a squash being thrown into a sack. Gracious Cianna, although elderly, without further ado, signaled with her head that she was about to begin, telling the following story: [vii]

lo cellevriello. [85] Lo frate, sorriesseto e pentutose de l'arrore, ghieze ad abbracciare la sore, cercannole perduono e decennole ca la voleva tenere cchiú de chello che l'aveva tenuta pe lo passato: pocca de l'arrore sujo n'era stata causa la mmardetta mogliere. Rienzo, 'ntanto, co bone parole accordannole, decette ca isso voleva dare a Mineco pe mogliere la sore soja, ch'era tanto amica de Cecca, e ca co tutta la casa soja se nne voleva venire a stare a Napole e gaudere tutte quante 'nzemmora.

[86] Azzettaje Mineco lo partito, tanto cchiú ca Belluccia schiattata non aveva fatto maje figlie ed avea arroinata meza la casa: ma pe dare quarche sodesfazione a Cecca disse a li serveture suoje ch'acciaffassero Colospizia Papara; ma chesta avenno 'ntiso lo chiàjeto, veduta morta la patrona, ed essennose canosciuta scoperta, 'nzonnanose lo male juorno si bè era de notte, se jeze a nasconnere dinto a lo cavallo d'avrunzo, credennose ca nesciuno nce avarria penzato. [87] E pocca tutte tutta la casa cercajeno, scise a lo vascio de lo cavallo d'avrunzo, che stea senza capo, la lacertella da coppa le spalle de lo cavallo raprette la voccuzza e decette: «Non jate cchiú cercanno, pocca la janara de Colospizia Papara, c'ha fatto tutto lo male patuto da Cecca, è ccà dinto: pigliate addonca chillo saccone ch'è llà 'n terra, cacciatene la paglia ed anchitene lo cavallo, e po' datence fuoco, ch'accossí deve morire sta razza de vordiello, janara, affoca-peccerille, vommeca-vracciolle, mamma de lo diascance». [88] Accossí decette la lacertella, accossí facettero Rienzo e Menechiello, e chella scrofa affocata da lo fummo e da la vampa crepaje comm'a bessica schiattata. E poje, fatto pigliare lo cuorpo, lo fecero ghiettare dinto a na latrina e chesta la facero fravecare.

[89] Ora Mineco non volenno cchiú tenere 'n casa chillo stromiento de la morte de na janara, vennette lo cuorpo de lo cavallo d'avrunzo, affummecato, a no mercante che stava a lo vico de le Campane, lo quale ne fece fare cannune ed aute 'mbroglie: ed essenno ghiuto no gran Cavaliero a chillo vico, e beduta na gamma de lo cavallo, addemmannaje si lo cuorpo s'asciava. [90] Decette lo mercante ca l'avea fatto squagliare, che se fosse ghiuto na semmana primma l'avarria trovato sano, se bè nce mancava la capo e lo cuollo, lo quale steva 'n casa de Mineco Stipa a l'Armiere. [91] Lo Cavaliero nce ghieze pe coriositate, e beduta chella bella capo addemmannaje se la voleva vennere, e 'n che priezzo la teneva. Mineco, che aveva corresponnenzia co la casa de lo cavaliero, pocca lo serveva de drappe, e co isso se nce aveva fatto na mano de migliara de docate, nce ne fice no presiento: ed oje lo juorno stace a lo cortiglio de no bello palazzo passato Sieggio de Nido, a la strata pe la quale se vace a lo Foro Nostriano, e lo palazzo stisso ha pigliato lo nomme de Cavallo d'avrunzo.

Endnotes

i The description of the plague is reminiscent of Boccaccio's in his Introduction to the *Decameron*.

ii *Bascio*, Ital. *basso*, a flat at street level in Naples, with an entrance door that serves also as window, a sign of poverty (*GDLI*).

iii *Doppie, zecchino*, gold coins; *ducato*, gold and silver coin (*GDLI*).

iv *Stròmmola*, a popular Neapolitan street game of spinning tops launched with a cord (Malato 1986, 154).

v *Seggio, Sieggio de Nido,* Seats of old Neapolitan nobility. The Neapolitan *Seggi* are mentioned in Sarnelli's *Guida de' forestieri* of Naples (ch.ix, 52).

vi *Cavallo d'avrunzo.* The Bronze Horse of this fairytale is mentioned in Sarnelli's *Guida de' forestieri* to Naples (Book ii, 54). Sarnelli claims that the statue had great virtues, which led to the superstition that it helped cure horses' diseases. Apparently, it was later broken up and used for the large bell of the Cathedral.

vii Metaphors concerning dawn, sunrise, and night skies are found in this tale and throughout the *Posilecheata*: *E benuta l'arba, co li pennielle de li ragge a pegnere li sciure, ch'erano deventate tutte de no colore pe li folinie de la notte* (At dawn when the sunrays set out to paint the flowers that had turned ashen colored from the night); *la matina, quanno l'annettacemmenera de l'arba, co la scopa de la luce va levanno le folinie da la cemmenera de lo cielo, addove comm'a focolaro erano state allommate tutta la notte li cravune de le stelle* (In the morning, when the dawn's sweeper wipes off the soot from the sky's chimney with a light broom, after the carbons of the stars had been lit up all night long like in a hearth). Similes include expressions such as *la cetate netta comm'a bacile de varviero* (the city got cleaned up like a barber's basin); *le chiantaje comm'a cetrule* ([she] dropped them like hot potatoes); etc.

[92] Ora, pe benire a la scompetura de lo cunto, Cecca vedde la vennetta che fece lo Cielo de Belluccia, e se pigliaje la dote soja de quinnecemilia docate, gaudennose co Rienzo sujo. Mineco se pigliaje pe mogliera la sore de Rienzo, ch'era na bella segnora. Colospizia Papara da l'ova de li sierpe non n'appe che benino da 'ntossecarese, e morette de fuoco, de fummo e de fieto. Belluccia sciaurata, se bè non appe maje cellevriello, pure n'appe tanto da poterelo semmenare pe coglierene la morte: e l'essere stata mogliere de no ricco mercante no' le servíje ped auto che pe avere 'ncoppa la sebetura na marmora, ma che le servette de perpetua 'nfammia, pocca nce fu scritto a lettere chiantute:

Non c'è peo de vellane arresagliute.

[93] Piacette a tutte lo cunto de na Cecca, da n'auta Cecca contato, pocca lo 'ntrico era bello, descritto bene, e rappresentato co grazia granne: e decettero ca tutte le sore serano fatto 'nore, e che beramente una non avea da cedere all'auta. Aspettavano mo che Cianna contasse lo sujo e desse compremiento a la recreazione, pocca accommenzavano le falluche a benire 'mmiero Posileco, lo quale se ghiettava dereto a le spalle lo sole comme na cocozza dinto de no sacco: e Cianna, ch'era graziosa, se bè vecchiarella, senza farese a pregare, dapo' fatto zinno co la capo ca voleva accommenzare, accossí decette:

LA CAPO E LA CODA

CUNTO QUINTO

[1] Se bè de tutte li vizie se pò dicere chello che decette no cierto foretano de li lupe, che addommannato che nce nne trovasse uno buono, responnette: «Sempe che so' lupe, malannaggia lo meglio!», puro l'avarizia è no vizio accossí brutto che fa benire l'avaro 'nzavuorrio a tutte. [2] E quanno cade dinto a quarche fuosso de desgrazie, nesciuno nn'ha compassione, comme isso non ha compassione de l'aute, potennole soggiovare: anze, comme isso non compiatisce manco a se stisso, facennose male a patere quanno porria stare da segnore, e morenno speruto dinto a lo grasso, comme ve farraggio vedere co lo cunto mio, se me starrite a sentire co la frèoma c'avite sentuto l'aute; se bè aggio paura che le fegliole m'avanzarranno tanto, pe la grazia de contare cunte, quanto io l'avanzo a lo contare de l'anne.

[3] Era na vota na femmena chiammata pe sopranomme Rosecachiuove, la cchiú cosa arraggimma de lo munno, la quale otra de le bellizze soje, azzoè de la capo a brògnola, de la fronte a lattucchiglie, de le ciglia spelate, de l'arecchie longhe e trasparente, de l'uocchie de gatta, de lo naso de cola, de la vocca chiaveca maesta, che pe non parere sebetura, comme s'avarria potuto credere pe lo fieto de lo sciato, non tenea manco n'uosso e stea 'ncrespata comm'a borza de camuscio, de lo cuollo sicco e luongo comme de no sturzo, ed otra de tant'aute isce bellizze, avea tanta bone qualetate che tutto lo paese sujo nn'aveva che dicere ed era la farza de lo contuorno: [4] pocca s'avesse veduto na scura figlia de mamma fare lo tratto pe la famme, non l'avarria ajutata de na spotazzella, tant'era grimma, aggrancata, spelorcia, formica de suorvo, stretta 'n centura, tenaglia de caudararo, lemonciello spremmuto, uosso de pruno, mamma de la meseria, e ba' scorrenno. E puro s'asciava bona paglia sotta ed avea quarche cosella, pocca se cresceva lo puorco, avea lo ciucciariello, tenea na bella massariella, e stea chiena comm'uovo. [5] Ora (vedite mone comme songo le cose de lo munno) avea chesta na figlia, chiammata Nunziella, ch'era tutto lo contrario de la mamma, avea li capille junne comm'a l'oro, lo fronte

CUNTO QUINTO

HEAD AND TAIL

(1) You could say about vices what a countryman said about wolves when asked if there was any good one: "As long as they are wolves, may even the best of them go to hell!" Avarice too is such a dreadful vice that everyone ends up hating the stingy. (2) When some misfortune afflicts them, no one shows compassion, just like they don't show compassion for others when they could be supportive. In fact, they don't even commiserate themselves. They suffer when, instead, they could live royally, and they prefer to die in starvation surrounded by fat, as I will show you with my tale, if you listen as patiently as you listened to the others. But I am afraid the girls beat me with their gracious tales, just as I beat them with my age.

(3) There was once upon a time a woman named Rosecachiuove (Nail-nibbler), the stingiest woman in the entire world. Aside from her gorgeous features, such as a head full of pimples, a lettuce-like curly forehead, peeled eyebrows, long and transparent ears, cat eyes, the nose of a magpie, a mouth huge like a sewer, and her foul breath reminding you of a grave, she was toothless and wrinkled like a suede purse, with a long neck like that of an ostrich. Beyond these and other fine beauty features, she had so many good qualities that everyone in town talked about them. In short, she was the joke of the hood. (4) If she saw a poor, starving broad, she wouldn't even think about giving her a spit, being so close-fisted, miserly, mean, indifferent, tight belted, a furnace pincer, a squeezed lemon, a plum's pit, mother of misery, and so on. Yet you would find some good straw underneath, and she owned a few things. She raised a pig, had a donkey and a lovely small farmhouse, and was well off, loaded like an egg. (5) She had a daughter named Nunziella who was her mother's precise opposite (see how things are in this world!), with golden blond hair, a forehead shinier than a mirror, sparkling eyes, a well profiled nose, a lovely little mouth, a whitish chest, soft hands, and small feet. But that's not all. On top of her beautiful face, she also had a good heart. She was

cchiú lustro de no schiecco, l'uocchie che te parlavano, lo naso sproffilato, la voccuccia graziosella, lo pietto jancolillo, la mano cenèra e lo pede peccerillo: anze ca chesto n'era niente, pocca a la bella facce responnenno lo buono core, era tanto comprita ch'ognuno ne rommaneva stoppafatto, e quanto era avara la mamma, tanto essa leberale: ma non poteva troppo allargarese, perché Rosecachiuove le stea sempe 'ncuollo, comm'a chiuovo che le passava lo core.

[6] Ora no juorno stanno quatto Fate a la ripa de no sciummo, che co l'acqua d'argiento jeva a pagare l'alloggiamiento de lo mare, pe l'affitto de lo lietto che le dava la terra, de la quale isso era l'affittatore, non sapenno comme spassarese a chell'ore accossí caude, che faceano mutare colore a l'erve pe la paura de li ragge 'nfocate de lo sole, se posero a tatanejare e descorrere de lo cchiú e de lo manco (ca de lo ghiusto non se nne parla maje), tanto cchiú ca la matina erano state 'ncògnete a bedere la festa de la Dea Pàlleta, addove erano venute tutte le gente de lo paese. [7] Ed accommenzaje la primma: «Haje visto, sore mia, comm'è fatta brutta la mogliere de Ceccone, e quanno se maretaje pareva na penta palomma?»

[8] «Chesto n'è niente — decea la seconna —, pocca le vasta chella bella grazia che tu pe fatazione le donaste: ca, singhe bella cchiú de Cocetrigna, se non haje no poco de grazia, va te 'nforna! Perché chillo jancore de le carnumme pare comme la neve 'ncoppa la lota».

[9] «Accossí è — decette la terza —, e creo ca ve ne sarrite addonate s'avite tenuto mente a Porziella, la mogliere de Sautafuosse, la quale pe na fatazione che le deze io è la cchiú bella de lo paese, ma è resciuta tanto sgraziata che chille vestite le chiagneno 'ncuollo».

[10] «Ma che ve pare — decette la quarta — de Nunziella, non è na bona fegliola, previta vosta?»

[11] «E che cosa bona — decette la primma — pò essere? Vasta che sia figlia a Rosecachiuove, sporca, sgraziata, e che darria ciento muorze a no fasulo!»

[12] «Che 'mporta chesto? — disse la Fata. — Non sempe cammina la regola: *Comm'è la chianta è la scianta.* Perché se vede ca da le spine nasceno le rose, e da n'erva fetente nasce lo giglio: accossí Nunziella da le spine de l'avarizia de la mamma è nata comm'a na rosa, pe l'affrezzione che sente de li guaje d'aute, e da lerva fetente de chella brutta caira è schiusa comm'a giglio de bellezza».

[13] «Ogne cosa pò essere — llebbrecaje l'auta: — ma chiste tale songo comme a li cuorve janche, e quanno ne truove quarcuna puoje mettere lo

so accomplished that everyone was amazed. She was as generous as her mother was stingy, but she couldn't let go too much, as Rosecachiuove watched her every step like a nail piercing her heart.

(6) One day, four fairies walked along the river, whose silvery waters were rushing to pay the rent for their home in the sea and for the bed the land provided its tenants.[i] Not knowing how to have fun during those hot hours when the grass pales from fear of the burning sunrays, they began to piffle and chat about this and that, as one never talks about serious matters, and about having gone incognito to the feast of the Palladian goddess, attended by everyone in town. (7) The first began: "My sister, have you noticed how Ceccone's wife turned ugly? She looked like a gorgeous butterfly when she got married."

(8) "That doesn't matter," said the second, "the little grace you bestowed on her through a spell is all she needs, because even if you are prettier than Ciprigna, if you lack charm, you can forget about it—a white complexion looks like snow on top of mud."

(9) "That's right," said the third. "I guess you noticed how Sautafuosse's wife Porziella turned out to be the prettiest woman in town due to one of my spells and how she ended up so graceless that her dresses cry out loud."

(10) "And what about Nunziella," the fourth said, "don't you agree that she is a good girl?"

(11) "How good could she be?" the first said. "Don't forget, she is the daughter of that dirty, graceless Rosecachiuove, who will chew a single bean one hundred times!"

(12) "Why does that matter?" the fairy said. "The saying, *The branch is like the tree*, isn't always on target. You can see how roses grow from thorns and lilies from foul-smelling grass. In the same way, Nunziella grew from the thorns of her mother's stinginess like a rose, worrying about other peoples's troubles. From the smelly grass of that sulky face she bloomed like a gorgeous lily."

(13) "All of this is possible", the other said, "but it all sounds like white ravens—if you find one you can consider yourself lucky—because never did a black girl give birth to a pretty child, white like milk, and never did a mangy goat give birth to a lamb with delicate wool."

(14) "All this talk is idle and gone with the wind," said the others, "let's try to understand this matter in its smallest details." "Agreed," the second said. The others replied, "You know what you should do? Dress up like an old

spruoccolo a lo pertuso: perché maje mora fegliaje e fice no bello nennillo
janco comme a lo latto, né crapa rognosa facette agniello co lana jentile».

[14] «Tutto sto trascurzo — decettero l'aute — è 'mmàtola ed a lo viento: cercammo de cacciarene le mmano, de sta facenna, e bederene che nn'è pe
nfi' a no fenucchio».

«Screvite ca io me firmo», decette la seconna; e l'aute: «Saje che buo'
fare? Viestete da vecchia pezzente e valle a cercare na lemmosena quanno la
mamma è sciuta, e s'essa se mosta de buono core e co quarche ammorosanza,
tu dalle na bona fatazione, e se no' fa che te ne nnommena». [15] Co chisto
appontamiento, essenno lo sole ghiuto a temperare li strale de li ragge suoje
a lo sciummo de l'Innia pe correre meglio la quintana de lo Zodiaco, tutte se
reterajeno aspettanno lo juorno appriesso, pe scotolare sto sacco e bedere se
nc' era porvere o farina.

[16] Venuto l'auto juorno, súbeto la Fata, fattose tornare la faccia comme se fosse vecchia de sessant'anne, se mettette no sajo viecchio, e accossí
stracciato che non ce potive appennere no fuso, ed abbistato quanno 'scette
Rosecachiuove se ne jeze a la casa de Nunziella, decennole: «Na lemmosena,
pe ammore de lo Cielo, a na poverella scauza e nuda e senza nesciuno ped
essa! Facitele na lemmosena, moviteve a pietate de sta compassione!» [17]
Nunziella che sentette sta voce accossí affritta, co tutto che steva arrostenno
na sardella ch'era rommasa la sera (perché la mamma l'aveva ditto: «Fammela
trovare cotta, ca po' volimmo ghire a la massariella nosta a fare la ghiornata»),
se sosette da lo fuoco, fece saglire la poverella, e le decette: «Bella femmena
mia, volesselo lo Cielo che te potesse dare chello che boglio io, ca te darria
porzí sto core! Ma aggio na mamma accossí arraggiata, che se sapesse ca io
dongo quarcosa a na poverella ne farria mesesca de sta povera vita: e non c'è
auto ccà de sta sardella: se ne vuoje la capo, sì la patrona, ca de lo riesto non
ne pozzo desponere comme vorria».

[18] «E ched è la capo — disse la pezzente —, auto che na fràola 'n
canna a l'urzo? Dammene quarch'auto poco!»

«Tèccote la coda porzí — decette Nunziella —, e se màmmama dice
niente, dirraggio: Scontamella a la parte mia».

[19] «Puozz'essere benedetta! — disse la poverella —. A gran merzé, lo
Cielo te lo pozza rennere!», e pigliatose la capo e la coda de la sardella se ne
ghiette a le compagne, contannole tutto lo fatto: le quale se contentajeno che le
desse chella fatazione che boleva, ca se lo mmeretava, la fegliola.

[20] Ora mo non passaje no quarto d'ora che súbeto tornaje Roseca-

beggar and ask Nunziella for alms when the mother is out of the house. If she responds with an open heart and kindness, you'll reward her with a good spell. If not, make sure she remembers you." (15) With this plan, as the sun went to cool off the arrows of its rays in the great Indian river to better run the Zodiac's merry-go-round, they all retired, waiting for the next day to shake that bag to see if there was flour or only dust in it.

(16) The next day, the fairy quickly changed her face to look like a sixty-year-old woman and put on an old and horrible, perfectly ragged tunic. She made sure Rosecachiuove had gone out, then went to Nunziella's house, imploring her, "For the love of Heaven, have pity, give alms to a poor, naked, barefoot broad without anyone to help her! Alms please—have pity for my miserable predicament!" (17) When Nunziella heard this sad voice while roasting a sardine left over the night before (her mother had ordered 'Cook it for me, we'll later go to our little farmhouse to work'), she got up from the fireplace, asked the poor woman to come up, and said, "My beautiful lady, if only Heaven would let me give you what I wish, I would give you even my heart! But I have such a stingy mother who would crush me if she knew that I gave something to a poor woman. This sardine is all I have. Help yourself if you like the head; I cannot give you the rest as I would like."

(18) The beggar said, "What's a head if not just a strawberry in a bear's mouth, give me some more!" "Fine, I'll give you also the tail," Nunziella said, "and if my mom complains, I'll say, 'Go ahead and eat my portion.'"

(19) "Bless you," the beggar said. "Thank you, may Heaven reward you!" She took the sardine's head and tail and went back to her companions, reporting what happened. They all agreed to reward the girl with a good spell, as she deserved.

(20) After barely a quarter of an hour, Roseca-chiuove returned, asking her daughter to serve her the sardine. She brought it to her in a small, clay dish without the head and tail. (21) When the mother saw this, she turned around like a wounded animal, grabbed her by the hair, and said, "Quick, go ahead, daughter of a pig, floozy, ugly maid, dirty broad, crushed barrel, womanly garbage—quick, spit out the head and tail if you don't want your head slammed against the wall or pulled with your ponytail!"

(22) "I did not eat them myself," the unfortunate girl said. "I gave them as alms to a poor woman." "What alms?! What alms?!" the enraged big devil replied. "Gluttonous ruin of my house—quick, beat it, get lost, you won't ever set foot in this house again. Go tramp around despised and without money

chiuove, e decenno a la figlia: «Portame la sardella», essa nce la portaje dinto a no piattiello de creta rosteca accossí comme steva, senza la capo e senza la coda. [21] Quanno la mamma vedette chesto se votaje comm'a n'orza feruta, ed afferrannola pe li capille deceva: «Priesto, figlia de scrofa, sgualtrina, vajassona, fonnachera, votta schiattata, priesto, schefienzia de le femmene, vòmmeca mo la capo e la coda se non vuoje essere schiaffata de capo a no muro o strascenata a coda de cavallo».

[22] «Non me l'aggio magnate io — deceva la scura fegliola —, ma l'aggio date pe lemmosena a na poverella».

«Che lemmosena?! Che lemmosena?! — llebrecaje l'arraggiata vava de Parasacco —. Cannaruta, roina de la casa mia: priesto sfratta mo da sta casa, e miettele nomme penna, e no' la vedere cchiú pe nfi' ca lo munno è munno, va sperta e demerta cchiú de lo denaro, ch'è meglio vedere a te sola terrafinata che la casa mia caduta pe lo mal essere tujo!» [23] E accossí decenno, dapo' d'averela 'ntommacata, ammatontata, abbuffata, carfettiata, 'ntofata, sgongolata, co sgrognune, sciacquadiente, serra-poteca, co no quatto e miezo, na mano 'mmerza, no 'ntrona-mole, no mmascone, no secozzone, no sbettorone, na govetata, no parapietto, co rasche all'uocchie e zengàrdole 'mponta a lo naso, ed avennole ammaccate li vuoffole e scommata de sango, la fece vrocioliare pe le grada abbascio, e serrata la porta co na grossa pontella se magnaje chella scura sardella, dannole cincociente muorze, e co sta bella magnata se ne steze tutto lo juorno.

[24] La negrecata fegliola, comme potte pigliare sciato, ca stette cchiú de n'ora addebboluta 'nnanze a la porta, se nne ghiette fora de la cetate, e tanto cammenaje nfi' che la sera, 'mmiero le bintetré ora, arrivaje a chillo sciummo addove stevano le Fate: e bedenno che lo sole, pe dare luoco a le stelle de pazziare, comme fa lo masto de scola co li scolare, se ghieva a nasconnere dereto la porta de l'Occedente, non sapenno addove ghire, pe la paura de non essere cannariata da l'animale sarvateche, se mese a chiagnere ed a sciccarese le zérvole, accossí decenno: [25] «Ah, che non ce fusse maje capetata a la casa mia, sarda de lo diantane, pocca pe ttene so' scapetata de sanetate e sto core mio s'arde d'arraggia e de crepantiglia. Uh, capo, uh, coda, che site state prencipio e fine de le roine meje! Ma che dico? Addove me straporta lo dolore? Che nce nc'entra la capo e la coda de chella scura sardella se de tutto n'è causa chella capo tosta de màmmama, che comme a cavallo caucetaro cchiú priesto darria no paro de panelle toste che no pilo de coda?» [26] E mente accossí voceteanno se lamentava la scuressa, la Fata, che steva llà becino, 'ntese le parole, se

and peace. It is much better to see a lonely derelict out there than to see my house ruined by your bad deeds!" (23) Saying this, she beat and bruised her, blowing her up and crushing her, battering her with her fist, toothbrushes, bottle tighteners, with a two-by-four stick, a slap, a punch at her jaw, a tingler, a jab at her chest, a kick with an elbow, spits in her eyes, and a pinch of the tip of her nose—bruising her jaws, making her bleed and tumble downstairs, and locking the door with a large prop. She then ate the miserable sardine in five hundred bites, happy for the rest of the day with that nice meal.

(24) The poor girl, catching her breath, slumped against the door for more than an hour and left the town. She walked until late in the evening, reaching the river of the fairies around eleven. As the sun began to hide behind the western gate to let the stars enjoy themselves—as teachers do with students—she began to cry and pull the locks of her hair, not knowing where to turn, fearful that she could be torn to pieces by wild animals: (25) "Ah, darned sardine, if only you had never shown up in my house. Because of you, I've lost my sanity, and my heart burns with rage and spite. Oh, head and tail, you are the beginning and end of my ruin! But what am I saying? What is my pain doing to me? Why fault the head and tail of that miserable sardine when it's all the fault of my stubborn mother who, like a wild kicking horse, would rather give away some hard old bread than a small fishtail?" (26) While the poor girl was shouting and lamenting, the fairy, who was nearby and heard her words, changed into a sardine with a golden head and tail and silver scales all over. She put a golden ring with an emerald as big as a hazelnut into her mouth and went towards the riverbank with an appearance out of this world. As the sun was about to tumble, just like the children do at Chiaja, and the sparkling rays of its face moved west, it made the sardine's head, scales, and tail scintillate with such splendor that it blinded you. (27) Nunziella saw this marvel and got closer to grab it, so the sardine threw the ring into her hand, moved away from her, and said, "Don't cry, my beautiful child, I am here to help you. I am the old woman whom you offered the head and tail as alms. To understand how much Heaven loves good deeds and how it rewards even small alms given with a generous heart, I am going to put a spell on you to be the most beautiful woman of this town, to have foresight and good fortune, so that you may get out of any trouble and find shelter before the night falls. Should you not be strong enough, you will come here and call me. I will show you what I am able to do." After that, the gorgeous sardine dove into the water and disappeared.

(28) Nunziella felt greatly relieved by this speech and like a new person.

strasformaje 'n sardella co la capo e la coda d'oro e tutte le scarde d'argiento, e puostose n'aniello d'oro 'mmocca, co no smiraudo quant'a na nocella, s'accostaje a la ripa de lo sciummo che parea na cosa fora de li fore: pocca stanno lo sole pe fare la capotròmmola (comme fanno li peccerille de Chiaja) co li ragge de la faccia, mente se revotava all'Occedente, facenno palommelle a la capo, a le scarde e a la coda de la sardella, faceva no gran sbrannore che te levava la vista. [27] Nunziella, vedenno sta bella cosa, s'accostaje pe pigliarela, e chella le jettaje l'aniello 'mmano, ed arrassatase le decette: «Non chiagnere, bella fegliola mia, pocca songo io ccà pe tene. Io songo chella vecchia a la quale tu diste pe lemmosena la capo e la coda: ed azzò che sacce quanto piace a lo Cielo lo fare bene, e quanto renne no poco de lemmosena fatta co buon armo, io te dongo na fatazione: che tu singhe la cchiú bella de sto paese e che agge tanta prodenzia, accompagnata da na bona fortuna, che puozze ascire da tutte li guaje, e non passarrà sta sera ch'asciarraje recapeto. E quanno le forze toje non vastano, vienetenne ccàne, e chiammame, ca te voglio fare a bedere che saccio far io»; ed avenno accossí ditto, la maravegliosa sardella sommozzaje a bascio, e non se vedde cchiúne.

[28] Nunziella se sentíje tanto sollevata da sto trascurzo che le parea d'essere n'auta da chella de primma, e súbeto accommenzaje a penzare comme avarria potuto fare pe smautire l'aniello, che le pareva d'essere de no gran valore. [29] Ma eccote che bede comparire no mercante che se nne veneva a la via de la cetate, ed essa, postas'a chiagnere e strillare, fece de manera che chillo mercante, lassata la via soja, venesse a bedere che cos'era. [30] Venuto lo mercante, subbeto Nunziella se 'nfilaje l'aniello a lo dito e accommenzaje a dicere: «Ah, bello segnore mio, de 'razia, se mme puoje ajutare non me lassare a sto luoco desierto, che m'aggiano a magnare li lupe. Io songo figlia de no segnore ricco ricco, lo quale essenno muorto, ed avennome arrecommannata a no zio mio, chisto pe gauderese de le robbe de pàtremo m'ha portato a la ripa de sto sciummo, e spogliatame de li vestite buone c'aveva, azzò che non fosse canosciuta, m'ha bestuta de ste stracce, lassannome chiantata comm'a cetrulo: co speranza che o io mme moresse de famme, o levasse la famme a quarch'urzo co ste carnecelle, quanno isso, lo lupomenaro, se la vò levare co le robbecelle meje. Ma pe bona fortuna, avennome tutta spogliata s'è scordato de levareme st'aniello, ch'era de la bon'arma de pàtremo, che creo ca vaglia quarcosa».

[31] Lo mercante, avennoce apierto l'uocchie, e trovannose squitato, se la portaje cod isso, co speranza de pigliaresella pe mogliera e de recoperarese co lo tiempo st'aredetate: e 'n frutto accossí soccedette, pocca se la portaje

She began immediately to ponder how to dispose of the ring, which seemed to be very valuable. (29) Suddenly, she saw a merchant appear on his way to town, so she began to cry and scream so loud that the merchant left the road to see what was wrong. (30) As he approached, Nunziella put the ring on her finger, saying, "My dear sir, please help, don't leave me in this deserted place; the wolves will devour me. I am the daughter of a very wealthy man who died and left me with an uncle. To enjoy my father's property, he brought me to this riverbank, had me take off my nice clothes, and get dressed with rags so I wouldn't be recognized. Then he dropped me like a hot potato, hoping that I would starve to death, or that the little flesh of my body would feed some bear, while he—the werewolf—could enjoy my property. Luckily, after undressing me completely, he forgot to take off this ring, which belonged to the good soul of my father. I believe it is quite valuable."

(31) The merchant understood, and as he happened to be a bachelor, he took her with him, hoping to marry her and eventually get his hands on her inheritance. And this is, in fact, what happened. He took her to his house and introduced her to all his relatives, who swallowed her little story with great pleasure. He married Nunziella, and they lived several months happily together. (32) But one day, as Nunziella was savoring the success of her invented story, her husband said something offensive to her, since no mention of her inheritance had ever been made. She retorted, "Your beard is worth less than the palace broom." (33) Hearing this, the husband got so enraged that he said, "Fine, since the palace broom is worth more than my beard, I want you to take me to your house, I'll see to it to recover your inheritance and come to an agreement with your uncle. Otherwise I'll drop you off where I picked you up." (34) These words caused a storm in poor Nunziella's head. Not knowing how to react but having faith in the fairy, she walked with her husband towards the river. When they were near it, she said to the husband, "Wait here for a moment, I'll be right back." She went to the riverbank, looking intently to see the sardine, but not even a toad showed up. (35) She then began to say, "What was the point of telling the little story of the inheritance and of the palace broom to end up without the gift of life and to be swept away by Death's garbage collector at Pluto's palace? What a wonderful job I've done! I heard that Charon ferries the souls across a certain river to the shores of Hell. I want to cross that river without the ferryman like a carrion, since neither the head nor the golden tail show up." (36) As soon as she named the head and tail, the sardine suddenly jumped out of the water, saying, "I do not want you to drown in a glass

a la casa e co gusto de tutte li pariente, c'avevano agliottuto la 'mmenzione comm'a pinolo 'nnaurato, se 'nguadiaje Nunziella e se gaudettero 'nzémmora pe paricchie mise. [32] Ma no juorno, stanno Nunziella tutta prejata de la 'mmenzione ch'era resciuta, le decette lo marito non saccio che cosa de despriezzo, pocca de la 'redetate non se nn'avea né nova né becchia, ed essa le responnette: «Vale cchiú la scopa de lo palazzo mio che sta varva toja». [33] Lo marito, sentenno chesto, se nne pigliaje tanta collera che le decette: «Orasússo, pocca la scopa de la casa toja è meglio de la varva mia, voglio che tu mme puorte a sta casa toja, che sarrà penziero mio de farete recoperare sta 'redetate ed accordareme co lo zio tujo: autramente io te torno a lassare addove t'aggio asciato». [34] La scura Nunziella a ste parole se sentette no truono 'n capo, e non sapenno comme se resorvere, fidatase de la Fata soja, s'abbiaje co lo marito a la vota de lo sciummo; e quanno fujeno llà becino disse a lo marito: «Aspetta ccà no tantillo, ca io mo vengo». E passata 'nnante, jonze a la ripa, e tenenno mente fitto fitto se bedea la sardella, no' le comparze manco na ranonchia. [35] Tanno essa accommenzaje a dicere: «E che nne voleva fare io a dicere sto cunto de 'redetate, de scopa e de palazzo, pe perdere la 'redetà de la vita ed essere scopata comme monnezza da lo monnezzaro de la Morte a lo palazzo de Protone? Eccote fatto lo becco a l'oca! Aggio 'ntiso dicere ca Caronte pe no cierto sciummo passa l'arme a la ripa de lo 'nfierno, ed io senza Caronte, comm'a carogna, me nce voglio abbiare pe chisto sciummo pocca la Capo e la Coda d'oro non comparesce». [36] Ma a mala pena appe nnommenato la Capo e la Coda, che subbeto la sardella, 'sciuta pe coppa l'acqua, le decette: «Non vorria che t'annegasse dinto a no becchiero d'acqua, pocca ogne cosa, pe 'mpossibele che sia, quann'haje a mene sarrà fatta: e statte secura, ca io non te mancarraggio maje: [37] Ora io saccio tutto chello che t'abbesogna, e tutto sta lesto. Chiamma maríteto e portalo a derettura pe la ripa de lo sciummo, ca da ccà a no miglio trovarraje lo palazzo mio, accossí bello, ricco e granne che nce pò stare no Rre; tutto aparato de velluto e de tomasco, co le feneste d'oro e le gelosie d'argiento, e lo solaro, pe nfi' de lo cortiglio, tutto de prete preziose, e nfra l'auto nc'è, dereto la primma porta, na scopa co le fila tutte d'oro e lo maneco de gioje che non hanno priezzo. Va' llà, e fa' chello che buoje. [38] Ora votate co la faccia dereto e bide a chillo pertosillo, ca llà stace la chiave de lo portone, e bide ca 'nnante a lo palazzo n'è na statola de marmora che se chiamma lo Giagante: chella farraggio fare che parla e che para che sia lo zio tujo, lo quale non volerrà che tu 'rapre lo portone de lo palazzo. Ma saje tu ched haje da fare? Quanno lo vide dille accossí:

of water, because everything—even if it seems impossible—can be resolved through me. Rest assured, I will never let you down. (37) I know what you need; everything will be done promptly. Call your husband, take him down the river's path. One mile from here, you will find my beautiful, sumptuous, and large palace made for a king, adorned throughout with velvet and damask, golden windows and silver shutters, and precious stones on the floor, even in the courtyard. Behind the first door, you will find a broom with golden bristles and a shaft covered by priceless jewels. Go there and suit yourself. (38) Then turn your head and you will see a small hole where you will find the key to the large gate. In front of the palace, there is a marble statue with the name Lo Gigante. I will make it speak as if it were your uncle who won't let you open the palace gate. You know what you'll have to do? When you see him, say these words: "The head and tail told me to enter! Keep quiet!" Don't worry, he will turn again into a statue like before. (39) But be careful, I give you this key provided you return it to me after eight days and leave the palace." After saying this, the sardine dove without waiting for thanks, although Nunziella showed her appreciation with the water that the gracious sardine had touched. (40) She then took the key and went back to the husband. Together they walked barely half a mile when they saw the palace, so tall that it seemed to touch the clouds and so beautiful that it drew admiring gazes just like a magnet attracts iron.

(41) They reached the gate and Nunziella was about to open it when Lo Gigante, in front of it, grasped her arm and said, "Get away from here, ungrateful niece—that's what I'll call you. When I got you undressed, I left you without even a name. This palace is mine. I am the heir of your father's property." Nunziella then said, *"The head and tail told me to enter! Keep quiet!"* Lo Gigante stepped back at once, turning into a marble statue three times the size of a human. (42) Poor Micco (Nunziella's husband) was so stunned that he resembled a statue himself, hesitating to enter after the gate was open. He finally went in, encouraged by his wife. Fifteen grooms dressed in superb liveries appeared, a dozen pages and about ten gentlemen dressed in country fashion but with golden drapes. Six ladies with a companion lady who looked like princesses descended to the courtyard to welcome Lady Nunziella. (43) Seeing this, Micco was stunned, amazed, and astonished by the splendor of the garnets, emeralds, diamonds, rubies, lapis lazuli, and other precious stones, but he was also excited, ecstatic, and happy to inherit such a beautiful palace. (44) They ascended the royal staircase and entered a hall that was so big that it

> *Capo e coda me l'ha ditto*
> *Che nce trasa! Statte zitto!*

E ba' allegramente, ca isso retornarrà statola comm'era. [39] Ma sta' 'n cellevriello, ca io te dongo sta chiave co patto che 'n capo d'otto juorne me la tuorne, e tu te ne jesce da lo palazzo». E accossí ditto sommozzaje a bascio, senz'aspettare d'esserene rengraziata: se bè Nunziella fice la creanza soja porzí co l'acqua che aveva toccato chella graziosa sardella. [40] Ed accossí, pigliatase la chiave, tornaje addove stea lo marito, ed accompagnatase cod isso a mala pena camminajeno n'auto miezo miglio che comparette lo palazzo accossí auto che pareva de toccare le nuvole, e accossí bello che se tirava li sguarde comm'a calamita lo fierro.

[41] Arrivate 'nnanze a lo portone, mente che Nunziella voleva raprire, eccote che lo Giagante che stava 'nnanze a la porta l'afferra pe lo vraccio e le dice: «Va via da ccà, nepote sgrata, s'accossí t'aggio da chiammare, pocca quanno te spogliaje de li vestite te lassaje porzí senza sto nomme: chisto palazzo è lo mio, ed io songo l'arede de le robbe de pàtreto».

Tanno Nunziella decette:

> «*Capo e Coda me l'ha ditto*
> *Che nce trasa! Statte zitto!*»

Ed eccote che lo Gigante se dà no passo arreto e resta na statola de marmora, ch'era pe tre bote la mesura de n'ommo. [42] Lo povero Micco (ch'accossí se chiammava lo marito de Nunziella) rommase na statola isso porzíne pe la maraviglia, e se bè era apierto lo portone non se fidava de trasire, quanno anemato da la mogliere a la fine de le fine trasette: ed eccote da quinnce staffiere co na librèra soperbissema, na dozzana de pagge e na decina de gentiluommene vestute de campagna, ma de drappe tutt'oro; e seje sdammecelle co na donna de compagna che parevano Prencepesse, le quale scennettero nfi' abbascio a lo cortiglio a recevere la sia Nunziella. [43] Micco che bedde chesto, da na parte restaje ammisso, stoppafatto ed agghiajato pe lo sbrannore che le ghiettavano 'n faccia li cravunchie, li smiraude, li diamante, li rubbine, li lapislazzare e tant'aute prete de focile; da l'auta banna non capeva dinto de la pelle, e se nne ghieva 'nn estrece e 'mbrodetto pe la contentezza de 'redetare accossí bello palazzo. [44] Sagliettero pe la gradiata Reale, e trasute a la sala, ch'era tanto granne che pareva lo cammarone de la Cavallarizza a lo Ponte, Nunziella, fatto

resembled the Cavallerizza's giant room near the Maddalena bridge.[ii] Nunziella asked her husband to turn around, showing him the broom behind the door with its golden bristles and the silver and gold shaft adorned with jewels. After using it three times he said to the wife: "I am your slave, kick me!" (45) They walked through the entire palace, which took half a day. They found a table loaded with fish and meat that could have fed an entire army, a true miracle. (46) I am not going to describe the numerous desks; velvet chairs with gold and silver studs; the refined paintings with ebony, ivory, and golden frames; closets filled with silverware; linen chests; huge rooms decorated with historied tapestries; and so many other things that a hundred years and one hundred thirteen thousand reams of paper wouldn't suffice to describe all the wealth. I do not have a brain that could manage all the details.

(47) By now the fairies returned to the riverbank, musing, "Who knows if Nunziella still remembers the poor now that she is surrounded by all that luxury? Because there are those who are full of compassion doing praiseworthy deeds until they get what they were looking for, but once they reach the top, they no longer have their feet on the ground, like monkeys on a perch, and don't bother any longer to help a poor fellow even pick up a straw. (48) For instance, what would a poor man do who earns just a carlino a day? That carlino doesn't belong to him. With his generosity, he would go with anyone, proposing, "Let's go for a glass of wine," and use it. But as soon as the same man manages to set aside a ducat, he endeavors to earn two, three, and with any luck four or and more, and he is no longer eager to spend, not even a trecalli."[iii]

(49) Nunziella's fairy replied, "The fingers of a hand are not all alike, just as people are not all the same. I hope Nunziella doesn't belong to that sort of folks. In fact, as a test, I told her that I was going to lend her my palace only for eight days. Should she change her behavior, I would change her lifestyle. (50) It is often true that some women do some favors to their neighbors, but after they become successful, we count for nothing. The smoke of honor blinds their eyes so that they don't recognize their friends any longer. When they look at someone, their new high rank makes them look at them from a distance, and worst of all, they are ashamed to deal with former friends, as they fear diminishing their status. That is what feebleminded women do who pretend to do virtuous deeds, while those with a genuinely good heart rarely change their nature, and I am sure Nunziella is one of those."

(51) Another fairy then answered back, "What good is all this talk? You

votare la faccia de lo marito, dereto la porta le mostaje la scopa, ch'era tutta de fila d'oro, co lo maneco d'argiento 'nnaurato tutto lavorato de gioje: pe la quale cosa, avennola isso manejato tre bote, decette a la mogliere: «Io te so' schiavo, ed hàime no caucio!» [45] Camminajeno po' tutto lo palazzo, che nce voze no miezo juorno, e nfra l'auto trovajeno na tavola apparecchiata ch'era na bellezzetuddene cosa, addove nc'era magnare de pesce e de carne, c'avarria potuto sbrammare n'asèrzeto. [46] Non ve stongo mo a contare lo gran numero de li scrittorie, la quantetà de le segge de velluto 'ncentrellate d'oro e d'argiento, le petture fine de li quatre co le cornice d'ebano, d'avorio e 'nnaurate, li belle stipe d'argentaria, le casce de cose de tela, li cammarune chine de panne de razza storiate, e tant'aute cose che non ce vastarriano cient'anne e tridece ciento migliara de réseme de carta si se volesse scrivere la recchezza: ca pe dicere le cose ad una ped una, non è cellevriello lo mio che passa pe sta carata.

[47] Ora mo le Fate, essenno tornate a spassarese a la ripa de lo sciummo, decettero nfra de loro: «Chi sa se Nunziella, mo che stace dinto a lo grasso, s'allecorda cchiú de li poverielle? Pocca nce songo cierte che pe nfi' ch'arrivano a chello che boleno songo tutte compassionevole e fanno tanta cose degne d'esserene laudate; comme poje songo puoste 'mperecuoccolo, [e] comm'a scigne 'ncoppa a lo rocchiello non toccano cchiú pede 'n terra, e non ajutarriano no pover'ommo co auzare na paglia da terra. [48] Comme ped asempio sarrà no pover'ommo che s'abbuscarrà no carrino lo juorno: chillo carrino non è sujo, co tutte n'è leberale, ed ognuno che le dice: "Jammo a bevere na meza", isso se trova lesto pe nfi' che ce nn'è. Ma fa che chisto stisso metta 'nsiemme no docato, subbeto le vene 'mpenziero d'acchiettarene duje, e se nce ha fortuna ne vò stipare tre, da li tre a li quatto, e ba scorrenno: ed accossí no' lo truove cchiú lesto a spennere, quanto fosse no tre chialle».

[49] Ma la Fata de Nunziella responnette: «Non tutte le deta de la mano songo socce, né tutte l'uommene songo de na manera. Spero che Nunziella non sia ped essere de sta razza, anze io, pe fare sta prova, l'aggio ditto che le 'mprestava lo palazzo mio pe otto juorne solamente: azzò che se essa cagnasse costumme, io porzí le facesse cagnare stato. [50] È bero che pe lo cchiú cierte poverelle che fanno quarche piacere a le becine, quanno po' veneno 'n quarche grannezza non simmo cchiú niente: subbeto lo fummo de lo 'nore le ceca l'uocchie e no' le fa bedere l'ammico: l'autezza de lo nuovo stato, se nce ne fa guardare quarcuno, nce lo fa bedere de lontananza, e chello ch'è peo teneno pe bregogna de prattecare co chille de mprimma, parennole de perdere de connizione. Ma chesto lo fanno le qualese, che fegneno de fare bene: ma

can tell the good melons by tasting them, and good ham by pricking it with a little wooden stick. I'll go back and ask for alms to see what she'll do and how she treats me. If she behaves well, we will behave better; if not, she'll deal with the consequences." (52) The fairy then changed at once to look like a beggar, killing a dog and splashing herself with its blood and putting a patch on one eye. She went screaming in front of Nunziella's palace, "Give me some alms, gentle folks. Take pity on a poor, crippled woman full of sores who fell from the wheel of fortune and has been ruined by bad luck." (53) The pages who heard the whining and witnessed this spectacle, instead of being moved to compassion, went out with a club ready to chase her away, telling her, "When are you going to break your neck and leave, damn you! Waking up the entire palace, without any regard for the sleeping gentry? Get some work, you dirty maid. Shameless idler! Take off your silly eyepatch. You are fat like a pig but go around pretending to starve. Work, get a job, find a boss, do laundry, serve in the hospitals, make the beds at the hospital for the incurable,[iv] empty chamber pots—filthy broad, gossipy, shitty, farty, shoe sole, cripple, villain, criminal, snotty, floozy, wrinkled, lame, hobbling, chanterelle, total fraud, ragged, worn out, tattered, troublemaker, lousy maid, goiter, crushed barrel, baby killer, bloodsucker, witch, gosling foot, mother of the devil, bad omen, pimp, deceiver of innocent girls, slanderous, loudmouth, scathing, screamer, depraved, wicked, ugly pig, harlot, scrap sower, disgusting, lice-infested, repulsive, show-off, ugly ape, pisser, whore, brothel, slacker, instigator, big fart, abuser, *shew shew,* crap, rogue, spineless, capricious, whorehouse clan, feeble minded, beastly, pretentious, dandyish, pooh! Crap!" Saying this, they threw a club at her.[v]

(54) Hearing this noise, Nunziella came out. She saw how the pages hounded the poor beggar. Instead of acting like a lady, she turned into a hellish fury, turning to these guys: "When are you going to quit, filthy little things that you are—rapists, snotty-nosed crybabies, complainers, wretched, possessed, fart-in-the pants, little devils, penniless servants, riff raffs! Shut up, may you all go to hell! Is that how you treat poor folks in my palace?" (55) Turning towards the gentlemen who laughed and enjoyed the pages' behavior, she began to scold them: "What's wrong with you that you are laughing? Animals that you are—arch donkeys, baboons, dull, stunned, slow, rustic, troublemakers, gluttons, logs of hell, good for nothing, idlers, day wasters, sleazy, sneaks, brainless, preposterous, disgusting pigs, saltless macaroni, jackals, urchins, fools, lasagna eaters, soup suckers, halfwits, old farts, broken pants,

chi veramente è de buono core difficelemente muta natura, comme io tengo pe cierto de Nunziella».

[51] Tanno n'auta Fata responnette: «A che serveno tanta parole? A la prova se canosceno li mellune ed a lo spruoccolo lo presutto: nce voglio ghire io a cercare na lemmosena, e bedere chello che fa e comme me tratta: si se porta bona, e nuje portammonce meglio, e se no', che nce penza essa». [52] Accossí ditto, subbeto la Fata se fenze d'essere pezzente, e acciso no cane tutta se 'nzangueneaje, e puostose de cchiú no 'nchiasto a n'uocchio, se ne jeze a strillare 'nnante a lo palazzo de Nunziella, decenno: «Faciteme na lemmosena, ah, belle segnure mieje, moviteve a piatate de na povera 'nchiajata, stroppejata, caduta da la fraveca de la bona sciorta e arroinata da la mala fortuna». [53] Li pagge che sentíjeno sto sciabacco e beddero sto spettacolo, pe scagno de se movere a compassione, 'scíjeno co na mazza e la voleano cacciare, decennole: «Quanno te rumpe lo cuollo e te nne vaje, che singhe accisa!, c'haje storduto tutto sto palazzo e non haje descrezzione ca li segnure dormeno? Va a fatecare, vajassa petra, pierde-jornata, senza vregogna! Levate sti 'nchiaste, ca staje grassa comm'a scrofa e baje facenno la speruta: fatica, miettete all'arte, trovate patrona, va fa' colate, sierve 'spetale, fa' liette a l'Incorabele, va ghietta cantare, chiarchiolla, cajòtola, cacatallune, cierne-pédeta, chiantella, guaguina, guitta, 'spetalera, sorchiamucco, sgualtrina, sbessecchiata, scianchella, scioffata, quaquarchia, pettolella, perogliosa, mezacammisa, zantragliosa, fonnachera, vajassona, vozzolosa, votta schiattata, affoca-peccerille, vommeca-vracciolle, janara, piede de papara, mamma de lo Zefierno, malagurio de le ccase, porta-pollaste, 'nganna-figlie de mamma, mozzecútola, lengoruta, forcelluta, gridazzara, 'mmiciata, cajorda, scrofolosa, perchia, semmena-pezzolle, fetente, lennenosa, schefenzosa, facce de gliannola, brutta scigna cacata, caca-trònola, nasella, scanfarda, piscia-pettole, lejestra, jenimma de vordiello, maddamma poco-fila, cacciannante, pedetara, mmerdosa, sciù, sciù, schifienzia!», ed accossí decenno tirajeno na mazza.

[54] A sto rommore affacciatase Nunziella, e bedenno ca li pagge se la pigliavano co chella scura pezzente, non fece cosa de femmena, ma de furia 'nfernale, e botatase a chille ragazze decette: «Quanno la scompite, scirpie, smeuzille, sautam'adduosso, peuzille, régnole, zengrille, speretate, pídete-'mbraca, scazzamaurielle, pane-a-parte, sbrammaglia! Zitto, che siate accise! Accossí se trattano li poverielle a lo palazzo mio?!» [55] E poje votatase a li gentiluommene, che s'erano riso e pigliato gusto de chello c'avevano fatto li pagge, le fice na bella 'nfroata, decenno: «E buje ve nne redite, neh? Anchiu-

boiled chestnut scraps, halfwits, rams, fools, idiots, hypocrites, chestnut eaters, mommy-feed-me-this, simpletons, dry spit, hooligans, ceremony shitters, peasants, little milords, dandies! (56) Eaters of cold food and drinkers of hot beverages! Pathetic servants, you walk around spick and span with a spit up your ass, hypocrites! Criminals, wranglers, neck breakers, nuisance, top rubbish, top cheats, top braggarts, voracious, pissed off, brazen, starving, naughty, bunglers, scoundrels, muggers, toilet cleaners, garbage collectors, rogues, losers,[vi] scrambled, riff raffs, brats, ugly servants, bastard mules, dishwashers, sons of bitches, branded, thieves, rams, cuckolds, ignoble fellows, bloodsuckers! Big fat gluttons! (57) Is this the example you give the pages? You think you have to eat bread with treachery? What more have you done for Heaven than that poor woman, pigging out as you please, while she can't even feed herself with a piece of bread? If you want to stay in my house, you've got to treat the poor the same way you treat me. If not, get the hell out of here, pull in your fishnet, pick up trash for the garbage collectors, pick up rubbish in the streets, look for nails in the water running down the creeks, become a porter at customs carrying baskets with ropes, pick up wax from funeral candles, plug latrine conduits, serve as grave diggers, break your neck, and don't get near this house! Don't make me tell you that I'm going to scold you. If I do, it won't be about money." (58) The poor gentlemen, to avoid her threats after so many insults, kept completely quiet without breathing, like a dog with its tail between the legs, like a he-goat who saw a wolf. They all went inside dismayed, frozen, feeling foolish, and stunned. Nunziella took the poor woman by her hand, kissing her and saying, "Don't worry, dear sister. Don't listen to the words of these devils and the poor judgment of these ugly beasts. Come with me; I am going to cheer you up." (59) She took her inside, calling the maids, had her washed, put her in a bed made of golden foam, and had a cake baked for her to have her recover. She then dressed her from head to toe like a grand lady and gave her a handful of ducats, hosting her three days. (60) But as the fourth day approached, the last of the eight days that she could stay in the palace, she said to her, "Bless you, my sister, go with God. I will leave soon too and descend the mountain, because I cannot stay more than another day in this palace. Take these little things and ask Heaven for my good fortune." (61) The poor girl thanked her profusely and went on her way. She returned to the other fairies, telling them all that had happened. The four of them couldn't stop praising the girl's kindness.

(62) At the end of the eight days, when it was time to return the palace

ne, arc'asene, babiune, babane, catarchie, chiafeje, catammare, chianta-malanne, cannarune, cippe de 'nfierno, caccial'a pascere, mantrune, pierde-jornata, porcagliune, varvajanne, macchiune, piezze de catapiezze, luonghe ciavane, majalune, maccarune senza sale, sciagalle, spellecchiune, mammalucche pappalasagna, zuca-vroda, baccalaje, guallecchia, straccia-vrache, scampole d'allesse, verlascie, vervecune, vozzacche 'nzallanute, sarchiapune, scola-vàllane, mamma mia 'mmoccame chisso, maccarone sàutame 'n canna, spite sicche, belle 'n chiazza, caca-zeremonie, pacchiane, caca-pósema, caca-zebetto! [56] Magna friddo e bive caudo! Settepanelle, ca mme ghiate linte e pinte co lo spito a cculo, e po' comme me vide mme scrive! Esca de corte, capo de chiàjete, scapizza-cuolle, scazzeca-luoco, accoppatura de li spolletrune, primmo vullo de li trafane, primmo taglio de li tagliacantune, guzze, scazzate, sbetoperate, sbrammaglia, sbricche, scauza-cane, spoglia-'mpise, scotola-vorzille, annetta-privase, caccia-monnezza, canaglia barrettina, zita-bona, jeffole, verrille, vajassune, mule capetiate, guattare, figlie de guaguina, mercate, mariuole, vervecune, tozzamartine, pignate chine, zuca-sanguenacce! Magna-magna! [57] Chisto è lo buono asempio che date a li pagge? Accossí v'avite da magnare lo pane a trademiento? C'avite fatto cchiú buje a lo Cielo de chella poverella, che buje v'avite da sbrammare a gusto vuosto e chella non se pò satorare de tozza? Si volite stare a la casa mia avite da trattare li poverielle comme a la perzona mia, e se no' sfrattate mo da lloco, ghiate a tirare la sciàveca, ghiate adonanno pezze pe li monnezzare, ghiate adunanno monnezza pe le bie, ghiate trovanno chiuove pe le lave, ghiate co la funa e la sporta a fare lo portarroba a la Doana, ghiate adonanno cera pe l'assequie, ghiate spilanno connutte de latrine, faciteve schiattamuorte, rompiteve lo cuollo, e non ce accostate a sta casa! Ma non me facite dicere ca ve voglio lavare la capo senza sapone, e se me nce mecco ve ne voglio fa' contare, ma non denare». [58] Li povere gentil'uommene che nn'aveano 'ntiso tanta, pe no' la fare dicere, zitte e mutte, e senza pepetare, comm'a cane co la coda 'mmiezo a le cosce, comm'a caperrone c'ha bisto lo lupo, schiantate, agghiajate, 'nzallanute, stordute, tutte de no piezzo se reterajeno dinto: e Nunziella, pigliatase la poverella pe la mano, la vasaje decenno: «Agge pacienzia, sore mia, non guardare a le parole de sti tentille ed a lo poco jodizio de stanemalune, ma viene co mico, ca te voglio arrecreare». [59] E portatala dinto, chiammaje le sdammecelle, la fece lavare, la mese a no lietto tutto scumma d'oro, le fece fare na torta, e po' l'arrecettaje: appriesso la vestette tutta da capo a lo pede comme na segnora e le deze na mano de docate, tenennola pe tre juorne. [60] Ma accostannose lo quarto juorno, ch'era

key to the landlady, to find an excuse for her husband, Nunziella told him, "My dear husband, let's leave this palace. I do not like the climate around here. Let's go back to your town—everything here has been taken care of. If you do not want to see me die, do me this favor." (63) The softhearted husband prepared the carriages, as he didn't want to displease his wife. Before leaving, Nunziella took the key for the gate and said to the husband, "Please wait for a minute. I'll be right back." She then went down to the river to meet the sardine, thank her, and put the key back into its place. She saw a familiar-looking old woman picking up crabs on the riverbank. As she was bending over too much, missing a stone, she fell into the river, and as she was about to drown, the sardine appeared. (64) Nunziella kneeled down and asked her to help the unfortunate woman who was about to drown. With her head out of the water the sardine began to grow so tall, turning into a beautiful young girl who grasped and held the hapless woman to prevent the river from carrying her away, pulling her on shore. (65) She then turned to Nunziella. "You must know, my child, that this is your mother, that ugly wretch who beat you and threw you out of the house. Because I disliked her anger, I made her plummet into the river so that she would die, sending her down like a log to burn in hell, but because of your pleas, I saved her. (66) To understand how virtuous deeds are never in vain, you must know that the beggar you treated well was one of my sisters. As a reward, I give you the palace and all its treasures. However, I want you to visit this riverbank eight days from now to honor the fairies' king, who gave you so many benefits. (67) May God bless you. Go back now. You'll find your husband with a sudden big headache. Don't worry, I gave it to him so he would beg you and say, "Let's stay here, my dear, we'll leave later." And you will answer, "Yes, my dear, I prefer to give up my life to save yours." Go back and reopen the palace and live there happily. He will love you even more, and you'll be happier than a queen. (68) And you, Rosecachiuove, give thanks to your daughter who gave you back the life you gave her. Be reasonable, don't give her grief with your stinginess. If not, you'll be sorry."

(69) Nunziella thanked the fairy and went with her mother to the palace with Lo Gigante speaking no more, had the carriages unloaded, and enjoyed life with her husband, whom she told that the old woman was her new companion lady, to avoid saying it was her mother. (70) When seeing all the riches, the old woman—instead of drowning in them and enjoying herself—didn't know what to do. She wanted to save and fix things and lock them up, take off the rubies and precious red stones from the walls and the floor, doing things

l'utemo de l'otto che nce avea da stare, le decette: «Sore mia, singhe benedetta, vavattenne connío, ca io porzí me l'abbío quanto primma pe lo pennino abbascio, ca non ce pozzo stare a sto palazzo cchiú de n'auto juorno: pigliate ste coselle e prega lo Cielo che me dia fortuna». [61] La poverella, rengraziannola e decennole: «A gran merzé», se ne ghieze, e tornata da l'aute Fate le contaje tutto lo socciesso, tanto che tutte quatto non poteano chiudere vocca laudanno la bontate de sta bona fegliola.

[62] Essenno addonca venuta la fine de l'otto juorne, e avenno da restituire la chiave de lo palazzo a la patrona, Nunziella, pe trovare scusa co lo marito, le decette: «Marito mio, jammoncenne da sto palazzo, ca non me nce conface l'àjero, e tornammo a lo pajese tujo, ca cheste robbe già stanno 'n sarvo: e se non me vuoje vedere morta, damme sto gusto». [63] Lo marito, che ne stea cuocolo e non volea dare desgusto a la mogliere, mese 'nn ordene li carriagge e primma de partire Nunziella se pigliaje la chiave de lo portone e decette a lo marito: «Contentate d'aspettare no poco, ca mo mo torno». Fatto chesto se ne ghieze a lo sciummo pe trovare la sardella, e rengraziatala, tornare la chiave a lo pertuso sujo. Quanno vedde na vecchia che le pareva de canoscere, che ghiea piglianno grance pe la ripa de lo sciummo: ma perché s'era troppo calata, venutale manco na preta cadette dinto a lo sciummo, e mente stea pe s'annegare eccote che comparze la sardella: [64] e Nunziella, addenocchiatase 'n terra, la pregaje ch'ajutasse chella scura, ch'addesa faceva lo papariello: e la sardella, cacciata la capo fora de l'acqua, accommenzaje a crescere, e crescette tanto che da sardella deventaje na belledissema giovane, la quale afferrata la negrecata vecchia la tenne, che lo sciummo non se la portasse, e la cacciaje fora a la ripa. [65] E botatase a Nunziella, le decette: «Sacce, figlia mia, ca chesta è màmmata, chella brutta càira che te deze tanta mazzate e te cacciaje de casa, ed io, 'mpena de l'arraggimma soja, l'aggio fatta precepetiare dinto lo sciummo, pe la fare 'scire de sta vita e mannarela pe l'acqua abbascio comm'a no cippo a lo fuoco de lo 'nfierno: ma pe le pregarie toje l'aggio sarvata. [66] Ed azzò che sacce ca lo fare bene non se perde maje, la pezzente a la quale tu haje fatto bene sti juorne era na sore mia, ed io pe buono miereto te dongo lo palazzo e quanto nc'è: non però voglio che da ccà ad ott'aute juorne vienghe accanto a sto sciummo, e facce quarche 'nore a lo Rre de li Fate, da lo quale haje recevuto tanta beneficie. [67] Ora, singhe benedetta, vavattene mo, e bide ch'a mariteto è benuta na gran doglia de capo: non avere paura, ca nce l'aggio mannata io azzò che isso te dica: "Stammonce, mogliera mia, ca po' n'auta vota nce ne jammo". E tu di': "Sí, marito mio, me contento perdere la vita mia

out of this world. Finally, she said to her daughter, "What will you do with all these grooms, pages, gentlemen, and ladies? One groom is more than enough; one girl is all you need. What's the matter, are you afraid of doing the laundry? Didn't you wear just a few rags until yesterday? Let's save all this money and all these treasures for a rainy day." (72) Hearing these things, the poor daughter choked and suffocated, as she couldn't swallow her sugar. On the eighth day, when she had to honor the fairies' king, she offered a banquet to all the poor women who could eat and drink on the riverbank while singing octaves and canzones to the glory of the king. (73) At the end of the party, toward evening, when people began to leave, the sardine fairy appeared, asking Nunziella what was wrong and why she was so sad. So she told her all the grief her mother gave her. (74) Changing back to the woman she was, the irritated fairy said to Rosecachiuove, "When are you going to stop, silly goat and great grandmother of the devil? Do you think you deserve to be the mother of such a good daughter who saved your life instead of taking revenge for all the troubles you gave her, taking you to a palace with all its riches, treating you like a queen? Meanwhile you, mother of misery and stinginess, make her swallow so many bitter pills that her throat is all flayed by now. Quick, dive, get lost—I don't want to have such a pest around!" (75) With this, she threw water in her face, and without Nunziella noticing, had her turn suddenly and secretly into a toad and the stolen rubies and diamonds into lumps. (76) Turning to Nunziella, the fairy said, "Bless you, my child. Enjoy life with your sweet husband and accept the prize for all your charitable deeds. Your mother can take a toothpick and eat dirt when she is hungry, that's all she deserves."

(77) After returning home with the ladies in waiting, when they arrived at the gate, her husband said, "My dear wife, I cannot bear to see the giant statue in front of the house. Let's take it down. Whenever I open the door, it seems like it is whacking me and pushing my head inside my body with its heavy hand." "That's done easily," Nunziella said. "You are the master, do as you please."

(78) The husband, a friend of the king of Naples who enjoyed statues and was looking for them all over the world, ordered to have it shipped to him. This was done, and it was used as a Jupiter statue, although later on it was used again to guard houses. Today, you can see it in front of the royal palace, the Neapolitans call it Lo Gigante.

(79) As to the toad, which still swells up, what do you think that miserable old woman is up to? As a toad, she is now doing worse than before, still

pe sarvare la toja". Torna a raprire lo palazzo, e stateve allegramente, ca isso te vorrà cchiú bene e starraje cchiú de Regina. [68] E tu, Rosecachiuove, rengrazia sta figlia toja, che t'ha rennuto la vita che tu l'haje data; e sta' 'n celevriello, no' le dare desguste co l'arzenecaria toja, ca te ne pentarraje».

[69] Nunziella, avenno rengraziata la Fata, se ne ghiette co la mamma a lo palazzo, senza che lo Giagante parlasse cchiúne, fice scarrecare li carriagge, e se gaudette co lo marito, a lo quale avea ditto ca chella vecchia l'avea pigliata pe donna de compagna, pe non dicere a primmo ca l'era mamma. [70] Ora chesta, mo, avenno visto tutte chelle recchezze, scagno d'affocarese e de satorarese non sapea che se fare: volea stipare, 'nzerrare e 'ncaforchiare, ghiea sciccanno li rubbine e li cravunchie da le mura e da lo solaro, facea cose de l'auto munno, e nfra l'aute deceva a la figlia: [71] «Che nne vuoje fare de tanta staffiere, pagge, genteluommene e sdammecelle? No staffiero è sopierchio, na zetella te vasta. Che? Te 'ncresce de fare la colata? Non sì stata nfi' ad iere co quatto stracce 'ncuollo? Stipammole, sti denare e sti tresore, pe chello che pò soccedere». [72] La scura figlia, che sentea ste cose, annozzava e 'ngottava che non ne potea scennere lo zuccaro, e benuto l'ottavo juorno, che avea da fare 'nore a lo Rre de le Fate, fece no commito a tanta poverielle, che a la ripa de lo sciummo magnassero e bevessero, cantanno ottave e canzune a grolia de chillo segnore. [73] Scomputa la festa, mmiero la sera, quanno la gente s'accommenzava a reterare, comparze la Fata 'n forma de sardella e addommannaje a Nunziella che aveva, che steva accossí colereca: ed essa le contaje tutto chello che le facea la mamma. [74] La Fata, de chesto 'nterretata, se straformaje 'n femmena com'era, decenno a Rosecachiuove: «E quanno te saziarraje, razza de caperrone, vava de Parasacco? Sì degna tu d'essere mamma de na figlia accossí bona, che scagno de te rennere lo male che l'haje fatto t'ha sarvata la vita, e t'ha puosto dinto a no palazzo ch'è la stessa recchezza, e te fa stare da Regina? E tu, mamma de la meseria, lesena anemata, le faje agliottere tanta male muorze c'oramaje nn'ha scortecato lo cannaruozzolo? Priesto, sparafonna, squaglia da lo munno, ca non voglio che nce stia sta peste»: [75] e accossí decenno le ghiettaje na vranca d'acqua 'n faccia, e ne no subbeto, nfra uocchie ed uocchie, senza che se n'addonasse Nunziella, la fece deventare no ruospo, e chille robbine e diamante c'aveva arrobbate le fece deventare tanta vrògnole. [76] Dapoje votatase la Fata a Nunziella, le decette: «Va, singhe benedetta, figlia mia, gaudete co lo marituozzolo tujo, e pigliate lo premmio de lo bene c'haje fatto: e màmmata, che se piglia no palicco e magna terreno quann'ha famme, c'accossí se mmereta».

filled with anger, and although she eats earth that's plentiful, she only eats little, out of fear that it could get scarce and she would starve. Bad habits are sad when they become natural, as the saying teaches us:

> *The wolf's bad habits last only as long*
> *as its hair changes, but not its nature.*

Endnotes

i Note the frequent use of similes and metaphors in this fairy tale: *No sciummo, che co l'acqua d'argiento jeva a pagare l'alloggiamiento de lo mare*; *pocca stanno lo sole pe fare capotròmmola come fanno li peccerille de Chiaja* (as the sun was about to tumble, just like the children do at Chiaja); *Rosecachiuove le stea sempe 'ncuollo, comm'a chiuovo che le passava lo core* (Roseca-chiuove watched her every step like a nail piercing her heart); etc.

ii The *Cavallerizza*, located near the Maddalena Bridge, is described with its dimensions in Sarnelli's Neapolitan *Guida de' forestieri* as a space to train horses (ch.vii, 42).

iii *Carlino, treccalli,* coins of little value (*GDLI*).

iv Described in Sarnelli's Naples *Guida de' forestieri* as a noble hospital with several art works, one by the Italian painter Giovan Francesco Penni (Fattore).

v An attempt was made at literal translations of the insults in Neapolitan in order to highlight their concepts. Emmanuele Rocco registers most of the terms in his *Vocabolario del dialetto napolitano* with citations for Sarnelli and Basile.

vi *Zitabona*, explained in Emmanuele Rocco's dictionary as Latin CEDO BONIS, a ceremony held by debtors near the courthouse, showing their buttocks to express their inability to pay.

vii *Monte Vesuvio*. A lengthy chapter of the *Guida de' forestieri* to Naples describes the fertile slopes of Mount Vesuvius producing delicious *Lagrime* and *Greco* wines. Following a Latin epigram about the volcano by Marcus Valerius Martialis (1ˢᵗ c.), Sarnelli chronicles the damaging fires of some twenty eruptions. The eruption of 1682 lasted two weeks in mid-August, accompanied by earthquakes that forced people to evacuate (ch.viii, 402 ff.).

[77] Ora Nunziella, tornatasenne a la casa co la compagnia, quanno fujeno 'nnanze a lo portone le decette lo marito: «Mogliere mia, io non pozzo vedere sta statola de sto Giagante ccà 'nnanze: se te piace, levammonnella, ca sempe me pare che quanno voglio raprire la porta non me dia quarche scoppola, e co la mano pesante non me faccia trasire la capo 'n cuorpo».

«Chesto è poco da fare — decette Nunziella —, tu sì lo patrone, fanne chello che buoje».

[78] Tanno lo marito, ch'era ammico de lo Rre de Napole, lo quale s'addelettava de statole e nne facea cercare pe tutto lo munno, ordenaje che se le mannasse, comme se fece: e chillo se ne servette pe statola de Giove, se bè co lo tiempo è tornato n'auta vota a guardare case, pocca è chella che oje se vede 'nnante Palazzo, e li Napoletane la chiammano lo Giagante.

[79] E pe tornare a lo ruospo, ch'ancora abbotta, che ve credite che faccia chella vecchia mmardetta? Ruospo e buono, fa peo de primma, e pe nfi' a lo juorno d'oje stace co chella arraggimma, e co tutto che magna terreno, e nn'aggia tanto quanto è gruosso lo munno, puro ne magna tanto poco, pe la paura che no' le venga manco, che se schiatta de famme. Tanto è tristo lo mal'abeto che deventa natura, comme nce 'mmezza chella settenzia:

Lo vizio de lo lupo tanto dura
Che pilo pò mutare, e no' natura.

SCOMPETURA
DE LA POSILECHEATA
OVERO
FESTA DE POSILECO DE LI 26 DE LUGLIO 1684

[1] Sto cunto de Cianna fuje veramente stimmato na cosa degna de l'ajetate soja, e tutte se maravegliajeno de la mammoria co la quale s'allecordava, se non d'auto, de chelle 'nciuriate fatte da li pagge a la Fata, e da Nunziella a li pagge e da li gentel'uommene suoje. [2] Ntramente venne la falluca pe tornareme a pigliare, e perché se faceva a maro na belledissema festa da lo segnore Vecerré (ommo veramente de la stampa de li Vespasiane e de li Tite, uno de li quale mmeretaje chillo bello alògio de «delizie de lo genere omano»: pocca mantene deritta la valanza de la jostizia e face che ognuno aggia lo sujo, e non lassa porzí de mantenere cod allegria e spasso li puopole che sotto d'isso gaudeno l'ajetate d'oro, cchiú priesto sonnata che beduta da chille che la scrissero: pocca se maje nc'è stata, è chella che oje se gaude sotta a lo coverno de sto Segnore, granne e pe nasceta, e pe costumme, e pe sapere): co l'accasione, dico, de la bella festa, che se faceva a maro, vierzo Mergoglino, vozero lo sio Petruccio e lo Dottore venire lloro porzíne co mmico dinto a la falluca, pe guadere de chille spasse. [3] Ed accossí io rengraziaje Cianna e le fegliole de li belle cunte c'avevano contato, ed azzò che n'auta vota me faoressero cchiú bolentiere deze a tutte cinco na patacca ped uno, decenno che nne pigliassero lo buono ammore: e scise a la marina nce 'mmarcajemo co no gusto granne, pocca sciatava no venteciello che te arrecreava, a la varva de lo sole lione.

[4] E bèccote lo maro quagliato da le tanta falluche che nc'erano, pocca non sulo chelle de Napole, ma porzí de l'isole e de li paise vecine, che formano lo bello cratere de la Serena, erano venute tutte, che pe chello che me pareva a Napole non c'era restata n'arma, tanta gente era 'sciuta a bedere la festa. [5] E mprimma vecino a lo palazzo de Medina nc'era no carro trionfante ch'era na bellezzetudene cosa, pocca era tutto 'nnaurato, co quatto rote rosse, terato da duje cavalle marine che parevano vive: 'ncoppa 'ncoppa a lo carro n'era na quaquiglia granne d'argiento, che serveva pe trono a Nettuno ed a la mogliere: tutto lo carro era attorniato da personagge che rappresentavano Tretune e Nereide, ed aute Ninfe e Dee marine, le quale co barie sorte de stromiente sona-

CONCLUSION
OF THE POSILECHEATA
OR
FEAST AT POSILLIPO ON JULY 26, 1684

(1) Cianna's story was well liked, suitable for her age, and everyone loved how she remembered the pages' curses thrown at the Fairy and Nunziella's insults directed at the pages and gentry. (2) Meanwhile, the boat arrived to pick me up, as a great feast at sea was offered by the viceroy (a man like Vespasian and Titus, deserving to be praised as "a delight of the human race," because he maintains the balance of justice and assures a decent life for everyone, without failing to provide joy and fun to his subjects, who enjoy a golden age—an age that was more dreamed about than lived in reality by those who wrote about it in the past. If there were ever a golden age, it is the one we enjoy today under the reign of this lord of a great lineage, morals, and learning). For this wonderful celebration at sea near Mergellina, Petruccio and the doctor wanted to join me in the boat to partake in the fun. (3) I thanked Cianna and her daughters for their beautiful tales, and for them to oblige another time, I gave each five and a half ducats, asking them for their loyal affection. I went down to the dock, and we boarded the boat with immense joy, as a light breeze refreshed us in spite of the burning sun.

(4) Boats crowded the sea. They arrived not only from Naples, but also from the islands and nearby towns of the beautiful Gulf of Naples. So many people had come out for the celebration that it seemed as if no living soul was left in Naples. (5) You could first see a triumphal carriage near the Medina palace: a golden marvel with four red wheels drawn by two marine horses that looked like they were alive. On top of the carriage, there was a large silver shell that served as a throne to Neptune and his wife. The entire carriage was surrounded by characters that represented the Tritons and Nereids and other marine nymphs and deities who played different instruments and sang to music that created a splendid harmony in the serene evening air. Surrounding this carriage were numerous feluccas, fishing boats and other vessels that looked like an army. (6) Further down at Mergellina, you could

vano e cantavano de museca che a l'àjero sereno de la sera facevano n'armonia de stopore. Or'attuorno a sto carro nc'erano tanta de le falluche, de li vuzze e de le barche, che pareva n'asèrzeto. [6] Cchiú 'nnanze, e propio a Mergoglino, nc'era na machena granne 'n forma de teatro, che stava 'mmiezo maro tutt'attorniata de frunne verde, che t'arrecreava la vista, e chisto era n'arteficio; attuorno a lo quale nc'era n'auta 'nfinetà de varche, vuzze e falluche, essennoce venute pe nfi' a le tartane carreche de gente: a la ripa po' de lo maro era na tirata de carrozze de sdamme e de cavaliere quanto poteva stennere la vista, e cose de zuccaro, e sorbette, ed acque agghiacciate ghievano e benevano.

[7] Ntramente comparze la falluca de lo sio Vecerré, accompagnata da doje galere ed aute falluche de guardia, che a la vista de lo luoco de la festa sparajeno na mano de cannonate. E che gusto era vedere tutte le feneste, l'àstreche, li soppuorteche chine de gente, accossí 'nzeccate pe lo gran numero che parevano sardelle, e tutte cann'apierte, chi a bedere che cosa fosse la bella machena de verdure, chi a conziderare la magnificenzia de lo carro trionfante, chi a sentire la museca, chi a mettere l'assisa a le provole, e chi a laudare la generosetate de chi faceva la festa! [8] Ccà nce trattenettemo nuje puro a fare chello che facevano l'aute: e subbeto che la notte sparze lo manto nigro 'ncoppa la terra, se bè la luna, ch'era 'nquinquagesima, pe bedere la festa essa porzíne nce lo stracciaje miezo, vèccote che tutte le case e li palazze de la revèra de Posileco, che fa no belledissemo teatro, cacciajeno tanta lumme, porzí co torce, che la luna se vregognava vederese soperata de luce da chelle stelle de la terra quanno essa chiarisce tutte chelle de lo cielo. [9] Dapo' se deze fuoco a la machena: e lloco te vediste la cchiú bella cosa de lo munno, tant'arteficie nc'erano dinto, che no' l'avarria creduto se no' l'avesse veduto: ogne sparata anchieva l'aria de stelle, ed una de chelle stelle ne figliava cient'aute: da ccà ascevano fontane de sciamme, da llà se facevano arche-balene de fuoco, tanto che lo maro non pepetiava, stopennose comme dinto a l'acqua arregnasse lo fuoco. [10] Pe la quale cosa, credennose che Borcano e Nettuno se fossero accordate 'nzémmora, isso porzí, scagno de astotare le sciamme, co farele refrettere dinto a lo sino sujo veneva a dopprecare lo fuoco, e la montagna de Somma che lo bedeva era rommasa storduta, credennose che llà fosse nato n'auto Vesuvio. Duraje sta bella vista quase n'ora tosta: e perché le falluche accommenzavano a botare carena, lo sio Petruccio co lo Dottore, passate a la varca de n'auto ammico, se ne tornajeno 'ncoppa Posileco, io co la mia me ne ghieze pe lo fatteciello mio, ed arrivato a tre ore de notte a lo muolo, sbarcaje sazio de gusto ed allancato de famme. E mannanno 'nnanze lo creato azzò che mettesse 'n frisco, me retiraje a la casa a pede a pede co na cocchiarella de mèle.

SCOMPETURA DE LO LIBRO

see a large engine shaped like a theatre at sea, surrounded by green fronds delighting your sight—an artifice surrounded by an endless array of boats, fishing boats and vessels, and even large ships loaded with people. Along the seashore, you could see a row of carriages with ladies and gentlemen as far as your eyes could reach, also sugary treats, sorbets, and iced water going back and forth.

(7) Meanwhile, the viceroy's barge emerged, accompanied by two galleys and other guard ships that, in front of the feast's site, shot a few cannonades. What delight it was to see all the windows, terraces, and alleys full of people stuck together like sardines with their mouths open, some admiring the barge with its green fronds, others the magnificent triumphal carriage, some listening to the music, some criticizing, others praising the generosity of the feast's sponsor! (8) We stayed there too, doing what everyone else was doing, as the night spread its black mantle over the land, although the full worm moon ripped it halfway in order to see the feast. You could see all the houses and palaces along the Posillipo shore turn on so many lights and even torches in a gorgeous scenery that the moon was ashamed to see, as its light that illuminates the stars of the sky was overwhelmed by the light of the stars on the shore. (9) They then burned the machine—you could see the most beautiful thing on earth, with so many artifices inside that you wouldn't believe if you hadn't seen it with your own eyes. Every explosion filled the air with stars, and every one of the stars gave birth to a hundred others. You could see fountains of flames come out here and fiery rainbows over there, so much that the sea couldn't breathe, surprised that fire ruled over the water. (10) Believing that the volcano and Neptune had made an agreement among themselves by mirroring them in its bosom, the sea too doubled the fire instead of extinguishing the flames. The Somma mountain was dazed when seeing it, believing that another Vesuvius was born.[vii] This beautiful spectacle lasted for about an hour. As the vessels began to turn their keel, Petruccio and the doctor boarded the boat of another friend and returned to Posillipo. I returned with my own boat, arriving at the dock at three in the morning, getting off satisfied from all the fun, but starving. I sent the domestic ahead to prepare fresh food, then walked back to my house with a spoonful of honey.

End of Book

TAVOLA
NON DA MAGNARE
MA
DE LI CUNTE
CHE SE FANNO DAPO' MAGNARE

TABLE OF CONTENTS
NOT FOR EATING
BUT
OF THE TALES NARRATED
AFTER DINNER

APPENDIX

BESTIARVM
SCHOLA

Ad homines erudiendos
Ab ipsa rerum Natura prouide
inflituta,

Et ab

✝ AESOPO PRIMNELLIO

E' MNIANOPOLI

Decem, & centum Lectionibus
explicata.

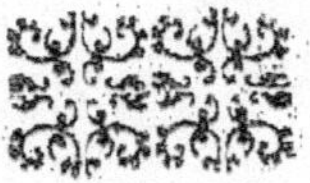

CÆSENÆ MDC. LXXX.

Apud Petrum-Paulum Receputum,
Epifcopalem Typographum.
Superiorum permiffu.

Frontispiece of Pompeo Sarnelli's *BESTIARUM SCHOLA ad homines erudiendos* (1680) (ed. Vito de Donato, Putignano: Vito Radio, 2007).

Appendix 1

BESTIARUM SCHOLA (1680)

The short comical-serious diversions of the *Bestiarum Schola* aim at castigating vices while entertaining through the great variety of talking animals. Each narrative or exchange is followed by a concluding didactic comment or maxim for members of the human race. Among the *Schola*'s seventy-six animals, the fox is the most frequent participant in the conversations, before the dog, lion, bee, donkey, and monkey, in that order. Jupiter is also present repeatedly, as are animals such as the beaver, deer, cicada, swan, elephant, butterfly, ant, cat, wolf, pig, fly, bear, parrot, bat, frog, snake, and mouse.

Following are a few *Lectiones* of *Bestiarum Schola*, with my translations of Damiano De Virgilio's Italian rendering of Sarnelli's Latin texts (Pompeo Sarnelli, *Scuola di bestie,* ed. Antonio Iurilli. Bari: Cacucci Editore, 2008).

LECTIO V   On the Need to Avoid Excess - The Owl and the Eagle
The birds were once divided into two separate confederations, each with a king. Those living in Greece were subject to the owl residing in Athens, all others had to follow the orders of the eagle. The owl's sovereign reign lasted a long time, until the news reached it that the eagle was able to look at the sun with its eyes wide open. Unaware that this was the eagle's natural gift, and that it was not owed to training, the owl yearned for a look straight at the sunrays, since it was unable to gaze at all things reflected by sunlight and to distinguish their features precisely. Having been blinded by the intense light, it was no longer able to distinguish the colors or shape of things. Therefore, the eagle gained absolute sovereignty, and the owl lost its regal authority, taking refuge in a cave, without ever seeing light again.

The Lesson shows how the same thing happens to those clever folks who pursue knowledge and erudition more than would be necessary, becoming incompetent and unfit for public service.

LECTIO XXXIII   Changing One's Dress Does Not Mean Changing Customs - The Hens

A few local hens sent to the Chinese empire hesitated to socialize when they noticed that the hens of those regions were dressed in wool rather than feathers. But as they found out that they practiced the same customs, they established relationships with great pleasure.

The Lesson shows how customs don't change with fashion, as a lyrical poet's verse reminds us: *Those who run across the sea find a new sky, but no new habits.*

LECTIO XXXVII   How to Manage One's Decisions - The Snake and the Hedgehog

A hedgehog asked a snake, after carefully watching its strides, "Why do you trail along, cringing with uncertain moves this way or that way, twisting in such sudden, tortuous spires that your body doesn't know where to direct its head? When you appear to move about this way, you suddenly go the other way, leaving no trace and no indication about where you are going." The snake replied, "This is why I was chosen as a symbol of prudence and discretion: the decisions and thoughts of prudent people must be inscrutable."

The Lesson suggests that those in power must keep the secrets of their plans so tightly that not even the closest associates are able to uncover them. Wisdom and expediency will advise time and place of the outcome.

Illustration of Lesson XXXVII by Diego de Saavedra Fajardo's *Idea Principis Christiano-politici, centum symbolis expressa* (1649) (*Scuola di bestie,* ed. Antonio Iurilli, p. 139)

LECTIO LIII   The Power of Diligence - The Ant and the Cicada

A cicada was surprised to see how stones were worn out from the continuous traffic of ants and how their busy going back and forth left a path. It wondered how such a tiny animal could leave such visible traces. One of the ants remarked, "You probably forgot the proverb, *Weak drops pierce a stone with diligence, not with force.*"

The Lesson teaches diligence—even with a light touch, it will get good results in any situation.

LECTIO LIV   Friendship to Be Avoided - The Chameleon and the Fox

They say that a chameleon that was longing to make friends approached a fox with these words: "You never found and will never find a better friend than me, because I am the only among all animals that does not eat or drink to feed itself, as I live only of air. Therefore, I do not need to bother my friends with tiresome requests, since I do not need what they have. And I am able to change color whenever I please, except for white." "To be your friend would be disastrous for me," the fox replied. "A friend who lives from air, changes color, and disdains candor cannot be trusted."

The Lesson suggests that a sophisticated person will never be a trustworthy friend.

LECTIO LVII   On the Necessity of Yearning for an Honest Rather Than a Long Life -The Phoenix and the Parrot

At a birds' assembly, the phoenix kept showing off its immortality, claiming that it had been living that way since the beginning of the world. After dying every six hundred-sixty years, it was reborn promptly, which made it feel very happy. After cracking up, a parrot remarked, "If I get this straight, your misfortunes cannot be measured with anyone else's, since you must follow the eternal cycle of such a long life. At the same time, you are more mortal than other birds, because you die several times all over. That same death means the beginning of new sufferings, while to us it brings peace."

The Lesson brings to mind one of Seneca's adages: *No one cares about living an honest life; everyone just wants a long life.* While everyone can easily live an honest life, no one can choose to live a long life. Another adage by Plato states: *We should not worry about life but about living with integrity.*

LECTIO LXIX   Chi si contenta gode / *Those Satisfied with What they Have Rejoice* - Jupiter and the Parrot

A parrot who couldn't bear any longer the sober lifestyle on the meadows and in the forests implored Jupiter to provide it with a special talent that people would value and the courts would hold in high regards. Jupiter awarded it speech, practiced only by humans. The parrot began to flatter princes at court who regaled it with abundant delicacies but that it could only enjoy locked up in an iron cage.

The Lesson teaches that those who are not satisfied with what little they have run into endless misfortunes.

LECTIO LXXIV   *On the Futility of Boasting One's Social Position* - The Lion and the Dog

A lion with a raised eyebrow treated a dog with conceit, claiming that there was no way it could stand up to comparison. But the smiling dog replied, "Half of our life— the time we spend sleeping—has the same bearing for both, and the way life ends is the same for all. As to the rest, aside from your arrogance, isn't it true that you lift your leg just like me when you pee?"

The Lesson teaches us that as long as we do not care about the conceit of titles, human life is such that it subjects everyone to the same miseries, since *Ashen Death knocks both at the poor man's hut and at the castles of kings.*

LECTIO XCIX   *Not All That Glitters Is Gold* - The Firefly

On a summer night when the crops were ripe and about to be harvested, all those small insects called fireflies because of their twinkle at night were flying about the spikes, shining when they opened their wings and darkening when they closed them. A young boy noticed them and caught one, believing it was gold. He kept it tightly in his fist so that it could not escape and took it to his father, saying, "Look here, I found gold!" But when he opened his hand, all he found was a gloomy, stinking dead insect.

From this Lesson we learn that such is the essence of all human things that seem endowed with some splendor. In fact, what are we if not some wretched beings; what is culture and fame? We are dust, culture is just a viewpoint, fame a gust of wind. And such is the END of all mortal things.

LECTIO C   All Things Human Are Imperfect - Esopo Pramnelli to His Readers
Dear Reader, perhaps some of you expect the one hundredth lesson. But my little book ends here, after ninety-nine lessons. It ends before arriving at the round number one hundred to illustrate its imperfection, just like all human things, following Cicero's statement in Book Two of *De inventione* that "Nature perfected no creature among the same species, as if it feared being unable to have anything to give all others by granting virtues to just a single one."

An Apophoretum of ten additional LECTIONES as a present to the students of the *School of Animals* is followed by a Dialogue Between Father and Son, Big Bear and Little Bear.

Appendix 2

Guida de' forestieri curiosi di vedere e d'intendere le cose più notabili della regal città di Napoli e del suo amenissimo distretto (1685), ed. Giuseppina Acerbo (2008) (https://www.memofonte.it/ricerche/napoli/#pompeo-sarnelli).

The first edition of the *Guide to Naples* opens with a dedication by Antonio Bulifon to Francesco Maria Pignatelli, archbishop of Taranto and *regio consigliere*; Bulifon's request for permission to print; his Letter to the Readers; a detailed list of Sarnelli's publications; and a table of contents. Divided into three books, the *Guide* discusses the history of Naples, its layout, notable buildings and art treasures. A large part of the *Guide* is dedicated to the very large number of the city's churches. A second, slightly revised edition with illustrations was printed in 1688, followed by numerous subsequent editions, including a bilingual Italian-French version with Bulifon's translations.

The following illustrations include the Italian table of contents, excerpts from Bulifon's preface to the readers, and passages from the original 1685 edition with my English translations.

Tavola de' capitoli de' tre libri seguenti.

Descrizione tanto dell'antica quanto della moderna Napoli, e di alcune sue cose principali. Libro primo.

Illustration of the outer door of Naples in Sarnelli's *Guida de' forestieri curiosi di vedere ed intendere le cose più notabili della real città di Napoli*, published in Naples by Antonio Bulifon. The illustration was designed by Sebastiano Indelicato and by the engraver Giovan Battista Brison. Flying Mercury holds up the book's title, a knight on a rampant horse and a wayfarer accompanied by a small dog are looking at the buildings of Naples. The illustration opens both the first and second editions (1685 and 1688). (http://www.memofonte.it/ricerche/Napoli/#pompeo-sarnelli)

Antonio Bulifon to the Curious Reader (Book I, p.XIIr ff.)

Although it has always been the custom for writers to explain their reasoning before setting out to treat any subject, and I asked the author for a preface of this book about to be published, he (that is, Sarnelli) answered that this was not necessary—in fact, it was rather superfluous, as it would hold back foreigners from beginning their visit. When I answered that it was a suitable ornament for the book, he replied, "Why should I write a preface? Perhaps to explain the book's purpose? Isn't it enough to just read the title of the book (…)? Or should I perhaps apologize for its layout and style? This is a topic that does not require adornment (…). What else? Should I discuss my research and labor? Here it is in a few words. All I did is prepare a manual with writings from the very thorough Engenio, the very learned Carlo De Lellis, the very industrious Mormile, and other Neapolitan historians. I added a few things that I researched, since they only wrote about their time, and the first two only about churches. I also benefited from the reprint of Summonte, although I do not agree with him on the origins of Naples (…). I should only add that when I write 'our Neapolitan,' 'our compatriot,' I do so because although I am not born in Naples but in Polignano, a very ancient town of the kingdom, I became a resident of Naples in my childhood (…)."

These were the reasons given by the author for not wanting to write a preface. After writing it, I fear that it is already too long. Therefore, I will only add that for your benefit I tried to employ one of the best writers for this book and that I had wood and copper engravings done for true illustrations of the most notable things, without worrying about their cost (…). Moreover, you should expect another book, the *Guida de' forestieri curiosi di vedere e considerare le cose notabili di Pozzuolo, Baja, Miseno, Cuma, eccetera*, which will be printed later, a work by the same author. (…)

About the Modern Site of the Royal City of Naples (Book I, ch.4, p.22 ff.)

Since Italy is commonly called 'The Garden of the World,' you will not go wrong calling Naples the Garden of Italy, or rather the Garden of Europe, because it rightfully deserves the title of "gentile" [graceful, kind] among all delightful and lovely cities. It has an excellent climate, a countryside called "felice" in antiquity. Its site has the shape of an incredibly beautiful theatre surrounded by the Tyrrhenian Sea to the south, forming a lovely, serene gulf. To the west rises a very fertile mountain next to it with a spiritual and temporal protection and defense, and on top of it, the castle of Saint Erasmus and the Carthusian monastery. Both of them change sentries at the same time—the soldiers at the castle with weapons in their hands, the deeply religious monks with divine prayers on their lips (…). To the north, it is surrounded by lovely hills that protect it from the rage of the north wind. To the east, you can see a very fertile plain that extends to the Acerrano fields and the Somma mountain. (…). The city is enlarged by seven main *borghi* called *suburbs* with gorgeous palaces, delightful gardens full of all sorts of fruits and vegetables for the entire year, and natural and artificial water fountains. They have so many residents that every *borgo* resembles a city. Almost all took their names from neighborhood churches. The first, bathed by the sea, is Santa Maria di Loreto. The second is Sant'Antonio Abate, the third Santa Maria della Vergine, the fourth Santa Maria della Stella, the fifth Giesù Maria, the sixth Santa Maria del Monte, the seventh and most beautiful is at the Spiaggia di San Lionardo, commonly called *Chiaja* since it is bathed by the sea. (…)

About the Administration of the City of Naples (Book I, ch.V, pp.32ff.)

According to tradition, supported by all writers, Naples was famous before the Romans and flourished among Italy's most illustrious Greek cities. Since its origins, it was governed as a republic, with magistrates that befit a well-ordered republic, as noted abundantly by the scholar Giulio Cesare Capaccio. When the flourishing Roman Empire began to subjugate Campania, it welcomed Naples among the free, confederate Roman cities. And although Rome suffered greatly because of the Carthaginian War, Naples did not fall short in expressing its friendship, offering very generously forty weighty golden cups to the Roman Senate. However, the wise senators only accepted one lighter cup, as they valued the love of Neapolitans more than the price of gold. Thus, the very loyal city of Naples was honored and kept in high regard throughout the governments of the consuls and the emperors.

When the Roman Empire declined, it was subjugated by the Goths and later by Bellisario, commander under Emperor Justinian. After the Longobards invaded and occupied most of the kingdom, Giovanni Campsino of Constantinople took possession of the part of Campania that was not Longobard, becoming king in 612, after Emperor Phocas's death. Following Emperor Heraclius's death, Naples returned to the empire up to the Saracens' invasion in 829 and their occupation of southern Italy from Gaeta to Reggio Calabria. Naples too was subject to their oppression for eighty years until the times of John X, who pushed them back from the Roman borders with the help of Marquis Alberigo of Tuscany, persecuted them up to the Garigliano, and defeated them in a large battle. Thus, the Saracens retired to the Gargano where they fortified themselves.

Naples was then toiled by the Greeks and Saracens until the arrival of the Normans as its new rulers. After the Normans' supremacy, Naples passed to the Swabians and their sole heir, Queen Costanza's rule. After Carlo D'Angiò killed Manfredi and defeated Corradino, Naples was subject to the French. One hundred eighty years later, it was ruled by the Aragonese and later by the Spanish, after the Catholic King Ferdinand and his army had driven away the French, who contended the kingdom's succession. Lastly, it was ruled by the Austrians through Giovanna, the third-born daughter of the Catholic king and mother of Emperor Charles V. Naples now rests in the very pleasant shadow of the Catholic king of Spain, Charles II.

Some Distinguished Buildings of the City of Naples (Book I, ch. VII, pp. 38ff.)

The most outstanding building of all is the royal palace, where the viceroys live. Its magnificence, number of rooms, splendid location, and noble design make it one of the most distinguished buildings of all of Italy, the work of the famous Sir Fontana. To be brief, I will not go on to describe it. I will only say that every day, around 10 o'clock, the companies of Spanish soldiers walk in front of the large square of this palace from one fort to another (…). Crossing a bridge, one gets from this palace to the Castel Nuovo, once the residence of the viceroys, a castle we described in the previous chapter. In ancient times, this castle served as guardian of the harbor—today's Tarcena—which was built in 1668 by Viceroy Pietro d'Aragona.

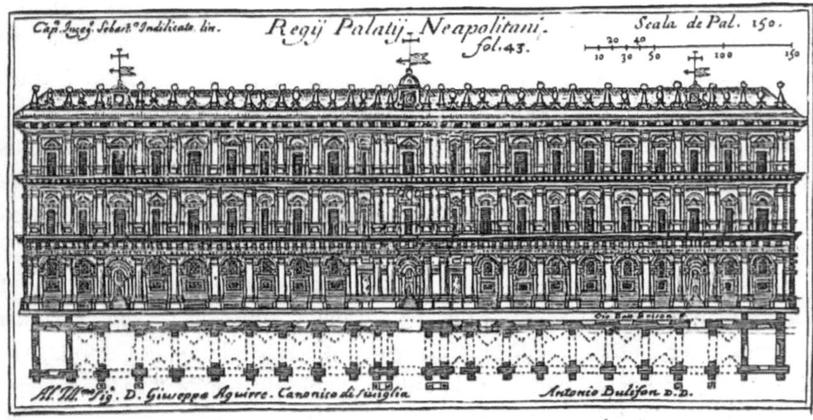

The Royal Palace of Naples. Second edition of the *Guida de' forestieri* for Naples (1688), eds. Federica De Rosa, Alessandra Rullo and Simona Starita. Naples, 2014, p. 38.

The Naples Cathedral (Book II, ch.1, pp. 57ff.)

This illustrious church, chief among all of the city's churches and the archbishop's chair, was founded by two kings: first by Charles I and later by Charles II, who brought it to perfection. (…)

This magnificent church was adorned with sculptures and porphyry columns by Antonio Baboccio da Piperno, a famous sculptor under Archbishop Minutolo. (…) Built under Cardinal Dezio Carafa for 14,000 scudi, the ceiling is highly valued for the paintings by Santa Fede, a celebrated painter (…). You will notice at the doors of a beautiful organ some figures of saints by Giorgio Vasari from Arezzo, a superb painter and architect who flourished in the 1550s. (…)

The Posillipo Mountain, Delightful and Lovely Mergellina, the Church of Santa Maria del Parto, and Sannazaro's Sepulcher (Book III, ch.1, p.327 ff.)

Posillipo is the most delightful and loveliest among the world's most beautiful, delightful, and lovely seashores, as the very name of the mountain clearly tells you, since the Greek word PAUSILIPUM in Latin means MOERORIS CESSATIO, a site so gorgeous and so full of delights that they mitigate all sadness (…). This place of peace and quiet was visited by the ancient Romans who came here to enjoy themselves, taking a break from the senatorial duties and tasks of the republic (…). Here you find magnificent palaces with lovely gardens built on the seashore and the mountain by Neapolitans for leisurely summer fun in its healthy climate. (…) In a place called Vomero on the back of Mount Posillipo, you can see the new noble palace of the Vandeneyn family, full of excellent paintings and abundant furnishings, with a view of the entire inlet of the sea (…).

Delightful Mergellina is located on the other side, towards the east (its name owed to the charming, submerging fish), a gift from the Neapolitan King Frederick to Jacopo Sannazaro that he highly valued for its beautiful location. (…)

About Mount Vesuvius (Book III, ch.VIII, pp.402-409)

The large Mount Vesuvius (…) is famous for its fertile shrubs and vines that produce very tasty, high-quality *Greco* and *Lagrime* wines, but also for its horrendous and harmful fires (…). This mountain threw flames from its top twenty-one times—six before the Christian era known to have been less ferocious than the other fifteen that followed and that are listed here.

The first occurred during the reign of Titus Vespasianus on November 1 of 79, when its eruption of fire, ashes, sulfuric mineral globes, and fiery stones killed many people and damaged cities and nearby villages, destroying the ancient towns of Pompeii and Herculaneum. Among those who died there was Pliny, brother of Caius Pliny the Second's mother, author of a natural history. The night before, he was with the imperial army at Miseno, a city near Baja that is now destroyed. While studying, he heard from his sister about the appearance of an unusual thick fog around Vesuvius, so he grabbed a few log-books and boarded the galleys in the harbor. Unaware that the Somma mountain was on fire, he proceeded to find out the cause of this uncommon prodigy, and although others were frightened and fled the fire, he went there fearlessly and willingly. As he approached the city of Pompeii, he saw the fire, observed as much as he could see, then suffered tightness of his chest, was overcome by the thick smog and sulfuric stench, fell, and died at once. In his *Triumph*

Mount Vesuvius, designed by Pesche in *Guida de' forestieri curiosi di vedere ed intendere le cose più notabili della real città di Napoli* (1685), ch. VIII, p.403. https://www.memofonte.it/ricerche/napoli/#pompeo-sarnelli.

of Fame, Petrarch refers to his death in the third chapter with the following verse: *Mentre io mirava, subito hebbi scorto quel Plinio veronese suo vicino, a scriver molto, a morir poco accorto* (As I was watching, I noticed readily Pliny from Verona, his neighbor, who wrote so much but died a foolish death). (…)

The fifteenth, most recent eruption occurred from Friday August 14, 1682 through Wednesday the 26th, when the Vesuvius was so horrifying that everyone was frightened, as its horrible fires were so intense that the sun hid two full days underneath thick clouds. You could hear the roars of the mountain's torn bowels continuously on four days as far as twenty-one miles. All the walls of Naples continued to shake for three hours, despite its eight-mile distance from Vesuvius. You can only imagine the worst happening in places near the mountain, because aside from the earthquake, the flames rose so high up and above the higher, nearby mountain that they fell into the Ottaiano forest, setting it on fire. Therefore, all residents of that area retreated to Naples, driven away by the threat of falling flames, the unbearable sulfur stench, and the hail of enflamed pumice-stones and ashes, which miraculously tried to bury the living by filling the entire area so that even Naples was covered by more than two inches. (…)

Notable Public and Private Libraries of the City of Naples. (Book III, ch.IX, pp. 411ff.)

After describing the most noteworthy things and principal churches outside of Naples, I wish to add information about the most notable public and private libraries of the city, something much demanded by honorable foreigners, to whom I will give satisfaction as best I can. They are the following, in alphabetical order for easier consultation. (1) *Sant'Apostoli, de' chierici regolari.* This famous library is set up in a large concave space, arranged symmetrically. It has rare books and books from all sciences. The library also has an archive of very ancient texts, in particular Tasso's *Gerusalemme Liberata*, an autograph of the celebrated writer, some manuscripts of Jacopo Sannazaro and Sir Marino, famous Neapolitan poets, and others. (...)

Appendix 3

Guida de' forestieri curiosi di vedere, e considerare le cose notabili di Pozzoli, Baja, Miseno, Cuma, ed altri luoghi circonvicini. Ritrovata colla lettura de' buoni Scrittori, colla propria diligenza dall'Abate Pompeo Sarnelli (1685).

The Phlegrean Guide takes foreign visitors on a tour from Agnano to Pozzuoli, Averno, Lake Lucrino, and the cities of Baja, Miseno, Cuma, Linterno, and the small island of Nisida. The *Guide* describes the sites of ancient monuments and ruins, evoking their histories based on ancient and modern sources and anecdotes, especially those by Virgil, Seneca, Pliny, and Sannazaro. The visitor is reminded of the area's beautiful landscapes along the Tyrrhenian sea, which were assaulted repeatedly and were chosen as places of leisure by the wealthy. Readers are also informed of the area's dynamic geology, with recurrent earthquakes and volcanic eruptions. The sites of ancient temples, caverns, and villas are described along the road, such as Cicero's mansion. Through historical, archeological, and literary references and citations, Sarnelli makes the *Guide* attractive to cultivated foreign visitors. At the same time, the *Guide* provides a menu of thermal baths for the cure of diverse illnesses at Pozzuoli, Agnano, the Solfatara, Averno, Tripergola, and Baja.

Following is a table of contents in the Italian original (Google Libri. Ital.440) and selected passages of the *Guide*, with my English translations.

Table of Contents

Ch. IV   *About the City of Pozzuoli* (pp.27-33)

The Royal City of Pozzuoli lies on the slope of a mountain near the seashore at a distance of eight miles from Naples. It was founded by people from the Greek island of Samos. The ancients named it DICEARCHIA for its just government, a name that was used until the arrival on Italy's coast of the Carthaginian Hannibal. Fearing an assault on the town, the Roman senate sent Q. Fabio with a troop of soldiers to keep watch. Seeing how the town was short of water, he had numerous wells dug, which gave it the name PUTEOLI. Others think that the name is owed to the sulfuric stench. (...)

Pozzuoli is located in a very felicitous region surrounded by the sea and a territory with a greater abundance of fruits perhaps than anywhere along the Tyrrhenian sea. It boasts gorgeous country residences described by Pilon. It was also the home of the Roman emperor Caligula. The Romans loved the city, so much so that after renouncing his dictatorship, Cornelius Sulla retired there to enjoy sweet peace and quiet.

The city suffered many great calamities due to Barbarians and earthquakes. Hannibal caused a lot of destruction and so did the Goths under Alaric.

The Longobards damaged it, as did many other warring Barbarians. Barbarossa tried to conquer it; he would have been successful if Viceroy Pietro Di Toledo had not routed him.

And what can we say about the earthquakes that turned the city into rubble? In 1198, the Solfatara crater erupted with a huge fire and very large stones, damaging the area. At the same time, the city suffered an earthquake that left no building unharmed. On December 30, 1448, the City got bruised by another earthquake, with many deaths. The 1538 earthquake was so horrible that almost all buildings were ruined—some swallowed by the earth—which left Pozzuoli almost empty (...). Viceroy Pietro Di Toledo revived the city by restoring it. To make this beautiful place habitable, he built a superb palace with a wonderful garden, decorating the city with elegant lively water fountains. The Neapolitan gentry followed suit, building similar noble palaces. (...)

As can be seen from the above, Pozzuoli was a famous town in antiquity. Today very few testimonies are left of its magnificence.

Ch. VIII   *Cicero's Country Mansion, Cluvio's and Lentulo's Gardens* (pp.49-50)

Between Pozzuoli and Lake Averno, you will see among the antiquities the sites of Cicero's country house and the gardens of Cluvius, Pilius, and Lentulus. Cicero called his residence, *Academia*. Pliny wrote, "The noteworthy country house on the seashore between Lake Averno and Pozzuoli with its famous portico and forests was named *Academia* by Cicero to resemble the Athenian Academy. It is here that he wrote his homonymous book *The Academic Questions*."

Only one part of this Academia is left with its ceramics and large lava paving-stones. You will notice the dome-shaped site of columns and statues. Today's owner uses it to house his flocks. That's the way of the world—worldly wisdom is foolishness in the eyes of the Lord. (...)

Ch. X   *The Baths at Averno and Tripergola* (pp.60-61)

To avoid omitting anything in these short notes, I will not mention the numerous baths in this area, just ten listed by Aretino.

i.   On the left side of Lake Averno is the *Arco Bath*. Its name is owed to the shape of the building. Its waters have similar properties as those of the baths of Civitavecchia, Siena, and Viterbo—they benefit the stomach and bowels.

ii. The *Rainieri Bath* is located near Tripergola. Its waters mingle with those of Trituli. They cure scabies and leprosy.

iii. The *Tripergola Bath*'s waters restore the body, alleviate excessive pain, cheer the heart, and remove stomach pain.

iv. The *Scrofa Bath* owes its name to the cure of scrofula. It is greatly appreciated by the leprous. It cures impetigo and scabies.

v. The *S. Lucia Bath* benefits the eyes, cures cloudy vision, and dries up tears and inflammations of the eyes.

vi. The *S. Croce Bath* cures contracted nerves, joint injuries, abdominal distensions, and tumors. It also cures gout, dropsy, and hypochondria. Drinking its waters greatly benefits the ventricle.

vii. The *Succellario Bath* is near the Sibilla grotto (...). Its waters taste like capon soup. It helps grow hair, cures leprosy, cleans teeth and gums, cures scabies, benefits the lungs and the spleen, alleviates burning sensations and pressure of the bladder, increases urine production, chases away kidney stones, and cures quartan ague and low-grade fevers.

viii. The *Ferro Bath* greatly benefits the eyes and ears, and cures headaches. Drinking its waters is a cure for the lungs, spleen, ventricle, kidneys, and womb.

ix. The *Palombara Bath*, whose name is owed to doves' nests, benefits arthritic pain, the kidneys, eyes, and stomach. Do not consume salty foods when drinking the water.

x. The *Salviana* or *Salmaria Bath* is helpful for women's periods. It also cures dry wombs and helps with infertility. Nature seems to have created this Bath for women only.

Ch. XIV *The City of Baja and its Baths* (pp.72-75)

The ancient, famous, delightful city of Baja was swallowed by time. Its only traces are found in the records of writers.

It was an ancient city, named after Bajo, Ulysses's companion. It was famous in the Roman era. Many of Rome's chief citizens owned beautiful homes there. It was so delightful that Seneca and Propertius fault it for inciting a dissolute lifestyle, owing to its unrestrained beauty. Claudius dared reproaching Cicero for having spent time in Baja. Horace, Martial, and Statius write of its delights in their verses. On his way to Rome, the Hebrew King Aristobulus visited Baja, where he found many beautiful mansions decorated with statues, columns, and marble walls and floors, which made him recognize the grandeur of Rome. (...)

Ch. XXI   *The City of Linterno, Today's* Patria (pp.104-105)

Between Cuma and Volturno, you can see the ruins of the ancient City of Linterno, a past Roman colony. Scipio Africano the Elder came here to retire after going voluntarily into exile from his Patria. He detested the ingratitude and abuse from fellow-citizens whom he had defended from their enemies so valiantly. He lived here without ever considering going back to Patria. He died here and was buried with the following epitaph: *Ingrata Patria ne quidem ossa mea habes.* (Ungrateful Patria, you will not have my bones)

All writers referring to this place claim that Linterno was sacked by the Vandals in 455, that the Tower you see today was erected later at the site of the tomb, and that to remember him, they kept the word *Patria*, now called Torre di Patria.

Following are illustrations of Chapter V from the 1769 bilingual Italian-French edition of the Phlegrean Guide based on Bulifon's translation of 1697. The Italian text is found on the left page, the French translation on the opposite page.

La Guida de' Forestieri curiosi di vedere, e di riconoscere le cose più memorabili di Pozzuoli, Baja, Cuma, Miseno, Gaeta ed altri luoghi circonvicini, spiegata con l'ajuto di gravi Autori, e con proprio riconoscimento di Monsig. Vescovo di Bisceglia POMPEO SARNELLI. E arricchita da Antonio Bulifone di molte figure di Rame, ed accresciuta di alcune curiosissime particolarità, con la Descrizione de' Bagni, e stufe dell'Isola d'Ischia molto salutevoli per guarire ogni sorte d'Infermità. Quarta edizione. In Napoli 1769. A spese di Saverio Rossi, e dal medesimo si vende accosto il Campanile di S. Chiara.

> *La Guide des Etrangers curieux de voir, & de connoitre les choses les plus memorables de Poussol, Bayes, Cumes, Misene, Gaete, Et autres Lieux des environs. Expliquèe a l'aide des bons Auteurs, & par la propre recherche De Monseigneur l'Evèque de Biseglia POMPEE SARNEL-LI. Et enrichie par Antoine Bulifon de plusieurs figures en taille douce, & augmentèe de quelques particularitez tres curieuses, & de la Description des Bains, & ètuves de l'Isle d'Ischia tres salutaires pour la*

guerison de diverses maladies. Quatrième Edition. A Naples 1769. Aux depenses de Xavier Rossi, qui en vende les copies au pres le Clocher Sainte Claire.

Della Città di Pozzoli

Cap. V
[p. 44]
È Pozzoli Regia Città, situata sul piano d'un monte presso al lido del mare, distante da Napoli meno di

De la Ville de Poussol
Chap. V
[p.45]
Poussol est une Ville du Domaine Royal, située sur le plat d'un coteau au rivage de la mer, eloignée de Naples environ de

[p. 46]
8. miglia, edificata (secondo Stefano) da' popoli venuti dall'Isola Samo.

Fu anticamente detta Dicearchia, per lo giusto governo, che aveva. Questo nome durò molto tempo, infin' a tanto, che Annibale passò a danni dell'Italia: onde il Senato Romano dubitando, che Annibale non assaltasse Dicearchia, vi mandò per guardia del luogo Q. Fabio con una colonia di Soldati; il quale vedendo, che il luogo pativa assai d'acqua, fece cavare molti pozzi, e dal nome d' essi acquistò la Città il nome *Puteoli*; benchè altri vogliono esser così detta della puzza del solfo.

Fu detta però Colonia Dicearchia, come scrive *Plinio nel 3. lib. Dein Puteoli Colonia Dicearchia dicti.* Eziandio *Colonia Augusta,* come lasciò scritto Frontino: *Puteolos Coloniam Augustam Augustus deduxit.* Fu parimente appellata *Colonia Augusta Neronia,* come riferisce Tacito; appresso *Colonia Flavia,* fotto Vespafiano, come in un marmo, che si riporterà trattandosi del Molo.

La sua grandezza, e la sua nobiltà si conosce infin da' tempi di Nerone, ne' quali era nella Città di Pozzoli l'Ordine Senatorio distinto dalla Plebe, come si legge nel *tredicesimo libro degli annali di Tacito: Iisdem Consulibus* (parlando de' tempi di Nerone) *auditae Puteolanorum legationes, quas diversas Senatores*

[p. 47]

huit miles : elle fut batie (selon Etienne) par une colonie d'habitans de l'Isle Samos.

Elle fut anciennement appelée Dicearchie, a cause de la justice, & rectitude de son gouvernement, & elle garda long tems ce nom-là. Quand Annibal vint ravager l'Italie avec une formidable armée de Carthaginois, le Senat Romain craignant qu'il ne prit d' assaut Dicearchie, y envoya une colonie de Soldats pour la garder sous la conduite de Q. Fabius, le quel voyant que la Ville manquoit d'eau, y fit creuser plusieurs puits; ce qui fit donner a cette Ville le nom Puteoli, quoy que d'autres disent qu'elle ait été ainsi nommée de la puanteur du souffre de son territorie.

Elle retint neantmoins le nom de Colonie, Dicearchie, comme l'ecrit Pline au 3. Livre : Dein Puteoli Colonia Dicearchia dicti *& meme on l'apella* Colonia Augusta, *comme Frontin l'a laisse par ecrit:* Puteolos Coloniam Augustam Augustus deduxit *: Elle fut encore appellée* Colonia Augusta Neronia, *comme Tacite le rapporte. Apres cela on trouve qu'elle s'apelloit* Colonia Flavia *sous Vespasien, comme on le voit sur un marbre dont on fera mention en parlant du Mole.*

Sa grandeur & sa noblesse etoient déjà fort illustres du tems de Neron, puis qu'on y distinguoit alors l'Ordre des Senateurs, ou des Nobles d'avec celuy du peuple, comme on le lit dans le 13. Livre des Annales de Tacite : Iisdem Consulibus (*dit il parlant du tems de Neron*) auditae Puteolanorum legationes, quas diversas Senatorius ordo,

[p. 48]

ordo, plebsque ad Senatum miserant: illi vim multitudinis, hi magistratuum, & primi cujusque avaritiam increpantes. Cumque seditio ad saxa, & minas ignium progressa, necem, & arma perliceret C. Cassius adhibendo remedio delectus, quia severitatem ejus non tolerabant, precante ipso, ad Scribonios fratres ea cura transfertur, data cohorte prætoria, cujus terrore, & paucorum supplicio rediit oppidanis concordia.

La sua antichità si conosce anche in fin da' tempi del medesimo Nerone, nominandola *Tacito* antica, come può vedersi nel *quatordicesimo libro degli annali*, ove egli scrive: At in Italia vetus Oppidum Puteoli, jus Coloniae, & cognomentum a Nerone adipiscuntur. Donde si vede, che sia stata Colonia de' Romani, e delle più potenti; mentre nelle sollevazioni delle Provincie, quali a Vitellio, quali a Vespafiano rivolte; si legge in *Tacito al terzo libro delle storie:*

Municipia, Coloniaque impulsae, praecipuo Puteolanorum in Vespasianum studio, contra Capua Vitellio fida municipalem amulationem bellis civilibus miscebat.

Ancorchè la Città di Cuma, della quale parlaremo più appresso, fosse situata in riva al mare, nulladimeno, perche la sua spiaggia non ha profondità per li Vascelli, si crede, che Pozzoli sia stato suo porto, celebre per l'Emporio

[p. 49]

plebsque ad Senatum miserant: illi vim multitudinis, hi Magiftratuum, & primi cujusque avaritiam increpantes. Cumque seditio ad saxa, & minas ignium progressa, necem, & arma perliceret C. Cassius adhibendo remedio delectus, quia severitatem ejus non tolerabant, precante ipso, ad Scribonios fratres ea cura transfertur, data Cohorte Prætoria, cujus terrore, & paucorum supplicio rediit oppidanis concordia.

Son antiquité paroit encore des le tems du méme Neron, puisque Tacite l'appelle ancienne, comme on le peut voir au 14 *livre de ses Annales, ou il écrit* : At in Italia vetus Oppidum Puteoli jus Coloniæ & cognomentum a Nerone adipiscuntur. *Ou l'on voit, qu'elle a été Colonie Romaine, & meme des plus puissantes, puisque dans les soulevemens des Provinces durant les guerres civiles, elle se declara pour Vespasien, a cause que Capouë qu' elle vouloit contrequarrer comme allant du pair avec elle, obeissoit a Vitellius.* Tacite 1.3. de son Histoire. Municipia, Coloniæque impulsae, præcipuo Puteolanorum in Vespasianum studio; contra Capua Vitellio fida municipalem æmulationem bellis civilibus miscebat.

Quoy que la Ville de Cumes dont nous parlerons cy-apres, fut située au rivage de la mer, neammoins a cause que sa plage n'a point de fond pour les Vaisseaux, on croit que Poussol etoit son Port de mer. Ciceron écrivant a Attique, dit au liv.5. ep.7.

[p. 50]

de' Cumani, di cui Cicerone scrivendo ad Attico ebbe a dire: *Quid potui non videre, cum per emptorium Puteolanum iter facerem? lib.5. epist. 7.* Portando li porti marittimi il trafico, così si crede, che questo era notabile, poichè si veggono tante fabbriche di botteghe, ed in particolare sotto la Chiesa di Gesù-Maria, dove quando il mar turbato caccia fuori l'onde con empito, si ritrovano sù l'arene Corniole, Ametisti, Giacinti, Crisoliti, Diaspri, Onicchini,

Berilli, Lapislazzoli con varj intagli, onde si comprende essere quivi state le botteghe degli Orefici.

Pozzuoli adunque è situato in una felicissima regione del Cielo, cinto da placida marina, ed è abbondante il suo territorio di frutti, forse più, che qualsivoglia altro del mar Tirreno; era circondato dalla parte della terra da amenissime ville, delle quali ragiona Filon Giudeo, che quivi di Roma seguì Cajo Caligola. E perciò tanto desiderato da' Romani, che L. Cornelio Silla avendo rinunciato la dittatura, ritirossi in Pozzuoli per godere d'una dolce, e placida quiete.

Ha patito questa Città molti, e notabilissimi danni, tanto da' Barbari, quanto da' tremuoti.

Annibale vi fece molta strage. I Goti con Alarico le cagionarono gran rovina.

[p. 51]

Quid potui non videre, cum per emporium Puteolanum iter facerem? *& parce qu'un Port de mer est aussi un lieu de trafic, & de commerce, il falloit que celuy de Poussol fut fort considerable, puis qu'on y voit encore tant de ruines d'anciennes boutiques, ou magazins le long de la mer, particulierement sous l'Eglise de Jesus-Marie, où les ondes de la mer poussées par l'impetuosité de la tempete jettent souvent sur le rivage quantité d'anciennes pierres gravées telles que des Cornalines, Ametistes, Jacintes, Crisolites, Jaspes, Onix, Berilles, & Lapislazuli, ce qui marque qu'autrefois les boutiques des orfevres etoient en ce lieu-là.*

Poussol est donc situé sous un Ciel qui luy envoye de tres douces influences; elle est entourée d'une mer tranquille, & son terroir est aussi abondant en toutes sortes de fruits, qu'aucun autre endroit de la mer Tyrrhene; son territoire etoit rempli de maisons de plaisance, dont la vuë etoit si charmante, que Philon le Juif en fait mention dans son ambassade; parce qu'il vint ici a la suite de l'Empereur Caligula, que les delices du lieu y attiroient souvent, ainsi que les principaux Romains de son siecle, jusques-là que Sylla apres s'etre demis de la Dictature, se retira a Poussol, pour y passer le reste de ses jours dans un doux repos.

Neantmoins cette Ville a souffert plusieurs fois de grands dommages, autant par les irruptions des nations barbares, que par les tremblemens de terre.

Annibal y fit un grand degat, les Gots

[p. 52]

I Longobardi le recarono non minori incomodi, e tanti altri Barbari le fecero sentire il furore de' loro ferri; ed infin Barbarossa Ammiraglio di Solimano Imperadore de' Turchi, tentò d'averla in suo potere, e l'avrebbe ottenuta, se la vigilanza di D. Pietro di Toledo Vicerè di Napoli non l'avesse fugato.

Ma che diremmo de' tremuoti, che quasi la ridussero a niente. Nel 1198. la Solfatara buttò fuoco sì grande con grossissimi globi di pietre, che danneggiò tutto il paese, e nello stesso tempo patì la Città un tremuoto, che non fu edificio alcuno, che non ne patisse.

A' 30. di Dicembre del 1448. fu altresì da' tremuoti la detta Città molto mal concia, il che succedette con gran mortalità d'uomini.

Il tremuoto del 1538. fu così orribile, che tutti quasi gli edificj furono rovinati, ed in parte inghiottiti dalla terra, onde la Città di Pozzuoli restò quasi dissabitata, e ne avenne la rovina di Tripergola, e l'assorbimento del lago Lucrino, ove sorse all'improviso quel monte, che oggi si vede, come più diffusamente diremo al *capo* 10.

Oltre a ciò a' 31, d'Agosto del 1695. una terribilissima pioggia fe grandissimi danni in molti luoghi d'essa, e particolarmente rovinò l'aquedotto, che conduceva l'acqua alle pubbliche fontane (...).

[p. 53]

sous Alaric la mirent a deux doigts de sa ruine, les Lombards ne l'incommoderent pas moins, les Sarasins, & plusieurs autres nations barbares luy firent eprouver les efets de leur fureur. Enfin Barberousse Admiral du Gran Turc Soliman tacha de surprendre cette belle Ville, mais il en fut empeché par la viglilance du Viceroy Don Pierre de Toledo.

Mais que dirons-nous des temblemens de terre qui ont presque reduit a rien une Ville si fameuse ? L'an 1198. la Soufriere jeta un si grand feu, avec des pierres d'une grosseur prodigieuse, qu'elle endommagea tout le pais, & dans le méme tems la Ville ressentit un tremblement de terre si violent, qu'il n'y eut aucun edifice qui n'en souffrit.

Le 30. Decembre de l'année 1448. cette Ville fut aussi fort endommagée d'un autre tremblement de terre, suivi de la mort de quantité de gens.

Le tremblement de terre de l'année 1538. fut si horrible, que presque tous le édifices furent ruinez, & en partie engloutis par la terre: de sorte que la Ville resta presque deserte; il en arriva aussi la ruine de Tripergola, & l'aneantissement du lac Lucrin, que la terre absorba, & se gonfla au méme lieu si subitement, qu'elle forma la grande montagne qu'on y voit aujour d'huy, comme on le dira plus amplement au chap. 10.

Outre les tremblemens de terre, Poussol souffrit un autre ravage causé par les eaux qui y tomberent avec tant d'abondance le 31. Aoust 1695. que la Ville en fut fort endommagée, entr'autres l'Aqueduc qui portoit l'eau dans la Ville aux fontaines publiques (...).[1]

[1] *Note on Bulifon's French translation*

Bulifon's French translation follows the Italian version closely, with an attention to clarity and stylistic elegance aimed at the cultivated, French-speaking tourists. In numerous instances, Bulifon amplifies his text with additions not found in Sarnelli's more synthetic somewhat Latinizing original Italian, as noticed in the following passages in the 1769 bilingual Italian-French edition (Italic marking additions):

- [Pozzoli] fu anticamente detta Dicearchia, per lo giusto governo, che aveva → Elle fut anciennement appelée Dicearchie, a cause de la justice, & *rectitude* de son gouvernement. (ch.V, pp.44/45)

- (...) benchè altri vogliono esser così detta [scil. PUTEOLI] della puzza del solfo → (...) quoy que d'autres disent qu'elle ait été nommée de la puanteur de souffre *de son territorie.* (ibid.)

- (...) infin' a tanto che Annibale passò a danni dell'Italia → Quand Annibal vint ravager l'Italie *avec une formidable armée de Carthaginois* (ch.V, pp.44/45)

- amenissime ville → maisons de plaisance, *dont la vuë etoit si charmante* (ch.V, pp. 50/51)

- delle quali ragiona Filon Giudeo, che quivi di Roma seguì Cajo Caligola → que Philon le Juif en fait mention dans son ambassade; parce qu'il vint ici a la suite de l'Empereur Caligula; *que les delices du lieu y attiroyent souvent* (ibid.)

- [Baja] fu così deliziosa, che Seneca, e Properzio la riprendono, come incentivo alla licenziosa vita per la troppa amenità → Elle etait si delicieuse, que Seneque, & Properce font des invectives contre elle, l'accusant de porter les Romanis à la débauche *par la multitude des plaisirs qu'elle leur fournissoit* (ch.XVI, pp.148/149)

- E Clodio ebbe ardire di rimproverare Cicerone, che trattenuto si fusse a Baja → & Clodius eut bien de la hardiesse de reprocher à Ciceron son sejour à Bayes, *comme si cela eut été capable d'amollir la vertu de ce grand homme.* (ibid.)

- Baja di Città opulente divenne poi infelice, poichè mancando l'abitazione, e la frequenza, mancò anche la clemenza del cielo → Bayes, de Ville riche, & opulente devint malheureuse aprés qu'elle eut été abandonnée (...), *l'air s'y étant corrompu par la desertion de ses Citoyens* (149-51)

- [Cuma] precedeba tutte le altre Città → [Cumes] elle surpassoit *en antiquité les autres villes de l'Italie, & de la Sicile.* (ch.XXIII, pp.188-91)

- lasciate tutte le turbazioni, e pensieri dell'animo → quittez tous embaras, et *soucis d'affaires*, et autres déplaisirs, *au contraire tachez à vous rejoüir* (ch.XXVII, pp. 220/221).

RULES that are very useful and necessary for visitors of the baths at Pozzuoli, with an elegiac description of the Baths at Pozzuoli. (English translation of the Italian text).

Chap. XXVII (pp. 220-223)

1   Never come to the bath unclean, because the baths stimulate and move bodily fluids.
2   When you arrive at the bath, leave all worries and anxieties behind. The bath features its virtue by producing gaiety, the same way a master works by using his tools.
3   Do not enter the bath without having fully digested.
4   Do not eat or drink water inside and outside the bath before cooling down, so that whatever is not digested won't leave the body, causing obstruction.
5   Protect yourself from the cold and wind while you are bathing.
6   Use only watered-down wine to quench your thirst.
7   Bathe only once a day to prevent excessive bowel movements weakening you.
8   Enter the water up to your shoulders, unless you have some wound that must never be bathed in the waters of the Cantarello, Sole, and Luna baths.
9   Stay in the water until your head is covered with sweat or as long as the water does not make you feel uncomfortable.
10   As soon as you get out of the water, cover yourself with a sheet. After sweating profusely, take off the sheet, dry off the sweat, stay for a while, then go home fully dressed and rest. Do not sweat any longer.
11   Don't amuse yourself by moving from one bath to another. Choose one among the numerous baths and use it.
12   Make sure the water of your bath flows out to the sea continuously. If not, it will turn cold.
13   When you are ready for a bath, throw out all its water if allowed, so that you will have fresh water.
14   Just like other remedies, the baths work gradually. Don't get upset if you are not cured immediately.

Appendix 4

In his *Memorie dell'Insigne Collegio di S. Spirito della Città di Benevento* (1688), Sarnelli describes its history and life in twenty-four chapters, from its foundation in the 11th century through 1688. The reader finds information about fraternities and religious rites. The *Memorie*'s last chapter chronicles, in a letter to the famous librarian Antonio Magliabechi, the earthquake of June 5, 1688 that destroyed the city of Benevento. The detailed account of Sarnelli's lived experience is accompanied by statistics of survivors and victims and a chronology of seven past earthquakes in Benevento.

Following is a passage from the *Memorie*'s chapter XXIV, with my translation.

Report of the Earthquake that Destroyed the City of Benevento on June 5, 1688, Written as a Letter to the Eminent Mr. Antonio Magliabechi, Librarian of S.A.S.

I received your letter from Abbot Vincenzo Antonio Capocio, a most virtuous friend in Rome where he practices with his many talents. You are asking me to share the sad story of the horrendous earthquake that occurred in Benevento. (…)

Among the Lord's arrows used to get rid of sinners in this world, I consider earthquakes to be the most dreadful. The plague, famine, and wars are great disasters, but they are avoidable, even though not for all. Earthquakes do not allow escape, they turn the very shelter into hazard, they do not care about people, and leave not even time for prayers. They kill instantly, disperse property, destroy entire families, and put the soul at obvious risk. Everyone fears their own demise. When surviving, they are stunned without knowing what to do, or they run away fast. Those left under the rubble have no priest to give them absolution, no one to help them, no relatives to mourn them. (…)

It was the fifth day of June, Saturday before Whitsunday, a day of celebration at our illustrious Collegio di S. Spirito in the Church of S. Maria di Costantinopoli, when as its abbot, I was getting ready to go there to celebrate the solemn first vespers. It was time to leave, but I decided to wait, because the distinguished archbishop, who was to solemnize the vespers at the Metropolitana Church, was not yet ready. To avoid idleness in my quarters, I sat down and continued to expand a few points of a sermon for the following Monday (…). Just after 8 p.m., I felt a strong jolt in my room. As I was busy writing, I did not pay much attention to what happened and heard no one in the bishopric who seemed surprised (…), but in an instant (it was 8:30 p.m.), without noticing another jolt, I saw the ceiling and roof of the room fall down on top of me. Getting up from my chair, the pen in my hand, I try to open the room's door, but the collapsed ceiling and roof lock the closed door. I touch my head lightly to protect it from injury, while the rest of the body from the shoulders down stayed exposed to the falling stones. After the jolt stopped, I was all beaten and bruised from the rubble of the roof and the nearby wall, so in this state, I repeated the words, *Omnia tua fecisti nobis Domine in vero judicio fecisti, quia peccavimus tibi, et mandatis tuis non obedivimus* (What you did to us, my Lord, was done in truthful judgment, because we sinned against you and did not obey your laws). At that moment, some people ran by, unhurt but frightened, fleeing the rubble, so I called for help, to no avail. (…) I moved my head out of the rubble and dropped down to the entrance hall of the bishopric. I felt the sharp pain from the severe bruises, and lied down on the floor motionless and unable to get up, as other jolts continued, causing indescribable fear.

By God's mercy, the wind began to rise after the quake stopped, blowing away the dust. Since the fallen bricks were fresh and not plastered, powder was everywhere and would have suffocated all survivors.

As I stood among the rubbles of my quarters, I thought that only the episcopy had been damaged and that people outside lamented out of compassion for our fate. As I said, you could not hear much of an uproar. But once I was down in the entrance hall, I could see how the surrounding houses were just piles of stones.

The eminent Archbishop Orsini, who was talking in his quarters with a gentleman of the diocese, also fell on the floor with the gentleman as the ceiling came crashing down (…). The gentleman died, but Orsini was unhurt. They began to exhume him from the rubble, together with other aids. He suffered many injuries on the head, right eyelid, hand, and right foot, without feeling any pain. (...)

The number of dead from the earthquake was 1,367. There were 155 missing people who left the city after the quake, and 6,312 survivors. Among the dead were some 200 foreign visitors.